MONSTER

BLOOD TRAILS, BOOK 2

JENNIFER BLACKSTREAM

SKELETON KEY PUBLISHING

MONSTER
A Blood Trails Novel, Book 2

USA Today Bestselling Author
JENNIFER BLACKSTREAM

To join my mailing list, visit
www.jenniferblackstream.com

Monster
©Copyright Jennifer Blackstream 2017, Skeleton Key Publishing
Edited by 720 Editing
Cover Art by Yocla Designs © Copyright 2017

Other Books by Jennifer Blackstream

Blood Trails Series (Urban Fantasy):

DEADLINE
MONSTER

Blood Prince Series (Paranormal Romance)

BEFORE MIDNIGHT
ONE BITE
GOLDEN STAIR
DIVINE SCALES
BEAUTIFUL SALVATION

The Blood Realm Series (Paranormal Romance):

ALL FOR A ROSE
BLUE VOODOO
THE ARCHER
BEAR WITH ME
STOLEN WISH

Join my mailing list on my website www.jenniferblackstream.com to be alerted
when new titles are released.

To all the canine partners out there, both on the force and off. Know you are treasured.

ACKNOWLEDGMENTS

To Capt. Flanigan for answering so many questions. And to Radar, for being the inspiring beginning of the Cleveland Metroparks Rangers Canine Division.

"The belief in a supernatural source of evil is not necessary; men alone are quite capable of every wickedness."
— Joseph Conrad

MONSTER

JENNIFER BLACKSTREAM

CHAPTER 1

"I have come to make you a deal."

That sentence, delivered in the craggy voice of my mentor, Mother Hazel, was the only warning I got. I glanced up from my crowded to-do list in time to see a grey and brown blur fall toward my desk. A cry of protest bubbled up my throat as I threw out a hand to catch it, but I was too slow. The heavy object landed with an ominous thud.

"Hey!"

I snatched up the cumbersome circlet of metal and leather with one hand and drew a finger over the mahogany surface with the other. My new desk for my new office. A symbol of my dedication to my fresh start in the private investigation industry. The grand piece of furniture had been too expensive, a ridiculous luxury that embarrassed me only slightly less than it pleased me. And now it had a large groove in it where the metal stud on whatever it was the old crone had dropped had bit into the smooth wood.

It mirrored my relationship with my waiting mentor to perfection.

Twin locks of grey hair fell to either side of Mother Hazel's face, brushing the floor as she tilted her head. An arched, bushy eyebrow was her sole acknowledgment of my distress. She straightened her short, stout frame and pointed at the object that had caused the blunt force trauma to my furniture. "Do you know what that is?"

"Nothing fragile, I hope," I muttered.

Mother Hazel met my gaze without a hint of humor. "Sarcasm is unnecessary. Can you identify it, or can't you?"

If I'd thought saying no would make her leave, I'd have said it. But even though I wasn't Mother Hazel's apprentice anymore, hadn't been for three years, I'd been her apprentice long enough that this trivial identification challenge was as familiar a routine as my morning coffee. And I knew she wasn't going anywhere until I jumped through her hoops.

Resigned to my fate, I studied the object. It was a brown leather collar, decorated with five iron studs spaced down its length at equal distances. The leather yielded when I folded it, the entire length well worn and soft. Too small to fit around any human's waist. Not a belt, then. "It's a collar." I squinted at the inner lining. What I'd dismissed as random scratches weren't scratches at all. "There are runes carved into it."

Mother Hazel offered no encouragement, no premature confirmation. Par for the course.

I concentrated on the symbols, pushing out with my magic. At the first brush of my power, the symbols burst into vibrant golden light.

"An abjuration spell." I licked my lips, and I could almost taste the magic, could almost see it glittering like a gold chain within the leather casing. "It's a suppression collar." I rolled the energy around my mind again, prodding at it with my senses. There were threads of silver wrapped deep inside the golden bonds. "And a tracking spell."

"You're describing the pieces, but what is the whole?" Mother Hazel pressed.

I put it down and reached out to straighten the long, gold-plated plaque with my name on it perched on the edge of the desk before folding my hands. "It's a device to prevent a shifter from changing form. It will also allow someone to track the wearer the same as if you'd implanted a GPS chip."

A calculating gleam shone in my mentor's eyes. In all the years I'd known her, that look had *never* boded well for me.

"Yes." She stepped closer, her protruding belly pressing against the desk. "It—"

"That's creepy," interrupted a high-pitched voice.

Mother Hazel and I turned in unison to see a pink pixie with thin gossamer wings pop her head over the top of the half-empty bookshelf in the corner. Peasblossom leaned her six-inch frame over the edge to peer down at the collar. "You had a nightmare about werewolves last night, and now she's bringing you a werewolf collar. That must mean something. I told you, dreams that wake you up screaming are not something you should ignore. But do you listen? Noooo…"

Mother Hazel's gaze sharpened, pinning me to my seat. "You had a nightmare about a werewolf?"

I shot Peasblossom a glare for the revelation, then gave my mentor my most reassuring smile. "It wasn't a nightmare. It was just a strange dream."

"Was it a werewolf or a shifter? Be specific."

I gripped the padded arms of my leather chair—also new—then forced myself to relax. "It might have been a werewolf. I'm not sure. I remember a black beast."

Saying the words out loud brought the images back. For one vertigo-inducing second, I was back in the dream. My legs pumped as I ran, muscles burning in protest. Sweat poured from my forehead. Labored breathing strained my lungs, turning my chest into one giant bruise, and a cramp stabbed into my side, trying to force me to stop, to give up. The beast crashed through the forest behind me. Twigs snapped under heavy paws, and wildlife scattered with screeches of fear, feeding my own terror. With every thud of my heart, I could swear I felt its hot breath on my neck, getting closer, ready to pounce. It was coming. There was no escaping it. No getting away.

I shivered and pulled my black fleece wrap tighter around me. It was spring, and the promise of a warm afternoon had made me forgo a hooded sweatshirt in favor of a simple long-sleeved black shirt over my usual multicolored leggings. I'd grabbed the wrap as an afterthought, a grudging concession to the chilly morning. Now I wished I'd brought both. I groped for the cup of coffee cooling in my oversized Batman mug, my hand shaking enough to throw off my aim, so I grabbed the mug holding my pens instead.

Mother Hazel pointed at me with a long fingernail. "That's what you get for making an enemy out of a dream sorceress." A frown marred the corners of her mouth. "Did you send her an apology gift?"

I released the pen mug and grabbed my coffee, spilling a few fat drops before I steadied myself to take a sip. It was still a few degrees too hot, but I didn't care. I took a deep breath through my nose, letting the fragrance of a medium roast waft over my senses. Some of the tension seeped from my shoulders, and I settled back in my chair. "Yes, I sent an apology gift three days after our…misunderstanding. A statue of the god Morpheus carved from amethyst." I took a sip of coffee, rolling it over my taste buds with a contented sigh. "I thought it was a well-chosen present, but apparently it was not sufficient for her to forgive my little indiscretion."

"You set one of her hotel rooms on fire." Peasblossom propped her chin up on one hand. "That's not a 'little indiscretion.' At least, you didn't think so when I tried to roast s'mores on the stove."

"You caught a dish towel on fire, and nearly burned the house down."

4

Peasblossom's wings flicked in annoyance. "At least *my* fire was an accident. You burned down Arianne's hotel room on purpose!"

"I set fire to my restraints to save my life! The bed was—" I held up a hand. "I'm not having this argument with you. You aren't using the stove again, and that's final." I looked away from the fuming pixie to Mother Hazel. "I said I was sorry, and I sent her an apology gift. I can't force her to forgive me."

"You made an enemy of a powerful sorceress because you insist on pursuing this…career of yours."

She said the word "career" the way a five-year-old would say "cooties," complete with the slight wrinkling of her nose.

"If you continue on the path you've chosen for yourself, you can expect more nightmares—and possibly much worse."

I rubbed my temples, trying to ease the headache forming there. We were meandering into familiar—and unpleasant—territory, so I opted to change the subject. "Can we talk about the deal you mentioned?"

"We are." She paced the room, casting a disapproving eye over my office's unadorned grey walls and the spotted windows that made up the northernmost wall. "Last night, a young boy called the police from the Rocky River Reservation of Cleveland Metroparks. He said there was a dead body among the trees."

I straightened. "A body?"

"Yes. Well, most of a body. A wolf found the corpse first, and there was a rather large amount of the man's midsection missing."

My stomach rolled, and I pushed away the chocolate chip cookie I'd intended to have for breakfast. "Ohio doesn't have wolves, not beyond those kept as pets by humans who don't know better." I looked at the collar, and the unease twisting my guts into knots grew heavier. "You think it was a werewolf."

"Perhaps. When the boy told the 911 operator about the

5

condition of the body, the dispatcher notified the Wild Animal Task Force. Are you familiar with it?"

I made a fist, resisting the urge to grab my laptop and do an internet search for wolves in Ohio in the wild hope that perhaps their numbers had exploded and we could blame the predation on a normal, run-of-the-mill grey wolf. Or maybe a coyote. It could have been a coyote. I could look up the bite radius...

"Sort of," I answered slowly. "The task force came about after some politician's wife claimed she was bitten by a wolf while visiting a reservation in the Cleveland Metroparks system. Her husband seized the opportunity to declare a resurgence of wolves into Ohio from Michigan, and he demanded the city take measures to protect park visitors from any attacks like the one on his wife." I shrugged. "The consensus among the rangers is it was a political ploy to win votes by painting himself as a guardian against the big, bad wolves. A classic motif for classic political grandstanding."

Mother Hazel snorted. "It was political, yes, but only because the mayor's wife did not have the mental capacity to process the truth of what bit her. That was no wolf. It was a barghest."

My eyebrows shot up. Despite being a canid, a barghest resembled a wolf only at first glance. A closer inspection would reveal front limbs more congruent with human hands than paws and a snout resembling a vampire bat more than a canine. "I thought her mental health vacation was added drama for the papers. If she saw a barghest, I guess that team of private doctors wasn't superfluous."

"Giving someone a bottle of medication to dull the mind until it can't register fear is not helpful." Mother Hazel's voice thickened with disgust. "She'd have been better off seeing a witch."

I nodded, for once in complete agreement. "True. Though if she doesn't believe in the Otherworld enough for her mind to process a barghest, then I suppose she never realized consulting a witch was an option."

"Too bad she didn't see your lovely online advert," Mother Hazel commented, meeting my eyes.

Warning bells went off in my brain. I could feel the lecture on why I should stick to being the village witch instead of mucking about as a private investigator on the horizon.

"All right," I continued, a little too loudly, "so she was bit by a barghest and her husband created a task force to battle imaginary wolves. So what?"

"The original members of the task force nearly died en masse, humans being unprepared to handle the likes of a barghest. However, there was one blessing to come out of the unfortunate situation. Liam Osbourne, the alpha of the Rocky River pack and the detective sergeant of the Cleveland Metropark Rangers, caught the ear of the horrified mayor. He recommended several officers who were 'well suited' to dealing with wild animals."

"Clever. Now they'll notify him for any animal attacks— which would mean he gets the call if there are any incidents involving a werewolf." I took another sip of my coffee, curling my fingers around the warm mug.

"And that is what happened last night as soon as the boy mentioned predation. The operator called Sergeant Osbourne, and upon investigating, he found a werewolf in the woods. The beast had the victim's blood on his face."

The spelled leather and metal seemed to throb in time with the story. My hands shook, and I put the coffee down before I could spill the rest of it. "And you want me to collar it?"

Mother Hazel squinted at a spot on the front window. "Yes and no. I want you to find out what happened to Oliver Dale. Do you ever clean your windows?"

"Oliver Dale being the victim?"

She nodded, still eyeing the window.

I frowned. If Sergeant Osbourne found the beast covered in the victim's blood, and the body bore obvious signs of predation, then it seemed like an open and shut case. So either she was toying with me...or there was more.

She let me stew for another minute, before going on. "The shifter the detective sergeant found was a member of his own pack. It is my understanding this wolf was in good standing, a trusted man and beast. Liam does not believe he killed Oliver."

I clasped my hands and rested them on my stomach. "That's a lot of trust, considering how he found him."

"Yes. It is a mark of Sergeant Osbourne's character that he is proceeding in an objective manner. Despite his personal feelings for this wolf, he seems determined to maintain propriety." She gestured at the enchanted metal and leather. "He called the Vanguard to request the collar."

I groped for my mug, suddenly desperate for caffeine. The Vanguard was the Otherworld's version of Interpol, an organized hodgepodge of representatives who helped coordinate inter-species criminal investigations.

"What operatives did the Vanguard assign to the case?" I held my breath as I waited for the answer. The Vanguard strove to be consistent and fair in its pursuit of justice, and there were measures in place to assure no one held too much power, or gathered enough clout to replace their own idea of justice with that of the organization. But no hierarchy could truly police itself. And, frankly, good or bad, members of the policing organization could be downright terrifying.

Mother Hazel dragged the pad of one finger over the window ledge, shaking her head at the layer of dust. "It has not gone that far. Liam was clear he desired only for someone to provide a means to quarantine his wolf while the coroner determines cause of death."

"So until the human coroner rules Oliver's Dale's death a homicide, no Vanguard." My shoulders sagged, and I leaned back in my chair. So she wasn't asking me to work with the Vanguard on a murder case. *Thank the Goddess for small favors.*

"Shouldn't take long." Peasblossom drummed her hands on the edge of the bookcase. "Even a human can tell when someone's been gnawed on by a wild animal."

"Which is why it is such a convenience that the Vanguard has agreed to accept our own Mother Renard as overseer," Mother Hazel said.

I froze, my relief evaporating like a snowflake on the brow of a fire demon. "You... You talked about me with the Vanguard?"

"Only Gertrude, in the call center. You remember Gertrude?"

Of course I remembered Gertrude. It was hard to forget a talking flea whose claim to fame was a brief dalliance with Hermes...

"So I'm supposed to activate the collar, then stay there and oversee the investigation so I can call in the Vanguard if he's guilty?" I asked.

"Yes. Though the Vanguard do not believe Liam would hide a murderer in his pack, the rules state that an interspecies murder must have a representative outside the race of the accused. You are that representative."

I tried not to think about Mother Hazel bringing me to the Vanguard's attention—in whatever form. I had a past I wasn't proud of; the last thing I wanted was to give Otherworld's Interpol a reason to notice me. "You said you wanted to make me a deal. What is it?"

Mother Hazel turned from her disapproving inspection of my dirty windows to nudge a near-invisible bit of debris on the office carpet with her foot. "You will take the collar to the hungry little werewolf in accordance with Liam's wishes. Once that task is complete, you will find out what happened to Oliver and you will report your findings." She studied me then, dark eyes penetrating and far too intense. "If you fail, then you will give up this silly private investigator business. You will continue on as a proper village witch. *Only* a village witch."

My stomach bottomed out, but I gritted my teeth and held her gaze. "And when I solve the case?"

Mother Hazel didn't blink. "I will owe you a favor."

If I hadn't been sitting down, I would have fainted. Peasblossom wasn't so lucky. She'd balanced on the brink of the bookshelf in an effort to better hear the conversation, so when she jerked in surprise, she lost her balance and plummeted. She was saved from an unpleasant collision with the floor only because Mother Hazel is much, *much* faster than she looks.

A favor. A favor from *Mother Hazel.*

If a witch existed that held more power than Mother Hazel, then I'd never heard of one—and I'd never met anyone who had. Mother Hazel was only the name she'd been going by when I'd first encountered her. She had other names—older names spoken only as whispers in the dark, and only by the exceptionally brave or the incredibly stupid. If she was offering me a favor—an *unqualified*, *unlimited* favor...

"I see your minimalist arrangement applies to more than your house," the crafty crone continued, as I fought to gather my scattered wits. "You favor a plain office too." She sniffed. "Not very becoming of a witch. If your workspace always looks as if you've just arrived, then people will assume you're lazy, not applying yourself as you should." She narrowed her eyes. "This reflects badly on me as your mentor."

"I don't see a need to clutter every available surface," I said, for once relieved at the familiar argument. I could have this conversation in my sleep. "I like space. And it's not so hard to keep things tidy if you make it a priority."

Mother Hazel smiled, and I tensed. There it was again—the look that hinted there was an I-told-you-so in my future. I *hated* that look.

It was exactly what I needed to snap myself out of the stupor her offered deal had plunged me into. I opened my mouth to retaliate against that look, but before I could speak again, she deposited Peasblossom on my desk and marched into the small bathroom against the left-hand wall, leaving the door open behind her. I could practically hear her assessing how clean the room was, making mental note of the bits of white fluff that would betray my use of paper towels to clean the mirror instead of using a squeegee or newspaper.

Peasblossom scurried across the desk, leapt onto my arm, and shimmied up to my ear. She clung to me like a living earring so she could speak directly into my auditory canal. "The werewolves will expect you to put the collar on and leave. There's no official cause of death yet, and don't think Sergeant Osbourne isn't counting on that technicality to keep the Vanguard out. They won't appreciate you hanging around while they try to solve the crime."

I leaned toward the open bathroom door, raising my voice so the judgy crone would hear me. "And the alpha has no issues with me helping him with a crime committed in werewolf territory, possibly by a member of his pack?"

Mother Hazel barreled out of the bathroom, scanning the office for more signs of my ineptitude. "It didn't happen in werewolf territory, it happened on public land. It so happens that the head of the park rangers is also the alpha of the local pack and a handful of the rangers are his wolves. It's his jurisdiction as detective sergeant, not as alpha." She studied a smudge mark on the wall. "Naturally, I spoke to him before coming to you."

It was a distinction without a difference. Each werewolf pack claimed the privileges of a sovereign nation among the people of the Otherworld, and they valued that designation. Given that human ignorance of the Otherworld made registering the land as their territory tricky, the subject of land ownership was grey. But regardless of paperwork, that park was werewolf territory.

"So he's all right with me investigating?"

"He would prefer to handle it himself," Mother Hazel said

nonchalantly. "But I'm sure he'll soon see the value in having a witch's help. People always do."

I swallowed a groan. Liam would not welcome my help. Especially not when the evidence against his wolf was so damning. She was sending me into a very unpleasant situation that would make me yet another powerful enemy.

But the favor...

My finger found the groove in my desk from the earlier damage. With a flex of my will, I filled it with a pool of green energy, then used a finger to draw it into smooth, flowing lines. The polished wood healed itself, leaving the furniture as pristine as it had been before my mentor's sudden arrival.

"I will never understand your obsession with keeping things new and unused," the old witch mused. "It's not good for you, you know." She pursed her lips. "Healing furniture is an outrageous use of magic."

I fought the urge to roll my eyes. "Being old and worn doesn't automatically make something superior."

The words escaped before my brain could give them a proper once-over, and my internal censor screamed in horror. Tension crackled between us, giving me plenty of opportunity to realize how my last outburst had sounded.

Mother Hazel didn't move, didn't react. Just let me squirm.

Typical.

"You don't think the werewolf killed him. Is that why you're sending me?" I asked, fighting through the awkward moment.

"Oh, I'm sorry. Are you too busy?" She made a show of looking around the stark office. "Do you have loads of other cases occupying your days? Has Agent Bradford retained your services for another FBI case?"

I winced and dropped my gaze to the even wood grain of the desk. No, Andy—Agent Bradford—wasn't on his way with an FBI case. I hadn't gotten any calls from him since the missing person case over a month ago. And even though I'd solved that case, I doubted I would get another call from him any time soon.

"You used me. You used me, and then when I was no longer convenient for your plan, you used your magic to drug me, and you left me behind. How the hell am I supposed to trust you now? How am I supposed to believe anything you tell me?"

His voice echoed in my head, hot with fury. For the last four and a half weeks, I'd tried to convince myself he was wrong, that what I'd done had been necessary to keep him safe. Yes, I'd needed him, and I'd invited him in on a dangerous plan. But he'd stubbornly refused to hide, refused to let me do my job.

I wasn't wrong, not entirely. Just wrong enough to feel guilty.

A movement outside drew my attention to the three large windows that formed the far wall of my office. Grateful for the distraction, I rose from the desk and glared at the house across the street—or rather, at the man who'd exited said house.

Mr. Grey, the landlord for the building that held my office, passed through the pool of sunshine circling the sprawling sugar maple that blessed his front yard. His brown hair was greasy, as always, his half-beard in obvious conflict about which direction to grow. A plain black shirt and pants looked as if he'd beaten them into submission, the threadbare material hanging limply on his frame.

I pressed my lips together. As a rule, I don't judge people by appearances, or even by rumors. When I rented this office, I'd done so determined not to assume my new landlord was the sour, unpleasant hermit everyone said he was. After all, Dresden was a tiny village. People gossiped.

"Tell me, how do you like having Mr. Grey as your landlord?" Mother Hazel asked.

I opted not to answer. If I knew my landlord, he'd paint a picture of himself all on his own.

Declan Grey oozed over the ground like an oil spill, heading straight for the trunk of the sugar maple. Shadows danced over his tight features as he raised a hand and put something inside the squirrel feeder, careful to tuck it away so the wind wouldn't blow it back out. He didn't smile, didn't laugh. Just put whatever food he'd brought them into the feeder then retreated inside.

Peasblossom perched on my shoulder, the breeze from her wings stirring the delicate hairs at the back of my neck. "He's poisoning them again, isn't he?"

In response, I drew a simple gesture in the air, breathing my magic into it. Silver lines of power swept toward the tree, passing through the large windows. The spell touched the feeder, flowed into a net that covered the small wooden box. Something sickly sweet pulsed against my senses, and I clenched my jaw. "Yes, he did."

"What a grouch."

"He's more than a grouch—he's a bully." I jerked the top drawer of my desk open. The small bowl of peanuts inside rattled with the force of the motion, but I ignored them, snatching one up and looking at it in light of the detection spell still alive in my mind. A faint blue glow surrounded the peanut, and I nodded and passed it to Peasblossom.

"This is the third time he's done this," I said grimly. "Forget that it's illegal to poison squirrels; it's *wrong.* If he doesn't want them around, there are other ways to handle it. *I* offered to help him with them." I glared at the pale blue door to the ranch-style house that appeared far too innocent to belong to such a cruel man. "He put up a squirrel *feeder,* for Pete's sake."

Mother Hazel studied me as if it were my face and not the conversation that was interesting. "And you've been using magic to neutralize the poison? That's a complicated spell. You must have studied very hard."

A flush rose up my neck. "I hired Dominique to do it."

Dominique was a powerful enchantress who owned the occult supply shop The Cauldron. Mother Hazel didn't so much as twitch an eyebrow, but I felt her judgment all the same. I didn't bother saying I'd tried the spell myself and failed. It wouldn't help matters. It also wouldn't help to point out that if she'd bothered to teach me any real magic during my apprenticeship, then maybe I'd be capable of more complicated spells. Such an accusation would lead to her pointing out all the skills I'd learned, languages I could speak, and knowledge I'd gained from years and years of reading. It was a battle I'd fought and lost before.

"Don't you want to 'have a word' with him?" I asked instead.

Again, she stared at me with that unsettling scrutiny. "You are the one bearing witness to his crimes. It is your prerogative to have a word about his tactics, don't you agree?"

Peasblossom held on to my earlobe, and we both stared at Mother Hazel. My mentor turning down the chance to "have a word?" It was one of her favorite things, if experience was anything to go by.

Peasblossom recovered first, holding the peanut against her chest and flying out the open window to place the spelled nut in the squirrel feeder. The endeavor took less than thirty seconds, Peasblossom being unwilling to linger with hungry squirrels about. Not that they would try to eat her, but they didn't always watch where they were leaping, and she'd been knocked out of the air by a flying furry body before.

Speaking of flying furry bodies…

"I don't suppose you've given any more thought to Majesty," I said lightly.

Mother Hazel crossed her arms. "Yes, the eternal kitten. I suppose it was only a matter of time before a human tried such foolishness. First they make the dogs teeny-tiny, and now they've robbed a cat of the most basic of rights—growing old. Monstrous."

"I've been calming his energy as best I can, but the spell is too thick, too complicated. It's bound to him in a way I can't unravel."

"What's done is done, and is not for us to undo." She pursed her lips. "That spell is evil and foolish. The person who cast it may be either or both."

That observation did not bode well. Magic like that, magic that forced nature in on itself, was unpredictable. Majesty could develop the ability to breathe fire or grow a set of antlers. Or he could explode. I took a breath to try again, to convince Mother Hazel to do something, anything, to help Majesty. She cut me off before I could get a word out.

"You haven't accepted my deal yet, Mother Renard," she said softly. "Was my reward not tempting enough?"

No more stalling. My nerves tightened until I feared they'd choke me, and I had to will my voice to come out as more than a squeak. "I'll do it." *Only a little squeaky—well done, me.* "Do you have the case file?"

Mother Hazel looked down her nose as if she were a mean-spirited school teacher about to assign homework over winter break. "No one will do the work for you this time. There is no file complete with suspects and dossiers and a vampire's little notes scribbled in the margins. You must do the work yourself. *All* the work yourself."

Anton would never have scribbled in the margins. There was a separate page for his notes.

The blush I'd thought disappeared had merely been hiding. It sprang back to full heat now. My first case had been brought to me by a vampire known for his...meticulousness. He'd hired me to solve a theft and provided me with a box of files detailing everyone he thought had the ability to carry out the theft. I'd identified the thief, but in retrospect, it did seem as if the training wheels had been on.

"Fine. I should get going, then."

Mother Hazel nodded. "The collar waits only for your command to activate it. Fasten it around the suspect's neck and the binding will lock into place." She pulled a slip of paper out of her pocket and handed it to me. "Here's the address. Liam is waiting for you."

"I assume I need the name of the werewolf to activate the spell?"

Mother Hazel grinned. That smile made my skin crawl, and I imagined I could see the shadows of iron teeth in her mouth.

"Oh, yes," she murmured. "I almost forgot. His name is Stephen Reid. *Officer* Stephen Reid."

CHAPTER 2

"She's sent you to investigate a *werewolf cop*. She wants you to prove he's guilty. Of *murder*."

Peasblossom, as always, spoke directly into my ear, her tiny hands clinging to the curl above my earlobe. The gooseflesh on my arms grew firmer with every hissed word, becoming almost painful as I fought to keep my attention on the road.

"Please stop speaking into my ear," I said, for the tenth time.

"Mmuurrddeerr," Peasblossom intoned, drawing it out with unnecessary drama. "A werewolf. A cop. A *werewolf cop*! Werewolves do not tolerate outsiders poking their noses into pack business."

"I *get it*." My knuckles whitened as I gripped the steering wheel harder, keeping my gaze locked on the unending line of orange construction cones. "Do you think I'm unaware of the situation?"

"You must be, or you would have turned down the deal." Peasblossom released my ear and fell to her bum on my shoulder. "It was a human mistake. Typical, really. Some dark creature dangles a pretty promise in front of you, and you're all too eager to sign on the bloody line. I'll bet you'd mend an evil altar if a nice old woman asked you to."

"Thank you so much for your vote of confidence. And I'll be sure to tell Mother Hazel that you called her a 'dark creature.'"

"She's been called worse. Much worse." Peasblossom pressed harder against my neck. "And she's *deserved* it."

I was vaguely aware of Mother Hazel's…history, but I didn't want to prompt the pixie to offer details. Not when I'd seen my mentor's home as it appeared in another dimension. Familiar chicken legs holding up her cottage in the center of a fence crafted from human bones, skulls with fiery red eye sockets watching the shadowy forest around it. Watching for the unwary soul who might next wander up to the old witch's home looking for help. One post always empty, waiting for a skull…

A change in subject was needed.

"We can't be certain that Stephen did it." My voice came out a louder than I'd intended, filling the small confines of my newly repaired Ford Focus. "There could be a perfectly reasonable explanation for why he had the victim's blood on his face."

"Such as?"

"He could have found the body already dead. It's sad, but accidents happen in the woods. The poor man could have fallen and broken his neck, or bled out from a cut on the femoral artery. If the wolf found him shortly after death, he might have still been warm, and—"

"And so he thought he'd have a snack?"

Admittedly, my alternative narrative was unlikely. I bit my lip. "Werewolves make mistakes. A temporary loss of control isn't the same as murder."

"He's not *just* a shifter. He's a cop and a ranger. Between the hard work his alpha would have put in helping him learn control after he started shifting, and the training he would have gotten as a police officer, he should have the self-control to resist having a nibble on some random human—dead or alive."

"What about foul play?" I countered. "Maybe someone—or some*thing*—influenced him, made him do it."

Peasblossom considered that. "You mean like a will-o'-the-wisp having a lark?"

"Yes!" I nodded emphatically, relieved to have an option that didn't include a murdering lycanthropic police officer. "Exactly, a will-o'-the-wisp. How many times have we saved someone's life after a will-o'-the wisp let a game go too far?"

"They can be right bastards, can't they?" Peasblossom gave a derisive sniff. "I'm not saying I never had a bit of fun with a wandering human, but you don't see pixies bobbing along and leading innocent drunks to die in bogs, do you? We have more class than that. More honor. Why, a pixie would take a bullet for you, lose their own wings to save a chap in need."

I tuned her out for the rest of the drive. Once Peasblossom got warmed up on the valiant nature of her kin, she could go on for hours. And since the alternative was being forced to discuss a case that—the possibility of fey interference aside—did not look good, I was only too happy to listen to her attempt yet another ballad for the noble race that was the pixie.

Stephen's neighborhood was a higher-end suburb of North Olmsted, well off enough that everyone's lawn was mowed and their shrubs trimmed, but not so fancy as to encourage thieves to put it at the top of their Christmas wish list. The houses were siding more often than brick or stone, and the fences were wood, not iron. More than one home had a sign in the front yard proclaiming they had a child in band or football. A family-friendly neighborhood.

When my GPS informed me I was two blocks from my desti-nation, I pulled over to the side of the road and stopped the car near a split-level home with a bicycle lying in the driveway.

"And the size of a pixie's heart, is challenged only by the size of its— Why did we stop?" Peasblossom leapt to her feet, grasped a strand of my hair, and leaned over as far as she could to peer out the window. "That's not his house." She peered down at the GPS. "It didn't tell you to stop," she said, pointing at the screen. "You keep going until you get to the little checkered flag. Did you forget how it works?"

"No, I haven't forgotten how it works," I said, exasperated. "I stopped here on purpose."

"If you're lost, you can say so," Peasblossom said. "I won't laugh."

I gritted my teeth. "I am not lost. I stopped here because I need you to fly ahead. Go to Stephen's and find a way inside. Liam should be there guarding him while they wait for me. With their hearing, they'll know when I pull in the drive, and I want you to make note of their reaction and remember anything they say."

Peasblossom fluttered to stand on the steering wheel, her glittering pink eyes giving the illusion of a multifaceted, insect-like gaze. "Oooh, I like spy work. You think they'll let something slip?" She paused and frowned. "Wait, I don't get it. Liam can't be in on it, else he wouldn't have called for the collar, would he?"

"I don't think he's in on it. I just want to understand the nature of their relationship. Is Stephen angry and shouting at his alpha? Is he begging for leniency? Demanding the chance to clear his name? I need to know if Liam believes he did it, or if this was all a bluff. When they hear me pull in, that will be Liam's last chance to appeal to Stephen before going through with the collar. Whatever he says will tell us a great deal about what we're getting into."

"Trouble, that's what we're getting into. We're investigating a murder where the number one suspect is a shifter *and* a cop." Peasblossom wagged a finger at me. "But I'm going to be supportive and not tell you what a foolish thing you've done taking this case."

"You're too good to me," I said dryly.

"Right that." Peasblossom's wings flicked behind her,

launching her off the steering wheel. She grasped the edge of the window and used it to fling herself into the wind. I watched her ride the air currents, darting about like a hummingbird, all effortless grace. For a fey who preferred to ride my shoulder whenever possible, and would climb my hair to get to my head, she was a very skilled flyer.

I gave her a head start, allowing myself ten minutes or so to collect my thoughts. Werewolves had incredible senses, and their ability to monitor physical reactions could be as informative as mind reading. To go in there with any kind of authority, I needed to present a confident front. I started to wipe my sweaty palms on my pants, then turned on the car's AC instead and held my hands to the air blowers.

"I will owe you a favor."

My erratic heartbeat provided the perfect accompaniment to the echo of my mentor's offer. I stared at the car vent, not really seeing it. It was an unheard-of bargain. Literally. I'd never in my life known of any witch, especially one of my mentor's ability, offering what amounted to a blank check in the magic world.

I looked at my reflection in the car's rearview mirror. "She thinks you'll fail." I furrowed my brow, considering what I'd just said to myself. "Probably. But she wouldn't have offered a deal if it wasn't *possible* for me to succeed. She does pride herself on being fair. Well, what *she* considers fair."

The clock on my dash ticked down another minute. I tore myself out of my musing to put the car in drive and ease away from the curb. "Either I'm good enough to be a detective or I'm not. If I'm not, then I shouldn't keep going anyway. And if I am... Well, if I am, then why not start my career with an ace up my sleeve?"

The GPS led me through a simple grid pattern of a neighborhood, and I followed its directions to a small, ranch-style building with pale tan siding and dark brown shutters. A short wrought-iron fence outlined the narrow stoop, and the sidewalk leading from the driveway to front stoop was free of debris, despite the fresh mulch that had recently been laid around the scattering of bushes lining the front of the house.

My knock sounded much louder than it should have, a sign my nerves were wound too tight. I took a deep breath in for the count of seven, then let it out for the count of eight. Then the door swung open, and I couldn't breathe at all.

There is no sensation comparable to standing in a shifter's aura. Leaning against a hot dryer in the middle of a heavy cycle on a cold night was the closest sensation I could think of. I blinked and concentrated on resisting the urge to sway forward.

Alert blue eyes settled on me, squeezing out the rest of my breath. "You must be Mother Renard. I'm Detective Sergeant Osbourne."

Werewolves aged almost as slowly as witches. Liam didn't look a day over forty-five, which meant he was probably over seventy—significantly older than his dark brown hair would suggest. Broad shoulders filled out the crisp lines of his stark white shirt, but his bulk had an understated shape to it that said it was genetic and not a result of the gym or manual labor. He'd rolled his shirt sleeves up to the elbows, giving the impression he was a hands-on sort of leader. I tilted my head to meet his gaze. Six foot three, I guessed.

I smiled and raised my hand. "Please, call me Shade."

"No title?" He raised an eyebrow. "Your mentor made it sound rather important that I address you properly."

I held the smile in place with some effort. "If it pleases you to call me Mother, then by all means. Personally, I find it more satisfying when someone can show me the proper respect without the reminder of using my title." That, and while Mother had been a natural way to address a witch once upon a time, it now made people outside the Otherworld give me odd looks. I still didn't understand how Mother Hazel had managed to convince the entire village of Dresden to use it without batting an eye.

His other eyebrow joined the first at the edge of his hairline. "All right, then." He bobbed his head and stepped to the side, gesturing for me to enter. "Please come in." A shadow fell across his face, making the lines around his mouth stand out more. "Stephen is in the den."

I stepped inside. A large grey sectional couch took up most of the living room, with a television dominating the rest. I walked the thin path between the coffee table and the TV, my feet sinking into the thick cream and navy-blue rug. It took a little concentration to avoid looking around for Peasblossom, but I managed. If there was one thing I trusted her to do with no coaching from me, it was snoop. Pixies possessed a natural nosiness that was unrivaled. Even among humans.

"Are you all right?"

I blinked, surprised to find Liam had stopped walking. I opened my mouth to say yes, and ask him why he'd asked, and noticed two things simultaneously. First, I stopped walking when he did.

Second, I was leaning on him.

Heat flared in my cheeks. My arm and his arm were joined without a sliver of light between us, and my nerves hummed under the touch of his aura. I stepped back, putting enough distance between us to be polite, but not so much that I seemed embarrassed and overcompensating. When I'd centered myself enough to look him in the eye again, I found the alpha studying me with a guarded expression that said I had ten seconds to come up with a reason for cuddling with him before I lost all professional credibility forever.

"You're radiating heat like a fire hazard," I blurted out.

A hint of disapproval pulled down the corners of his mouth. "I'm sorry?"

I resisted the urge to take another step back, not wanting to look like I was retreating. It wasn't easy to hold my ground. I wanted to lean closer again, feel more of his energy. *He thinks you're flirting. Say something. Fix this!*

"I get that you're upset," I said, trying for a Mother Hazel smile—equal parts empathy and condescension. "It's understandable, given the situation. But your energy is chaotic. I can feel it burning like a furnace ten seconds before it explodes. My instinct is to calm that energy before it gets out of hand, especially when I'm going to be working some fairly complicated magic. I was trying to be subtle because I don't want to embarrass you. I'm sorry if I made you uncomfortable."

There. He's the one losing control, and I'm the capable witch trying to help. Mother Hazel would be so proud.

He studied me, the creases between his brows deepening. He obviously didn't believe me, but like most people, he seemed uncomfortable calling a witch a liar. *Excellent.* I watched him parse his options, holding my witchy smile firmly in place.

"I apologize," he said finally. "It's a difficult time. I didn't realize you were so sensitive to shifters' energy."

"Please don't apologize. It's quite all right."

I shoved my hands into the pockets of my red trench coat, curling them into fists to smother the tingling in my fingertips that begged to touch him again. For pity's sake, had it been that long since I'd been near a shifter?

Liam stopped before we could cross the threshold from the living room to the hallway, and it was through the grace of the Goddess herself that I didn't collide with him. Tension squeezed his shoulders as he turned to face me.

"You are not what I was expecting."

His voice was calm, but that didn't soften the critical quality of his tone.

I stiffened, letting some of the congeniality leak from my smile. "Oh?"

"Not at all, in fact," he continued. "When I spoke to Mother

Hazel initially, I thought she would handle the situation herself. When she said she was sending you…"

"You had a different image in mind," I guessed.

He looked down at my leggings. The emerald and black abstract design hinting at diamond shapes in a paint-slash grid pattern were one of the more understated pairs I owned—only two colors. I hadn't thought twice about wearing them to this meeting. Now with the detective staring at them, I felt the familiar sting of judgment.

My hackles rose. "I see."

He was still staring at my leggings. I held a hand up and snapped my fingers between his face and mine. His eyebrows shot up in surprise.

"Let's get one thing clear, shall we?" I straightened my spine. "I am a witch. And I am a damn good one. I don't have to prove that to you. The fact that Mother Hazel sent me should be sufficient. I'm sorry my leggings perturb you, but they are comfortable, and I like them. Since they are my clothes, my opinion is the only one that matters."

He looked as though he wanted to argue, but to his credit, he refrained. "I apologize. I meant no disrespect." He paused. "But I have to ask…have you ever dealt with a feral werewolf?"

My heart skipped a beat, a sudden deluge of memories battering the walls I'd built to protect myself from that particular memory. My stomach rolled, and I swallowed before I tried to speak. "Yes."

"You have?"

Tension squeezed my jaw so hard that I had to fight to get my answer out. "Yes."

I hoped that would be the end of this particular line of questioning. There wasn't a lot of leeway in what one should expect from a feral shifter. Blood, death, and a special breed of terror. Details varied, but the meat of it remained the same. He didn't need details of my particular encounter to have an idea of what I'd seen.

Liam didn't speak, didn't move. He wanted the story.

I took a few slow breaths to calm my pulse, organizing my thoughts so I could tell him the story while remembering as few details as possible. I had plenty of nightmares without adding fuel to the creative fire, and given my most recent nightmare, the last thing I wanted to think about was an out-of-control werewolf.

"I was still an apprentice, living with Mother Hazel. Two hours past sundown, a young man knocked on the door. He was covered in blood. He said a wolf had eaten his parents. He'd been running through the woods when Mother Hazel's hut appeared before him—which isn't as strange as it sounds."

My voice maintained a near-monotone, a cold, dry recitation of facts. Even then, I could feel the pain waiting, the nightmares churning as they waited for me to remember, to let my mind return to that night I'd promised myself never to think of again. I was quiet for a long minute, shoring up my mental blocks against the memories. *The facts, stick to the facts.* Liam waited.

"I'd been her apprentice for over a decade, and I'd gained just enough confidence to think I could do anything." I snorted. "Sad that an influx of knowledge is so often accompanied by grand stupidity. When she told me to wait in the cottage, I ignored her. I followed her." I swallowed, but managed to maintain eye contact. "He was eating the mother's body when we got there. It was…" I shook myself. "Mother Hazel bound him." I averted my eyes before I said the next part. "The boy was wrong. A wolf didn't eat his mother and father."

"The wolf was his father," Liam said quietly.

I nodded. "The boy had seen him go into the woods, heard a wolf howl and snarl, and he'd assumed his father had been attacked. His mother screamed at him to run, so he did." The screams echoed in my memory. Not the victim's. The poor woman died before I arrived. The screams I heard were the father's. The wails of despair after Mother Hazel returned him to his human form and he learned what he'd done.

"It is unusual for a shifter to be feral only in one form," Liam said. "Usually, the madness leaks into the other form, wherever it starts. But it's when it affects only the beast that it is truly terrifying. The disparity between man and wolf, the complete separation… That's why balance is so important. Without it, you have a man and a monster, separate creatures instead of two parts of a whole."

I peered past him into the hall and toward the back rooms where I assumed Stephen was. "Do you believe he's feral?"

"No." He followed my gaze. "It would be easier if he were. There's protocol for feral werewolves, steps to be taken to attempt rehabilitation. My path would be clear. But Stephen shows no signs of being feral. Even that night, when I found him with blood all over his face, he didn't fight me."

"And yet…" I prompted.

Liam's face hardened. "He's withholding. He respects my authority, and he does what I ask, but his story… He is not telling me the whole truth. And that is unacceptable. Absolutely unacceptable." He shoved a hand through his hair and stared at my coat as if trying to see where the suppression collar was, where I'd hidden the piece of leather and metal. "This is not something I do lightly. This collar…it's very serious."

"I understand," I said gently.

"If you'd asked me twenty-four hours ago if Stephen were capable of this, I would have given an unqualified no."

"You asked me if I'd ever dealt with a feral werewolf, but you don't believe Stephen is feral." I let the question hang in the air.

"Feral or not, Stephen will understand what that collar means." Liam's tone was grim. "It's one thing to be told it's going to happen. It will be another when it's happening, when his wolf realizes it's happening. That collar is a sentence worse than death for some shifters." He held my gaze. "I will protect you. But you should prepare yourself for the worst."

The worst. My imagination exploded, overflowing with dark images of blood, and teeth, and claws, my brain echoing with the sound of my own screams. I lost my breath for a second.

Liam opened the door.

I wasn't ready.

CHAPTER 3

Heat slammed into me like a fairy tale witch escaping a fiery oven. Chaotic energy swirled around the room in a maelstrom of emotion. Unlike the pleasant buzz of Liam's heightened aura, this was more intense, unpleasant. The force of it should have lifted the furniture, smashed anything that wasn't nailed down. I squinted as if I stood in the path of a strong wind, trying to focus on the man responsible for it all.

Stephen reclined in a dark brown leather chair, watching me with eyes the color of a stag's pelt. His dark hair was smoothed away from his face in a gentle wave, and his beard shaded his jaw line and upper lip without hiding his mouth. The violence of his energy suggested his wolf was very close to the surface, the fury of it screaming of a werewolf about to snap. And yet he remained relaxed in the chair, his feet propped up, and his head resting against the cushion.

"Officer Reid, I presume?" I held out my hand. "I'm Shade Renard. Please call me Shade."

His eyes glinted, changing to the gold-brown of a tiger's eye stone, as if his wolf paced restlessly inside him while his body remained still. He stared at my hand for a split second, giving my brain plenty of time to torture me with fantasies of having the limb bitten off. Suddenly, he levered himself out of the chair, and I almost swallowed my tongue as the pressure of his aura and my own surprise threatened to knock me off my feet.

"I wish I could say it was nice to meet you," he said, taking my hand.

"I understand."

He wasn't as tall as Liam, but he was close, at least six foot. His hand closed around mine in a warm, firm grip. He didn't try to intimidate me, dominate me by crowding my personal space. There was no fevered hunger, nothing to suggest he was deciding which fleshy bit would taste best. Even his voice was calm. My stomach sank. His control was incredible—not the sort of shifter that would lose control and take a bite out of someone. If he'd taken a bite, he'd meant to do it.

"Not a pleasant situation, I'll agree," I said, trying to keep my voice upbeat. "Needs must, though, right? Quick and painless, that's the goal." I straightened my shoulders and unfastened my coat so I could unzip the black tactical pouch fastened around my waist. "Stephen, if you could tell me in your own words what happened last night?"

Liam's aura flared, adding a second wall of fire behind me. I kept my eyes down as I rifled through my pouch, trying not to sway on my feet as shifter energy battered me from all sides. How was a witch supposed to concentrate under these conditions? My hand brushed a push dagger, a bag of hard candy, and a hairbrush before my fingers found the collar.

I didn't realize until I looked up from my search that Stephen was looking at Liam, not me. I frowned.

"I'm sorry, Shade," Liam said. "We can't discuss an ongoing investigation. I hope you understand."

Steady. Breathe. "When Mother Hazel called you to inform you I was coming... What exactly did she say?"

"She said you would be coming to activate the suppression band."

"That's it?" I asked, already dreading the answer.

Liam crossed his arms. "That's it."

Damn her eyes. "She said I was only coming to bring the collar?"

"Yes." A hint of exasperation crept into his tone. "What's going on?"

I held the collar in front of me, but made no move toward Stephen. "I'm not here to activate the magic and leave. I'm here to work the case. At Mother Hazel's request."

Stillness crept over the werewolves. No emotion, no outward reaction. Instinct screamed at me, a primal urge to flee, now, before they could decide I was a threat and act accordingly. *Relax, Shade,* I chastised myself. *No one's going to hurt you.* Still, I wished Peasblossom was on my shoulder. She'd no doubt make an inappropriate observation to break the tense silence.

Finally, Liam inclined his head in a small bow of respect. "Of course I'm grateful for Mother Hazel's interest in helping. But I assure you it's not necessary." His deep voice was polite, but strained. "I requested the suppression band, but I in no way meant to invite anyone into this investigation."

"No need to invite me," I said with forced cheer. "Mother Hazel hired me. It's all settled."

I raised the collar, and whatever Liam had been about to say died instantly. Stephen twitched as if he'd fought not to take a step back, his gaze zeroing in on the leather circle.

No one spoke or moved. This wasn't just a monitoring device, a simple means of Otherworld house arrest. It would keep Stephen from shifting. It would cause him pain if he tried to hurt someone. And it would make him an easy target if he left his land.

Liam watched Stephen with an expectant look, a silent plea. I'd seen that look before. Usually on the face of a parent giving their child an ultimatum they hoped they wouldn't have to go through with. The alpha didn't speak, but I could see the words in his expression.

This is your last chance to tell me the truth.

Stephen's jaw clenched. He set his feet shoulder width apart and raised his chin. One hand closed over the opposite wrist behind his back. At first, it seemed defiant—a declaration that he had nothing to say. But the veins in his neck bulged, and sweat coated his temples. I suspected the stance was as much to stop himself from shaking, to keep himself from running, as it was a show for Liam's benefit.

"Do it," Liam said quietly.

Stephen kept his gaze straight ahead while I reached up. My heart pounded as I remembered Liam's warning about wolves panicking when the time came for the spell to activate. Stephen swallowed hard, then, with a surprising show of control, bent at the waist, making it easier for me to fasten the clasp. His aura grew hotter, a painful crackle against my skin as my fingers brushed his neck.

I traced a finger over the smooth leather. *"Vincio."* Gold magic coiled around the collar, snapping as the spell sank beneath the leather and touched the silver. I thought I heard a sound in Stephen's throat, a noise somewhere between a groan and a whimper, swallowed before it could pass his lips.

The energy in the room died, the sudden absence of all that fire staggering. All that remained was the steady buzz of Liam's aura against my side.

Nobody moved. My mind tortured me with images of Stephen's beast inside him, the howl of mourning as the metaphysical cage door slammed closed. I looked away, unwilling to see the pain in Stephen's face. I didn't know what was worse. The pain I knew he was going through, or the fact that his rigid control, his implacable serenity as I'd fastened the device around his neck, was the most damning evidence against his story he could have offered.

I dug around in the pouch, frustrated as a knot of twisty ties and paper clips kept me from getting a grip on the business card I wanted. I threw them out of the pouch onto the floor, then held the card out to Stephen.

"I'm a good listener," I said, forcing calm into my voice. "I don't judge. When you're ready to talk, please call me."

Stephen didn't accept the card. I hadn't really expected him to. I laid it on the arm of the recliner he'd been sitting in then collected the debris I'd scattered on the carpet and backed toward the door of the den. His gaze followed my movement, but the rest of him remained frozen in place. I couldn't read his emotion right now. Thank the Goddess.

"Thank you for your help, Shade." Liam picked up the card and slid it into his pocket. "I'll see you out."

I held his gaze and took out another card, putting it in the same place on the chair. "Lead the way."

The muscle in his jaw flexed, but he didn't take the second card. I waited for him to start for the door, keeping myself between him and the card, then fell into step behind him. I didn't speak until the den door closed behind us, giving Stephen the privacy to mourn his new circumstances.

"Detective, I understand your reluctance, but I really am here to help with the investigation."

"No, I'm afraid you don't understand." Liam held open the screen door that led onto the front stoop. "The coroner hasn't declared this a homicide yet. The suppression band is a formality, nothing more."

Well, that was a lie. If Liam had requested a collar before the death was ruled a homicide, then he'd been angry. Either Stephen had killed that man, or he'd lied to Liam. Either way, that collar was no "formality."

So much for playing nice. I sighed and straightened my spine to give myself all the height I could manage. "No, I'm sorry, detective. The fact of the matter is, my mentor instructed me to solve this murder—and she does believe that this was a murder. Even if I wanted to leave now, I can't. Disobeying her would be the same as one of your wolves disobeying you. And I'm sure you can understand how serious such a defiance would be. It would be easier for us both if we cooperated."

A tiny weight tugged at my hair, followed by the familiar sensation of Peasblossom climbing up my spine. My nerves calmed, both from the reassuring contact with my familiar and the promise of more information in the near future.

I stepped away from Liam, noting the way his eyes followed me with that easy intensity only predators managed. "You obviously want the truth, or you would never have called the Vanguard. And you clearly doubt Stephen has been completely honest with you, or you wouldn't have asked for the collar. Accept my help. Work with me. We will find out what happened."

"To be clear," Liam said calmly, "did your mentor send you because she lacks faith in me as a detective? Because she believes I cannot solve this case on my own? Or does she doubt me as the alpha of my pack? Because she's under the impression I would turn a blind eye to a member of my pack killing someone?"

"If you want to turn my presence into a personal insult, I can't stop you," I said. "But it changes nothing. I'm here. And I will remain here until I can tell my mentor with absolute certainty how Oliver Dale died." I tilted my head. "For what it's worth, I have faith in you as both a detective and an alpha. As such, I doubt it will take more than twenty-four hours for us to find the truth. Together."

Liam watched me for a long minute. He took more time to size me up than before, looking past the leggings. I imagined he gave my fanny pack a disparaging look, but I sensed camaraderie on the horizon, so I ignored it.

"All right." He glanced at the house before looking at me. "I'll walk you to your vehicle, then you can follow me to the station."

I waited for Peasblossom to settle in the neckline of my coat before following Liam to where I'd parked at the bottom of the driveway.

"So how much did Mother Hazel tell you?" he asked.

I rooted in my pouch for a notepad and a pen. "She said a boy called 911 and reported a body that looked like it an animal gnawed on it." I frowned down at the Transformer, wondering how the toy had gotten in my pouch. "The dispatcher called you because you're the head of the Wild Animal Task Force and you went to investigate. That's when you found Stephen in wolf form with blood on his mouth." I found the notebook and beamed at the pen tucked into the spiral binding. Perfect.

"Basically, yes. When I got the call, I contacted Stephen. He was on duty that night, patrolling the park."

"But you didn't get an answer." I removed the pen and flipped open the notebook.

Liam's mouth tightened. "I knew there was a problem, but at first I thought something else had attacked Oliver, and Stephen had engaged it. I had to consider the possibility that he might be hurt—I don't have to tell you the kind of dangerous creatures roam the forest at night."

"Barghests and crocottas." I shivered. If humans knew what sort of monsters lurked in the forests, they'd burn them to the ground and salt the earth.

"To name two." He stopped at my car and leaned against the hood, bracing his hands against the slate-grey metal. "When I found Stephen with blood on his face—*human* blood"—he shook his head—"I had no choice but to prepare for the worst. I called Blake, my second-in-command. He's a detective, so I assigned the case to him. He went to the station where the witness was waiting. I told him to take the kid's statement, then get to the scene and lock it down before calling the forensics team."

"And you questioned Stephen."

"Yeah. He said he spotted the body when he was on patrol. When he got there, he smelled barghest. He thought he'd interrupted it and it might still be close by, so he shifted in the hope he might track it down before it found a replacement meal."

Barghests didn't need to feed often. A single large meal a month was usually sufficient. Unfortunately, when it did come time for them to eat, they were ravenous, and very violent. A meal could be a fully grown deer, but they favored humans if they could manage it. Only a human dinner would feed their magic as well as their physical body.

Liam paused, and I didn't press him to continue. He studied the small trees lining the road for a moment, gathering his thoughts. "Hunger when you're a wolf isn't the same as hunger when you're human."

I leaned against the driver's-side door, absorbing the warmth from the sun-heated metal. "Given the different brain structure, it's not surprising. The amygdala is more dominant in wolves than in humans."

Liam looked at me. "That's right."

I crossed my arms, mirroring him even as I resisted the urge to scoot closer. Now that he wasn't being a jerk, the temptation to bask in his aura returned. I slid farther away. "I'm a witch, detective. You shouldn't act so surprised when I know something."

"I didn't realize being a witch meant studying medicine," he said.

"It means studying everything. I have the equivalent of at least five PhDs in terms of human education."

"My apologies." He gazed across the street, into the distance toward the Rocky River Reservation. "Stephen told me he forgot to eat before he went on duty. After he shifted, what had been annoying hunger pains became something more. And there he was, standing over a still-warm, bleeding body. He took a bite before he could stop himself. As soon as he had meat in his belly, he regained his senses and ran off after the barghest."

I didn't look at him, didn't trust what expression was on my face. It was a pathetic story. Liam had to know how pathetic his story sounded.

"He's not feral, as far as I can tell," I said.

"No, he's not feral. If he'd gone feral, he would have attacked me. Possibly hunted down the boy."

I didn't point out that he could have been interrupted by new prey and simply abandoned one meal for the temptation of a better one. Feral werewolves weren't like wolves or men, but rather the most twisted version of each—very unpredictable. If Oliver Dale had already been dead, a fresh kill might have been appetizing enough to lead him away. Liam knew that already.

"Tell me about Stephen."

"Born a lycanthrope, both parents also lycanthropes. Mother and father were both very loving and very supportive."

"That's good," I said. "Loving, supportive parents who are in a position to help him throughout the transition after his first shift. That must have made it easier for him."

"Too easy, perhaps," Liam agreed. He stared at the front window as if he could will Stephen to come out and apologize, admit he'd held back and confess everything. "Sometimes I think he'd have benefited if his parents had challenged him more, doted on him a little less."

"What makes you say that?"

He shifted his weight, leaning more heavily against my car. "A lot of things come naturally for Stephen. He's strong; he's fast. Played football in high school and college. Could have gone pro, but chose to join the force instead." He glanced at me. "How much do you know about our hierarchy?"

"I'm not sure what names you give the different positions in your pack," I said. "In my experience, that varies from pack to pack. But my understanding is that there's an alpha, then a second- and third-in-command, and two enforcers that act as personal bodyguards to the alpha. There are other positions a pack fills as necessary."

Liam nodded. "I'm called the *kongur*."

"Old Norse for 'one who steers the helm,'" I noted.

"Blake is my second-in-command, the *jarl*. My third-in-command, the *stallari*, isn't on the force, so you probably won't meet her. The *hersir* are my enforcers. Stephen is one of them." He braced his hands against the hood of my car. "When someone joins the pack, they have the option of challenging someone in an existing role to take their place in the hierarchy. Stephen challenged one of my *hersir* and won." He looked at me. "Easily won."

"But?"

"But he never even considered challenging for *stallari*. I don't think he could win against Blake for *jarl*, but he had a solid chance for *stallari*. Stephen wouldn't even try."

"You think he was afraid?"

Liam scoffed. "No. I think he took a position high enough in the hierarchy to be dominant to most of the pack, but not so high that he would have more day-to-day responsibilities. And if someone wants to challenge for alpha, they have to start with my third-in-command, my *stallari*." He scratched his chin. "I feel like a father telling his son to live up to his potential. I keep telling him, if he'd put in a little more effort, he could have anything he wanted. But he's happy where he is. So he says."

"Do his parents know about what happened?"

"No. They moved to Montana a few years ago. I'm not going to contact them until I know something. If Stephen wants to call them, he can."

"I doubt he will," I said, crossing my arms. "You said you feel like his father. Did you ever have to discipline him?"

"No. Stephen is stubborn when it comes to leaving his comfort zone, but he doesn't disobey me." He stared at the house, frustration deepening the crease between his eyebrows. "Until now. I don't know what happened."

"Were there reports of any other injuries, or dead animals?" I asked. "Anything to suggest there might have been someone or something else in the woods last night?"

"Another ranger—a human, Emma—found a dog that was in bad shape. But it hadn't been attacked; it was just a pet that got away from its walker. Poor beast got itself caught on a tree root near a ravine and almost hung itself."

I stared at him, my stomach dropping. "Please tell me the dog is okay. She found it in time."

The corner of his mouth twitched up at my concern. "Yes. Emma got her to the hospital. Significant bruising around the neck and some light damage to her throat; a broken bone or two in her leg. Emma had to cut her down quickly and wasn't able to get in a position to catch her. But she'll be fine."

I relaxed against the car. I didn't own a pet myself—Majesty was *not* my cat—but I lived in a neighborhood where more people owned a dog than didn't. I knew how loved they were, how very much a part of the family a pet became.

"So did the coroner send you his initial findings for Oliver Dale?"

"He did. So far, cause of death is blood loss. It's unclear from what."

So it could have been Stephen.

We stood there in silence for a few long minutes.

"You know," I said slowly, "barghests aren't the only creatures roaming the woods. There are others whose sense of humor can be as deadly as teeth and claws."

"Such as?"

I shrugged. "Will-o'-the-wisps can affect someone's logic. They sort of hover in your mind, project emotions or thoughts into your brain. Usually they lead you into a bog, or too close to the water where a kelpie or rusalka is waiting, but... Well, it's not impossible that one of them might have seen Stephen sniffing the victim to get the barghest's scent and decided to have some fun."

Liam stared into the blank space. "So they could have tricked Stephen into eating the body? He could be telling me the truth as he knows it?"

I really wanted it to be true. But I couldn't lie. "It's possible."

"Possible," Liam echoed. He kicked a piece of loose gravel to skitter across the driveway. "But not likely."

"Not likely." I cleared my throat and stepped in front of him. "Still, an investigator must consider all possibilities and avoid jumping to conclusions."

He arched an eyebrow at me. "True."

"And you know, truth is stranger than fiction."

"Often." He smiled and stood from the car as well, dropping his arms to his sides. "And who knows, the final coroner's report may list cause of death as natural. A heart attack."

I twisted my mouth into what I hoped was a reassuring smile. "Sure."

"All right, then, Shade Renard. Follow me to the station and we'll get started." He paused, then added, "And call me Liam."

I nodded and opened my door, sliding inside as I watched Liam walk to his official vehicle. It had been a rocky start, but at least he was trying. I climbed into my car and shut the door behind me.

"Stephen did it."

Peasblossom made her announcement from my dashboard, her wings catching the sunlight and throwing shards of gold over the car's interior. I sighed and pulled onto the road, allowing Liam to back out and then following him.

"What makes you say that?" I asked.

"Besides the blood on his mouth?"

I rolled my eyes. "Yes, besides that."

Peasblossom kicked her feet where they dangled over the

edge of the dash. "He's lying to his alpha. That's serious business. What else could be serious enough to make him lie?"

"A valid point. Did you overhear anything useful before I got there?"

"I think I missed an argument. After a really long staring contest, Liam started pacing the room. He told Stephen he didn't find any evidence of a barghest. Stephen tried to suggest the barghest might have retreated to the astral plane, but Liam shouted at him, said there was no DNA from a barghest at the crime scene, and the wizard didn't pick up any magical traces either."

"They have a wizard?"

"Apparently."

Wizards, in my experience, tended to be too holier than thou for my taste. They held a certain bloodthirsty political drive reminiscent of the days they'd been part of a royal court, often on equal or greater standing with the king or queen. Mother Hazel had no use for them. I made a mental note to look into this wizard.

"So Liam dismissed the barghest as a complete fabrication."

"Yes."

"Did he say anything else? Anything that might tell us if he's convinced Stephen did it?"

"No. Stephen wouldn't talk to him at all, not a word." Peasblossom's forehead wrinkled. "Stephen looked like he wanted to say something. I mean, he didn't seem defiant or smug or anything. He looked upset, like…" She gave up and crossed her arms. "Werewolves are stupid."

"Interesting." I tapped my finger on the steering wheel. "So either he did it, and he can't bring himself to tell Liam, or someone else did it, and for some reason he feels revealing who it was to his alpha would be worse than admitting he did it."

"Could someone else have done it, but they're threatening

him to keep quiet? Maybe threatening to hurt his pack, or even the alpha himself?"

An image of Liam hovered in my mind's eye, and my skin buzzed with a sensory memory of his heated aura. "I have a hard time believing Stephen would feel Liam needs protecting."

"So you think he did it."

"There has to be a reason she was keen for me to take this case. She offered an unqualified favor for solving it—not an offer she'd extend on a whim."

Peasblossom crawled over the dash and stood behind the steering wheel. "So you think he did it?"

I scowled and arched my neck to look over her. "I'd say proving a werewolf police officer is guilty of murder would qualify as pretty serious."

Liam turned down a road lined on either side with thick trees. I followed, glad for the lack of traffic as my mind continued to process my meeting with the suspect.

"Something's bothering you," Peasblossom said.

"It's probably nothing. It's just the way Liam talked about Stephen, telling me to be ready for a feral wolf. I was expecting an attack. Maybe not a salivating, golden-eyed ball of fur and claws, but something equally terrifying. Stephen was completely calm. I just... I'm surprised his alpha misjudged him by such a large margin." I bit my lip. "I've seen a feral werewolf. I've seen people who kill for pleasure, or kill indiscriminately. I've seen people who killed by accident. Stephen didn't have any of those qualities. He looked...frustrated and resigned. And he's a cop—if he wanted to kill someone, you'd think he'd plan it better. Liam caught him running on the other side of the park. Why leave the body? And there's a river, why not wash himself off, at least?"

"Well, if he didn't eat him by accident, like Liam said, and he didn't plan to kill him, then what's left? Someone or something made him do it?"

"I don't know." I thought back to the werewolf, remembering the roiling energy churning beneath the composed surface. The stiffness in his body as he'd leaned down to let me put the collar on him. That had been, perhaps, one of the greatest shows of control I'd ever seen. It wouldn't surprise me if Stephen were alpha himself one day. *Kongur.* Assuming the Vanguard didn't take him away…

"It would be nice to prove his innocence instead of his guilt," I admitted.

Peasblossom sat down, her little face looking sad. "I don't think that's going to happen."

CHAPTER 4

"The sign says 'Official Personnel Only.'"

I ignored Peasblossom and followed Liam's vehicle past the warning sign to the parking lot behind the ranger station. "I can read. But that's where Liam's going, so that's where we're going. I'm not going to park up front and then wander inside looking for his office."

"Don't trust him?"

No, I don't. "Of course I trust him. He may not have been happy at my involvement in the investigation at first, but he's come around. I just don't want to waste time getting separated. This is a murder investigation."

"Says you. The alpha says that hasn't been determined yet. If it was a barghest, it's accidental. Animal attack, not murder."

I pushed back against my seat and squirmed, trying to scratch an itch by rubbing my back against the seat. "I'm not buying the barghest attack theory. Didn't you feel the energy in that room?"

Peasblossom shivered. "Of course I did. That was a very distraught werewolf."

I let out a relieved breath as the itch surrendered to the muted scratching. "But he didn't shift. Not even a little. He didn't shift; he didn't snap at me. That level of discipline doesn't happen overnight—and it doesn't snap because he was peckish." I tucked my car keys into the side pocket of my waist pouch, careful not to store them in the enchanted main compartment. *Fool me once.*

"So it won't be a human coroner who makes the call on whether or not this is a homicide," Peasblossom said. "When the human coroner finishes, they'll have someone from the Otherworld have a turn."

"Right. And whoever performs that autopsy will determine if it was a werewolf or a barghest." I lowered my voice as Liam exited his car. "There must be a reason Mother Hazel based a wager on this case. And I don't think it was a rogue barghest."

I got out of my car as Liam approached, watching his face for any sign he'd heard me. He didn't appear agitated, so I guessed not.

"This way," he said.

I fell into step behind him. He gripped the knob of a door labeled Official Personnel Only, but froze before pulling it open. My pulse jumped as his nostrils flared. Blue eyes fixated on my neck.

"Is something wrong?" I asked, my voice higher than I'd intended. His energy flared against my aura, and I swayed forward, then immediately scowled and leaned back.

"That smell. It was in Stephen's house too." He scented the air. "What is that smell?"

"I do not smell!" Peasblossom leapt out from behind my neck, glaring at Liam.

Now it was Liam's turn to lean back. "A…pixie?"

I sighed. "Peasblossom, this is Detective Sergeant Liam Osbourne. Liam, this is Peasblossom, my familiar."

The skin around his eyes tightened. "You have a pixie as a familiar?"

I lifted my chin. "Yes."

His lips parted, but he closed his mouth without saying anything. He opened the door for me, and a less charitable woman may have observed he fled into the building to escape the pixie. Peasblossom flopped down on my shoulder to continue glaring after him, surreptitiously sniffing her arm.

"There are humans here," I said under my breath.

"Yeah, yeah," she muttered. With one final sniff, she resumed her hiding place under my hair.

Conversation filtered out of the offices we passed, quieting when Liam came within ten feet. He nodded to several people, but didn't stop to converse with anyone. The authority in his stride seemed to discourage anyone from crossing his path, and it didn't take long for us to reach our destination. The room we entered was a large rectangle, with beige walls. Three long tables formed lines on either side, with two chairs at each positioned to face a large whiteboard. A small snack area took up half of the back wall, complete with a coffee maker and a small fridge.

The room's three occupants stopped what they were doing when we entered. My attention immediately gravitated to a ranger leaning between the two chairs at the table against the far wall closest to the whiteboard, his large hand resting on a map. His buzz cut looked soft and fuzzy, and for one weird moment, I wanted to pet him. The hard expression in his dark brown eyes suggested that would not go over well. A beard and mustache covered the lower half of his face, thick enough that I couldn't see his jaw, but not long enough to worry about having someone use it as a handhold in a fight. His gaze flicked from me to Liam.

"Shade Renard, meet the Wild Animal Task Force. Everyone, this is Ms. Shade Renard. Mother Renard. She'll be assisting with the investigation." He gestured to the ranger first. "This is Detective Blake Giles."

Blake nodded at me, but didn't seem terribly happy with my

presence. I told myself that was just him being a stern second-in-command and I shouldn't take it personally.

"This is Vincent Aegis," Liam continued. "He's our forensic lab technician."

He gestured to a middle-aged man sitting catty-corner behind Blake. He wore a grey cotton shirt under an open dusty-blue dress shirt and khaki pants. His wild brown hair flared about his head as if he ran his hands through it a lot—or perhaps had stuck his finger in an electric socket. At Liam's use of the title "Mother," he startled and put down the small athame he'd been holding.

"I'm sorry," he said, holding up a hand. "You're a witch?"

I arched an eyebrow. "I am."

"She is not here to replace you, Vincent," Liam assured him. "Ms. Renard's mentor, Mother Hazel, was kind enough to hire her to help us."

His tone made it clear how much help he thought I'd be. I didn't rise to the bait, choosing instead to fix Vincent with a warm smile. "You're the wizard," I guessed, gesturing at the wooden staff propped against the table next to him.

"I am." He paused. "Mother Hazel. I know that name, don't I?"

"Everyone else does," I agreed with a sigh.

He toyed with the athame. "And she sent you here to work this case?"

"Yes. I hope I can be of help."

Vincent didn't respond. Blake stared at me harder now, as if contemplating physically ejecting me from the room. I met his gaze and held it.

"I'm a half-ghoul."

I blinked, startled by the feminine voice, and swiveled my head to face the speaker. She stood apart from the other occupants, closer to the window. Her voice was soft, her declaration a gentle announcement, as if she felt obligated to warn me of her nature. For my part, I did my best not to stare. I'd never met a half-ghoul before.

The ghouls I had encountered—usually when I came to exorcise them from a graveyard—were skeletal, rotting creatures, with pallid faces and eyes bulging from dilapidated sockets. This woman was beautiful, with delicate features and straight dark blonde hair that fell around her face to brush her shoulders. She wore a pink shirt and blue jeans with a battered pair of tennis shoes. White gloves encased her hands.

"It's nice to meet you…?"

"Kylie. Kylie Rose."

"Kylie is an autopsy technician," Liam explained. "She'll examine the body when Dr. Dannon is through."

"I take it Dr. Dannon is human?"

"Yes. I wanted to choose an Other coroner for the task force, but Dr. Dannon served with Doctors Without Borders, and he has a great deal of experience with animal attack victims. There was no argument I could make for not letting him handle this autopsy."

Liam's voice was so conversational, so easygoing, that I almost didn't notice the anticipatory tension to his stance. He hadn't told me I'd be meeting a half-ghoul, probably because he wanted to see me make a fool out of myself. Half-ghouls were rare enough that there were those who denied their existence. And no one I'd ever met interacted with them by choice.

Unfortunately for Liam, I'd spent far too many years with Mother Hazel to be scared off by a half-ghoul.

"It's lovely to meet you, Kylie." I circled the tables to offer her my hand.

She hesitated a second, then took it. "Nice to meet you."

I nodded, then turned to Vincent and Blake. "It's lovely to meet you as well, Vincent, Blake. I look forward to working with all of you."

Vincent rose as if suddenly remembering his manners. His abrupt movement shoved his chair back into his staff and there was a mad moment of scrambling as he caught it just in time to keep the heavy wood from slamming into the floor. "A pleasure, Ms. Renard," he said, his voice pleasant, if breathless. He offered his hand.

"Please, call me Shade," I said, accepting the handshake.

I'd already taken another step to offer my hand to Blake when I noticed the German shepherd lying on the floor, its black muzzle cradled on beige paws. It rolled brown eyes up at me, and I started to smile, my lips parting to greet the pretty canine.

Something stopped me before I could use the honeyed voice people reserved for pets and small children. The intelligence in the German shepherd's gaze wasn't unusual; most dogs had a very human gaze. But the casualness of its posture didn't match the energy I sensed vibrating under the surface. I frowned, leaned closer. Without thinking, I raised a hand. *Revelare,* I thought, pushing outward with my magic.

Silver energy flowed forward, brushing against the dog. Its collar tugged at my spell, bursting to life with purple brilliance. I blinked. An illusion spell. I looked back at Liam, a question on my lips. Then it hit me, and I realized what the collar was. I stared at the wolf. "You're a werewolf."

The dog didn't react.

Blake scowled. "She's not going to change for you, if that's what you're waiting for. She's on duty."

I ignored his salty tone and nodded to the dog in greeting. "It's a pleasure to meet you...?" I raised my eyebrows at Blake.

The muscle in his jaw twitched. "Sonar."

I waited.

"As far as you're concerned, her name is Sonar," Blake said.

Liam stepped closer, using his position to intercede in the tension building between me and his *jarl.*

"Don't take offense, Ms. Renard. It's a matter of security. Sonar is what you might consider an undercover operative. There's no need for you to know her real identity, and the less you know, the less chance there is of revealing something by accident. It could be awkward if you called her by her real name in the presence of any human personnel, and worse if someone Other heard you." He nodded toward Sonar. "In point of fact, it's important that you treat her as you would any other dog."

I glanced at Sonar. She still lay there. Watching me. "Seems awkward."

"Well, if you hadn't been nosy with your magic, and let her keep her secret, it wouldn't be awkward," Blake pointed out.

I didn't like Blake.

"What if something happened to you?" I asked him. "What would happen when they reassigned Sonar to someone else?"

"Wouldn't happen," Blake said. "That's not how a K9 partner works. Once the force assigns an officer a puppy, that dog is theirs, permanently."

I turned that piece of information over in my mind. "So if an officer got a puppy, trained it, then had to retire due to injury or some other accident...?"

"Dog retires too."

"That's..." I stopped, a smile pulling at my mouth despite the tension in the room. "I like that." I looked at Sonar and remembered she wasn't really a dog. "I mean, I think it's wonderful that the police force takes the bond between an officer and his canine partner so seriously."

I thought Blake's expression softened, but a second later, he was giving me the stink eye again.

"I don't meant to be nosy," I started, ignoring Blake's eye roll. "But I thought it was bad for a shifter to stay in animal form for too long. Wouldn't being on duty for eight hours straight be...taxing?"

"We go home for our lunch hour and she shifts back," Blake said, his tone making it clear he didn't think it was any of my business.

"That seems like it would be more challenging, not less," I said. "Isn't it a little tiring to change back and forth like that in such a short amount of time?" I'd known werewolves that could do it, but they'd all been high-ranking members of their pack. It wasn't something I'd have expected from your average werewolf.

Blake scowled, putting himself between me and Sonar. "Are you here to help or play twenty questions?"

Very defensive of his partner, I noted. I looked at Sonar, who was watching me with a considering gaze. She didn't move from her position on the floor despite being the topic of conversation. Before I could comment further, Liam spoke up again.

"Now that introductions are finished," he said, "let's begin. Blake, why don't you summarize where we are for Ms. Renard?"

"Shade," I insisted.

Liam waved a hand. "Summarize for *Shade*."

Blake rolled his eyes, but stepped closer to the table, tapping the papers in the folder close to the edge. "Last night, sixteen-year-old Greg Tyler was walking his neighbor's dog, Gypsy, outside an apartment building down the street. The dog got away from him and chased a squirrel toward the reservation. Greg tried to catch her, but eventually had to turn back. A neighbor in the same apartment building, a Mr. Oliver Dale, witnessed Gypsy's escape and followed her in his car."

"So our victim is the helpful neighbor," I said.

Blake's expression turned grim. "No. According to Greg, Dale's apparent eagerness to help was anything but comforting. In his statement, Greg said Dale hated Gypsy. When he pursued her, Greg feared for the dog's safety and called her owner, Anthony Catello, in a panic. Anthony left work to retrieve his dog and told to Greg return home."

"And did he?" I asked.

"For about an hour. Then he said he couldn't stand it anymore and he left to find Gypsy himself."

Again, Blake's tone said more than his words. I winced. "He's the one who found the body."

"'Fraid so."

I shook my head. I hadn't seen the crime photos yet, but I didn't need to see them to know that no teenage boy should have to see what was left after a werewolf took a bite out of a body.

"He took it better than some," Blake said finally. "He had enough sense to call 911."

"And what about Anthony Catello?" I asked.

Blake's mouth tightened. "Guy's got a record as long as my tail. One of our rangers, Emma, was on duty last night, and she had the dubious honor of encountering Mr. Catello when he came looking for Gypsy. According to her statement, Catello appeared severely agitated, ranting about his neighbor out there trying to kill his dog. He was flailing his arms around, and Emma caught a glimpse of a firearm, so she confiscated his weapon."

"He didn't have a concealed carry permit?"

"Wouldn't have mattered if he did. When law enforcement engages you, even if it's to say hello, if you're carrying a firearm, you're required to say so. He didn't. Emma had the authority to take his weapon, permit or no."

I winced. "I suppose he didn't react well to that?"

Blake snorted. "No shit. Emma took the gun and sent him home, told him she'd find Gypsy."

"Gypsy is the dog you mentioned earlier, isn't she?" I asked Liam. "The one who nearly died after getting her leash caught and hanging herself?"

"Yes," Liam confirmed. "Emma found her just in time."

"Not that Catello appreciated it," Blake muttered. "Anyway, after Emma got Gypsy down, she contacted Stephen, who was also on patrol. Stephen agreed to cover for her while she took Gypsy to the hospital." He picked up a few files and dropped them in front of me. "These witness statements give the same information I went over."

I thumbed through them, skimming quickly. "There's no statement from Mr. Catello."

"I'll be going to see him today," Liam said. "Stay here and review the forensics with Vincent and Kylie."

Peasblossom snickered.

"No, I'll come with you," I said, replacing the files. "I'm good with people, and I can always read the forensic reports afterward." I tapped the papers and spoke to Vincent and Kylie, "If you could make me a copy?"

Liam's hands curled into fists, then he released them with visible effort. "Ms. Ren— Shade. Anthony Catello has a record. And not for nothing, but it's mostly aggravated assault and criminal menacing."

"A strong suspect, then—even more reason I should be present for this interview." I turned to face the half-ghoul, trying to head off the warning from Liam, even though I knew it was pointless. "Kylie, is there anything you can tell me about how Oliver died that might help when I question Mr. Catello?"

Kylie nodded. "In addition to the damage to the victim's midsection, there was a small injury at the back of his skull, we think from where it struck the ground when he fell. He also had a red welt on his palm that could be a rope burn. Preliminary cause of death is blood loss. Estimated time of death is between eleven p.m. and three a.m. I'll have a better time of death after Dr. Dannon finishes the autopsy and I can perform my own...tests."

"She's going to eat part of the body to determine time of death," Peasblossom whispered. Her voice held the satisfaction of a kid revealing gross but true information to an adult, relishing the reaction she knew was coming.

I tried very hard not to wrinkle my nose. *Ew.* I looked to the wizard, hoping for less visceral information. "Anything from the scene analysis that might help?"

Vincent twisted the athame in his hands. "I'll have all the videos ready to view soon."

"And the analysis?" Liam pressed. "The fur and blood collected at the scene? Have you been able to confirm there was a barghest?"

Vincent released the small blade and crossed his arms. "My magic provides the bigger picture, but it is science that gives us results for the official report, and science takes time. I will have iron-clad results by tomorrow evening at the latest."

"The sooner the better. In the meantime, work with Blake. I want that barghest found."

I studied Vincent's face as Liam turned away. He didn't have the confidence of a wizard who could give his boss the proof he wanted that there'd been a barghest in that forest. He looked like a wizard trying to avoid telling an alpha werewolf that his subordinate was lying. That there'd been no barghest.

Blake nodded. "We'll find him."

I swore Sonar nodded too.

"All right." Liam took a deep breath, as if bracing himself for something unpleasant. "Shade?"

He gestured toward the door, and I waved goodbye to the room and followed him out. This time as we passed through the station, I paid close attention to how the other employees reacted to Liam. Most halted casual conversation; all said hello and smiled. Three of them straightened, not like soldiers coming to attention, but more like someone instinctively reacting to a superior. By the time we left the building, I was comfortable betting I could pick out at least three more werewolves, one officer, and two office personnel.

It seemed as if there was more overlap between the Cleveland Metropark Police and the Rocky River pack than I'd thought. Was that why Mother Hazel put me on this case? Was Liam right —did she think there would be a cover-up?

"Before we question this witness, there is one thing I need to make clear."

Liam's voice pulled me out of my thoughts, and it took me a moment to focus on what he was saying. "Yes?"

"You are a civilian. Catello has a temper, and he's dangerous. I'm letting you come along, but I expect you to stay behind me. Do not put yourself into danger." He opened his car door and paused, facing me, before climbing into the car. "Are we clear?"

Irritation rose, sharp and fast, prickling my intentions to play nice with the alpha werewolf. Every time I thought we'd come to an understanding, he said something to make me realize he was only barely tolerating my presence.

"Get him, Shade," Peasblossom whispered.

A frown tugged down the corners of Liam's mouth, and I knew he'd heard her. I opened my car door and climbed inside the SUV, trying to grab the ends of my own temper before I said what was really on my mind. I counted to ten as I fastened my seatbelt, waiting until Liam slid into his seat before speaking. "You keep doing that."

He paused with his key in the ignition. "Doing what?"

I turned to face him, letting my face slide into the expression Mother Hazel termed the "witchy look." Similar to the look a parent gives a teenager when they start to think they don't need to obey the rules anymore. "You keep forgetting I'm a witch. I thought we could do without titles, but perhaps you do need the reminder. Mother Renard will be fine for now."

Liam's expression shut down, all emotion draining from his face as he started the car and pulled out of his parking space. "You feel I've disrespected you?"

"You have most certainly disrespected me." I dug around in my pouch for a mint. If I wasn't driving, I was prone to car sickness, and throwing up in Liam's vehicle wouldn't do anything for my credibility with the werewolf.

"Since when is looking out for someone's physical safety disrespectful? You do realize that's my job?"

I squinted into the pouch. Was that a horse bridle? "I know what your job is. It's you who seem to misunderstand mine."

"You're a village witch."

"And a private investigator." I beamed as I finally closed my fingers around the tin of mints. *Success.*

"Are you a licensed private investigator, or when you say private investigator, is that a self-designation based on your own assessment of your skills?"

My mouth fell open, and I almost lost my mint.

"Now you've done it," Peasblossom told him from under the protective curtain of my hair.

"Tell me, Detective Liam Osbourne, what is it you think village witches do?"

If he registered the warning in my tone, he didn't show it. "My understanding is that you fill several roles. Mostly that of a doctor and a midwife, but also a farmer and an herbalist."

"And I do fill those roles. I also protect the people of my village from threats, both mundane and those of the Otherworld. I've dealt with goblins, troglodytes, and ghouls on a regular basis. I've retrieved children from the astral plane. I've seen things that would curl your fur, and gone to sleep with nightmares I wouldn't wish on my worst enemy. I do not sit in my house all day brewing potions, nor do I spend all my time babysitting. I am more than capable of taking care of myself, and to suggest that I need your protection against a human brute is not only disrespectful, it's insulting."

"I meant no insult. I'm sorry you took it that way."

I bristled at the backhanded apology. My magic rose with my temper, and I had to remind myself that setting his car on fire to prove my point would be childish. "Tell me, detective, if it were your female ranger, Emma, sitting here instead of me, would you have said the same thing to her? Told her to stay behind you? Not to put herself in danger?"

"No," Liam said. "Emma is a trained police officer. She knows how to handle herself."

"And how do you think she'd react if you did give her such a warning?"

He grinned. "She'd punch me in the face."

A conversational victory was within my grasp, but the humor in Liam's voice made me close my mouth on my next sentence. I turned in my seat so I could study Liam more closely. The smile had softened the hard lines of his square jaw, and a twinkle in his eyes made the blue less like winter ice and more like a spring sky. "You like her."

He arched an eyebrow without looking at me. "I'm sorry?"

"Emma. You like her."

"I do. She's a strong woman, and a valuable officer."

"And pretty?"

Now he did look at me. "Yes. But you're barking up the wrong tree."

"Ha, he said barking." Peasblossom snickered.

I brushed at Peasblossom, urging her to be quiet. "Am I? You seem awfully happy when you talk about her."

He opened his mouth then shut it. "All right. Yes, Emma and I had a date—one date, years ago. It was right before she transferred here to my unit."

"So you called it off because you didn't want to date someone under your command."

"Exactly." He met my eyes briefly. "And there has been nothing since. Nor will there be. Which is fine."

"Fine."

The word reflected my doubt more than I'd meant it to. Liam sighed.

"Emma is beautiful, smart, and strong. I asked her out, and she accepted. We had one date. I did not have time to form a deeper attachment, and neither did she. We made the mutual decision not to pursue it when she came under my command,

and that was that. Please don't imagine that either of us pined for the other. As a private investigator, I hope you're capable of focusing on facts and not some imagined drama."

"Is it common for werewolves to date non-werewolves?"

Liam shrugged. "I don't know about common. Werewolves tend to seek strong mates, so there's a tendency to skew toward other werewolves, but a strong woman is a strong woman, no matter the species."

Werewolf mating habits hadn't been an area covered very extensively in my studies. I considered what he'd said. "So, do you only date humans for fun, or do you date them with the intention of keeping them as a permanent mate?"

"I think you'll find werewolves don't often date for fun. Casual sex, maybe, but dating someone, getting to know them, usually only happens if it could be serious. If we don't see a future in it, we don't bother. You'll find exceptions, I'm sure, but in my experience, that's the way it is." He shrugged. "That doesn't mean I intended to take Emma as my mate. We date to get to know people like anyone else; we don't get serious with everyone we go out to dinner with."

I started to say something, but he kept going.

"Lycanthropy isn't a disease. It's not passed through blood or semen."

"I know. It's a curse, with a very specific trigger. You have to bite someone with the intention of turning them. Or, sometimes, if the werewolf is agitated enough, the madness is enough to replace intention."

"We don't consider it a curse," Liam said tightly.

I flushed. "Sorry. I meant no offense."

He shrugged it off. "You need to understand, werewolves aren't a huge population. Packs are small in most areas. If we limited ourselves to only mating with other werewolves, we'd end up in the same inbreeding boat with the old royal families— and probably with their marriage customs, too."

"Good point." I drummed my fingers on my waist pouch. "So if you do mate with a human, do you…" I searched my brain for a nice word to use. Something besides "infect" or "curse."

"Our instincts guide us to find a strong mate," Liam said patiently. "When the time is right, we share our true nature. If our mate wants to be part of that, then we share that gift with them. If not, then that's fine too." Defensiveness tightened his shoulders. "We aren't brutes who can't be trusted not to hurt someone we love just because they're physically weaker."

I considered that for a while. I'd never really stopped to consider werewolf mating idiosyncrasies. It was very interesting. "So, are you dating anyone now?" I asked.

"No."

"Are you looking for someone?"

He shrugged. "It's doesn't top my list of priorities, but yes. I'm not required to have a mate as alpha, but two strong leaders are better than one."

I sucked on my mint, turning it over in my mouth as I considered that. "Do you want a human mate?"

This time he turned to study me for longer than was safe while driving. It wasn't until I made eye contact that I registered the arched eyebrow. It took me another ten seconds to realize how I'd sounded.

"Not me," I mumbled, cursing the blush heating my cheeks. "I wasn't… I didn't mean…" I huffed out a breath. "Blood and bones."

Liam didn't say anything.

I opted not to continue the conversation. I obviously couldn't be trusted not to make an idiot of myself. To make matters worse, now that my accidental innuendo was out there, I was once again hyperaware of Liam's aura. In the small confines of the car, it was impossible to get away from that warm, tingling energy.

Peasblossom crawled closer to my ear. "Get your hormones under control before you embarrass me!"

I closed my eyes and tried to will the pixie into silence as I resisted the urge to use an invisibility spell. This was what they meant when they said curiosity killed the cat. The feline obviously died of embarrassment.

Thankfully, true to Liam's word, it wasn't long before we arrived at the apartment complex. It was a three-story building, with a brownish-red brick exterior for the first half and cream-colored stucco for the upper floors. The brown roof extended down past the first floor with breaks to allow third-floor windows. The landscaping was neat, but sparse, and the asphalt wanted repaving.

I said a small prayer of thanks as we got out of the car, and the cool air dispelled the heat of the werewolf's aura. Just to be on the safe side, I kept five feet of space between us as we crossed the parking lot. "Did you call ahead to talk to the manager?"

Liam led the way toward the front entrance, his stride making it clear that it was my job to keep up. "Yes. He said Anthony is in apartment 4B. Oliver Dale was to the right of him, apartment 4C. He said he'd send the maintenance man to let us in."

Peasblossom clung to my ear, unwilling to give up the ability to project her voice directly into my auditory canal despite the strong, cold breeze blowing her wings back. "He's walking too fast for you on purpose!"

"Yes, he is, and he can bloody well wait for me." I slowed my pace. "Someone is going to notice our arrival. Have a look around. If anyone gets chatty when they see Liam, I want to know what they say."

"I saw a window garden on the second floor. If any fey live there, maybe they witnessed something."

"You are so clever. Yes, talk to them, then wait for me by the SUV."

Preening at the compliment, Peasblossom launched herself off my shoulder and disappeared in a pink streak of light. Liam stood at the exit, holding it open for me as if he'd remembered his manners. Something akin to amusement lightened his eyes, and he dipped his head as I walked past him.

There was no one waiting for us outside apartment 4C, so we moved on to Anthony's door. Liam knocked, and I had a quick decision to make. Stand beside him and risk letting his aura coax me into another embarrassing breach of personal space, or stand away from him and let him think I'd conceded to his protection from the human with the violent record.

I stood beside him. Liam sighed, but didn't comment.

A woman in her mid-thirties answered the door. She had pale brown skin, and dark hair that bounced in soft waves around her shoulders. The white shirt and black pants she wore had the look of work clothes to them. Except for the dog hair on the pants. I shook my head. Black pants, white dog. Never a good combination.

The polite smile on her face wavered when she saw Liam's uniform. "Hi, can I help you?"

"Good afternoon, miss, I'm Detective Sergeant Osbourne of the Cleveland Metropark Rangers. I'm looking for Mr. Anthony Catello?"

Canine whimpering came from the back room, soft, but insistent. The woman glanced over her shoulder, then said in a raised but smooth voice, "It's all right, Gypsy. I'll be right back, sweetheart." She stepped away from the door, then stopped, giving us an apologetic wince. "I'm sorry, I should get back there. Anthony stepped out, but he should be back soon." She hesitated. "I can tell him you called?"

"That's Gypsy back there?" I asked.

"Yes. Anthony asked me to sit with her while he ran out for some supplies for her. He's going all sorts of crazy trying to make her feel better after what happened to her last night."

"Sounds like he really loves his dog," I said.

"Oh, he does." She cleared her throat, shifting awkwardly in the dance of someone trying to get rid of unwanted company without appearing rude.

"I'm sorry, I didn't introduce myself. I'm Shade Renard." I reached out a hand to shake hers.

She tried to smile as she took my hand. "I'm Rosie, Anthony's neighbor."

When she pulled her hand back, I noticed a red line across her palm. A very familiar red line. "Oh, my, what happened to your hand?"

She looked down. "Oh, that's nothing. Gypsy got out the other day, and I tried to help by grabbing her leash." Her smile turned rueful. "She didn't stop."

I shared a look with Liam. Oliver Dale had the same red line on his palm. Perhaps he'd gotten a hold of Gypsy that night after all.

"So it seems Gypsy makes a habit of getting away, then?" I asked.

"Not when Anthony is with her, no, she's a very well-behaved dog. It's only poor Greg. She seems to delight in giving him a hard time, and—"

She stopped suddenly and stared at Liam. "Wait a minute. Are you here because of Gypsy?" She tightened her grip on the door as if she'd slam it closed, a sudden ferocity making her brown eyes spark. "He called you again, didn't he? Well, whatever he said, it's not true. Gypsy stayed in the hospital all night, and now she's on strict bed rest. She's hasn't done a damn thing to him."

"Who are you talking about?" Liam asked.

She crossed her arms. "Oliver Dale. That miserable man." She gestured at the apartment in question. "I don't know what his problem is, but this is beyond ridiculous. Gypsy is not a wolf; she's a Czechoslovakian wolfdog." She gritted her teeth. "I can't believe he called the police. Just because animal control doesn't believe his lies about Gypsy, he felt he had to go over their heads?

Well, tell him I'm sorry, but I don't have time to cater to his fantasy today. I have to take care of Gypsy."

She started to close the door. Liam stepped forward, holding out a hand to stop her. "This isn't about Gypsy, miss, and if you—"

A door slammed at the end of the hallway, cutting him off. An angry male voice boomed down the hall.

"Who the fuck are you?"

CHAPTER 5

Liam's aura skyrocketed from cozy fireplace to roaring bonfire so fast that I fell back a step. He angled his body to put me behind him, forming a protective wall of alpha werewolf between me and the man barreling down the hallway. I opened my mouth to object, but snapped it closed when I peered around him to get a good view of Oliver Dale's neighbor.

Anthony Catello was huge. Not big-boned, or fat, but muscular in a way that screamed violence. Unlike Liam and Stephen, this man had worked hard to turn himself into a tank, and every muscle vibrated with purpose, screaming his strength, his *power* to the world. The beard shadowing his jaw said he hadn't gotten around to shaving in a few days, and grease smudges on his cheeks made some patches darker than others. A black tank top stretched to cover a wide chest, and blood stained his pale grey sweatpants. The blood was faint and smeared, giving the impression he'd gotten it from holding his injured dog as opposed to being wounded himself.

"Who are you?" Anthony repeated in the same booming volume. He marched up to Liam, not stopping until he was well within the werewolf's personal space.

Liam's face betrayed nothing but polite patience, a violent contradiction to the power radiating off him. "Mr. Catello, I presume?"

"Who wants to know?" Without waiting for an answer, Anthony glanced at Rosie. His voice downshifted from fury to soft gratitude, though his body language remained angry and defensive. "Thanks for sitting with her. Is she okay?"

Rosie smiled nervously, glancing from Anthony to Liam. "She's fine, but she's still hurting."

The whimpering from inside the room grew louder, more frantic. Gypsy had heard her master. Tension seized Anthony's body, and he jerked forward, trying to shoulder his way past Liam.

Liam kept himself between Anthony and the doorway. "Sir, I need to speak with y—"

"Bite me," Anthony growled. He didn't try to push Liam out of the way, but his body language made it clear he was ready for a fight. "Get out of my way."

Liam's jaw hardened. "We can chat here, or you can ride to the station with me. Your choice."

Anthony sneered. "This is about Dale, isn't it? You think I had something to do with him turning up dead last night."

"When did you find out about Mr. Dale's passing?" Liam asked.

Anthony opened his mouth then closed it. "None of your fucking business."

Tension crackled in the air, an almost physical weight that made it difficult to breathe. Rosie hovered near the door, her eyes wide. It was obvious she wanted to leave, but was afraid to move. Anthony looked ready to punch Liam if he didn't step aside. Liam didn't seem inclined to clear the way.

Gypsy chose that moment to resume whimpering, her cries growing louder, more insistent. Anthony twitched, leaning toward the door.

"I'm not gonna ask you again," he ground out. "Get out of my way."

"We need to talk. Now. The dog can wait."

My mouth fell open. Anthony snarled, fingers curling into a fist, rising toward Liam's face. Liam didn't move, just stood there as if he'd let the other man hit him.

"I'm here about Gypsy!" I said quickly. My voice came out higher than I'd intended, more panicky than I'd like, but there was no helping that. My heart pounded as Anthony's dark brown eyes slid to me, and he paused with his fist clenched and trembling at his side.

"What?" he demanded.

Magic crackled against my palm, the instinct to call a defensive spell tingling against my fingertips. I cleared my throat. Magic was never a first resort. So said Mother Hazel.

I pointed to the open bedroom door behind Rosie, where the whimpers emanated from. "I know you didn't have the money to keep her at the animal hospital for very long—not that you would have left her there anyway. You love her too much for that; everyone at the hospital said so. I'm here to do what I can to help."

Anthony's gaze flicked to Liam, then to me. "You're from the animal hospital? You're not with him?"

His suspicion rang out crystal clear, and I was very, very certain that lying to him would be a bad idea. "I don't work at the animal hospital, no. I just help where I can." I stepped away from Liam, using physical distance to highlight the disassociation. "Gypsy sounds scared. She's getting worked up, and that's not good for her condition. She might tear her stitches."

Anthony's face tightened, as if he were the one in pain. He looked toward the bedroom door.

"I'd like your permission to go inside and check on her." I gestured to the pack around my waist. "I have a salve that would make her feel better. No charge. I just want to help her."

"The dog can wait," Liam interrupted.

I stifled a groan. *The dog?* If I didn't know better, I'd swear Liam was goading Anthony into hitting him. Anthony growled, and his fist rose higher in the air, once again angling toward Liam's face. The promise of violence hung between them, and the hairs on the back of my neck rose.

Sod it.

I called my magic, and purple energy rose through my body, spilling into my voice. "It's hard to see someone you love in pain." I slid in front of Liam with the care of someone easing into a bath that's a few degrees too hot. His aura bit into me like embers drifting off a bonfire, but I ignored it, concentrating on filling my words with as much power as I could. "I promise you, if you let me see her, I can make her feel much, much better. I can help Gypsy. Right now. Let's go inside. I'm sure the nice officer will wait out here while we take care of Gypsy. Then the two of you can talk."

Lavender energy tinged the air between me and Anthony, easing past his defenses. Some of the tension eased from his jaw, and his hand fell to his side, fingers no longer curled in a fist. He hovered on the edge for a second, still angry, still wanting to lash out at Liam. A fresh wave of whimpers was his undoing. Rosie was right. Anthony loved his dog.

"She's in the back room," he said gruffly. "Follow me."

I stepped back, forcing Liam back a step as well. Unlike Anthony, Liam was no calmer now than he'd been before. In fact, his energy grew even hotter, and I smothered a hiss of surprise as I jerked away from him. Anthony stepped into the apartment, and Rosie took the opportunity to give him a small wave goodbye and then slip into the hallway. She gave me a nervous smile, nodded at Liam, and then scurried down the hall to vanish into her own apartment.

Anthony headed for the back bedroom, leaving me to follow

him. Before I could take a step, Liam's hand closed on my shoulder.

"What are you doing?" He kept his voice tight and low so Anthony wouldn't hear him. "We talked about this."

"You remember the beginning of the conversation, but obviously not the end." I waved toward Rosie's apartment so it would look as if I was saying goodbye to her if Anthony happened to glance back. "I'm trying to calm him down so he'll answer our questions. He wasn't going to say one word to you with his dog crying for him in the back room." I gave in to the urge to give him a disapproving wag of the finger. "I doubt he was going to cooperate with you at all after you kept telling him '*the dog* can wait.' I swear, it's like you wanted him to hit you."

Liam took a deep breath, flexing his hands at his sides. "As you may have noticed, Mr. Catello isn't feeling particularly helpful. As a witness, I can't force him to cooperate. However, if he had hit me, it would have been assaulting a police officer. I could have arrested him and taken him to the station where we have observation rooms. I could have held him in an interrogation room whether he liked it or not."

I shut my mouth, a flush warming my cheeks. "You did want him to hit you. You were goading him to make him mad."

"Yes."

I lifted my chin. "Well, now we've learned the importance of communication. It's all right, though; my way will work just as well. He'll talk to me—freely."

"You aren't a cop." The vein in Liam's temple pulsed, but he kept his tone low and controlled.

"No, I'm a witch. And I promise you, he'll talk to me. Unless, of course, you insist on holding me here until he gets suspicious." I stepped away from him, deliberately moving over the threshold. "You have my card with my number. Go into Oliver's apartment and listen through the wall. If you have something you want me to ask him, text me."

Liam blinked, and I closed the door before I could decide if it was shock or outrage that pushed his eyebrows into his hairline. Shock. Probably.

As usual, getting a peek at someone's apartment when they hadn't been expecting company proved very enlightening. Anthony wasn't much of a decorator, and his apartment was largely functional. He had a comfortable couch that, while not filthy, had likely never gotten familiar with a vacuum cleaner. His television was large and flanked by speakers that seemed a lot bigger than they needed to be. A weight bench in the corner was the most used piece of furniture in the place, and the amount of weight on the bar resting over it made me reaffirm my dedication to not making Anthony angry.

I found the man in question sitting on the edge of the bed talking in a low, soothing voice. Unsurprisingly, he'd given his beloved dog the lion's share of the mattress, extra sheets and blankets piled up to form a cozy nest for her. Gypsy buried her face in Anthony's lap as he murmured soft sounds of encouragement.

Gypsy did resemble a wolf. So much so that if Rosie hadn't told me what breed she was, I would have sworn this animal could be a member of Liam's pack in wolf form. Her fur was a beautiful cream color, almost white. Pointed ears swiveled in my direction, and she tensed, her eyes rolling to where I stood in the doorway.

"It's okay," Anthony soothed her. "She's here to help you. She's a friend."

I waited, not making any move to come closer until Gypsy relaxed against Anthony, her eyes drifting half-closed even as she continued to watch me.

"You are so beautiful," I told her. I studied the bandages on her leg as I crept closer, noting the fresh blood. She'd torn some stitches. "Who's a good girl?"

I laid my hand on her head, next to Anthony's fingers. He

continued whispering to her as well, hushing her and praising what a strong girl she was. Her breathing was even, but strained, each exhale holding the ghost of a groan. Shudders ran through her body any time she tried to move her injured leg.

I called my magic, tracing the patterns of a healing spell over the silky-soft fur, and speaking the incantation in a soft whisper that blended with Anthony's voice. Blue light flowed over my hand in tiny rivulets, washing over Gypsy and sinking through the bloody bandages into the wounds beneath. Gypsy melted farther into her master, her breaths coming easier.

As if they were one creature, Anthony relaxed as well. The headboard groaned as it took more of his weight, but the sound didn't stir Gypsy. Her eyes remained closed, her head cradled in her master's lap. For a moment, I watched them. Anthony had closed his eyes along with Gypsy, and seeing the two of them there, comforted by each other's presence, painted a very different picture of Mr. Catello than I'd had when I arrived. He didn't seem like a killer.

My phone rang. Gypsy didn't move, too lost in the warm fuzziness of magically induced healing, but Anthony cracked an eye open.

"Sorry." I pulled my phone from the side pocket of my waist pouch and thumbed down the touch screen to see a text from an unknown number.

Get his alibi.

Liam. I pressed my lips together, my thumb hovering over the buttons, ready to reply with a sarcastic *Why didn't I think of that?*

"Bad news?"

I put the phone away and tried to muster a smile. "Someone who labors under the false impression he's my boss. I'm an independent contractor of sorts, so I'm my own boss, but sometimes the people I work with enjoy telling me how to do my job."

Anthony snorted. "Yeah, I get that a lot. I'm a mechanic, and a lot of guys who bring their car in feel the need to tell me what's wrong with their vehicle and how to fix it."

"If they know what's wrong and they can fix it themselves, then why bring their car to you in the first place?"

Anthony shrugged one enormous shoulder. "People are assholes. There's no fixin' stupid."

"Too true." I unzipped my pouch and dug around for clean gauze. I pulled out a glue gun I'd been searching for yesterday, along with a jumble of paperclips and a bottle of bright pink bubble bath. Anthony raised his eyebrows but didn't say anything.

"So that ranger seemed awfully interested in talking to you." I found the gauze and a bottle of water and laid them on the bed next to Gypsy.

"He can bite me," Anthony snapped.

I returned the rest of my junk to the pouch and scratched Gypsy's neck, smiling at the way she pressed into the gesture. "I heard you mention a dead body. And you knew the dead man's name. I take it you didn't like him?"

"Dale was sick, the biggest asshole in the whole damn building. He *kicked* Gypsy. He calls animal control on her at least twice a week. I know them by name now—Frank and Chris. They know damn well Gypsy's no wolf, and she's no danger to anyone. After a few months of Dale's harassment, now, when he calls them, they come by for a beer and talk about what a total dick that guy is."

He smiled, an ugly expression that raised gooseflesh on my arms.

"Well, what kind of guy he *was*," he amended. The smile broadened. "I heard he was eaten by a coyote or something. I hope he was alive through the worst of it."

He meant it. He meant it in a way that threatened to bring up the mints I'd had on the way over. I unwrapped Gypsy's bloody bandages, examining her leg as I rinsed away the dried blood. "Eaten by a coyote? What gave you that idea?"

He stroked Gypsy's back. "The kid that walks Gypsy found the body. He called me."

My heart pounded, and I used the bottled water to clean her wounds as best I could. "Where were you when he called you?"

Suspicion tightened the lines around Anthony's eyes, and his hand stilled in Gypsy's fur. "What did you say your name was again?"

Before I could answer, my phone buzzed again. I jumped.

"Who is that?" Anthony's voice lost its friendly tone. He sat up, looking much more like the very angry man I'd first seen in the hallway and less like the placid puppy owner of moments ago. Gypsy stirred, a whine trickling from her mouth. She pressed her head against Anthony's chest, pushing her head under the hand that had been scratching her behind the ear.

I ignored my phone, dipped inside myself for my magic, and let it spill into my words in a flow of violet energy. I could stick with my original lie, use magic to push past the suspicion in his voice, but that would be less effective if I wanted to ask more questions. Time for the truth, with just enough magic to smooth the transition. "My name is Shade Renard. I'm a private investigator."

Rage filled Anthony's eyes, but I rushed to finish before he could speak.

"I'm sorry I misled you, but it was necessary. I needed to know how you really felt about Oliver Dale."

"Why?" Anthony demanded.

I met his eyes. "I was hired by a woman who asked me to prove Oliver Dale tried to kill her dog."

Anthony froze. "What?"

"I can't share names because of confidentiality, but she lives near the building where Oliver Dale works—used to work. She says he was feeding her dog poisoned treats. Nothing strong enough to kill her outright, but enough to make her sick. Sick enough that she'd eventually die."

Gypsy succeeded in pressing her head into Anthony's palm, and he leaned back against the headboard, resuming the ear scratching. "Sounds like him." He studied my face, eyes still narrowed. "Why did you lie?"

My phone buzzed again. Again I ignored it. "I've been having an awful time getting people to open up to me. Oliver Dale intimidated people, and most of them won't say anything against him for fear of retaliation." I petted Gypsy's head, scratching behind her right ear. "I'm sorry I lied, but I thought if I could convince you to let me in, then maybe you'd answer some questions about Oliver Dale. And besides, I really can make Gypsy feel better."

The charm I was using to make myself more convincing wasn't a heavy magic, more of a soft persuasion. Fortunately, Anthony's hatred of Oliver Dale, and my claim to be investigating the dead dog-hater for animal abuse, brought him just enough to my side that the magic did the rest of the work. His brow softened, the suspicion melting away. "I can understand that, I guess."

I sighed and wrapped clean bandages around Gypsy's leg. I'd healed the wound, so the bandages were no longer necessary, but I couldn't very well tell Anthony I'd used magic to heal her in seconds. "The police don't even believe my client. They said since she's never seen Oliver give her dog the treat, they can't do anything about it. She's sure it was him, though, so she called me. I talked to the people at the vet to see if they'd had any other complaints against him. I was there when Gypsy came in, and I heard them read your address on her tag. I figured you live in the same building as Oliver Dale, and you have a dog, so maybe you'd know…"

"Yeah." Anthony snorted. "The cops never believed Dale was a monster, but they'd come banging on my door if something happened." He leaned closer, and only a sudden move from Gypsy made him stop before shoving his face into mine.

"Dale was evil. Not just an asshole, but really evil. He dressed nicer than me, hid his shit behind a fancy suit, but the truth is, you'd be better off walkin' with me down a dark alley than that guy."

The scent of sweat and blood combined with the unique metallic-grease combination of a mechanic's shop filled my senses from Anthony's nearness, and I resisted the urge to lean away. "It sounds like he did more than call animal control on your dog. More than kick her."

"He did this." He gestured at Gypsy's bandaged leg.

"You think he did this to Gypsy? How do you know?" I sat a little straighter. "If you saw him do this, then that would help me with my case against him. Were you at the park when it happened?"

"No. I tried to get in the park to find her after Greg called me about Dale, but some bitch cop sent me home." His jaw tightened. "I told her Dale was gonna hurt Gypsy. Bastard chasin' her into the forest like he was gonna help find her. He wouldn't piss on Gypsy if she was on fire. I tried to explain that to the ranger, but the bitch wouldn't listen. Told me to go home, she'd handle it."

If I hadn't been staring at him, I'd have missed it. The moment when the anger in his eyes flickered, and I saw what lay behind it. Fear.

"You believe he chased after Gypsy so he could hurt her. You believe he did this."

"Not hurt her," Anthony said tensely. "Kill her. Dale hated her, hated her more than any man should ever hate a dog that's never done a thing to him." He shook his head. "Everyone's always watchin' me, thinkin' I'm gonna lash out and hurt someone. But Dale... No one saw it but me. They saw he was an asshole, yeah, but the evil, the violence..." He pulled Gypsy closer to him, and she didn't whimper, just pressed harder against him, as if she sensed he needed comfort. "Me and Gypsy saw it."

"You followed him." It wasn't a question. "When Greg called you and told you Dale bolted after Gypsy, you went to the park looking for him."

"Damn straight I did. What was I gonna do, stand there like some coward while that monster killed my dog?" His voice broke on the last word, but he ignored it. "I went into that park to save Gypsy. And I would have found her before she got hurt, too, if that cop hadn't made me leave."

"So you weren't in the park when Gypsy got hurt, or when Oliver was killed. Where'd you go?"

Anthony frowned. "Why?"

I petted Gypsy again. "If it had been me, and it was my dog out there with a man I thought meant to kill her...I wouldn't have left."

Anthony studied me for a long time. "You remind me of that lady cop," he said finally. "You're nice to Gypsy, and you talk like you understand me, like you feel bad for what happened to my dog and what I'm going through. But you think it was me. Just because I got a record, I'm the one that killed the bastard."

"You have a record?"

Anthony didn't flinch. "I don't care what you think of me. I don't care what anyone thinks of me. It doesn't matter now anyway. Dale's dead, and I didn't kill him, no matter what the cops say."

"I'm sure they don't think you killed him. I mean, you said yourself, the cop made you leave. So you weren't even there. Do you have an alibi, someone that can tell the cops beyond a doubt that you weren't there when it happened?"

His stare had the same cold weight as the barbells in the living room. "You sure you're not with the cops?"

I held my ground. "I told you, I'm a private investigator. My client—"

"Your client said Dale was poisoning her dog. But he's dead now, so she can stop worrying. Right?"

Frustration pulled my skin tight. "I'll never get the chance to prove Oliver Dale was hurting my client's dog. And it might be petty, but that pisses me off. I don't want this guy's death to fall on another dog owner he tortured. Let me help you."

"Help me?" Anthony scoffed. "What do I need your help for?"

"Based on everything I've seen and everything you've said, you're a perfect suspect for Oliver Dale's murder. I can help you prove your innocence."

My charm was still active, still working against Anthony's defenses to make me more believable. But it was obvious he wasn't a trusting man at the best of times, and it was a simple, subtle spell. I couldn't make him trust me.

"You helped my dog," he said. "I got no beef with you. Get out now." He jabbed a finger at the floor near the door. "And take the bitch ranger's sweatshirt with you."

I stood from the bed, knowing an out when it'd been offered to me. I picked up the sweatshirt he'd mentioned, wincing at the amount of blood soaked into the cartoon drawing of angel wings around the letters NOHS. I pointed to Gypsy, who had opened her eyes to watch me get off the bed. "She's going to be okay. She's a strong dog."

"I know." He scratched Gypsy behind the ears, studying me. "I drove back to my shop to make sure I locked up. When I left the park. No one saw me, though."

So no alibi. I pulled out a card and laid it on the foot of the bed. "Call me if you decide you want my help. No charge."

I left without another word. Liam was exiting Oliver Dale's apartment as I closed Anthony's door behind me, skimming the text messages I'd ignored inside.

Liam didn't seem happy. Without a word, he took in the bloody sweatshirt in my arms, his nostrils flaring. Then he made a gesture for me to follow him and stormed down the hall to the stairs that led to the ground floor.

"He has a strong motive and no alibi," I started conversationally. "He says Greg called him when Oliver took off after Gypsy. He left his shop to find them, but Emma sent him home. Then he says he went back to his shop to make sure he locked up, but there's no one to vouch for him."

Liam halted as soon as his foot hit the floor of the lobby. I almost ran into him, but managed to stop myself. He faced me with his arms crossed, aura flaring around him like a heat wave. "You ignored my texts."

"One asking for the alibi—which I just told you he doesn't have—and three messages ordering me to get out of the apartment. Your confidence in me is overwhelming." I put my phone away. "He loves that dog. You can tell a lot about a man by how he treats animals."

"You can tell a lot by how he treats people, too." Liam gripped the edge of the banister at the bottom of the stairs, biceps bunching as he squeezed. "He's got a temper, and he's not shy about it."

"Point taken." I looked back up the stairs toward the hall we'd just left. "Did the manager come by to let you in Oliver Dale's apartment?"

"Yes."

I nodded and took a step back up the stairs. "I should have a peek while we're here. I might find something useful."

Liam pivoted and headed straight for the exit. "I already searched it while you had your little chat with Mr. Catello. There's nothing but a bunch of medals and trophies."

Irritation pinched the corners of my eyes, and I debated going to check out the apartment without the cranky were-wolf. I discarded the idea, though. Given his mood, I had no doubt Liam would leave without me, and I didn't want to lose daylight having to walk back to the reservation. I gritted my teeth and followed after him. "What kind of medals?" I asked.

Liam snorted. "Mostly high school. Apparently, Oliver Dale was North Olmsted's golden boy. Star quarterback. That guy saved every trophy he ever got." He paused before opening the door to his SUV. "I saw a trophy in there from his Pee-Wee team."

I raised my eyebrows. "So not a humble man."

"I'd say not. There wasn't a single picture of friends or family. Just Oliver, Oliver, Oliver, and all things demonstrating the glory of Oliver."

I was about to point out that if he'd hold his horses long enough for me to look inside, I might find something, but before I could speak, he gestured to the sweatshirt.

"Is there a reason you're holding bloody clothes?"

I blinked. "What? Oh, this." I wrinkled my nose. "Anthony… requested that I return this to Emma. I guess she used it to wrap Gypsy after she found her."

The wind picked up, reminding me that winter hadn't completely yielded to spring, whatever the calendar might say. I shivered and got in the SUV. Liam dug around in the back seat then climbed behind the wheel again.

"Here," he said, handing me a large plastic evidence bag. "I don't need my vehicle smelling like blood for the next week."

I kept my door open a crack as I stuffed the crusted sweatshirt into the plastic. "Why don't you want me to see Oliver's apartment?" I asked.

He turned and opened his mouth to answer, then frowned. "Why are you holding your door open?"

The plastic crackled as I tucked the bag on the floor by my feet. "I'm waiting for Peasblossom."

As if saying her name had summoned her, Peasblossom darted through the part in the door and landed on my head.

"I'm back!" she announced. She crossed her arms and looked at Liam. "You weren't going to leave without me, were you?"

JENNIFER BLACKSTREAM

"No."

The alpha's tone made his feelings on the matter clear, and I spoke up before Peasblossom could take offense. "Did you hear anything useful?"

She plunked down on my shoulder, kicking her legs as she talked. "Lots of people doing that double-talk thing."

"What double-talk?" Liam asked.

"You know, where they say one thing, but their face says another? Lots of people talking about 'poor Oliver' and the 'horrible' thing that happened to him, but they're all smiling."

Liam started the SUV and eased out of the parking space, heading for the main road. I leaned back against my seat and drummed my fingers on the armrest of my door.

"There has to be someone who didn't hate him," I said.

"Not that I found." Peasblossom lay down on her stomach, wings fanning the air and tickling the fine hairs at the back of my scalp with a light breeze. "No one seems to care that he's dead." She stilled, tilting her head. "Well, except for Mother Hazel. She cared enough to offer you that deal, so she obviously has some sort of stake in his death."

"Deal?"

I winced at the sharp tone of Liam's voice. Blood and bones, I hadn't intended to tell him that part.

"Shade, what deal is she talking about? You didn't mention any deal."

"It's not relevant," I said calmly. "It's between me and my mentor." I raised a hand to cut off his protest. "But if you must know, my mentor would prefer I restrict my duties to those of a village witch."

The vein in Liam's temple throbbed, his aura inching up a few degrees. "She doesn't approve of your private investigating?"

"No, she does not. However, I believe I've convinced her that's there's no changing my mind."

"And the deal?"

I fought the urge to roll my window down a few inches to help disperse some of the heat rolling off the angry alpha. "She put me on this case. If I fail to solve it, I have to give up my private investigation business."

"And if you succeed?"

"Then she owes me a favor."

It was a testament to Liam's self-control that he didn't veer off the road. As it was, he jerked the wheel enough when he turned to stare at me that the resulting swerve sent my heart into my throat and drew a squeak of protest from Peasblossom.

"A favor? From Mother Hazel?"

I closed my eyes, averting my face, as if that would somehow ease the discomfort from the heat of Liam's aura as it surged out of control. "Yes, a favor. But don't think for one second that our deal will dictate my behavior on this case. I'm here for the truth, and that's it." I slanted a look at him, wishing I could meet his eyes. "Just like you."

His hands tightened on the steering wheel. It groaned a warning, and tension rolled off him as he fought to calm himself.

"You're suggesting it's not relevant that your livelihood rests on solving this case?"

"It changes nothing."

"It changes everything!" He stopped and sucked in a deep breath. "Shade, this is not a television show. There is no guarantee we'll solve this case; no case has that kind of guarantee. I will not allow your personal business to—"

"Please stop right there."

I had enough control over my magic that nothing exploded. But the anger in my tone was enough to silence the werewolf, and my hands shook in my lap.

"If you were about to suggest that I would let my personal life lead me to rush a conviction, or even influence me to push for a resolution that was not one hundred percent supported by the facts, then I'd advise you to rethink your position. I told you when I arrived that I want the truth. Now, if Stephen is innocent —and I hope he is—I will happily remove that collar and walk away. However, if he is guilty, then don't you want to know?"

"There is no one hundred percent in real life." Liam shoved a hand through his hair. "Stephen's life is at stake. Do you expect me to believe if we don't find a stronger suspect, you won't be a little tempted to rush to judgment on Stephen?"

"You mean the werewolf with the victim's blood all over his face who admitted eating the body and is obviously hiding something?"

Liam jerked back, shooting me a wide-eyed stare before forcing his attention to the road. Peasblossom slid out of sight under my hair, her fingers digging into my shirt to hold on.

"You're the one who won't let me interview him," I said. "Are you sure you don't think he's guilty?"

"I want the truth." He squeezed the steering wheel again, but not so hard. "Whatever that is."

"Then let's find it. Together."

A long minute passed. Finally, the blistering energy rolling off the alpha eased, and I could breath again.

"All right."

"All right." I cleared my throat and settled back in my seat despite my racing heart. "So where to now?"

"We need to interview Greg again."

"You think he might tell you something he didn't tell Blake?"

"Blake talked to him right after he found a dead body, when he was worried about Gypsy. I want to talk to him now that he knows Gypsy's fine, and he's had a chance to process everything." He glanced at me. "I'll interview him. Observe, but do not take over."

"Wouldn't dream of it."

He narrowed his eyes, then sighed. "Listen, the first time— and sometimes the second time—we interview someone, whether they're a suspect or a witness, the point is not just to check off means, motive, and opportunity. I'm not accusing anyone, or aiming to catch them in a lie. The first conversation is all about the timeline—getting the person's story with as many details as possible. Details like what time was it, what did he do first, what was he wearing, who was there. Ask the same questions over and over. The more information I get, the better the chance that I'll find out if he's telling the truth."

"You want as much information as possible, because you never know what might be contradicted by someone else," I guessed.

"Right. Little details matter. If I ask him if he grabbed a snack before he left, and he says he snagged an orange, then later he tells me it was a bag of chips, then that's a lie I caught him in. And if he told one lie, he probably told more. It's easier to catch people in little lies."

"Because they don't spend the same amount of time plotting the little details."

"Exactly." He was silent, considering for a moment. "If I need help, I'll tap my pen on my notepad. That'll be your signal to step in. Until then, you let me do the talking. All right?"

It was a small step forward, so I took it. "All right."

My concession seemed to chase the tension from his shoulders. An amicable silence filled the car as we drove. It was almost enough to silence the nagging voice in the back of my brain that wondered why he hadn't wanted me to look around Oliver Dale's apartment.

Almost.

CHAPTER 6

The Tylers lived in a small house less than ten miles from the Rocky River Reservation. The neighborhood wasn't as nice as Stephen's, the yards smaller and the homes closer together. A few of the houses had heaps of junk collecting at the sides, mud-crusted children's toys and broken lawn furniture, making them an eyesore on what was otherwise a quaint street. The Tyler home was among the more cared for, the white siding clean of the dirt that coated most of the other houses, as if the owner took the time to wash them on at least a semi-regular basis. It was a Saturday, and the beige Toyota in the driveway promised someone was home.

"Remember, I'll do the talking this time," Liam said, pulling his Jeep into the driveway. "Greg is still a minor, so we need his mom's permission to talk with him."

I paused with my hand on the door handle. "But he's a witness, not a suspect."

"He is a witness, but he's also one of two people besides the victim that we can prove was in the park when Oliver Dale was killed. And he has a record."

"For breaking and entering," I said, remembering the boy's file

84

from my earlier perusal. "That hardly qualifies him as a potential killer."

Liam got out of the car and circled around to my side, glancing at the house as he opened my door. "I'm not saying he killed him. I'm just saying we need to be open about the possibility. That means doing this by the book. If he did have something to do with Oliver's death, I don't want the case falling apart when it gets to court."

"And doing it by the book means playing nice with his mom so she lets us talk to him." I shoveled a lapful of junk back into my waist pouch. It had taken me longer to find the mints this time.

"Yes."

I zipped the pouch before meeting his eyes. The tension between us still hadn't dissipated. I was irritated he hadn't waited so I could look through Oliver's apartment, and he was annoyed I'd commandeered the last interview. I hesitated to cause more friction.

Still…

"And you think an officer of the Cleveland Metropark Police will be more reassuring to the mother of a juvenile offender than a fellow female with no uniform or gun? Someone who isn't part of the organization that arrested her son for B&E?"

I tried to keep my voice light, secretly satisfied I'd finally gotten the chance to use B&E in a sentence. Liam didn't appreciate my efforts.

He tightened his grip on the still-open door. "Believe it or not, I am trained to speak with people who aren't happy to see me. I can handle this."

I shrugged. "All right, you handle it. I look forward to watching your training in action."

The last bit came out more sarcastic than I'd intended, but he let it go. He led the way up the driveway to the front porch, and as we walked, I couldn't help staring at his bare forearms. It was March, and since this was Ohio, that could mean a temperature anywhere between forty and sixty degrees. Today felt more like forty, but you'd never know it the way he marched around with no coat, and his shirt sleeves up to his elbows. I knew lycanthropes ran hotter than humans, but surely the rolled-up sleeves was a little much?

At least he's not wearing flip-flops.

That thought sent me back to last year, when I'd been called out in the middle of January to a college campus to deal with a *clurichaun* in a fraternity. No less than two of the fraternity's members had worn flip-flops to class—despite over six inches of snow outside. Even the *clurichaun*, drunk and half-mad as he was, had mocked them.

"Shade?"

"Hmm?"

He didn't respond right away. A feeling of déjà vu crept over me, and I shook off the haze of memory to look at the detective.

Yep, I was leaning on him again.

Blood and bones.

"Sorry." I lurched forward from the standstill we'd come to as I drifted down memory lane and Liam realized I was invading his personal space. A gentleman would have let it go, ignored the social *faux pas* and continued on to the front door so we could question our witness and possible suspect.

"You wanna tell me why you keep touching me?" Liam asked.

He hadn't moved from his spot. I stopped without turning.

"Don't we have more important things to be worrying about?" I asked.

"Yeah. So if you could answer quickly, that'd be swell."

"Who says swell anymore?" Peasblossom said against the back of my neck.

"Apparently, werewolves do." I turned to Liam. "At least this one does. And as I've mentioned before—he can hear you."

"But what I don't hear is an explanation for why you keep

leaning on me." Liam's arms hung loose at his sides, but there was a tension in his stance that hadn't been there a second ago.

"Sorry," I said finally. "Won't happen again." I started to turn back to the house.

Liam locked gazes with me, and the force in the blue-eyed stare startled me into standing still. Unease slid down my spine. He was taking this way too seriously.

"I'm sorry if it annoys you," I said carefully. I shrugged. "I don't know why. Maybe it's because it's cold outside and your aura is really warm."

The tension in his shoulders wrenched tighter. "I've heard of spells that can siphon off someone's life force through touch," Liam said, never taking his eyes from mine. "I'm sure Mother Hazel knows such a spell."

My jaw dropped. "Excuse me?"

"Why do you keep leaning on me?" he asked again. "Why did Mother Hazel send you?"

I shook my head, too shocked to be embarrassed anymore. "And here I was worried you'd think I was flirting. No, I'm not siphoning your life force." I said the last part with as much mockery as it deserved. "But thank you for the accusation; that's…that's very flattering."

"Way to lay on the sarcasm," Peasblossom said appreciatively.

"Mother Hazel offered you an unqualified favor for taking this case, and you said yourself you don't know why." Liam took a step closer. "Why are you really here?"

"I've fallen into a nightmare." I twisted my head to look at Peasblossom. "Do you know why I'm leaning on him?" I asked. I didn't bother to whisper. He'd hear me anyway. "Do you feel like touching him?"

"He's too big for me," Peasblossom said matter-of-factly. She tilted her head and gave Liam a once-over. "You really don't understand why you want to lean on him?"

"Peasblossom," I snapped. "This isn't funny."

"Fine, fine. So touchy." She snorted and smacked my back. "Ha! Get it? Touchy?"

"Peasblossom!"

"All right, all right, geez." She scowled and settled into a sulk. "Shifters have warm, buzzy energy, and you're a witch, so you can feel it. Liam's upset, so he's giving off more heat." Peasblossom shrugged. "Feels comfy to me."

"Why do I keep leaning on him?"

"Why do people touch wet paint?" Peasblossom said exasperatedly. "Who knows? Maybe you need a hug—what's the big deal?"

I pressed my lips together and faced Liam, squaring my shoulders and lifting my chin. "I swear on my magic and my life, to my knowledge, I'm not using magic on you or against you. I don't know why I'm leaning on you." I paused, then rolled my eyes. "Your aura does feel good. Near as I can tell, that's all there is to it."

Liam studied me hard. When he took a quick step toward me, I let out a squeak of surprise, my eyes widening when he leaned in and scented the air above my skin. I was still staring, dumbfounded, when he leaned back.

"I believe you." He looked like he was going to say more, then thought better of it. Before I could question that look, he resumed his brisk walk up the driveway to the front door of the Tyler home.

"That was very embarrassing," I muttered.

"It looked embarrassing." Peasblossom leaned out, holding on to a lock of my hair to keep her balance as she studied my face. "I hope you weren't leaning on him because you're attracted to him."

"Why?" I pulled at the lines of my coat, letting my brain settle before I followed Liam.

"Because if you're aroused, then he'd have smelled it just now."

I froze, staring at Peasblossom.

"I'm just saying," she said, holding up her hand. "That would be really, really embarrassing."

I pushed all thoughts of Liam and shifter auras out of my face and half ran up the driveway. I didn't have time for this.

"Not that it wasn't already embarrassing," Peasblossom added.

I ignored her, arriving on the front porch as Liam raised a hand and knocked on the door.

A minute later, it swung open and a petite blonde appeared wearing a pair of black dress yoga pants and a pale blue button-down shirt. When she saw Liam, the smile on her face wilted and wariness creased the corners of her mouth. "Hello?"

"Good morning, I'm Detective Sergeant Osbourne of the Cleveland Metro Police Rangers. I'd like to speak with Greg Tyler, if I could?"

The hand not holding the door open braced on the frame, barring our path. "I'm Mia Tyler, Greg's mother. Is this about Oliver Dale?"

Liam nodded. "It is."

"Greg already told you everything he knows."

Her tone wasn't unfriendly, but her body language made it clear she intended to keep our visit short, sweet, and outdoors. If I didn't already know her son had a record, I would have guessed it now. She was in full-out protection mode, and Liam hadn't said a word about Greg being anything more than a witness.

"He spoke to my sergeant, Detective Blake Giles. I was hoping I could speak with him myself?" Liam gave her a smile warmer than any expression he'd given me. "It's routine, nothing serious."

Mia didn't look convinced. "Greg isn't here right now. I'll tell him to contact you." She started to close the door.

"Mrs. Tyler," Liam said, his voice still calm, "I need to speak with Greg as soon as possible. I know you're busy, and I'd hate to keep coming back. I just have a few questions. Where is Greg right now?"

"I don't know." She met his eyes as if she could will him off her porch. "Probably with friends. He's sixteen. I don't keep track of him every second."

"Does he have a cell phone you could call?"

"Why don't you give me your card and he'll call you when he comes home?" Mia countered, lifting her chin.

She wasn't giving in. Liam reached into his pocket, took his card from a small stack, and handed it to Mia. She snatched it out of his hand and started to shut the door again.

Without thinking, I burst into a fake coughing fit, raising my arm to cover my mouth.

Mia paused, startled, watching me through the gap in the half-closed door. "Are you all right?"

It was an automatic response more than any true concern for my welfare, but I didn't need her sincerity. "I think so." I gave a few more coughs, roughening my voice. "But could I trouble you for a glass of water?"

Suspicion tightened the lines around her eyes, and she didn't answer right away.

"I can't believe you're trying the old 'get in the door by faking a cough' routine," Peasblossom muttered against the back of my neck. "It won't work."

I coughed again, ignoring my familiar's judgment. Unfortunately, Liam heard her as well. His expression seemed less than supportive.

Sod it. Plan B.

I called my magic as I drew breath for a final round of coughing, threading warm strands of purple energy into my voice. I'd never tried to tie a charm spell to a cough to make it more convincing, and the magic balked at the attempt, refusing to latch on to the rough bits of sound. I hummed between coughs as if I were trying to clear my throat. It wasn't easy with Mia and Liam gaping at me as though I were about to hack up a lung, and fake or not, the cough hurt my throat. I kept on, though, and finally, the magic relented. The air between me and Mia glittered, and Mia's suspicion melted into concern.

"I'm sorry, yes, come in, I'll get you some water."

Liam followed me inside, his gaze boring a hole between my shoulder blades as Mia led us into a spacious living room. To the left, a half-wall partitioned off the kitchen, the stove visible from my viewpoint near the threshold. I stopped in the center of the room, holding my hand to my throat as if warding off another cough. The buzz of shifter energy pressed against my back as Liam stood behind me, closer than was polite. He waited until Mia disappeared into the kitchen before speaking.

"Are you all right?"

"My throat hurts," I rasped.

"Any reason you didn't use your magic in the first place?"

I should have told him it was because he'd insisted I let him handle it unless he gave me a sign—which he hadn't. "Mother Hazel," I told him instead.

I could feel Liam's confusion at that, but this wasn't the time to explain my mentor's opinion on witches who used magic to solve mundane problems. Magic was a last resort, not a first, and she'd ground that philosophy into me from the first moment she became my mentor.

Our hesitant hostess returned with a glass of water, and I accepted it with real gratitude, taking a big gulp before slowing to smaller sips. The cool water soothed my abused throat, and I sighed.

"You have a lovely home," Liam said, breaking the silence. He squinted at a picture sitting on the desk in the corner. "I think I know him. Isn't that Anthony Catello?"

I followed his gaze, surprised to see Anthony's face smiling at me from the small silver frame. The protective—and somewhat foul-mouthed—dog owner stood beside a beaming teenage boy I recognized from his mug shot as Greg Tyler. Greg's curly brown hair erupted around the edges of a blue knit cap, and his eyes shone with excitement. Mia stood on Greg's other side, also smiling. They all wore dark parkas and jeans, and their cheeks were rosy, as if the day had been cool. A perfect family portrait.

Though the guns in their hands rendered it less Hallmark and more *Guns & Ammo*. And the targets in the background suggested the picture had been taken at a shooting range.

Mia followed Liam's gaze. "Yes, it is. How do you know Anthony?"

"I spoke to him a short while ago. Since he was on the reservation last night, we wanted to see if he'd seen something or someone that might help us find out what happened to his neighbor, Oliver Dale."

"Greg said it looked like an animal got him. A coyote or something." Mia crossed her arms. "Are you saying it wasn't an animal?"

"It likely was an animal attack," Liam agreed. "Which is why we're concerned. We need to know what kind of animal we're dealing with, so if Greg saw anything—a coyote, a black bear, or a bobcat, for example—then that would help us find the animal faster."

Some of the tension leaked out of Mia's shoulders, and she let her arms fall to her sides. "I'll tell Greg to call you, but I'll be honest, he's a city boy. I'm not sure he'd know a bobcat if it licked him on the nose."

Liam chuckled. "Well, I sure would appreciate any help he can give me." He inclined his head toward the photograph. "Mr. Catello was fortunate that Gypsy wasn't hurt. If there was a hungry animal out there, it could have been her that crossed its path. And based on what I saw of Mr. Catello, if some animal had hurt his dog, he'd have tracked it down himself."

"He does love that dog," Mia agreed. "And you're right. I'd pity the wild animal that threatened Gypsy when Anthony's around."

"What's your relationship with Anthony?" Liam asked.

Mia went to the desk and straightened the picture. "We dated for a short time."

"Did you part ways recently?" Liam asked.

"No. It was months ago." A hint of defiance crept into her tone, and she narrowed her eyes. "I'm sorry, how is that any of your business?"

Liam pointed at the photograph. "I was just wondering. It seems unusual to keep pictures of an ex around."

"Do you know how hard it is to get a picture of a teenage boy smiling?" Despite her irritation, Mia's face softened. "That is a great picture of Greg. He was so happy that day. His grouping was damn near perfect, and he was bursting with pride every time Anthony complimented him." She shrugged. "Besides, Anthony and I parted amicably. We're still friends. And he and Greg are still close."

"I understand," I said. "Teenagers get very moody around this age, don't they?"

Mia sighed. "That they do. Everyone talks about how bad teenage girls are, but I can't imagine they're worse than boys. I swear, as if having a human garbage disposal emptying my fridge isn't bad enough, he's just so...so..."

"Moody?"

"Yes. He's trying so hard to be a man, to convince me he's not a kid anymore. It's an adjustment for both of us. And not having his dad around hasn't made it any easier."

"Where is his dad?" Liam asked.

A shadow fell over Mia's face, and she raised her arms to hug herself. "He passed away five years ago. Complications from an undiagnosed head injury from playing football. Chronic traumatic encephalopathy, they called it." She turned to the wall and another photograph hanging there. It was a family portrait, Mia and Greg and another man. Greg was much younger, maybe ten. He stood behind his mom and in front of his father, smiling in the way boys did when told to smile, but his posture was relaxed. It was a happy portrait.

"I'm sorry for your loss," I said.

Mia lowered herself onto the couch, one hand gripping the arm. "It took us too long to recognize the symptoms. Doctors talk about head injuries in sports, but twenty years ago, no one realized the damage those tackles really did. You didn't expect the consequences to show up a decade later."

"Did he play professionally?" Liam asked.

"No. Just high school, but he could have gotten an athletic scholarship to college if he wanted to." Her jaw tightened. "He started at North Olmsted, but when his family moved, he played for his new high school, Olmsted Falls. They were North Olmsted's big rivals, and I think his former teammates hit him harder than they had to. Bad feelings, like he'd deliberately betrayed them."

North Olmsted. I glanced at Liam, and he met my eyes. Oliver Dale had played football for North Olmsted.

"High school sports are taken a lot more seriously than they should be, if you ask me," Liam said. "At least now they're being more careful with the kids. More so than when your husband played. What year was that?"

"He graduated in 2000."

"He was young when he died, then," I said sympathetically.

"Not even forty," Mia whispered. She looked back at the photo. "It was hard enough for me, but for Greg... I guess there's no way to prepare a boy for losing his father."

For a second, I thought she would cry. Instead, she took a slow, deep breath, then looked up at Liam. "Listen, I'm not stupid. Greg's been in trouble before. And Oliver was a grade-A bastard who made Anthony's life a living hell. You want to interrogate Greg because you think he or Anthony had something to do with Oliver's death."

Liam lowered his shoulders, trying to look less intimidating.

"I'm not here to accuse Greg of anything. I'm only trying to gain a better understanding of what happened last night. You're right: Mr. Dale didn't have a sterling reputation, and it's easy to believe his death wasn't an accident. Mr. Catello doesn't exactly put his best foot forward, and he showed up last night armed, angry, and convinced Mr. Dale was hunting his dog."

"He was right to worry that Oliver would hurt Gypsy," Mia said. "That man never met an animal—or a person—that he didn't consider an inconvenience at best. He was a bastard and everyone hated him. Hell, I can't think of a person who won't dance on his grave, including Anthony." She pointed a finger at me. "But if there's one thing stronger than Anthony's hatred for Oliver, it's his love for Gypsy. He wouldn't have done anything until he found her, wouldn't have taken so much as a second to rough Oliver up before he got her back safe and sound. Greg called him when he found Oliver's body, and Anthony was already on his way to the animal hospital. I promise you, he wouldn't have left her. Not even to kill Oliver."

If she was right, then Anthony would have looked for Gypsy until Emma called him from the hospital, and then he would have gone straight there. That would mean he didn't have time to kill Oliver.

I bit the inside of my cheek. But Mia could be wrong. Maybe Anthony found Oliver with Gypsy and killed him to keep him from hurting her. What if that mark on Oliver's hand had been caused when Anthony ripped Gypsy's leash away from him? Maybe they struggled and Anthony stabbed him or even shot him. The full autopsy report wasn't finished yet. Gypsy could have run off again during the struggle, and Anthony chased her, but Emma found her first. We didn't know for sure Anthony had left the park when she sent him home. He could have returned by a different route.

My head ached, and I took another sip of water. There were too many possibilities.

Mia picked up the picture of Anthony with her and Greg. "Anthony comes across as a brute, but he's a good man. After we broke up, he maintained his relationship with Greg. Took him under his wing." She smiled and brushed a finger over Greg's face. "Greg is one of the only people Anthony will let walk Gypsy. Greg is so proud of that." She tilted her head. "My mom used to tell me you can tell everything you need to know about a man by three things: how he treats his mother, how he treats customer service, and how he treats animals."

Smart woman. I stopped with my lips on the edge of my glass, thinking over something else Mia had said. "Mrs. Tyler, Anthony's neighbor told us that Gypsy gave Greg a hard time, that he struggled to control her. If you don't mind my asking, why was Anthony so willing to entrust Gypsy to Greg when he wasn't ready?"

I'd half expected Mia to be defensive, but she smiled. "Anthony told me Gypsy was helping Greg find himself. He said animals respond to confidence, and Gypsy would respect Greg when Greg learned to respect himself."

Liam considered that, and I caught a hint of respect in his gaze. "Mr. Catello is smarter than he comes across on first meeting."

Mia barked out a laugh and nodded. "Yeah."

"If you like him so much, may I ask why you broke up?" Liam asked.

Mia shrugged and replaced the photo on the desk. "I like Anthony, but we had nothing in common. Shared hatred isn't enough to build an entire relationship on."

"Shared hatred?" I asked.

Mia hesitated. "Yeah. Shared hatred." She squared her shoulders. "I work for Myers Insurance."

"The same company Oliver Dale worked for," Liam said. "So you knew Oliver Dale. Personally, not just through Mr. Catello."

"Unfortunately, yes."

"You say you hated him. Was that hatred professional or personal?" I asked.

Mia scowled. "I *never* dated Oliver. I don't care what he told other people; I never gave him the time of day. We worked together, that's all."

"Did he tell other people you...dated?" I asked, trying to be tactful.

She clenched her hands into fists. "It was all part of his plan to discredit me at work. He liked to tell people I was coming onto him, using my 'feminine wiles' to sleep my way up the corporate ladder. It was *bullshit.*"

"That's approaching sexual harassment," I told her. "Did you ever tell your boss?"

"I considered it, but it didn't seem worth it. Sexual harassment can go one of two ways for a woman—either she has proof in the form of a witness or video and the man gets arrested, or it's her word against his, and she ends up getting a reputation as an unprofessional slut. Oliver was careful not to do more than gossip, enough to ruin my reputation, but not enough to hold him accountable for it in any real way." She stood, keeping one hand on the arm of the couch. "It's messed up, but I admitted to myself he would always get away with it. I had a harder time swallowing the fact he cost me two promotions."

"How did he do that?" Liam asked.

"Different ways." Mia threw herself into furious pacing, as if she couldn't bear to stand still anymore. "We use a shared team spreadsheet to track basic group information for the manager to follow. There's a column for 'ID Card Release.' Oliver changed the values, put 'Yes' in some of my older groups so when I pulled the name from the filter, I thought they'd removed the suppression, and I stopped checking those groups. Which means those ID cards never went out. He made me look incompetent, and always when I was up for promotion, so it was worse—it looked like I cracked under pressure." She jabbed a finger at Liam. "I earned a second shot at a promotion, despite his interference. Do you have any idea how hard I had to work to earn that second shot?"

I hadn't understood a word of what she said, but I got the gist. "How did this shared hatred bring you together with Anthony?"

"I went to Oliver's apartment building one day to talk to his neighbors, see if I could dig up some dirt, something I could use to make him leave me the hell alone. Return fire for gossip, if you will. That's when I met Anthony."

Her eyes glittered as if she were recalling a happy memory. "He understood. Understood what it was like to have Oliver trying to destroy my life. He talked about all the shit Oliver pulled with him, reporting sweet Gypsy to animal control, calling her a wolf when he knew damn well she's a dog. Oliver claimed she was a threat and needed to register as a dangerous animal, when there wasn't a child in that building who didn't bring her treats and beg to play with her."

She rolled her eyes. "That dog had the patience of a saint. She never snapped, even when the younger ones tugged on her tail or tried to sit on her head. If anyone needed to register as a hazard, it was Oliver, not Gypsy." She shoved a hand through her short hair. "I talked to a lot of people in that building. Everyone hated him. E-v-e-r-y-o-n-e. I won't pretend I'm sorry he's dead. And neither is anyone else."

"I understand, and I thank you for your candor, Mrs. Tyler," Liam said. "For the record, can you tell me where you were between the hours of eleven o' clock and three a.m. last night?"

Mia snorted. "Am I a suspect now?"

"It's just—" Liam started.

"A routine question," Mia finished. "Yes, I know. I was here, sleeping, until I got a call from the police around three thirty saying my son was on the reservation and I needed to come and pick him up."

"Was anyone with you?" Liam asked.

She met his eyes. "No."

So no alibi. "Did Greg often walk Gypsy so late at night?" I asked.

"Yes. Anthony owns his own body shop, and he works an odd schedule, so if he's there too late, he'll ask Greg to walk Gypsy and then stay the night, and he brings him home or to school in the morning."

I raised my eyebrows. "He has Greg spend the night so he can stay late to walk his dog? Even on school nights?"

"As long as Greg gets to school on time, it's all right with me. But that should give you some idea of how much Anthony loves that dog. I don't think Gypsy's been alone for more than an hour at a time her entire life."

"Were you at all worried having Greg out alone at that hour?" I asked.

Mia shook her head. "Greg is sixteen, but he had to grow up fast after his father died. He never walked her very far from Anthony's apartment, and the people there know him and look out for him."

"Did Greg mention any details about that night, another neighbor joining the search for Gypsy, or anything unusual at the park?" Liam asked.

"No. I asked him what happened, and I'd imagine he told me the same thing he told you. He was walking Gypsy, and she slipped away from him. He saw Oliver go after her, and everyone knows Oliver hates Gypsy, so Greg called Anthony right away."

"Did he continue following Gypsy?" Liam asked.

"Not right away. Anthony told him to go home—like I told you, he's a good man. He wouldn't put Greg in danger, even for Gypsy."

"But Greg did go to the reservation," I said.

Mia bit her lip. "I didn't even hear him come home. When I asked Greg about it, he said he came home, but he couldn't stand sitting here doing nothing, so he left again."

"Mrs. Tyler, I noticed the three of you are at a shooting range in that picture. Does Greg have access to a gun?"

Mia's jaw tightened. "No. I'm the only one with a gun, and I keep it locked up."

"Where?"

She narrowed her eyes. "It's in a locked drawer beside my bed, and no, you can't see it. In fact, I have errands to run, so I if you'll please leave…"

Liam tipped his hat to her. "Thank you for your time. And I'd appreciate it if you would ask your son call us the minute he gets home."

I followed him out, then paused. "Teenagers can be intimidated by serious conversation," I told Mia. "If you have trouble getting him to open up, try talking while doing something else. Dishes, or driving, or at the shooting range. It helps take the pressure off when they don't need to think about eye contact, or keeping the conversation going. A little distraction can go a long way."

Mia didn't say anything, but after a minute, she nodded. I gave her a smile and followed Liam outside.

"Did you find a gun?" I asked Peasblossom.

"What makes you think I was looking?" Peasblossom asked, indignation pushing her voice higher. "You didn't say to snoop, so maybe I didn't snoop."

I waited.

A tiny huff of breath tickled the back of my neck. "No, I didn't find the gun. It's not in the drawer she said it was in, though."

"That doesn't bode well."

Peasblossom crawled between my shoulder blades to peer around my neck. "Neither does that."

I looked up to find Liam standing on the passenger side of the SUV. As I came closer, he held up a set of keys, then tossed them to me.

"You drive," he said.

I didn't catch the keys. They clattered onto the driveway, and I bent to pick them up, still staring at Liam. "I'm driving?"

He nodded and opened the passenger door. "Back to the station, yes."

I shared a look with Peasblossom. "Why is he having me drive his car?" I looked back at Liam, trying to read his expression through the windshield of the SUV. "No one has ever asked me to drive their car. Not outside of an emergency." I frowned. "And never a man."

"There's a reason no one asks you to drive their car," Peasblossom said. "You have an iron foot."

Still confused, I edged around the SUV to the driver's side. "It's lead foot, not iron foot."

"Whatever, your foot's too heavy."

Liam didn't say anything when I got in the car. It took a minute for me to adjust the seat and the mirrors, since Liam and I were nowhere near the same height. He arched an eyebrow as I moved the seat forward.

"You shouldn't sit so close to the steering wheel."

"I have to reach the pedals, don't I?" I responded testily. I didn't like driving other people's cars. When I had everything settled, I started the car and pulled out of the driveway. It wasn't until I'd driven down the block that it hit me why the werewolf had asked me to drive. I hit the brake harder than I needed to at a stop sign and twisted to stare at Liam. "You want me to drive because you think I'm going to try something on you when you're distracted."

Liam braced his forearm on the door's armrest, but the tension vibrating the air in the SUV belied his casual pose. "It's nothing personal. I have to be careful, that's all." He inclined his head forward. "You can go now."

I scowled and shot past the stop sign. Peasblossom pinched the back of my neck and I hissed.

"Slow down," she demanded.

"You still think I was leaning on you for some nefarious purpose," I said tightly. "You think I'm trying to 'siphon off your energy.'"

"I think you're Baba Yaga's apprentice, and you're here against my wishes on a case that hasn't even been declared a homicide." Liam's voice was calm, but firm. "I can't afford to take any chances."

I wanted to point out that I could cast a spell while driving, but that wouldn't help matters. "So is this how it's going to be for the duration of the investigation? You treating me like a dangerous suspect, always preparing for an attack that will never come?"

"I'm going to have a word with Vincent, and then I'll let you know."

He shifted in his seat, and I glimpsed his cell phone in his hand. He was sending a text, but I couldn't make it out, not while simultaneously keeping my eye on the road.

"He just texted Mother Hazel," Peasblossom whispered. "He asked her if she sent you."

I tried not to be offended. I tried to look at it from Liam's point of view. He didn't know me, not really. And Baba Yaga did have a...grey reputation. One of his wolves, a man he treated like a son in need of direction, was lying to him, accused of something Liam didn't think him capable of. He needed someone to blame, another possibility. And I'd turned up on his doorstep when he'd been expecting Mother Hazel.

I stared at the road ahead and almost laughed. My entire career rested on this case.

And I'd just become a suspect.

CHAPTER 7

Liam's phone beeped, alerting him he'd received a response to his text.

"Satisfied?" I asked, my voice frosty.

"She confirmed she sent you." He glanced at me. "You're taking this too personally. I think if you're honest with yourself, you'd admit you'd do the same thing in my position."

"That wasn't Mother Hazel," Peasblossom told him.

Liam tensed, and I grinned. Normally I would chastise Peasblossom for baiting the werewolf, but in this case, I'd let it slide.

"What do you mean, that wasn't Mother Hazel?" Liam asked.

"She's being contrary," I said. "It was Mother Hazel's answer, but it wasn't Mother Hazel sending the text. It was Gus."

"Gus?"

"Gus is a gremlin," Peasblossom told him.

Silence fell over the vehicle. Liam waited for us to continue the explanation, and Peasblossom and I waited for him to keep asking questions. Apparently, we were both feeling a little petty.

"Who is Gus?" Liam asked finally.

Peasblossom opened her mouth, and I knew with the utmost

certainty that she was going to tell him Gus was Mother Hazel's gremlin. I took pity on him and spoke first.

"Gremlins are smaller, more benign relatives of goblins. They have the ability to convert themselves into wild energy, and for some reason no one completely understands, that energy is particularly compatible with today's technology. Mother Hazel can use technology, but she doesn't like it. So when I bought her a cell phone, she immediately gave it to Gus as a hub to live in. Gus thanks her by forwarding her calls as necessary and responding to texts. Sort of a secretary."

Liam looked at his phone. "Gremlins. I heard a rumor that what humans call computer viruses are actually gremlins infesting their programs."

"Yep. But they don't usually do that on their own; that happens when someone angers a technomancer." I shook my head. "Or when technomancers get greedy and decide to use their gift to fleece unsuspecting humans instead of working for a living. Most gremlins are harmless, though they do like to reroute emails to junk folders if people don't take the time to add trusted senders to their contacts."

I pulled into the parking lot of the ranger station, maneuvering the larger vehicle back into the employee-only parking lot. I unfastened my seatbelt and slid out of the car, careful not to drop the keys. Liam had already gotten out of the car, and I locked the doors then closed my door behind me. I smoothed down the lines of my coat and took a deep breath. No more being petty. The trust between Liam and I had been strained, and it was my job to fix that. I had to stay calm and be reasonable. Assuage his fears. I nodded.

I never saw Liam come around the corner of the vehicle. Suddenly he was just there, in my personal space, towering over me. The scent of the forest clung to his skin like a faint aftershave, and underneath that, a masculine scent I couldn't quite describe. It filled my senses, and I stumbled back and hit the side of the SUV. My breath caught in my throat as Liam followed me, keeping our bodies close enough that there was barely room for a breeze. He stood there, almost pinning me against the vehicle with the force of that heated aura.

I was too shocked to call my magic, but I wasn't afraid. There was no sense of violence to the werewolf, no real threat. Nothing but the intensity in his eyes and the pressing buzz of his aura pushing against mine.

"Um…" I cleared my throat. "What are you doing?"

Liam pressed a hand to my shoulder, studying my face. His nostrils flared as he scented the air. I narrowed my eyes. "Liam?" I asked warily.

He didn't answer, just lifted his hand, this time to rest against my jaw, bare skin to bare skin. He stepped closer, and the heat of his energy burrowed deeper into my body. I tried not to squirm even as my thoughts erupted into chaos. Liam leaned closer and put his face over my neck. He drew in a long, deep breath, his mouth ghosting over my skin but not touching it.

Finally, he stepped back. The cool air rushed between us, a sharp contrast to the heat of a second ago. My knees trembled and I leaned against the SUV while I gathered my wits.

"I don't smell a change in you," he said, sharp blue eyes looking me over from head to toe. "No disease. Your vitals all seem strong."

"Um…" I squinted, trying to concentrate on what he was saying. "I'm sorry, you sniffed me to see if I'm…diseased?" It hadn't sounded right when he said it, and it didn't sound any better when I said it.

"And you didn't smell aroused at first, either," Liam continued. He tilted his head. "Not at first."

I slapped him. It wasn't a conscious choice, not something I'd ever seen myself doing. But I did it, and it felt *right*.

Liam blinked. He opened his mouth to speak, but I beat him to it.

"I don't know what's wrong with you," I growled, "but if you really think I'm here to hurt you, then insulting me seems like a really stupid thing to do." I shoved my hands down at my sides, resisting the urge to slap him again—or worse. "I am sorry I leaned into your aura. Twice. I didn't mean to. I wasn't trying to 'siphon your life energy' and I wasn't flirting." I shook my head and lurched toward the building. "Definitely not flirting."

"Wait."

I tensed, but he was smart enough not to touch me, not to put a hand on me to stop me. I didn't turn, just waited for him to speak.

"The people in that building are under my protection. It's my job to take the little things seriously. And I'm sorry if it offends you, but the leaning on me thing is weird." He came to stand in front of me so I could see his face. "I needed to make sure it wasn't something that could put my people in harm's way."

"You can be careful without being an ass," I said evenly.

He scratched his chin. Then he nodded. "The arousal comment was uncalled for. I'm sorry."

I refused to blush. He didn't deserve it. "Don't sniff me again."

He blinked. The corner of his mouth twitched. I pressed my lips together, but it was too late. I smiled. He chuckled. I laughed.

"All right, that sounded weird," I admitted.

"Not among werewolves," Liam said, amusement in his voice. "All right. So you don't cuddle with me, and I won't sniff you. Deal?"

"Deal."

We shook on it, and Liam led the way to the building, holding the door open for me.

"You know he's still going to ask Vincent if you were trying something funny," Peasblossom pointed out, her breath tickling the hairs at the back of my neck.

"I know," I said. I shrugged, knowing Liam could hear what we were saying. "But I'm not lying, so it'll be fine."

"Telling the truth doesn't mean you don't get blamed," Peas-blossom said. "Remember when you accused me of eating the cookie? But I didn't, did I?"

I scowled. "You ate all the chocolate chips out of it. That counts as eating the cookie."

"It does not!"

I abandoned the conversation as we wove through the station, heading for Liam's office. He led me into a small room with plain white walls. A monstrous desk took up a quarter of the room, the surface piled with papers, files, and a scattering of paperclips, binder clips, and sticky notes. Liam stopped at the desk, frowning at the mess. "This case has put me behind."

"I can see that." I perched on the edge of one of the chairs opposite the desk.

Liam's desk chair held a pile of folders, and he didn't bother moving them to sit down. I guessed he didn't spend a lot of time sitting. I studied the photos on the walls and file cabinets. He had pictures of his officers, including the canines. There were vaca-tion pictures too. Wolves featured prominently. Some of the pictures had children's school photos stuck into the corners. I couldn't help but smile. Liam might be a little too high-handed for me, but it was obvious he cared about his officers. And his pack.

"Peasblossom said that Mia's gun wasn't in her desk drawer like she said it was," I offered when a few minutes of silence had dragged on.

Liam paused with his hands full of papers and looked up at me. He scanned both my shoulders as if he were looking for Peasblossom. "Are you sure?"

Peasblossom poked her head out from the curtain of my hair. "Of course I'm sure. Pixies are always sure."

"Well, that's one lie, then." Liam shook his head and began shuffling papers on his desk. "We'll have to talk to her again after we find Greg."

"Does everyone have a gun now?" I asked.

Liam harrumphed as he shoved a pile of folders to the side. "Yes. At least, all the people who shouldn't have guns have them." He braced his hands on the desk's surface. "I still don't have that final coroner's report."

I toyed with the zipper on my pouch. "So, we have a victim who loved himself and hated everyone else."

"And was hated by everyone else in return," Liam added.

"And last night he entered the park intending to kill his neighbor's dog."

"That's the general consensus." He fished his cell phone out of his pants pocket. "We need that report."

I scooted back in the chair, reclining until my head rested on the wall behind me. "Anthony follows him, but he's turned away by Emma, who understands an angry felon running about with a gun hunting the man trying to kill his dog is a bad idea. Anthony gets in his car and drives off."

"He says he drove to work," Liam continued, "but he has no alibi, so it's possible he drove to a different area of the reservation and resumed the hunt for his missing dog." He swiped his thumb over the phone screen, then tapped out a text message.

"A more likely scenario, given his well-documented love for Gypsy," I added.

Liam laid the phone on his desk. "Meanwhile, Greg Tyler, dog walker and juvenile offender, leaves his house against Anthony's orders to continue his hunt for Gypsy, and instead finds the body of our victim. His first call isn't to the cops, but to Anthony."

"Maybe…" I said slowly, "he called Anthony first because he was afraid Oliver attacked Gypsy, and Gypsy fought back."

"So he called Anthony because he was worried Gypsy might have been the one to attack Dale?" He stared at his phone as if willing it to buzz with a new text message alert.

"It makes sense. Greg loves that dog, and so does Anthony. If they thought Gypsy did it, they might delay reporting in the hopes that any evidence against Gypsy would be contaminated."

"Or eaten," Liam added.

I drummed my fingers on the arm of the chair. "I can understand why they might have done that. I mean, Oliver Dale was a bad person by all accounts. If someone I loved had attacked him, say in self-defense, I can't say I wouldn't be tempted to keep my mouth shut. Hope the cops blamed some wild animal."

Subtlety had never been my strong suit. With a mentor like Mother Hazel, it was a miracle I had a grasp of the concept at all.

Liam's shoulders tightened. Slowly, he lifted his face to look at me. "If you have something to say, Mother Renard, say it."

Right to it, then. Fine. "Why won't you let me talk to Stephen?"

"Because I already talked to Stephen. I talked to him for several hours."

So much for our blossoming camaraderie. I straightened in my seat. "And I'm not questioning your ability. But it is possible I might learn something from talking to him, get him to open up—"

"And how would you get him to open up to you more than he opened up to his own *kongur*?"

The accusation in his tone tightened the muscle in my jaw. He hadn't come right out and said it, but the insinuation was clear.

"We're back to me playing the part of the evil witch, then, are we?"

"I didn't say—

"If you're suggesting that I would use magic to force Stephen to say something against his will," I said in a low voice, "you are very, *very* wrong."

"You say that like I haven't been watching you influence people all day. And I didn't—"

"You've been watching me charm people into being friendlier and more open to talking to me, not manipulating them into saying what I want them to say. What I've been doing is the magical equivalent of offering someone their favorite candy, or telling them I'm friends with someone they love and respect before talking to them. It's a subtle influence that will only get me so far. What you've seen me do wouldn't work on someone who hated me, or had a strong reason not to help me."

I shook my head, reminding myself that Liam didn't understand me, and he didn't understand magic. I would let the insult slide. Again. "Manipulating someone's mind is another matter. And even if I were the sort of witch to throw mind-magic around willy-nilly—which I'm not—it wouldn't work that way on a shifter."

Liam's eyes sharpened, pinning me in place. "What do you mean?"

"I can answer this one!" Peasblossom shouted.

I winced and put a hand to my ear, hoping the next words out of the pixie's mouth wouldn't go straight through my ear drum.

"Shifters have two minds," Peasblossom continued, "human and beast. The magic to affect one is different than the magic to affect the other, because affecting a human isn't the same thing as affecting an animal."

"She's right," I said. "The complexity of a spell that would manipulate both would be a lot of effort, and it wouldn't be subtle enough to make it effective."

"I've seen witches affect shifters just fine," Liam said. "Sleep spells, for example."

"Sleep spells are different," I said, trying to keep my voice calm. "Humans and wolves have a similar concept of sleep, so the effect is the same. But manipulating a shifter's mind in the way you're suggesting I would with Stephen, negating his free will and forcing him to tell me things he doesn't want to, or even convincing him to say something, confess something that might not even be true... A wolf would have no concept of that. And it would feel the attempt at affecting his will and react...poorly."

Liam considered that. We stared at one another in silence for a while. It was reminiscent of the standoff we'd had in the parking lot, and I swallowed a sigh. I'd been foolish to think the mistrust could be so easily put aside.

"I'm sorry if I offended you." He rolled his neck, tendons popping loudly in the small confines of his office. "I didn't mean to insult you. I'm just…" He shook his head. "Stephen didn't do this."

I took a deep breath. It would be easier to agree with him, but that wouldn't help anyone. "But he is hiding something."

"Yes, he is," Liam admitted.

His voice held the weight of the knowledge that someone he cared about had done something bad, and he wouldn't be able to protect him from the consequences. That tone eased away the rest of my anger. He was worried for Stephen.

And he should be.

"Dr. Dannon isn't answering my text," Liam said finally. "I'm going to call him. We need a definite cause of death."

"I left Emma's sweatshirt in the SUV. I'm going to go grab it while you're on the phone." I stood. "Is she here today?"

"Her shift hasn't started yet, but she should be here soon. I need to talk to her anyway, so if you wait a second, I'll go to the SUV with you and then we can stop at her cubicle together."

"I need a moment with Peasblossom, and then I'll join you back here, if that's all right?"

His jaw tightened, but he nodded. "Fine."

I left the office as he snatched his phone off the desk and punched in the coroner's number. As soon as we were in the hallway, Peasblossom tapped me on the back of the neck.

"He doesn't like you," she said matter-of-factly.

"He doesn't like me because we had a little misunderstanding that's been blown way out of proportion because he's frazzled by this situation with Stephen," I said. I pushed open the door and stepped outside, bracing myself against a stiff breeze that smelled of snow.

"Maybe he doesn't like witches in general," Peasblossom offered. "Witches are an acquired taste. You're a little scattered, if you want the truth. And he thinks you wanted to come out here alone because you want to talk to me about how guilty you think Stephen is."

I sighed and pressed the button on the key fob to unlock the SUV. "He's convinced I consider Stephen an easy conviction and a shortcut to that favor from Mother Hazel. It would be nice to prove Stephen's innocence instead." I opened the door and retrieved the evidence bag with the bloody sweatshirt. A thought occurred to me, and I paused before closing the door. "Could you ask around, search for witnesses? If someone or something else manipulated him, there has to be chatter. Someone would be bragging."

"Some creatures love to boast, don't they?" Peasblossom played with the edge of her flower petal skirt. "Not very humble. But you can't expect every species to be as evolved as pixies, can you?" She huffed. "Too bad it didn't happen in the city. I have a whole army there, lots and lots of ears."

"And you built that army in less than a day, didn't you?" I said. "Imagine if you built another one here. You'd have armies everywhere."

Peasblossom's eyes glittered. "Armies everywhere. I like the sound of that."

"Of course you do. Go find a witness. We need to know what's keeping our werewolf friend silent."

The pixie nodded and bounced on her toes, ready to take off. Then she stilled and looked at me. "Does it seem to you like I do all the work?"

I glanced at her out of the corner of my eye. "You mean like going to the store to buy honey instead of taking on the bees to get it yourself?"

She cleared her throat. "Point taken."

I smiled after her as she took off, vanishing into the woods in a wink. All joking aside, I'd be lost without the little pixie. I went back inside and found a ranger to direct me to Emma.

I found her sitting behind her desk, fingers poised, unmoving on the keyboard. Her brown skin was smooth and wrinkle-free except for the deep lines around her eyes. Her hair curled out in springy waves from her head, and even sitting down, I could tell she had the long, lean build of a dancer. The dark circles under her eyes, along with the zombie-like stare she'd leveled on her keyboard, made me approach cautiously, not wanting to startle her.

I knocked on the wall of the cubicle. "Hello?"

She spun so fast that I fell back a step, startled by her wide-eyed stare. As soon as she processed my appearance, she relaxed, then reached for a glass of water on her desk. "I'm sorry," she said, "I didn't hear you coming. Can I help you?"

"I'm sorry I startled you. I'm Shade Renard; I'm here helping Sergeant Osbourne." I hesitated. "Are you all right?"

"I'm sorry? Oh, yes." She laughed and put her water down to rub both hands over her face. "I must look like a wreck. I didn't get much sleep last night."

"I would imagine not. Anthony said you were at the animal hospital with him all night."

"You spoke with Mr. Catello?" She toyed with her glass, turning it in circles on her desk. "Did he also mention Gypsy's injuries were all my fault?"

I cleared my throat. "He may have given me that impression."

"He's right." She dropped her hands into her lap. "Maybe if I'd let him help find Gypsy, we would have found her before she got hurt."

I leaned on the cubicle wall, the sweatshirt in the plastic bag pinned between my leg and the partition. Emma was obviously upset, so now wasn't the time to return the bloody reminder of last night's events. "It's not your fault. If not for you, Gypsy could have much worse than an injured leg. If Anthony can't see that, then that's his problem."

Emma shrugged. "I have three dogs of my own." She lifted a picture from her desk. The image in the pale wood frame showed Emma sitting on a grey couch that had seen better days. Three dogs fought for the place of honor in her lap.

"What are their names?" I asked.

"The blue-nose pit is Nova. Her owner abandoned her at birth, and she is now the most spoiled creature you've ever met. The corgi is Crash. He keeps the yard free of squirrels, ducks, and cats." She paused, her brow furrowing. "Except one cat. He seems to have made friends with my neighbor's calico. And the last one is Aro; he's a German shepherd. Some monster threw him out of the truck because he didn't have the black and tan coloring of most shepherds. He's getting over a fight with his ball."

"A fight with his ball?"

Emma grinned, and the expression chased some of the shadows from her face. "He was chasing it and went too fast and tripped over it. He seems to think the ball did it on purpose. It's been a week and he's just now nosing around it again."

I laughed and propped my chin on the edge of the cubicle. "They all sound like such characters."

"That they are." A shadow fell over her features, and the corners of her mouth fell. "I couldn't imagine how I would feel if one of them were lost in the park. There's so many ways they can get hurt. And if there was someone else in the park, someone who wanted to hurt them…" She rubbed her thumb over the three furry faces. "I can't say I would have reacted to someone getting between me and one of my dogs any differently than Mr. Catello did."

"Gypsy's ordeal seems like it hit home for you. Stephen mentioned you were really upset when you called him."

She snorted. "That's an understatement. I sobbed like a little girl with a skinned knee. God, I felt so…awful. Poor Gypsy." Her voice thickened with the threat of tears, and my heart went out to her.

"Emma, you did everything you could. It's because of you that Gypsy is still alive."

She sniffed and nodded. "I guess so." She straightened in her seat, tapping her hands against the surface of her desk. "I'm sorry, you said you're helping Sergeant Osbourne—did you need something from me? What case are you helping with?"

"I'm a private investigator working with the Wild Animal Task Force to figure out what happened to that man they found in the park last night."

Emma frowned. "What?"

I hesitated. "No one told you?"

"Sergeant Osbourne called me and asked me if I'd seen any predators, said there'd been an attack... He didn't say anyone had died."

"Last night after you left with Gypsy, a boy called 911 and said he found a body. It turned out to be a man named Oliver Dale. A significant portion of his stomach was missing, as if some animal had gotten to him."

Emma's lips parted, her mouth moving before any sound came out. "Eaten? Oh my God, is Stephen okay?"

Her first instinct was to ask about Stephen. Interesting. "Yes, he's fine." I paused. "Are you two...close?"

Emma nodded, her eyes still too wide. "We've worked together for years. But it's not just that—Stephen took over my zone last night when I took Gypsy to the hospital. If he got hurt because I wasn't there to back him up..." She swallowed hard and shook her head. "But you said he's all right? Is he here?" She stood, her hands shaking as she looked around.

"I'm not sure." I couldn't tell her that Stephen was on werewolf house arrest for snacking on a dead body. Blood and bones, why hadn't Liam told her what happened already?

The alpha in question came around the corner, waving a handful of papers in the air. "Coroner's full report came in."

"Sergeant, where's Stephen?" Emma asked.

"He's canvassing the area around the park." Liam looked at me, his expression neutral. "Did you…?"

"I told her about the body." I held his gaze. "I thought she already knew."

"It's not her case, and I don't share unpleasantness unless I have to, especially not with someone who's not on duty. I was going update you today when you came in," he told Emma.

"I'm glad Stephen's all right," Emma said with a weak smile.

"He is, he is, don't worry. It'll take more than a coyote to take Stephen down, trust me." He raised the papers he was holding in my direction. "My office?"

I nodded and followed him out, leaving Emma staring into space. As soon as he crossed the threshold, Liam turned. "The coroner made his ruling," he said grimly. "Homicide. Oliver Dale was shot."

CHAPTER 8

I faltered in the doorway, shock pushing my eyebrows into my hairline. "Shot?"

Liam nodded and slapped the file in his hand on his desk. "Beveling on the bone suggests a .40 caliber. There was also evidence of hydrostatic shock."

Hydrostatic shock referred to the wave of pressure caused by a penetrating projectile. The pressure of a bullet entering the body could radiate outward, causing damage surrounding neural tissues.

"Definitely shot, then." I bit my lip as I picked the file up off Liam's desk. I frowned at the evidence bag in my other hand.

"I thought you were going to return that to Emma?" Liam asked.

"She's really upset about what happened to Gypsy, still blaming herself for not finding her before she got hurt. I didn't think now was the time to hand her a sweatshirt covered in Gypsy's blood." I set the file back on the desk and unzipped the pouch at my waist. "I'll give it to her later, when she's had a chance to get a little distance from last night's trauma." I grabbed the evidence bag smashed it as much as I could before angling the

117

corner at the enchanted pouch. "Why would a werewolf shoot someone?"

"He wouldn't."

Liam sounded distracted, so I glanced up. The werewolf was staring at the pouch, watching with a combination of interest and horror as the large bag disappeared into the small confines of the enchanted compartment.

"It's bigger on the inside," I told him.

"I see." He shook himself and fixed me with a smile. "Anyway, this is good news. Oliver Dale was shot, he didn't die from animal-inflicted wounds."

It would have been more beneficial to our working relationship to let that go. Especially with our recent...misunderstandings. But I couldn't. I nodded to the gun holstered to Liam's side. "I assume Stephen carries a weapon as well? Especially while on patrol?"

Liam's face shut down, eyes cooling to an icy stare. "Yes."

I waited, but he didn't continue. "What caliber?"

A shadow passed over Liam's face, but he didn't look away. "A werewolf doesn't need a gun to kill someone. You know that."

I didn't bother pointing out that just because a werewolf didn't *need* to shoot someone, it didn't mean he *hadn't* shot someone. I'd asked my question, and Liam understood what I meant. If he didn't want to acknowledge it now, that was fine. Eventually, he'd have to let me interview Stephen, and I'd ask the ranger then.

"How many rangers were on duty last night?" I asked instead.

"Six. Why?"

I finished jamming the evidence bag into the pouch and zipped it up. "Emma only asked about Stephen."

Liam shrugged. "I've suspected for some time that something was developing between those two. They're the same rank, so I didn't see the harm in it."

I sat up. "And you didn't think that was worth mentioning?"

"Why would I?"

I stared at him in disbelief. Romance was never irrelevant. And if I wasn't so certain he'd blame that opinion on my ovaries, I'd have told him so.

"To be clear, you're telling me you dated Emma, and now Stephen is dating Emma."

Liam snorted. "Don't make this into a soap opera. As I told you before, Emma and I had one date; that's it. It doesn't bother me in the slightest that she's dating Stephen now."

"That wasn't what I was getting at," I said testily. "My point is, Emma has now dated two werewolves that we know of."

"So?" Liam's brows pinched.

"So, I can't help but wonder if she knows you're werewolves?"

"No, she doesn't. None of the human employees do."

I bit back the urge to laugh in his face right then. Instead, I folded my hands in my lap. "It's not possible? There is zero possibility she knows Stephen's a werewolf?"

Liam started to answer, then stopped. "Nothing is *impossible*," he said grudgingly. "But I'm telling you, she doesn't know."

"I could find out for sure."

His eyes narrowed. "How?"

I leaned back in the chair, trying to look as casual as possible. "I could ask her."

Liam stared at me. For a second, he didn't say anything, as if he were waiting for me to say more, as if there had to be more to my plan than what I'd said. I didn't say anything.

"Ask her," he repeated. "You don't see a flaw in that plan?"

"None whatsoever. It's easy, it's direct, and a simple hypnotic suggestion would make her forget I ever asked her."

"No."

I crossed my arms. "I promise you, it would work. Once the mind's curiosity is satisfied, it's much easier to convince someone to forget what they know. I could ask her about werewolves in a roundabout fashion, get a feel for what she—"

Liam smacked his palms flat on the desk and leaned forward. "This conversation is over. You are not talking to Emma about werewolves, end of story."

Anger shot through my veins like a kick of molten caffeine. I held very, very still, waiting for my temper to settle, breathing through the urge to do something petty and satisfying to wipe that superior tone from Liam's voice. When I could speak without spitting a spell at him, I kept my voice as even as possible.

"Is it possible, Sergeant Osbourne, that the reason you are so dead set against my speaking with Emma about werewolves is because you realize that if she's not as ignorant as you think she is, then that could make her a witness?"

Liam stiffened. "Excuse me?"

I shrugged one shoulder, not taking my eyes from his. "If Emma believes in werewolves, then wouldn't it make sense to ask her about Stephen? Did he seem agitated? Did he complain of being hungry? Did you see him attack someone and eat them?"

A muscle twitched in his jaw, and his broad chest rose and fell with a deep, slow breath. "Emma was at the hospital. She wouldn't have seen anything."

"She was at the hospital around midnight," I corrected him. "We don't have an exact time of death. She could have seen something."

"I talked to her. She saw nothing."

"*You* talked to her," I scoffed. "You didn't tell her about the body. What exactly did you ask her?"

"I asked her if she'd seen any predators around, coyotes, or coywolves. She didn't see anything. If she'd seen a wolf, she would have mentioned it. Especially if she knows Stephen is a werewolf."

"She might know Stephen is a werewolf, but not you. From what you've told me, she's a lot closer to him than she ever had the chance to get with you. It's possible she knows what he is, and she knows what she saw. It's possible she saw a werewolf and doesn't want to tell you because she's afraid you'll think she's crazy."

Liam held up a hand, and if I hadn't seen the veins bulging out of his temples, I wouldn't have realized how angry he was. "This is pointless. There's a bullet out there that could give us the answers we need. Why don't we work on finding that bullet—that *physical evidence*—before we leap to conclusions?" He picked up the phone. "I'll call Blake and Sonar and have them look for it."

I didn't argue. There was no point. "Sounds like a plan." I stood from my seat and gave him a strained smile. "I'm going to get a cup of coffee. I'll be right back."

He didn't even look at me as I slipped out of the office. I waited until I heard him on the phone, then made a beeline for Emma's desk. Whatever Liam said, now that it had occurred to me that Emma might know about werewolves, she had far too much potential as a witness to ignore. I had to find out if she was a believer. If she was, she and I needed to have a chat about Stephen and what happened last night.

I tried to tell myself that Liam's outright refusal to even consider asking Emma about werewolves came from an instinct to protect his pack, to not let humans know there were werewolves amongst them. After all, humans hadn't evolved so far that fire and pitchforks wouldn't make a roaring comeback if anyone could offer proof of a werewolf's existence, let alone one's presence on the police force.

But a little voice in my head whispered that it was equally likely Liam was in denial. Perhaps he feared what Emma would have to say if she found she could speak freely about her lupine coworker...

"Excuse me, can I help you, miss?"

I blinked and realized I was standing by Emma's cubicle, staring at her empty chair. A woman stood beside me, and I recognized her as one of the secretaries Liam had greeted the first time I'd come here. "Yes," I said, turning away from Emma's desk. "I'm looking for Emma?"

The woman gave me a polite but curious smile. "She's not here at the moment. I believe she's on patrol. Could I see your visitor's badge?"

"Visitor's badge?"

Liam hadn't said anything about a visitor's badge. In an unkind moment, I wondered if that had been intentional, a way for him to trip me up, or make sure I didn't go wandering around unattended. I smiled and reached for my magic, ready to use a little extra charm if it became necessary.

Before I could say or do anything, my back warmed with the buzz of shifter energy.

Angry shifter energy.

"I've got this, Amy, thank you," Blake said.

Amy gave Blake a more genuine smile then she'd given me. "No problem. Let me know if you need anything."

I arched an eyebrow as Blake's smile brought a tinge of pink to the woman's cheeks.

"I will, thanks," he said.

Blake's expression remained pleasant until Amy left earshot, then he glared at me, dark brown eyes hard and unfriendly. "Why are you poking around back here without an escort?"

I looked down to find Sonar giving me an equally suspicious glare. It was a strange look on a German shepherd.

"I'm searching for the coffee machine." It wasn't exactly a lie. I had planned to stop for coffee; I'd just thought I'd be doing it with Emma so we could have a chat with our caffeine. "Did Liam call you about going to look for the bullet?"

Blake's expression didn't soften. "Yeah. He didn't mention you'd gone for coffee, though."

I furrowed my brow and looked from Blake to Sonar. "Well, that's odd. I can't imagine why he wouldn't tell you about my beverage plans. It being so crucial to the success of our mission." I waved a hand. "Let's not hold it against him. I'll see you in his office in a moment."

I turned toward the hallway that led to the room where I'd first met Vincent and Kylie. If I couldn't talk to Emma, maybe I could talk to them. I doubted they would be as dismissive of Emma's potential for enlightenment as Liam had been.

Blake's voice stopped me in my tracks. "You don't need to go to the meeting room. There's another coffee maker this way."

Nosy werewolf. I turned with a polite smile pasted on my mouth. It wasn't until then that I noticed the smell of hamburgers. My stomach rumbled, and I looked down at the four takeout bags in Blake's hand. "Is all of that for you?"

"No, some of it is for Liam." He shifted his weight from one foot to the other, and for a split second he almost looked embarrassed. Then he lifted his chin. "I didn't know you were going to be here, or I'd have brought you something."

Sonar butted her head against his leg. When he looked down, she laid her ears flat against her head and made a short woofing sound. Then she looked at the bags, then at me. Blake scowled.

"Fine. You can have one of mine," he grumbled.

I smiled at Sonar, then nodded to Blake. "That would be lovely. Thank you." I paused. "But I will get that coffee first, if that's okay?"

"Fine. This way."

I gave him a smile and followed him to a small open area that was surrounded by offices. I found the Keurig and then looked through the cupboards above it for a mug. Rows of eleven-ounce mugs, without a fifteen-ounce mug in sight. I wrinkled my nose. *Criminal.* "So, how did it go with Vincent? Any luck finding a barghest on the astral plane?" I unzipped my pouch and shoved my hand inside, feeling around for a proper mug.

"No."

Didn't think so. I set my mug on the counter. "I understand

Sergeant Osbourne's desire to find proof that Stephen's story is true. It must be har—"

"Stephen's story could be true," Blake interrupted. "Just because we haven't found a barghest, doesn't mean Stephen doesn't believe that's what he smelled. There are other explanations than he's lying."

I didn't speak right away, taking the time to root around for one of my K-cups instead of using the dubious selection the ranger station offered. I was particular about my coffee. "Does Emma know about werewolves?"

The abrupt switch in conversation seemed to catch Blake off guard. He frowned. "No. She's human. None of the humans here know what we are."

Finally, I pressed the start button on the coffee maker and faced Blake. "You're sure? One hundred percent positive?"

"Yes, I'm sure." A hint of annoyance crept into his tone. "Why?"

I looked down at Sonar. She didn't move, but something about the way she looked into my eyes suggested she didn't share the men's certainty that Emma was in the dark.

"But you think she's a good cop?" I asked, looking back up at Blake.

The bags of fast food crinkled as he tightened his grip. "Yeah, she's a good cop. What the hell are you getting at?"

I held up my hands and looked around, making sure no humans were in earshot. "I'm just curious how you and Liam could be so convinced that a woman you both consider a good cop could date two werewolves and still think there's no way she could know you're not human."

"Two werewolves?" Blake echoed.

I stopped with my hand halfway to the steaming mug of coffee. "You didn't know she dated Liam first?"

All emotion left Blake's face, professional cop facade sliding into position like a mask. "I'm a cop, not a gossip. I focus on facts, evidence, not my boss's romantic life."

I snorted then opened the small fridge and helped myself to some cream. Peasblossom thought private investigators should drink their coffee black, but I wasn't there yet. "Does Emma carry a cell phone on her?"

"Yeah."

I poured the cream into my coffee. "Can you tell me the number?"

Blake narrowed his eyes. "No."

"Don't want me to find out if you and your alpha are wrong about Emma's perceptiveness?" I guessed.

"What does it matter?" Blake demanded. "Why are you so caught up on whether she knows what we are?"

"Because if she knows, then we can ask her more questions."

"Like what? Liam already asked her about Stephen's mood, and he was fine."

"Did he ask her if she saw a werewolf?"

Blake pressed his lips together and took a deep breath, visibly forcing himself to calm down. "You're a piece of work. Are you that eager to collect on your little favor that you want to see an innocent man punished for a murder he didn't commit?"

"What fav—" I halted with the coffee halfway to my mouth.

My surprise must have showed on my face, because Blake bared his teeth in what only a very generous person would have called a smile. "Yeah, Liam told me about your deal with Mother Hazel."

He took a step closer, crowding my personal space in a way not unlike Liam had done earlier. His energy hummed against me, warm and inviting despite his attitude. Thankfully, I wasn't feel all that fond of Blake right now, so there was no urge to lean closer.

"If you think Stephen's your ticket to that favor," Blake said, his voice low, "then you've got another thing coming. This hunt you're on for a witness to prove he's guilty won't turn up squat."

I took a sip of my coffee. "Sort of like your hunt for the barghest."

Sonar, who had been quietly sitting by Blake's side, growled at me.

I looked down at her and shook my head. "Don't look at me like that. Whatever your alpha or your partner thinks, I don't want it to be Stephen."

"Maybe not, but you can't tell me you're aren't tempted to sacrifice him to get that favor," Blake countered. "Werewolf takes a bite out of a dead body, it's not so hard to convince someone else, even convince yourself, that he did it."

"Harder than convincing yourself he didn't, I'd imagine," I said.

Blake's face flushed, but I continued before he could interrupt.

"Let me ask you this. Mother Hazel offered me a favor if I could solve this crime. Do you think she meant that she would reward me for a solution, right or wrong?"

Blake paused, shifting the fast food bags to his other hand. He didn't answer.

"I'm not sure how much Liam told you," I went on, "but Mother Hazel also said if I fail, I have to quit. She doesn't want me to be a private investigator, and she's been crystal clear on that point. So even if I went to her and told her Stephen did it— as you seem to think I'm so keen to do—then it would be in *her* best interest to tell me I'm wrong." I tilted my head. "Unless you think she'd put my interests ahead of hers? A falsehood against a truth? Perhaps you think Mother Hazel wouldn't mind my lying to her, or feel it reflected poorly on her if her apprentice got something so horribly wrong?"

The anger faded from Blake's expression until he looked more uncomfortable than anything. Even Sonar wasn't baring her teeth at me anymore.

"Things don't look good for Stephen," I said. "I know that. But I also know that none of your pack members will rest until you know the truth. I know that when I return to my mentor, and I tell her my conclusion, I had better not be wrong."

Sonar's ears lifted, no longer lying flat against her head. She raised her face to Blake, and he looked back at her for a long moment. Finally, he nodded.

"Fine. I'll give you the benefit of the doubt—for now." He turned to leave the room. "Best find that bullet."

I wasn't going to get an apology, so I didn't wait for one. Instead, I followed my growling stomach's lead and trailed after the werewolf with the hamburgers.

Liam wasn't in a great mood when we got back to his office. "What the hell took you so long?" he asked, eyeing me before shifting his attention to Blake and Sonar.

"We were out getting food," Blake said, putting the bags on the table. "On our way inside, we found her at Emma's cubicle."

Liam's eyes darkened, and when he looked at me, it took an effort not to step back. "I thought I made myself clear. You're not interrogating Emma about werewolves."

I focused on the fast food bags. Blake hadn't moved to retrieve his food. Or to offer me any. "You were right by her desk," I said to Blake without looking away from dinner. "Did you talk to Emma before she went on patrol?"

Blake frowned. "Yeah."

"And did she ask where Stephen was?" I took a sip of my coffee, but my stomach rumbled angrily. Now that there was food, it didn't want coffee anymore.

"Yeah." Blake glanced at Liam. "I told her he was trying to contact next of kin."

Liam closed his eyes and let out a slow breath.

"What's wrong?" Blake asked, a trace of uncertainty creeping into his tone.

"Liam told her Stephen was canvassing the surrounding area for witnesses," I said. I wrapped both hands around my coffee to resist the urge to root through the bags of food myself. "Perhaps if you two had taken their relationship into consideration, you would have realized earlier that that would be among the first questions she'd ask, and it would have occurred to you to get that answer straight from the beginning?"

Silence dragged on, and the room grew so thick with the energy of angry shifter that I considered trying to breathe my coffee. Would have been thinner than the air around me.

When I didn't say anything more, Liam drew in a deep breath. He grabbed one of the fast food bags and snatched a hamburger from the greasy paper. After taking a king-sized bite, he focused on Blake. "Any luck with the barghest?"

"No. Wince took me to the astral plane three times, to three different locations, but no luck."

"Wince?" I asked.

Blake didn't look at me. "Vincent. You met him earlier."

Ah, a nickname. And not a kind one. My stomach growled again. This time Liam looked at me and arched an eyebrow. He nudged two of the bags of food toward me and Blake. Blake nodded and retrieved a couple of burgers, handing one to me and putting the other on the desk. Sonar rose onto her back legs and nosed the wrapper open. I stared as she wolfed down the burger in two seconds flat. She met my eyes and licked her lips.

"Cheers," I said, raising my burger to her.

Liam finished his burger and dug in the bag for another. "We need to find that bullet."

Before anyone could respond, a high-pitched voice rang out from the vicinity of the doorway. "I know where it is!"

Blake jerked around so fast at the sound of Peasblossom's voice that he slammed his elbow into the filing cabinet beside him. A string of curses filled the air, and he searched the room around him with eyes that looked more gold than brown. "What was that?"

"My familiar." I held out my hand, and Peasblossom landed on my palm, her face pinched in confusion as she watched Blake rub his injured elbow.

"What's wrong with him?"

"Nothing." I laid the hamburger on the wrapper in my lap and broke off a piece of meat. "Here, eat this."

Peasblossom covered her mouth. "No. I don't like hamburger."

"You need to eat something."

"I already ate!"

I narrowed my eyes. "What did you eat?"

"I'm sorry," Liam interrupted. He pointed at Peasblossom. "Did you say you found a bullet?"

"Yes! Well, sort of. Violet said someone shot her house last night. Some bigjob fired something straight through the wall—something with iron in it." She paused. "Not just iron. Metal, with a bit of iron. Not enough to burn, but it gave her a headache." She glared at me. "Tell her we have to go find the bullet now and I don't have time to eat any disgusting hamburger."

"Who's Violet?" Liam asked.

"A pixie." Peasblossom's voice held a touch of censure, as if Liam should know Violet.

I put the piece of hamburger down and raised the sandwich to take a bite. Peasblossom didn't want it, and I knew better than to battle over food. I'd have to wait until she wanted something, then make eating dinner a prerequisite to getting it. "Excellent work, Peasblossom. Did you find anything else?"

Peasblossom leapt onto my shoulder and snuggled up against my neck under the fall of my hair. "No will-o'-the-wisps messed with the wolf. And no one saw what happened. A dryad is lusting after a human ranger. Oh, and a leshy found a barghest tooth."

"A barghest? Was there a barghest around last night?" Liam

put the burger he'd been unwrapping on his desk and leaned forward.

I smothered a groan. If I heard the word "barghest" one more time...

Peasblossom shook her head. "Not last night. There's a barghest that uses this forest as a hunting ground, but one of the dryads said it's not his time of the month to feed. She said he ate two weeks ago—swallowed a deer."

"Barghests eat humanoid creatures, not deer," Blake interrupted, speaking around a mouthful of sandwich.

"Well, the werewolves are obviously doing a good job of keeping them from their favorite food, then," Peasblossom said primly. "It ate a deer."

"Barghests can eat other creatures," I said slowly. "But other creatures only satisfy their physical need for nutrients. To feed their power, and increase their ability to survive against their own predators, they need to eat humans and other humanoids. If it ate a deer, then it might still hunt for something to feed its power." I stopped and almost smacked myself. The werewolves needed no more encouragement to believe this particular false hope.

"No one saw a barghest last night," Peasblossom repeated.

I looked at the rangers. "Blake didn't find one on the astral plane near here either."

Peasblossom snorted. "Of course he didn't find a barghest on the astral plane. What good is a werewolf's senses on the astral plane?"

Blake bristled at that. "I suppose you can do better?"

Peasblossom's face wrinkled in genuine confusion. "Of course."

"What about this bullet?" Liam asked, interrupting before Blake could respond. He snatched up another burger. "Where is it?"

"I'll show you," Peasblossom said. "It's not far. Follow me."

CHAPTER 9

"Peasblossom, how much farther is it?"

I asked the question as nicely as I could, but I was dangerously close to snatching the little fey out of the air and threatening to pin her wings together. I wasn't sure how long we'd been walking. Long enough that her promise of "not far" felt like a lie.

"It's that tree right up there." Peasblossom pointed ahead.

I put a hand over my rumbling stomach. If I'd known the walk would take this long, I would have brought my fries with me. "For future reference, this walk did not qualify as 'not that far.' It was, in fact, very far."

"It wasn't when I was by myself," Peasblossom grumbled, kicking at the seam of my shirt where it traced the top of my shoulder. "You bigjobs take forever."

Liam had remained silent the entire walk, scanning his surroundings as if a barghest would appear out of nowhere to clear Stephen. Despite his state of high alert, he seemed more at home amongst the trees, as if he breathed easier out here in nature than in his office, with its stacks of paper and dusty windowsills. If I stared at him, I imagined his wolf inside, relishing the outdoors, looking forward to the next night when it would be free to run, nothing between its fur and the cool night breeze.

Blake kept looking to a spot toward the left. His distraction continued snagging my peripheral vision, until I followed his gaze and noticed police tape marking off a section of the forest floor not far from us.

"Is that where the body was found?" I asked.

Blake nodded. "I'm surprised the tape is still up. Usually the creatures in these woods can't wait to tear things like that down."

I craned my neck, but couldn't see much of the area from here. Not that I expected to find much. The earth had probably already soaked up the blood, and I'd seen the crime scene photographs. Still. "I'd like to examine the crime scene after we're done here."

"We're not incompetent," Blake said, annoyance plain in his tone. "I supervised that scene myself. And whatever his personality, Wince is a competent wizard who specializes in forensics." He snorted. "And he's been working in forensics for years; he didn't up and decide to—"

"I didn't mean to offend you," I interrupted, irritation sharpening my voice. "I'm sure you and Vincent did an excellent job. I'd still like to see for myself."

"Fine. But do it on your own time. I'm not wasting a day rehashing all the work we've already done."

It was Oliver's apartment all over again. Liam didn't want me talking to Stephen or looking around Oliver's, and now Blake didn't want me poking around the crime scene. I paused, forced my mind off that path. No, that wasn't true. Talking to Stephen was the only thing I'd been outright barred from. I could look at both scenes if I wanted to. As long as I didn't mind letting the investigation progress without me while I did it, being left out of the loop when new clues were discovered. I frowned. There had to be a way around that. Maybe if I went to the scenes while the rangers were sleeping...

Sonar raised her head, nose twitching as she caught a scent. She took off at a lope, and Blake and Liam immediately broke into a jog to follow her.

"What is it?" I asked.

"That's it!" Peasblossom announced, pointing to a tree up ahead. "That's Violet's house. Hello!"

Sonar was a few feet shy of the tree when a blue light twinkled like a speck of glitter against the pale grey of the trunk. Too late, Sonar reached the towering beech, paws rising as she rose onto her hind legs, sniffing the bark. The blue speck darted forward, and Sonar let out a yelp of surprise.

Werewolves had keen senses, and even in human form, they could scent a chipmunk in the underbrush. But pixies had a gift. A gift for being unseen, unsensed. They were tiny, and unlike most creatures with natural glamour, they could partially mask their scent. Liam wasn't searching specifically for a pixie, so he never had a chance.

Blake and Liam reached for their weapons. They hadn't seen the speck. I opened my mouth to call out a warning, but before a sound left my lips, Liam stumbled, eyes widening as he found himself with a face full of blue pixie.

"What the—?" he sputtered.

"Why is there a dog on my tree?" the blue pixie demanded. Her cerulean eyes twinkled like shards of sapphire, glowing faintly with her temper.

"Peasblossom, you haven't introduced us to your friend," I said, stifling a smile.

"Violet, this is my witch, Shade," Peasblossom said. "Shade, this is Violet." She pointed at Liam and Blake. "And the other two bigjobs are Liam and Blake."

Violet was six inches in height, the same size as Peasblossom. Her hair matched her eyes, and she wore a dress made of new leaves, so pale a green they were almost yellow. She gave Liam and Blake a once-over. She did not look impressed.

"The dog," she repeated. "Why is it on my tree?"

"Her name is Sonar," I told Violet. "She's looking for a bullet—"

"A bullet!" Violet shouted as if she'd forgotten about the incident until this second—which she probably had. "That's right! Someone shot my house." She stared at Liam's gun, now hanging at his side. "You!" She threw out an arm, pointing at the weapon in question. "Come to shoot my house again, have you?" She zipped upward, flying tight circles around Liam's head. "I'll give you such a beating!"

Neither of the three werewolves seemed capable of a reaction beyond staring in shock and dismay at the angry pixie. She darted down and bounced off Liam's head in what would be a vicious kick by pixie standards.

Liam looked at me. His face was blank, but there was something in his eyes. A very clear plea for assistance.

"Violet," I said, stepping forward, "Liam did not shoot your house."

Violet ignored me, darting down to stomp on Liam's head again. "He's got a gun, hasn't he? And he's here. Returned to the scene of the crime!"

I'd bet money when she said "scene of the crime," she referred to her house being shot, not the murder. It was also apparent she hadn't actually seen Liam, but rather was making assumptions on his presence and his possession of a gun.

"He has a gun too," Peasblossom said, pointing at Blake.

Violet paused in midair, her attention zeroing in on Blake's sidearm. She narrowed her eyes. "Was it you?"

Blake blinked, tension seizing his body as if he had to fight to not take a step back. "No."

Sonar sat on the ground, keeping her distance from the pixie's house, but angling her nose in its direction. Liam noticed her attention and focused on the tree for a moment before taking a steadying breath. "Miss—Violet, I assure you, I didn't shoot your house, and neither did my detective."

"Liar!"

She stomped on him again, and the muscle around his eye twitched.

"Can you describe the person who shot your house?" Liam asked, taking a pen and notepad out of the front pocket of his shirt and clicking his pen with unnecessary dramatic flair.

Violet landed on his head, looking as though she wanted to give him a final stomp just in case. "Well, he was a bigjob."

Liam scribbled on his notebook, and I wondered if he'd written "bigjob."

"Did you see this person, or are you making inferences based on the evidence of what happened to your home?"

The pixie crawled closer to his forehead, clinging to his hair and leaning down to get a better view of his notebook. "I didn't see him. I'd have given him what for if I had, believe you me." She leapt into the air, using his skull as a springboard. "Look at what he did to my house!"

All three werewolves moved closer to the tree, examining the damage. The bark had been chipped away in a section the size of a half-dollar, surrounding the small, dark hole with the golden brown of naked wood. The bullet's point of entry was close to the knothole that led into the home the pixie had made for herself in the tree. Liam flipped his notebook to where a ruler was printed on the back cover. He held it up to the hole. "Small caliber, probably a .40." He looked down at Sonar. "Any blood?"

Sonar barked once. Near as I could deduce, that meant yes.

Liam looked into the hole. "It doesn't seem to have gone straight through. Where is the bullet now?"

"Gunderson took it out," Violet told him.

"Gunderson?" I echoed.

The pixie landed on Liam's notebook, staring down at what he'd written with a critical eye. "Yes."

"Who's Gunderson?" I asked.

"A dwarf," Blake answered. "He's an artisan of sorts. His shop's not far from here."

Liam started to close the notebook, then remembered the pixie was still standing there.

"That's right," Violet said. "I knew he'd get that bit of metal out for me, and he did. Didn't take him a minute. And he said he'd help me fix my tree if I wanted. Good man, that Gunderson."

"What did he do with the bullet?" Liam asked.

She sniffed. "I don't care. At least it's not in my house anymore." She pressed her hands to either side of her head. "It was giving me a headache."

"I have just the thing for that." I unzipped my pouch and dug around for a minute—or two.

"This could take a while." Peasblossom perched on my shoulder and patted the space beside her. Violet tilted her head, then accepted the invitation and sat next to Peasblossom.

The werewolves took turns examining the bullet hole and the surrounding area as I found mail that should have gone out last week, a set of D&D dice, and a handful of index cards. Finally, I found what I was looking for. "Here."

Violet's lips parted as I handed her the honey packet, humorous reverence stealing over her as she hugged it to her chest. Peasblossom fidgeted, looking from Violet's honey to the pouch. I considered telling her she couldn't have any until she ate her dinner, but that just seemed cruel. And she was helping. I gave her a honey packet as well. A second later, Violet vanished, and if the sound of surprise from Blake was any indication, she'd darted into her house.

"I guess she's done with us," I said.

Liam put his notebook away and looked at Blake. "We'll head to Gunderson's and see if he has that bullet. You head to the station and check and see if any of our suspects have a .40-caliber weapon registered in their name."

Blake nodded, and he and Sonar headed in the direction we'd come.

"Gunderson's shop is just on the outside of the park," Liam said, gesturing with his thumb as he moved away from Violet's tree.

I nodded and fell into step beside him. Now that we'd found the bullet hole, and were close to having the bullet to go with it, I had a vague sense the case was nearing a solution. If Stephen had shot Oliver, we'd be able to trace the bullet to his gun. If it wasn't a match, then it would be the closest we'd come to dismissing the werewolf as a suspect since the case started.

I wouldn't be sorry to see this case end. And I hoped it ended with someone who wasn't Stephen. If I wanted to continue as a private investigator, then a friendly relationship with the police was desirable. Certainly, avoiding friction was to be preferred. On that note…

I cleared my throat. "You told Blake about my deal with Mother Hazel."

"Yes."

I waited, but he offered nothing more. Irritation bit at my nerves, but I pushed it down. *Stay calm; stay friendly.* "Why?"

"Because it is relevant."

Again I waited, and again he said nothing. I curled my hands into fists.

"You cannot still believe I'm here to pin this murder on Stephen?"

Liam didn't stop walking, or even slow down. "I don't know why you're here. Why did Mother Hazel insist you take part in this investigation when it's clear you aren't qualified to do so?"

My temper flared. This again. Every time I thought we'd moved past it, every time I dared to believe we'd reached a peace in our working relationship, he said something to make me realize I was still the unwanted outsider. My palms warmed with the promise of rising magic. "Excuse me?"

"You interfered when I tried to question Anthony Catello. If you hadn't, then I could have had him at the station, being questioned by experienced investigators."

"I interfered with Mia Tyler as well, and if I remember correctly, I'm the reason you got in at all." I pressed my palms flat against my legs, trying to wipe away the nerve-tingling urge to call my magic. It was unsettling how often this happened now, my temper calling to my magic. I hadn't had this trouble before... I frowned. When had it started?

Liam shook his head. "You still don't understand. Do you think we only question witnesses who are eager to talk, that we only interview suspects who volunteer to come down to the station? People shut us down all the time, sometimes because they're guilty and sometimes because they don't want to get involved. I'm trained to work around that. I know how to make people talk to me."

"So do I. And I did."

Liam opened his mouth, then snapped it closed. When he spoke again, his voice was calmer, more even.

"Listen. Don't take this personally. You want to be a PI; I understand that. I understand the desire to get justice for victims, to see bad guys put away. And everyone needs to start somewhere, so don't think I'm judging you because of a lack of experience. But please understand: this isn't just any case. Stephen isn't just an officer under my command; he's a part of my pack. I'm his alpha, and it's my job to protect him." He faced straight ahead, tension pulling his shoulders tight. "And if he's committed a crime, it's my job to punish him."

He looked at me then, and the intensity in his gaze almost made me stumble.

"You want me to accept your help, really include you in this investigation? Then help me understand why Mother Hazel wants you here. Why now? Why this case? Does she think

Stephen did it? Does she think I'll look the other way because he's my wolf?"

"She didn't say anything to make me think she had anything but the utmost respect for you and your professionalism," I said.

"Then does she think it was someone else? Does she think I'm not capable of finding out who did it?"

I ran a hand over my head and down my hair, curling the end around one finger. Getting frustrated wouldn't help anyone. Liam was frustrated enough for the both of us anyway. "I don't know why she sent me. I don't know what's special about this case, why she chose this case to base her deal off." I hesitated, then admitted, "But you're right to wonder. Mother Hazel does nothing without a reason."

"That's what I'm afraid of."

I stopped walking. "But neither do I. Do something without a reason, I mean." I looked at Liam, trying to catch his eye. He refused to stop or even pause, just kept walking. I gritted my teeth and followed. "And I have no reason to want Stephen punished for a crime he didn't commit. I don't want it to be him."

Liam didn't look at me, and he still didn't stop, but he nodded. I couldn't think of anything else to say, nothing that might reassure him. I let the distance stretch between us, but stayed in his peripheral vision. His energy hummed against my senses, and the last thing I needed was to find myself leaning on him again in a moment of distraction.

I turned that thought over in my mind. I'd never reacted to shifters this way before. There'd been no urge to lean on Stephen, though his energy was less, a dryer in the middle of a cycle and more like a bonfire. Most likely because of the impending collar. Blake's energy had been quiet the few times I'd stood close to him. So was it shifters in general that I felt the urge to be close to? Or Liam?

Neither was a terribly comforting thought, and my shoulders bowed in relief when we crossed over an access road and I saw

Gunderson's shop. The grey stone building with the red-slated roof sat at the edge of the forest, its twin chimneys bellowing smoke into the evening air. A smaller building beside it offered a view of large wood stacks through its open face. Liam pulled open the red double doors and gestured for me to go in first.

A bell over the door announced our arrival, and a man's gruff voice followed on the heels of the last chime. "I'll be but a moment!"

"Oh my," I said.

Artisan indeed. Shelves upon shelves lined Gunderson's shop, each one holding an eclectic array of items, only half of which I could identify. I saw a gold chain holding an absinthe-green gem the size of my thumb, a wooden box covered with gears and wires, pocket watches of every metal and shape I could think of, and a plethora of other wondrous objects.

"This work is breathtaking." I ran a finger over a silver chain connected to a vial of black liquid that shone like polished obsidian.

"It's kind of you to say."

I released the chain and found a man's face rising above the low counter, brown eyes shining and what I could see of his face over the bushy grey beard heavily creased with age. He smiled at me before ducking out of sight. I heard a trapdoor shut and a bolt slide into place, and then he straightened and put both hands on the counter. Pockets lined every inch of the leather apron he wore, each filled to bursting with bits of metal, thick glass tubes, and tools, so that he clinked when he moved.

"Mr. Gunderson, I presume?" I asked.

The dwarf nodded. "I am. And who might you be?"

"This is Mother Renard," Liam said. "Mother Renard, meet Mr. Gunderson, the finest artisan this side of the veil."

"Your work is stunning." I paused. "Do you have anything that might work against non-corporeals? Shadow creatures, perhaps?"

Gunderson's eyebrows went up, and he waved a hand at me. "Yes! Yes, I do— Wait right there; don't move. I have something for you. Wait right there; don't move!"

The dwarf rifled in a drawer behind the counter, his movements quick and excited. "I've built a new device, and it would take a magic user to activate it. I haven't been able to try it out. Drat, where is it?"

I watched with interest as he half disappeared in a drawer that was much deeper than I'd initially thought. He crowed in triumph and hauled something out of the drawer and onto the counter.

It looked like a bracer, the base of it supple brown leather. But the myriad metal and glass bits all over it suggested it wasn't just a bracer. "What does it do?"

"It stores sunlight! Only, instead of exciting the electrons in silicon cells, the photons from the sun harvested by the photo-voltaic panels collect in a solar pool formed by the wearer's own magical aura. This part here"—he gestured to a bowl-shaped gear —"will bend your aura beneath this panel here." He pointed at a small solar panel no bigger than a silver dollar. "The resulting dimple will hold the solar energy collected by the panel. Then, when you need to use the sunlight you've stored, you flex your aura. The sunlight will filter through this small lens here, magnified through this lens here, and Robert's your father's brother, you have a beam of pure sunlight!"

"That's fascinating." I took the contraption with gentle hands, careful not to jar any of the delicate gears. "How much do I owe you?"

"Not a penny. I don't know if it works yet. Try it, and let me know."

I nodded. "I will. Thank you."

"If I might interject," Liam said, "I'd like to talk about the reason for our visit."

"Yes, yes, of course. What can I do for you, Sergeant Osbourne?"

"You removed a bullet from a pixie's home earlier today. I wondered if you still had it?"

Gunderson frowned, spreading his thick, stubby fingers over the countertop. "I hope it wasn't important."

"Why do you say that?" I asked, though I was pretty sure I already knew the answer.

"I added it to the smelting pot. It was a worthless bit of metal, warped beyond repair. Waste not, though, that's my motto. It'll be part of an invention soon." The dwarf's eyes took on a faraway look as his mind no doubt wandered to future inventions.

"Well, we won't be getting a match from that, will we?" Peasblossom said.

Liam twitched, then caught himself. I grinned. Another gift of the wee ones. Despite their capacity for constant chatter, pixies could maintain a long silence if they wanted to. They could make you forget they were there.

"I'm sorry, Sergeant Osbourne. I'd no idea you'd be needing it." Gunderson shook himself out of his daydream and folded his hands over his robust stomach, looking genuinely apologetic.

Liam's phone vibrated, and he took it out of his pocket. His gaze twitched side to side as he read the text message, then he replaced his phone and smiled at Gunderson.

"No harm done. If it was as damaged as you say it was, it was unlikely we'd have gotten a match anyway." He turned to me. "Thank you for your help, Shade. And you, Peasblossom."

Peasblossom preened at being acknowledged, but I knew when I was being ditched. And Liam's demeanor had brightened suspiciously fast. "It was my understanding that there was no quitting time when there's a murder to solve?" I said, letting my suspicion seep into my voice.

Liam stopped with his hand already on the door. "I'm not going home. I'm going to the station."

"Then I'll come with you. Mr. Gunderson, do you have anything I could package this up with so it doesn't get damaged?"

The dwarf's gaze darted between us, then he nodded. "Of course."

"Shade, there is no reason for you to stay. I'm going to my office to meet with Blake. If any of our suspects own a gun that matches the caliber of bullet we found, I need to draft a warrant, and that takes time. Besides," he added, "you mentioned that you wanted to see the crime scene, didn't you? You have a little daylight left—more if Mr. Gunderson's creation works, which I know it will."

I ground my teeth. He seemed determined to get rid of me, so there was no point arguing. Yet.

"I won't be able to get a warrant before the court opens tomorrow anyway," Liam added. "I'm sure you'll be here bright and early?"

I crossed my arms. "Yes, I will."

My voice sounded more petulant than I'd intended, but it was what it was. Liam was up to something. And unless I wanted to call him out in front of the shopkeeper, there was nothing I could do about it. I stood there stewing as the door closed behind the werewolf.

"Not like Sergeant Osbourne to leave a lady to walk home alone at night," Gunderson said. "I'll be walking you to your car, then."

"I appreciate the offer, but I'll be all right. I am a witch, you know." I lifted the freshly wrapped package. "Besides, I have this now, haven't I?"

Gunderson beamed. "You will tell me how it fared for you? I've lots more ideas like that one."

"I will, thank you again."

It took me two steps to realize I was alone. And I shouldn't be. "Peasblossom?"

A muffled squeak came from somewhere near my arm. Gunderson and I both looked at the package.

"Oh, my, have I...?" he asked, grey eyebrows rising to his hairline.

I sighed and unwrapped the brown paper. Peasblossom glared at me from her hiding spot inside the bracer.

"Well, if this is what I get for helping you find a critical piece of evidence, then you can find your own way back!" she snapped.

Arguing that it was her own fault she'd been trapped wouldn't do me any good, so I didn't waste my breath. Instead, I redid the paper and string and stood there while the pixie stomped up my arm and sat down on my shoulder, hard enough I'd bet it hurt her more than it hurt me. I rolled my eyes and slid the package into the pouch at my waist, easing the gift into the bottomless confines of the enchanted bag. Gunderson wisely kept silent about the pixie's predicament and waved goodbye.

The sun was kissing the horizon as I left the shop. Liam's desire to be rid of me irritated me even more as I noticed how little daylight I had left. Even with the bracer, assuming it worked, it would be more effective to scout the scene tomorrow. I looked off in the direction he'd gone. What drove him out in such a hurry? And so determined to leave me behind?

"Lost, aren't you?" Peasblossom sneered. "Well, I'm not helping."

The zipper of my pouch sounded loud in the serene shadows of early evening. The bracer had already sunk into the depths of the bag, and I didn't even touch it when I groped inside for the potion I needed. I pushed a travel coffee mug, an extension cord, and a dozen napkins out of the way before I found the vial I wanted.

The last of the sun's rays turned the bottle bright red as I upended it, drinking down the moss-flavored brew. I coughed, the rock dust in the potion clinging to my throat. I fumbled for the travel mug, hoping there was still some tea left inside.

Fortune was with me, and a swallow of lukewarm tea pushed the rest of the potions bits down.

Magic sprayed over my vision, a map hovering before me as if someone had traced out the forest paths with a child's silver crayon. One by one the paths vanished, leaving only the quickest way through the woods.

"That's cheating," Peasblossom grumbled.

"No one told you to climb inside the bracer," I said, returning the empty bottle and the travel mug to the pouch. "Why didn't you say something when he started wrapping it up?"

"What was I going to say? Hey, I'm snooping here?"

"I think you were being considerate," I said. "I think poor Mr. Gunderson didn't see you, and rather than embarrassing him, you let yourself be trapped."

Peasblossom was silent for a moment. "It was considerate of me, wasn't it? Not to embarrass the old fool?"

"You're one of a kind."

The pixie shifted around to lie on her stomach across my shoulder, kicking her feet in the air. "I really am."

The darkness thickened as I pressed deeper into the woods, the shining line of the spell still racing forward, a beacon leading me on. I passed beneath a tree heavy with a murder of crows, their beady black eyes watching me as I wandered too close. I ignored the avian disapproval. If I kept a good pace, I could make it to my car and be home in time to put in a few hours researching Majesty's condition. There had to be a way to find out who did that to the kitten and—

The hairs on the back of my neck rose. A sensation like cold winter slush poured down my spine, and the long black shadows formed by overarching tree branches slithered like tendrils, reaching for me with grasping fingers. A scream bubbled in my throat, and for one horrible moment, I couldn't breathe.

A deep, rasping sound came from behind me. Not human. Bigger. Sound swelled in my throat, threatening to pass my lips in a scream that promised more to come. Tears flowed like liquid panic. Whatever it was had affected my mind, pushed me from confusion to terror in the span of a breath. I hovered on a mental precipice, and I did not want to know what would happen if I fell.

I willed myself to stay calm, to hold on just for a second. Very, very slowly, I drew out a spell, moving my fingers as little as possible. Peasblossom was still on my shoulder, but as soon as I'd gone still, she'd sensed the danger. Her tiny body trembled as she scuttled down my arm and hid beneath my sleeve, clinging to my wrist, her rapid heartbeat pressed against my erratic pulse.

Green energy rose at my command, surging forward in the shape of a sleek, lean-limbed cat. It raced over the muscles in my legs, filling each strand with strength and power. I held the image in my mind as I said the incantation under my breath. The creature inhaled sharply, as if it sensed what I was about to do.

I ran.

The magic invigorated me, giving me the endurance I needed to escape. I had the gift of the cheetah, a cat whose talent was speed, and only speed. I bolted through the forest, and the humming silver thread of my earlier spell kept me on track, preventing me from crashing face first into the trunk of a tree, or tumbling bum over teakettle into a ravine. The spell saved my life, because I certainly didn't have the presence of mind to watch where I was going. Not with that thing pursuing me.

It was following me. I could feel it, could feel that skin-searing cold. But I couldn't hear it. There was no crashing through underbrush, no snapping branches or disturbed leaves. Not even the beating of wings. There was only silence behind me. And if it wasn't running, and it wasn't flying, it was…incorporeal.

"Peasblossom," I wheezed, taking a risk and trying to speak despite the current physical demands on my lungs. "Can you see what it is?"

"I don't want to." Her voice was thin, panicked and barely discernible over the rush of blood in my ears.

"Please," I gasped.

There was a muffled cry from beneath my sleeve, and then Peasblossom stuck her head out and pried open her eyes to look behind us. A wail poured from her throat, and she dove back underneath my shirt, her trembling ten times worse.

"What is it?" I hurtled over a fallen tree.

"I don't know!" she shrieked. "A monster! Black, shadowy, pointed ears, long tail, four legs. It's running on the air!"

My heart leapt into my throat and I choked. That description. It sounded... It sounded like the creature I'd seen in my dream last night. Exactly like it.

I knew what it was.

Cursing with every fiber of my being, I pulled on my magic. I didn't bother to be quiet or subtle this time, but screamed the incantation, throwing my hands through the gestures like a madwoman who'd run through a spider web. Violet strands of energy whipped the air, then spun as if caught up in a whirlwind. They wrapped about me in a cocoon of purple light, sank past my skin to my heart, my soul. Heat pulsed out as the spell locked into place, chasing back the fear the creature had infused me with. My heart slowed, if only a little, and my next breath didn't threaten to shatter my ribs. Magic-fueled determination seized my spirit, and I leaned forward into the spell. The monster would not catch me. Not tonight.

The silver path before me flickered.

"No," I shouted.

The magic ignored me. Another flicker, and then the path vanished. I dismissed the second spell, biting back another cry as the emerald image of a cat fled my body to vanish into thin air. My legs trembled, and I stumbled a few steps before falling to my knees.

"Don't stop! Don't stop! Run!"

Peasblossom's cries forced me to my feet. I called my magic, but my limbs shook violently as I paid the price for forcing my body faster than nature intended it to go. I'd dismissed the cheetah spell too fast, cut it off when the direction spell died, because running full speed when you didn't know which direction to run was a recipe for a concussion—or worse. Without the cooldown period for the spell, there was nothing to save me from the full brunt of the consequences.

"Peasblossom," I rasped. "Fly. Get away."

"I won't leave you!"

My throat constricted so I had to fight to speak. "You'll die if you stay—now *fly*!"

"No!"

A car horn cut off whatever I might have said. I raised my face and sobbed with relief. A car slowed, its headlights revealing how close I was to the road. Emma peered at me from her window, her eyes wide. With the last of my strength, I forced myself to my feet and gave a final burst of speed to push me to the car.

"Ms. Renard, are you all right?" Emma caught my hand as I fell into the passenger seat. My entire body shook, and it took three tries to close the door. I stared out her window into the darkness of the trees.

Teeth glinted in the moonlight.

"Drive!" I yelled.

CHAPTER 10

"What was that?"

Emma's calm voice contrasted sharply with the wide-eyed stare I'd glimpsed through her window. I didn't answer right away. I couldn't have if I'd wanted to, if I'd known what to say. I was too busy gulping in lungfuls of air, breathing through the pain as my body fought through the aftereffects of shrugging off a spell too fast. Every muscle in my legs felt brittle, as if each strand were a frayed piece of wicker being wrenched into the shape of a basket. Each breath brought a fresh round of stabbing against my lungs, and sweat poured down my temples.

"I'm not sure." My stomach twisted at the lie, but my expression was already a mask of misery, so I hoped she wouldn't notice.

Silence filled the air.

"Was it a demon?"

I sat up so fast that I slammed my elbow into the door. "Ouch!" My legs spasmed, screaming protest at being used to push myself up in the seat. I grabbed my calves, trying to keep them from exploding as pain shot down every nerve ending at once. "Argh!"

"Are you all right?" Emma's voice held a touch of amusement, but her face remained serious.

Pressing my palms flat against my thighs, I eased back in my seat, willing myself not to scream. A voice in my head echoed her question, and I latched on to it, grateful to have something to think about beside the agony crushing my body into one tight ball of misery. "You believe in demons?"

Another silence followed my question, this one thicker than the last. I'd all but convinced myself I'd imagined the whole interaction when Emma sighed.

"Is that thing still chasing us?"

I forced my eyes open long enough to look out the rear window to be sure, but I doubted I'd see anything. Arianne wouldn't have turned a dream shard loose without restrictions; she was too careful for that. I guessed it would flee at the first sight of a human.

"We're fine now. It's gone." I slumped back in my seat and closed my eyes.

"Good. This conversation will go a lot faster if we put our cards on the table."

She pulled over to the side of the road and put her hazard lights on before turning to me. The ticking of the hazard lights made me open my eyes, but before I could ask what she was doing, Emma spoke again.

"I know they're werewolves."

My jaw dropped before I could stop it, and I closed my mouth with an audible click of teeth. "You... Who?"

She pursed her lips, her smooth brown skin wrinkling around the corners of her mouth. "Liam, Stephen, and Blake. And don't pretend you don't know; you'll insult both our intelligences."

She'd left out Sonar. I groped for the door handle, not with the intention of making a break for it, but to give myself an anchor to reality. To suspect Emma knew about werewolves was one thing, but to have it confirmed in such a…blatant way was unexpected. "How?"

Emma settled in her seat, pulling a leg up as though we were old friends having a long-overdue chat. "My grandmother. Our ancestors come from Haiti, and it was important to her I learned where I came from. She had lots of stories to tell me, and the way she talked about the Never Never…" She shrugged. "I knew it was real."

"The Never Never," I repeated. "It's been a while since I heard it called that. Most of the people and creatures I interact with around here call it the Otherworld." I settled in my seat, acclimating to the conversation and the fact that Emma knew about her coworkers. A small, petty part of me wanted to call Liam and tell him I'd been right. I resisted. "How long have you known?"

"From the moment I met Liam." Emma chuckled. "My grandma had a routine for me to go through before I went on a date with anyone new. Always eat Italian, wear real silver, and put your underclothes on backward."

"Italian for the garlic in case your date is a vampire, real silver to discover a werewolf, and reverse your clothes against the glamour of a fey." I grinned, looking at Emma in a whole new light. "Your grandma is a smart woman."

"She was." Emma arched an eyebrow. "Between you and me, there was a time I was convinced the underclothes-on-backward thing was her way of discouraging sex too early in a relationship. Nothing ruins the mood like giving your date the impression you can't dress yourself properly."

Despite her joking demeanor, there was a heaviness in Emma's voice, the tone of someone speaking of a loved one lost too soon. And when you lose a loved one, it's always too soon.

"I'm sorry for your loss."

She nodded, fingers toying with the edge of her seatbelt. "It's been a few years now. Still hurts, but I like to talk about her. It's good to remember."

"Is that how you discovered your coworkers are werewolves? You wore silver on your date with Liam?"

Emma's eyebrows rose. "He told you about that? Our date?"

"Was he not supposed to?"

"Oh, I don't mind." She waved a hand. "I'm just surprised. It was one date a long time ago."

"You stopped dating because he was going to be your boss."

"Yes. Fortunately, we'd only had the one date, nothing serious. It wasn't hard to move on as friends." A car drove past us, headlights filling the car's interior with too-bright light for a few seconds. Emma squinted and frowned. "Those brights aren't necessary."

As if the driver had somehow heard her, the lights shifted from brights to low beam. Emma nodded in satisfaction, then started the car again. "You never told me what was chasing you. You seemed scared."

An image of the creature roared into my mind's eye, and I shivered. Very slowly, I pulled one leg up and gently massaged the tight muscles, needing something to do with my hands. "It was a dream shard."

"A what?"

Peasblossom stirred under my sleeve, but didn't make her presence known. I concentrated on our link, sending her calming thoughts. "A few weeks ago, I made the tactical mistake of upsetting a sorceress that specializes in dream manipulation. She created the creature that attacked me by taking a remnant of the nightmare I had last night and breathing energy into it." I didn't add that this was just a guess on my part. I was confident I was right.

Emma shifted uneasily, her gaze darting to the rearview mirror. "She made a creature from a piece of your dream?"

"Yes. And then sent it after me."

"What does a dream shard do?"

I swallowed hard. Remembering the creature brought back

the icy sensation of its first attack, the single touch that had nearly frozen me with fear. "They try to pull their victims into the nightmare that spawned them. If they succeed, the dreamer's mind plunges onto the astral plane, and their body falls into an unnatural sleep. The dream shard keeps them trapped in the nightmare and feeds off their terror." I must have shivered again, because Peasblossom tightened her hold on my wrist, pressing her tiny face against my pulse in an offer of returned comfort.

Emma offered a nervous laugh. "Remind me never to make a sorceress angry."

"Easier said than done," I muttered.

A cloud passed over the moon, thick and heavy with the threat of rain. It plunged the interior of the car into deeper darkness, making Emma's next question sound more sinister than it should have.

"Are you a sorceress too?"

"No. I'm a witch."

She shifted in her seat, straightening her spine as if stretching to check all her mirrors. "Will the dream shard come back?"

"No." I took a deep breath. "No, it shouldn't." My insides still trembled like gelatin during an earthquake, and if the pain in my legs got any worse, I was going scream. If I was wrong, and that dream shard did return, we were in trouble. I certainly wasn't running anywhere anytime soon. Perhaps a potion... I unzipped my pouch.

"So how's the investigation going? I heard the coroner ruled it a homicide."

I pulled out a mini shampoo bottle and frowned. "He did. Our victim didn't die from an animal attack; he died from a gunshot."

Emma's fingers tightened on the steering wheel. "A gunshot? Did they find the bullet?"

I hesitated, but only for a second. "Yeah, buried in a pixie's house."

Emma shot me a quick are-you-serious glance. "A pixie's house?"

"Yep. She wasn't happy about it, either—the iron was giving her a headache."

"That makes her a witness, right?" Emma said, a hint of excitement in her voice. "Did she see anything?"

"No, she didn't see anything." I looked at Emma and noticed the lines around her eyes that hadn't been there a second ago. I almost kicked myself as I realized that if she knew Stephen was a werewolf, she'd likely guessed he was a suspect in the murder. "You're worried about Stephen."

She nodded. After a moment, she cleared her throat. "But now they can prove he was shot, they'll stop looking at him, right? A werewolf doesn't need to shoot someone."

It sounded a lot like what Liam had said. And my response was the same. "Stephen carries a gun."

"So?" Emma snapped. "I carry a gun. All the rangers carry a gun. Hell, have you see the gun laws? *Everyone* carries a gun now. Did you talk to everyone that was here last night? Everyone?"

I didn't respond right away. Emma's pulse was visible under the thin skin of her throat, and she was holding the wheel hard enough that she was halfway to fusing it to her palms.

"How long have you two been dating?"

"Almost two years." Emma shook her head. "He didn't do this. I am one hundred percent positive he didn't do this. He's not that kind of man."

"Tell me about him," I said. "I haven't had a chance to get to know him. Everyone keeps telling me he's not feral, he's not bad, he's not capable of this. Tell me what he is like."

Immediately her face softened. "He's sweet. A gentleman, as corny as that sounds. He has this quiet determination he brings to everything he does. It doesn't matter if he's fixing a sink or chasing down one of those idiots who sees the reservation as a keen place for a drug deal; he gives it everything he has. And he's smart." She glanced at me, then at the road. "He could be chief someday if he wanted to."

"Well, that would be interesting," I said.

"What would?"

"Stephen as police chief."

Emma tensed. "Why would that be weird? You don't think he'd be a good chief?"

"That's not it at all," I assured her. "I'm just saying, it would be strange for Stephen to outrank his alpha."

"His alpha?"

"Never mind. It's pack politics, and explaining it would add more complication than enlightenment." I leaned back in my seat, relieved to notice that the discomfort in my legs was easing. "The way Liam talks about him, it seems like Stephen isn't interested in being more than he is right now. Something about not taking the sergeant's exam?"

"It's not that he doesn't want to be more," Emma said. "Stephen understands that rising too fast means you miss things."

I tried to move my toes inside my thick winter boots. "Miss things?"

"Yeah. Stephen does want to advance, but he wants to make sure he understands every level first. As an officer, you interact with people more. You do more grunt work. You deal with the tasks the higher-ups don't have to do and don't want to do, and you get familiar not just with the tasks, but with the other people who have to do them. Stephen says he'll move up when he understands everything he can about the work and the people at this level. And then he'll do that again when he reaches the next level."

"So by the time he's chief, he'll understand where everyone is coming from," I finished. I nodded. "I understand his reasoning."

Emma stole a glance at me before returning her attention to the road. "But you think he's wrong?"

I shrugged. "Not in theory, no. He's right—a leader does need to understand where everyone else is coming from, at all levels.

The problem is, time changes things. People come and go; society exerts different pressures. Even job descriptions change, and how those jobs are carried out."

"He's not spending decades in every position," Emma said.

"No, but there's another factor. A leader needs to know how to communicate. They need to stay in touch with representatives at every level." I stretched my legs and rotated my ankles, forcing myself to breathe through the discomfort. "Take Liam, for instance. He started out at a lower level, both in the pack and on the force. So he got to know those people and he knew their jobs. But when he became alpha, and detective sergeant, he didn't shut everyone out and assume he knew all there was to know about what they did, what they needed, and where they were coming from. He built relationships with people; he communicates with them regularly. That's how he stays in touch, and he stays current."

"There's a difference between someone telling you what their life is like and living that life yourself," Emma said, her voice sharper than it had been a moment ago.

I nodded. "And there's a difference between theory and practice."

"Stephen will make a great chief someday," Emma said evenly. She lifted her chin. "And probably a great alpha." She straightened in her seat. "And it won't be just theory for much longer. He has a plan, everything scheduled out. He'll take the sergeant's exam next year, then three years after that, he'll take the captain's exam."

"Three years?" I echoed. I didn't know much about ranking among police officers, but that sounded like a very short amount of time.

"I told you, Stephen is good. He's strong, and he's smart, and once he decides to do something, he does it."

I didn't answer right away. Part of being a witch meant learning about people. It was a large part of the reason I wasn't more advanced in my spellwork. Mother Hazel had made me spend most of my time either studying books, or out in the world studying and helping people. One of the first things I'd learned as someone who was called in when things went wrong is that people are often very poor judges of their own ability. The fact that Stephen seemed to be planning big things without currently doing anything to attempt big things made me believe he was such a person.

Emma turned into the driveway of the station, and I turned to watch the play of the parking lights over her face. This wasn't the time to point out her boyfriend's cognitive flaws, so I tried a different tactic. "If this were your investigation, how would you handle it?"

"I would talk to everyone who was at the park." Emma shot me a look. "And I mean *everyone*. I would find out if anyone there had a connection to Oliver Dale. I'd consider church attendance, gyms, even high school. I would keep looking until I found a connection."

It was a wonderfully generic piece of advice. Hiding a sigh of disappointment behind a groan of pain, I moved my legs again, ready to disembark. I pointed to my car, and Emma pulled in next to it. "Thanks for the ride. I'll ruminate on what you said." I opened my car door.

"Shade?"

I stopped with one foot on the driveway. "Yeah?"

"Liam and Blake lied about where Stephen is when I asked them, so they obviously think he did something wrong. I don't know if there's some sort of pack politics getting in the way that I'm not privy to, but I'm telling you, Stephen didn't do this. No one will come to me for this case because I'm human, but that's part of the problem. Oliver was shot. You need to consider looking outside the Otherworld for this one."

"We are," I promised. "In fact, two-thirds of our suspects are human."

Emma didn't seem comforted, but she didn't say anything when I closed the door. Peasblossom waited for the headlights to disappear before poking her head out of my sleeve.

"I'm hungry. Give me another honey packet."

"You're not having any more honey until you have dinner." I opened my car door and slid behind the wheel. For a while I sat there, staring into the woods. "I wish I'd gotten a look at that crime scene."

Peasblossom fluttered her wings, lifting herself to the dashboard, then perched with her legs dangling over the clock. "Think you'll find something the wizard and the ghoul didn't?"

"The woman with ghoul fever," I corrected her automatically. I looked at Peasblossom. "Have you ever met someone with ghoul fever?"

"Gods, no. Disturbing, that's what that is. You're aware you get ghoul fever from consuming human flesh?"

"Yes." I shivered a little at that and closed my car door. "I do not understand how she can bear to work around dead bodies. You'd think she'd be tempted to have a snack."

"Sort of like werewolves working with dead bodies?"

I ignored her pointed tone. "Yes, but werewolves don't usually get to a dead body until it's cold, and meat is less appetizing to a shifter after decay sets in. Ghouls, on the other hand, love a decomposing meal."

"I'm not eating dinner," Peasblossom grumbled. "You've turned my stomach. It's honey or nothing."

"You're not getting any honey." I drummed my fingers on the steering wheel. "I need to talk to Vincent again. Without the werewolves hanging around. I got the impression he knew there was no barghest and was putting off having to tell Liam."

"You don't have his phone number. Do we need to go inside and ask?"

I glanced at the door to the ranger station, but dismissed the idea almost immediately. "Sergeant Osbourne isn't feeling cooperative right now." I eased into reverse and angled out of the parking spot. "I'll find the number myself. Who knows, maybe he's in the phone book."

Peasblossom snorted. "A wizard in the phone book? Not bloody likely." She paused. "You could call Andy…"

I stared down the dark road that wound past the ranger's station without seeing anything. "He hasn't answered any of my phone calls or returned any of my messages. I don't see the point in calling again."

"Fine. How about Bryan?"

"He's on vacation. Florida with his mom and brothers."

Her pink wings buzzed angrily, catching the light from the digital clock and splintering it into a thousand shards of blue-green light. "Okay then, let's hear *your* idea!"

"Peasblossom, I'm not trying to shoot down your ideas. They're good ideas. I just…" I sighed and ran a hand through my hair. "I don't want it to be Stephen," I admitted. "He seems like a good guy."

"Unlike the victim." Peasblossom paced back and forth. "If he was the bastard everyone says he was, then I see no reason it couldn't have been any number of people. Maybe we should look for someone even worse than him."

"Don't swear." I tapped a finger on my waist pouch, thinking. "From what everyone's said, it would be hard to find someone worse. The man intended to kill a dog, for crying out loud."

"We can't prove that for sure."

"That red welt on his palm is rather damning. It matched the mark on Rosie's hand, the one she says she got when she tried to catch Gypsy's leash."

Peasblossom threw up her hands. "So he was a bastard. Lots of suspects, then, and plenty who aren't Stephen."

"Don't—"

Someone knocked on my window. I jumped, jerking my foot down on the gas and shooting us into the road. Heart in my throat, I slammed on the brakes, swiveling my head from side to side and expecting to see a car bearing down on me, a collision only seconds away. The dark road remained clear, and I struggled to regain my breath as I checked the rearview mirror and slowly backed into the driveway again.

Kylie stood there watching me, her features calm for someone who'd narrowly avoided being roadkill. My car's taillights cast a reddish glow over her smooth, pale features, giving her an unsettling appearance. Her eyes followed mine as I backed up to put her even with my driver's-side window, and for a second, her eyes changed. Empty white orbs flickered before returning to normal. Any doubts I'd had about what she was vanished.

I forced myself to roll the window down and greet her like a sane human being. "I'm so sorry. Are you all right?"

"It's my fault for startling you." Her voice was soft, something about her inflection too flat.

I waited for her to say more. When she didn't, I cleared my throat again, the sound too loud in the sudden silence. "Is there something I can do for you?"

"My car is in the shop. I got a ride here, but Sergeant Osbourne says he'll be working late. He suggested you might give me a ride home, since I'm on your way."

I made a mental note to have a word with Liam about offering me up as a taxi. "Of course."

Peasblossom had hid in my shirt as soon as she'd realized who Kylie was, and now she jabbed a finger into my spine. I held my smile in place and pressed against the seat to warn her that another jab would mean being squished. A frantic pat said she got the message.

Kylie got in the car and settled in with her hands on her lap. "Thank you."

"What's your address?" I asked.

She gave it to me, and I put it in my GPS. With an angry pixie grinding her heels into my spine, I pulled onto the road. It took a mere twenty seconds for me to realize that I'd always underestimated how many muscles there were in my legs, and how many of them were required for something as simple as shifting my foot from one pedal to the other.

"Are you all right?" Kylie asked, polite but curious.

I winced. "I'm fine. Pushed myself a little too hard, that's all."

Kylie glanced down. "A bath with Epsom salts would help. If you have a Jacuzzi, that would be even better."

"I'll definitely try it, thanks."

I smiled at her and the glow of the dashboard lights caught her white gloves. Again it struck me as odd.

"They're to prevent contamination."

I blinked. "I'm sorry?"

"My gloves."

I blushed and hoped the darkness of the car's interior would hide it. "They're lovely. They seem too nice to wear at a crime scene?"

"I didn't mean preventing contamination of a crime scene."

Oh. I swallowed hard. Contamination—as in ghoul fever.

Peasblossom chose that moment to pop up from the neck of my shirt. "You catch ghoul fever from eating dead bodies," she said. "Not from being touched by a ghoul."

"Half-ghoul," Kylie said. "And that's true—most cases of ghoul fever are passed through cannibalism. But there have been a few instances when a scratch from a half-ghoul sufficed to pass it along."

"Not likely, though," Peasblossom insisted.

Kylie looked down at her lap. "Likely enough," she whispered.

Peasblossom paused, and I felt a pulse of regret down our empathic link. I wanted to tell her it was okay, she hadn't meant to upset Kylie, but saying that would only drag out the awkward moment.

"Sergeant Osbourne mentioned before that your mentor is Mother Hazel," Kylie said, breaking the silence.

"Yes." I nodded. "You've met her?"

"I've heard of her."

"Most people have. I hope knowing I was her apprentice doesn't make you think poorly of me."

I'd meant it as a joke, but Kylie didn't so much crack a smile.

"It speaks very highly of you that a witch as powerful as Mother Hazel considered you worth training."

Peasblossom sat on my shoulder, and I took advantage of her new position to lean back more fully against my seat. "It does, I suppose. It has its downside, though."

"You mean her disapproval of your desire to be a private investigator?"

"Excuse me?" I asked, glancing at her before returning my attention to the road.

"Sergeant Osbourne told me about the deal she offered you."

"Did he?"

My irritation must have showed in my voice. Kylie watched me, and her white gloves made a soft rustling sound as she folded her hands.

"That upsets you. That he told me?"

And everyone else, I thought bitterly. "It's not that he told you; it's the *reason* he told you. Liam told me to my face that he believes the deal between me and my mentor predisposes me to rush for a conviction. I find it insulting that he thinks so little of my professionalism. My sense of common decency."

Kylie shrugged one shoulder. "It is up to you to prove yourself. You have no reputation yet as a detective. And outside your village, your reputation as a witch is limited to being Mother Hazel's apprentice. But all that will come in time. Good or bad."

I frowned. I couldn't quite tell if she'd meant that to be encouraging or not. Her voice was only a note above a monotone, which made it hard to gauge. Especially when I couldn't see her face.

"How well do you know Stephen?" I asked. As long as I had

her attention, I might as well see what information she could offer. And she didn't seem inclined to sugarcoat anything.

"Well enough. I've worked with him for seven years."

"And what is your impression of him?"

"Efficient, but personable. Good with victims' families; a strong, analytical mind. He'll make a good father someday."

It was the perfect opening. "Do you think he'll start a family with Emma?"

"Possibly. They seem to get along well."

She didn't sound surprised by the question. "So you know about their relationship?"

Kylie shrugged again. "It is difficult to keep such things secret when one works with werewolves, so they didn't put much effort into hiding it. The evidence was there for those who looked for it."

"And did anyone look for it?"

"No." She paused. "Well, perhaps Sergeant Osbourne. But he is alpha, so it is his business to know what is going on with members of his pack—especially when there is the risk of a human finding out more than they are meant to."

I hadn't considered that. "Was he worried that Stephen might tell Emma about the werewolves on the force?"

"Probably not. Stephen knows better than to discuss such matters without his alpha's permission."

I'd only met Stephen briefly, but I had to agree. His self-control was impressive. "Stephen told Liam that he found the body when the victim was already dead. He said he shifted to better get the scent of the perpetrator, then lost control and ate part of the body."

Kylie didn't react, remaining still in her seat. "I know."

"Do you believe him?" I asked.

She was silent for a minute, staring out the windshield at the road with the same empty gaze. The silence dragged on long enough that I thought she wouldn't answer. It was on the tip of my tongue to apologize, to tell her I wasn't asking her to speak against her coworker, when she spoke.

"The werewolves and I share a responsibility. We all have hungers we must control, and jobs that test those hungers every day. Stephen is too experienced to make such an elementary mistake."

"Everyone makes mistakes. It's possible, isn't it?"

"Even if I were to agree that it's possible he lost control, it doesn't match with the rest of the story."

"How do you mean?"

She looked at me, and it took a concerted effort not to flinch. In that moment, I became a model driver—eyes on the road, full attention on keeping my hands at nine and three.

"If I made such a mistake and allowed my hunger to rise to where it overwhelmed the years of self-control and willpower I've built up to avoid such temptation...a few bites would not be sufficient to restore my senses."

I shifted uneasily. "So you're saying—"

"If Stephen's hunger was strong enough to overwhelm him, he would have eaten much more than a few bites." She looked out the window. "Also, I imagine the shame that would have followed his failure would have driven him to run, either to his alpha to beg forgiveness, or away from his alpha in self-loathing. Liam would not have found him on the reservation."

A thought occurred to me, and I pressed my lips together, not wanting to say it out loud.

"What is it?" Kylie asked.

I sighed. "I just thought of another problem with Stephen's account. You're right, he's a well-trained police officer."

"Yes."

"So why didn't he mention the victim was shot? He found the body, still warm, recently dead. Wouldn't it have been a little obvious to a ranger he'd been shot?"

"I see." Kylie stared into the distance, her face betraying little of her thoughts. "Yes, that is troublesome. This is my house."

The last sentence was so abrupt that I nearly passed her driveway. I shot Peasblossom a warning look where she was perched on the center console with my GPS. She'd turned the volume all the way down so she could change the destination without me noticing. "We're not going to Goodfellows right now. And I wasn't kidding about the no honey. You have to eat real food."

Peasblossom kept looking me in the eye. Slowly she put the GPS down, braced her foot on the edge, and shoved it off the console. It bounced off the center dash and hit the floor with a dull thud.

I gritted my teeth and pulled into Kylie's driveway. "That was petty."

Kylie waited for the car to stop, then opened her door. "Thank you for the ride, Shade. It is good you're someone a person can count on for help."

There was something about the way she said that last bit, something about her tone that made me think she meant something more than getting a ride home. She closed the door before I could respond, and I stared after her as she walked up the sidewalk to her front door and disappeared into the dark house.

"Well," Peasblossom said slowly. "That was weird."

"What do you suppose she was getting at?" I asked, still staring at the closed door.

"I don't know. And I don't care. I'm tired. Take me home."

I bit my lip but put the car in reverse and backed out of the driveway. "Remind me to ask Liam if there's anything else I need to know about Kylie..."

CHAPTER 11

"You are not royalty, and if you keep acting like you are, you'll force me to take drastic measures. I told you, you can't be here. Now *get out!*"

Majesty looked into my eyes from his position on my desk a few feet away, feline gaze never wavering. His thin kitten body belied the cold confidence in his stare, the arrogance that ran through every line, every muscle. He lifted a grey paw, the morning sunlight streaming through my office window giving the fur an ethereal shine.

"Don't do it," I warned him. I tensed to take a step forward, but stopped, not wanting to startle him. The desk was new, and polished. If I scared him, he might use the keyboard as a launch pad, and I didn't want my laptop to slide off to die a horrible death on the floor of my new office.

Helpless, I could only watch as Majesty stepped onto the first key. The blinking cursor vomited a line of *aaaaaaaaaaaaaaaa* across the computer screen, followed by *vbbbbbbbbbbbbbb* and *iooooooooooooooo* as Majesty continued to climb into his chosen napping spot. I gritted my teeth.

"Get off my computer. You'll get fur in the keys, and so help me if you break it, I'll have you buzzed. Have you ever seen a hairless cat?"

The kitten didn't blink. His furry bottom landed on the right end of my keyboard, sending another scattering of randomized alphabet over the screen. With all the languid calm of a king lying on a bed of silken sheets, he eased onto his side. Velvety eyelids drifted closed, and the air filled with a soft, steady purr.

My eye twitched.

"Run him under the faucet!" Peasblossom suggested from her safe perch high on the bookshelf. "That'll teach him!"

"I'm not running him under the faucet." Counting to ten to keep my temper, I waited for Majesty's sleek body to give up the last bit of tension, then snatched him off my keyboard. The little devil had the nerve to mewl in protest, offering a tepid glare from half-lidded eyes. "See here now, you cannot sleep on my keyboard. And you cannot be in my office. You're violating my lease."

"You ran *me* under the faucet," Peasblossom grumbled. "I don't see why he's too good for it."

"I ran you under the faucet once, when your dress was on fire," I reminded her. "And you were on fire because you didn't listen when I told you not to fly back and forth over the candles." I returned my attention to the kitten. As always, the hum of magic from the innocent-looking feline throbbed against my senses, a constant reminder of the spell that had frozen him in time, his body unable to age as it should. Every day the magic felt stronger, more…chaotic. It would have to escape sometime, and it was anyone's guess what would happen when it did.

It was possible that Majesty understood a lot more than you'd expect of a kitten. At least, that was my theory. I took a deep breath and tried again. "Look, my lease for this office states—"

"No animals," came a deep voice.

I closed my eyes. *Of all the rotten timing.*

Bracing myself for the coming unpleasantness, I opened my

eyes and faced my landlord. Declan Grey wore his usual faded black suit, looking not so much like a businessman as a chimney sweep that had fallen on hard times. Or an undertaker. Deep lines creased the skin around his hazel eyes, no doubt a result of all the squinting he did. Like now.

"Mr. Grey, I—"

"That," he said, pointing to Majesty, "is a violation of your lease. It will be fifty dollars for the violation, and your rent will go up an extra fifty dollars a month as well."

My mouth fell open. "Mr. Grey, I did not bring Majesty to work with me. He stowed away in my bag. I have no intention of—"

Declan blinked, surprise momentarily chasing some of the sourness from his face. "You call the cat Majesty?"

Heat filled my cheeks. "I didn't name him."

"So, you refer to him by his title?"

If it had been anyone else, I'd have said he was teasing me. But Mr. Grey did not tease. From what I could tell, he didn't smile or laugh either. What was more, his expression suggested that while his derision for the cat was considerable, he understood why I might consider myself beneath the fluffy beast.

"He will not invade this office again," I said evenly. "I trust you can forgive a single transgression? I am a valued member of this community, after all."

"Yes, Dresden's own medicine woman," he said, his tone mocking. "A midwife and nanny who parades herself as a doctor."

Perhaps I could recommend a proctologist to get that stick out of your bum.

"Fifty dollars for the fine," he said. "But in consideration of all the 'good work' you do for the community, I will postpone the increase in rent for the next violation."

He said "good work" in a way that robbed the words of sincerity. My fingers twitched at my side, the urge to cast a spell almost unbearable. Once again, I wondered when my temper tied itself to my magic.

"Not that I think you'll be here for a second violation." He glanced around my office, still unfinished. His attention lingered on the computer keyboard that still bore furry evidence of Majesty's nap, and one eyebrow twitched upward before his gaze returned to me. "You don't seem to have any clients. I guess people don't want to hire a nanny to solve serious matters."

"Actually," I said, "I'm in the middle of a murder case. I'm working with the Cleveland Metropark Rangers."

"I was unaware they had a program that let children ride along pretending to be police officers. How fortunate for you that there's no age limit on that program."

Magic crackled inside me, and I looked away before the sight of that sneer could make me do something I'd regret. "If you'll excuse me, I need to meet Sergeant Osbourne at the station, and I don't want to be late."

"But you will be." He took a long, smooth stride to the door, battered jacket fluttering behind him. "Don't forget the fifty dollars. I expect it to be in my mailbox by sunrise tomorrow."

The door closed behind him, and I gave myself three deep breaths before I trusted myself to move.

"I don't like him," Peasblossom announced, popping out from the book she'd hidden behind.

"Neither do I." I glared at Majesty where he'd curled up in my arms while I was talking with the landlord from hell.

The demon spawn was asleep.

"Unbelievable," I muttered. "Come on; we have to drop him off at home on the way to Rocky River."

I packed up my laptop—my entire reason for stopping by the office in the first place—and hauled myself through the door. Peasblossom wisely chose not to comment when I allowed the sleeping kitten to stay in my lap for the drive home. I didn't want him to wake up and make a nuisance of himself, that was all.

Peasblossom tugged the miniature pad of Post-its into position on her lap as she leaned against the passenger seat and grabbed the piece of pencil lead she used to write with. "All right," she said, "time to review our goals for the day. Goal number one: find out which of our suspects owns the right caliber gun to have fired the bullet that broke Violet's house."

"Goal number two: talk to Vincent and find out if there's anything else he's hesitating to tell Liam."

"Ah, yes, the wizard. Whose phone number was *not* in the phone book, and whose number we could have had last night if a certain witch had gotten off her bum and gone into the station to ask for it instead of hiding in her car from a mean werewolf detective."

I groped for the cup holder, only to realize with true sorrow I'd resisted the desire to grab a can of Coke before I left. "Goal three: talk to Stephen. And make goal four visiting Oliver Dale's apartment." Something tugged at the back of my mind, and I bit my lip.

"What?" Peasblossom rested her piece of lead on the paper. "You're making that face."

"What face?" I asked absently.

"The one that means you're ignoring something you shouldn't ignore and you're deciding how bad the consequences of ignoring it will be."

I arched an eyebrow at her. "That's one of my looks?"

"A popular one."

I sighed. "I'm thinking of Stephen. Why did Mother Hazel give me this case? Was it to prove Stephen's innocence because he looks so guilty? Or was it to make sure he's convicted despite the fact that everyone seems to like him? Does she think Liam can't solve this case on his own? Or that he won't do what was necessary? What role am I meant to fill?"

"Sheesh, no wonder you're making that face."

Orange construction cones offered an interesting alternative route, and for a moment I allowed myself to focus only on not giving in to the urge to ignore them and drive straight down the highway that seemed perfectly clear as far as I could see. Peasblossom scribbled on the Post-it, no doubt adding her own goals to the list. Shopping at the local market for more organic honey would feature prominently.

For a split second, I wished I had someone to talk to. Someone who'd been an investigator longer than I had, someone who could give me a straight, objective, non-Otherworld view of the facts. Like an FBI agent.

"You're making that face again." Peasblossom tapped the lead on the paper. "What's wrong?"

"Our last case," I said quietly. "We didn't leave things in a good place with Andy."

Peasblossom put down the bit of pencil lead, but didn't interrupt.

"I know I'm being silly. It's not like I knew him very well; we weren't friends. But still, he was part of my first case, and I had this stupid idea that he was going to be an ally, someone who would help me grow from wanting to be a private investigator to actually being a private investigator. I helped him, helped him with something no one else on his team could have handled." I squeezed the steering wheel. "I know there were more cases I could have helped with. And he wanted to learn. He would have worked with me again, I know it. And now…"

"He doesn't hate you," Peasblossom said. "He's just mad. People get mad. Give him time."

"But what if it's affecting the way I handle this case now?" A thread of thought unraveled in my brain, and I tried to follow it before I lost it. "What if I'm trying to prove Stephen didn't do it because I don't want another colleague angry with me? I should have pushed Liam to let me talk to him. I should have insisted, done whatever I had to do to convince him it wasn't optional. Stephen was there, he had the victim's blood on his face, and he admitted to *eating* the body." I waved a hand, almost striking the rearview mirror. "And yet here we are, twenty-four hours later, and I still haven't talked to him." I smacked the steering wheel. "I'm new to being a PI, but I've been a witch for a long time. My strength is in talking to people, getting them to open up. And I haven't used that skill on the one person who matters most."

Peasblossom considered that, her tiny brow furrowed in thought. "I think," she said slowly, "there might be a different lesson here."

"Oh?"

"You didn't trust Andy to handle himself against an Otherworld suspect. You tried to protect him for his own good, and he got mad. Maybe you're doing the same thing to Liam."

I frowned. "How?"

"Well, you're worried that Stephen did it, and you're trying to prove someone else did it because you don't want to upset Liam. But it seems like what you're thinking is that if Stephen did it, it's up to you to prove that, or else the wrong person will go to jail."

"I don't follow."

Peasblossom twirled her bit of lead. "You're upset with yourself because you think you've been giving Stephen a pass because you don't want Liam to be angry with you like Andy is. But what if you're not pursuing Stephen because you learned something from working with Andy? You learned that you need to trust your partner, trust their instincts. Liam is a cop, and an alpha. It's possible you haven't been pushing Stephen as a suspect because you trust him. Like you should have trusted Andy."

"So I'm not avoiding pushing Stephen as a suspect because I want Liam to like me," I said slowly. "I'm not focusing on Stephen as a suspect because I trust Liam the way I should have trusted Andy. I trust his professionalism and his instincts, and if he says he doesn't believe Stephen did this, then that means something." I slid a glance at Peasblossom, surprise mixing with awe. "You know, you really are very wise."

The pixie threw her hands in the air, flinging the shard of lead to bounce off the door before vanishing in the gap between the seat. "That's what I keep telling you!"

I laughed, my spirits rising. Peasblossom was right. I was working this case, and eventually, I would need to talk to Stephen. But I wasn't working alone. I had Peasblossom, and I had Liam, however awkward our partnership might be. Together we would find out who killed Oliver Dale. No matter who it turned out to be.

When I arrived at the ranger station, my good mood was back. I had bounce to my step, the walk of someone with renewed determination and optimism—right up until the moment I got to Liam's office and got a look at his expression. His face was somber, but there was a distinct excitement in his body language. Happy, but trying not to look happy. As always, his sleeves were rolled up to the elbows, and he stood beside his chair instead of moving the files off it so he could sit.

"Good morning, Shade." He raised his mug of coffee in greeting and took a sip.

"Good morning," I said warily. "Has there been a break in the case?"

Liam gestured for me to have a seat. "There has. Last night we got a search warrant for Anthony Catello's apartment."

I froze with my hand on the back of the chair. "You what? You said you couldn't get a warrant until the court opened this morning."

Liam waved his free hand. "I'm sorry, I must have misspoken. I forget you're new to this."

A blatant lie *and* an insult. I lifted my chin and refused to sit.

"Anyway, as I was saying, we got a search warrant."

"On what grounds?"

He raised an eyebrow. "On the grounds that he had the means, motive, and opportunity to commit the murder. He was at the park near time of death, with a .40-caliber gun. He hated

Oliver Dale, and he believed that on that night, Oliver was an immediate threat to his beloved dog's life."

I shook my head. "Emma took his gun away from him as soon as he got to the park."

Liam gestured again for me to sit across from him. I didn't.

He put his coffee down on the desk. "Let me offer an alternative narrative. What if Anthony didn't get to the park at midnight? What if he got there closer to eleven, or eleven thirty? What if he caught Oliver hurting Gypsy?"

I started to speak, but Liam silenced me with a raised hand.

"He could have shot him then, killed him to keep him from hurting his dog. The shot scares Gypsy, and she takes off. She's injured, but not so much she can't outrun her owner. Anthony gets in his car and drives around, waiting for a chance to catch her. He sees his chance, gets out of the car, and that's when Emma confronts him and takes his gun."

I said nothing. So far, he could be right.

"That's why he was so agitated," Liam went on. "Because he already knew Gypsy was hurt. And he already knew Oliver had done it. Emma tells him to leave, but he doesn't; he drives off. Emma finds Gypsy, who by this time has hanged herself in her mad dash to escape the gunshot. She takes her to the animal hospital, calls Anthony, and he shows up. He's furious with her because, in his eyes, it's her fault he didn't find Gypsy sooner—because she stopped him when he'd set eyes on her."

"Is the gun Emma took from him a .40?"

"No, but we don't know for sure that Oliver Dale was shot by a .40. We don't have the bullet, and there is a margin of error for Dr. Dannon's measurements on the bone."

I got the distinct and uncharitable impression that if Stephen carried a 9mm instead of a .40, Liam would have considered the bullet hole measurement hard evidence of his innocence. "It's only a theory," I said. I remembered my conversation with Kylie and stepped closer to Liam's desk. "And another thing. Why didn't Stephen mention that Oliver Dale had been shot? It would have made him less suspicious, wouldn't it? Better than everyone thinking Oliver died from an animal attack—a possible werewolf attack. But Stephen didn't mention that. He just said the body was bloody."

"Doesn't mean anything," Liam said. "Any number of predators could have gotten to the body before Stephen found it. Even a small amount of predation could obscure a bullet wound."

Now I let the sarcasm loose. "Ah, yes, the elusive barghest. Or are we abandoning that excuse now it's been proven false? Are we saying coyote? Perhaps a large rabbit?"

Liam's face darkened. "You don't know Stephen, and you don't know me. If Stephen did this—"

"If Stephen did this, you'd never know, because you take him at his word." All the good will I'd had in the car, the epiphany I'd had with Peasblossom, flew out the window on a flood of anger. "You never really considered him a suspect."

Liam's aura flared, the warm buzz exploding into the same bonfire I'd felt inside Stephen. The hairs on the back of my neck stood straight up. Outwardly, nothing changed, but my fight-or-flight instinct was suddenly raring to go.

"Careful, Ms. Renard," he said softly. "You are...uncomfortably close to challenging my authority."

"Careful, or what?" I straightened my spine, unimpressive as my stature might be. I fed the adrenaline scalding my veins into my temper, pushing it out like a shield in front of me. "You won't let me talk to him. If the situation were reversed, can you honestly tell me you wouldn't be suspicious?"

"*I've* talked to him, and for your information, Blake has talked to him."

"All pack," I said. I let my thoughts on that show in my voice.

He took a step around his desk, slow and deliberate. "Which is what makes us qualified. Unlike a witch with dreams of being a private investigator—a dream even her own mentor has no faith in. You talk about the situation being reversed. Tell me, if you were me, would you trust a magic user to interrogate someone under your protection, knowing she has an ulterior motive for wanting the case solved? By any means necessary?"

His aura burned at the edge of my own, a strange combination of pain and excitement. I closed my hands into fists. "If I wanted it solved by any means necessary, I'd jump on the bandwagon to hunt down Anthony Catello. I'd give up on fighting you and just go along with whatever you said."

Another step brought Liam into my personal space. Not sitting in the chair meant my back was to the wall, and I hadn't realized how close I was until I tried to take a step back and my heel hit the drywall. The fact I'd taken a step back without meaning to pissed me off, and I narrowed my eyes. Liam tilted his head, and a shine of gold slid over his blue eyes. His beast coming out to have a peek at me. I dug my nails into my hands, distracting myself with the pain.

"But that wouldn't count, would it," he said, close enough that he didn't have to use a normal voice to be heard. "Since you had no part in identifying him as the murderer?"

I clenched my jaw, ignoring the pressure building up where our auras pressed together. We were both angry, and just like his temper brought out the energy of his beast, mine brought up a swell of my magic. If I couldn't see the space between us, I'd have sworn we were touching. "Are you serious? You think I played no part at all in this investigation? You think I've contributed nothing?"

"Do you see it differently?" He took another step.

My hand shot out, braced against his chest to keep him from coming closer. A spell tickled my palm, the word to cast it dancing on my tongue. I held it back, pausing when Liam opened his right hand.

There was too much heat between us, too much energy from our chaotic auras. I couldn't concentrate on the stone I glimpsed in his hand. It was small and black, smooth, as if it had been polished.

Liam looked down at the stone, and a crease appeared between his brows. Confusion. He looked at me and, without warning, leaned in. With his face between our bodies, he drew in a deep breath.

For the second time in twenty-four hours, I slapped him.

This time, he expected it. His hand rose as I swung, our palms colliding in a loud crack of sound. He took a step back and slipped the stone into his pocket.

My cheeks flamed, and I had no idea if it was rage or humiliation. Whatever it was, I needed to get out of here. Now.

I ran into Blake on my way out of Liam's office. Literally.

"Hey!" He grabbed my shoulders to keep me from catapulting backward, holding on only long enough to make sure I kept my feet. Sonar tensed at his side, as if she thought I'd fall on top of her.

"Excuse me," I said stiffly. The sound of my blood rushing through my veins filled my ears like the sound of a distant ocean, and I was still so angry that I could hardly see straight. It took more effort than I wanted to admit not to fire off a spell, something painful to wipe that intense look off Liam's face.

"Don't worry about it." Blake looked from me, to Liam, and back. I expected him to make a snide comment, especially since there was no way he hadn't heard our conversation. But instead, he looked...cautious. "What's going on?" he asked.

"Nothing. Shade and I were just discussing the case." Liam returned to his spot behind his desk and picked up his coffee.

I didn't move. I didn't trust what I would say or do if it did. Sonar watched me, her canine eyes seeing more than I wanted her to. Her nose twitched as she scented the air, and her snout rose as if following a scent trail. She took a step toward Liam, then stopped.

"I'm sorry if you liked Anthony," Liam continued, speaking to me with the voice one would use to tell a child there's no more ice cream left. "But the fact is, whether or not he killed Oliver, Anthony is not innocent. When we executed the search warrant, we found a box of guns in his apartment—literally, a box full of guns. None of which were licensed. We're testing them now, and we've already found one that matches a bullet fired during a robbery at a local gas station."

"I don't—" I started.

"There's more, so listen before you draw a conclusion," Liam said calmly.

I crossed my arms and forced myself to face him.

"We also found evidence that there were kids staying there. A lot, by the looks of it. Catello had a room dedicated to video games—state-of-the-art television with a new console and enough games to start his own rental place. The room was littered with bags of potato chips and other snacks, empty cans of soda."

"No beer?" I said.

Liam arched an eyebrow. His eyes were blue again, no sign of his wolf's golden gaze. "No. But there were at least six carburetors and a few boxes of other car parts. Now why do you suppose someone would have that sort of thing in his apartment?"

"Maybe he's teaching auto repair classes? Or perhaps he brought work home with him. He is an auto mechanic."

Liam inclined his head. "Possibly. Or they could be evidence of a chop shop. We'll find out when we talk to him."

"I'd like to talk to him too."

"Please, Shade, go home. You can tell your mentor you helped solve the case, and now we're crossing the t's and dotting the i's. No one here will contradict that."

He looked at Blake, and after a second of confusion, Blake nodded.

"Yeah, sure. We'll back you up."

I looked down at Sonar. She didn't nod along with the rest of her pack. Instead, she sniffed the air again. I wished I could talk to her, talk to her when she was in human form. I wanted to know what she sensed.

I gave myself the count of five to get control of my voice so I could speak without shouting. "Last night you sent me home knowing damn well you would apply for those warrants. You made me think you were done so I'd get out of your way."

"I'm sorry you feel that way," Liam said over his coffee mug. "It wasn't my intention. If you like, I'll call you after I've spoken with Mr. Catello. I'll even send you a copy of my final report."

I was so angry that I couldn't speak. Before I could unclench my jaw enough to talk, an officer leaned in the doorway, glanced at me, then focused on Liam. "Sergeant?"

"Yes?"

"We had a report that Mr. Catello was spotted at the Tyler house. We sent people over, but he left before they got there. Do you want us to sit on the house?"

Liam gritted his teeth. Suddenly, he wouldn't look at me

I smiled, letting a petty wave of satisfaction roll off me. "You haven't caught him yet."

"It's only a matter of time." Liam glared at the officer. "Stay there and wait for him."

I smoothed my hands down my coat, my mind already spinning over my next move. If they hadn't arrested Anthony yet, then I still had time. "I'll say goodbye, then." I turned to the door. "Let me know when you catch him."

"Shade, stay out of this," Liam said. "Catello is dangerous, even for a witch."

I ignored him. He'd made it perfectly clear he didn't want my help, and he wouldn't let me participate anymore. As far as I was concerned, I didn't owe him a damn thing. I stood in front of Blake, waiting for him to get out of my way.

"We haven't broken the news to Stephen yet," Liam said in a low voice. "You and your mentor can rest assured that nothing is being rushed for the sake of clearing our own. Stephen will remain collared until we have proof he didn't kill Oliver."

"I'm sure," I said. "I'm particularly sure because you can't remove the collar without me, and I'm not touching it until the case is solved to my satisfaction."

Blake took a step forward, but Liam came out from around the desk again and he stopped.

"And when we prove it was Catello," Liam said, "I trust I can call you to remove the collar?"

"Of course." I didn't look at him. The urge to smack him again was too strong.

"Shade?" Liam asked.

I counted to ten and took a deep breath, aware of Sonar's steady gaze on me. Slowly, I turned. "What?"

Liam stood by his desk, no longer holding his coffee mug. He wasn't standing as straight as he could, so not trying to be intimidating. And the tension in his shoulders suggested my mention of not removing the collar before I was satisfied wasn't something he took lightly.

"I don't know you well enough to know why you want to be a private investigator," he said quietly. "But as a man who's met more than one person entering the field, let me give you some advice."

I didn't bother to hold back my sarcasm. "Oh, please do."

Blake shifted on his feet, his aura prickling along the side of my body facing him. Liam glanced at him, and he took a step back.

"It's not like the movies," Liam continued. "Or the books. It's not always the person you least suspect. Sometimes, it is the scary guy with the guns and the foul mouth. Sometimes, it is the most obvious person."

I met his eyes then, staring at him as if I were taller, as if I could look down my nose at him the way I wanted to so badly. "You know, Sergeant Osbourne, you're right. Partially."

"Partially?"

I shrugged. "Well, if it was the most obvious person, then it wouldn't be the angry man with the gun whose ballistics don't match your own assessment. It would be the werewolf with the blood all over his face and his teeth marks on the victim's body. Wouldn't it now?"

CHAPTER 12

"I think we should stop here and review a list of reasons pursuing the angry man with a box of guns is a bad idea."

Peasblossom clung to my ear, holding her face as close to my eardrum as she could without plunging her mouth inside my ear canal. The sensation ground against my raw nerves, and it took a lot of effort not to swat her like a bug, but I had practice. Lots of it.

"Peasblossom, if the werewolves find him first, then I won't have a leg to stand on when I report to Mother Hazel. I'll have to quit my investigation services and go back to being just the village witch." I veered off my path to my car to kick a small rock lying on the smooth asphalt. It shot over the parking lot with satisfying force to disappear into the surrounding trees. "As infuriating as the wolves are, they're right. All I've done is read reports they've already typed up and tag along to question witnesses. Mother Hazel will not count that as solving the case."

"You talked to Anthony when he wouldn't talk to Liam," Peasblossom pointed out.

"And learned nothing new. I was in that apartment, but I didn't see any of the evidence Liam mentioned."

Peasblossom hugged my ear harder. "We found the bullet hole, so they knew what kind of gun the killer used."

"The wolves would have found it tonight. Besides, now he's saying that information was misleading."

I slammed my car door behind me. Peasblossom leapt off my ear to stand on the steering wheel, her arms held out as if to stop me.

"The police are already looking for Anthony," she said. "What makes you think you can find him first?"

"That cop said Anthony was at Mia's. Maybe she'll know where he is."

"And you don't think the police will think to ask her?"

"I don't think she'll talk to them." I smiled. "She'll talk to me." I started the car and grabbed the gear shift, throwing it into reverse with unnecessary force. "I've been going about solving this case like a private investigator. It's time I solved it like a witch."

Peasblossom glared at me from the dashboard, where she'd landed after my abrupt eruption from my parking space. "Does that include driving like maniac? You can't solve the case if you're dead."

I laughed, and even to my own ears it sounded too high, too... unhinged. "Then I shall endeavor not to die. Now be a sweetheart and plug Ms. Tyler's address into the GPS?"

Grumbling, Peasblossom did as I asked, making a big show of grunting and groaning to heave the GPS out of the cup holder and onto the passenger's seat. I dropped my phone beside her, and she smacked the screen with an open palm, accessing my files with practiced ease. Mia didn't live far, and less than twenty minutes later, I pulled over and parked a block before her house.

"See any police?" I asked.

Peasblossom hit the button to roll the window down, then flew out and up. A gust of cold wind swept inside the car, and I shivered. After no more than two minutes, Peasblossom zipped back through the window. I rolled it down and turned up the heat as she resumed her perch on the dashboard.

"No police cars, but there's a car sitting across the street a few houses down with two people inside. They look fairly attentive."

"Good to know. I'd rather they didn't see me, so I'll need a disguise."

"If any of them are werewolves, I'd be more worried they'll smell you."

I snorted. "There's no way Liam or Blake will sit on a house where the suspect may or may not show up. They'll have wolves lower in the pack do that, or human officers. None of the other werewolves have met me, so even if they smell me, they won't recognize me."

Peasblossom didn't look convinced, but that didn't bother me. After going through the past twenty-four hours feeling like a third wheel, having my contribution questioned and insulted at every turn, I was finally on my own.

Excitement raced through my blood, and my magic rose to my call like an enthusiastic pet. I held an image of myself in my mind and concentrated on my appearance. I drew the magic over my features, turning dark brown hair to pale brown, and chocolate eyes to green. My curves flattened out, and I grew a good six inches. The leggings I wore turned black and flared out into dress pants, my long black shirt growing shorter and shrinking into a white button-down shirt. I even added a gold necklace with a faux-diamond paw print and a charm bracelet to match.

"You look like a proper businesswoman," Peasblossom said. "No one will recognize you."

"I know you meant that as a compliment, so I'll take it that way." A thought occurred to me, and I looked at Peasblossom. "Can you glamour the license plates? It'd be a shame if we were interrupted because someone figured out this is my car. Not that I think Liam would consider me enough of a hindrance to tell them to be on the lookout for me, but still."

"On it!"

I waited for Peasblossom to lay her simple glamour over the aluminum plate, and as soon as she finished, I drove the rest of the way to Mia's house. With my disguise and the car's glamour in place, I pulled into her driveway as though I had every right to be there. I ignored the car holding two human rangers I recognized from the station and knocked on the door.

Mia answered with a sour look, her shoulders squared as if prepared to do battle. "Can I help you?"

"I hope so. My name is Beth, and I'm from the twenty-four-hour veterinary hospital. Two days ago, a gentleman's dog came into the clinic, a beautiful female Czechoslovakian wolfdog named Gypsy?"

Mia's shoulders dropped, and concern drew deep creases around her eyes. "Is something wrong?"

"Could I come in for a moment?"

She nodded and gestured for me to come inside. "Please."

"Thank you." I went in without looking at the rangers, careful to keep my face and voice composed to match my disguise and false pretense. "I'm sorry to bother you like this, but something's come up, and Mr. Catello gave your number as a backup in case we couldn't get a hold of him."

"No, it's fine," Mia assured me, waving a hand. "What's wrong? Is Gypsy okay?"

"She is, but she's at risk. The woman who worked on Gypsy is a recent hire at our clinic. I was looking at Gypsy's x-rays as part of a standard review, and I noticed a small hairline fracture in one of her vertebrae. It's tiny, easy to miss in the heat of the moment."

Mia paled. "Vertebrae? You mean her spine? Oh my God, it is serious?"

"It will heal itself in time," I said. "But it's very important that I speak with Mr. Catello. Gypsy needs a splint until it heals, otherwise she could aggravate the fracture. The consequences could be devastating."

Mia bit her cheek. "He's…out of town."

"He doesn't have a cell phone?"

Mia shook her head. "No, it was… He lost it."

It was more likely that Anthony had turned off the cell phone so the police couldn't use it to track him. I wrung my hands. "I have to find him. I'll never forgive myself if anything happens to that poor dog."

A door slammed toward the rear of the house and a young man stomped in. He was tall and lanky, five eight and barely one hundred and sixty pounds. A blue skull cap hid most of his shock of black hair, and he wore baggy blue jeans that were in serious danger of being pulled down to his ankles by the chains hanging from his pockets.

"How long have the fucking cops been sitting across the street?" he demanded.

"Watch your mouth," Mia barked. "They're waiting there in case Anthony shows up. Ignore them."

"Ignore them? They're turning our house into a goddamn prison!"

"Language!"

The anger tightening the teenager's features didn't let up. He squared his shoulders in a way that mimicked the stance his mother had held when she'd first answered the door. "Who are you?"

"Greg," Mia warned.

"It's all right," I told her. I held out a hand to Greg. "My name is Beth, and I'm the veterinarian who helped Gypsy the other night."

Greg's face softened the tiniest bit, though he didn't accept my offer of a handshake. His leather-bracelet-laden wrists remained resolutely at his sides. "Is everything all right?"

"No, I'm afraid not. I found a hairline fracture in Gypsy's x-rays, and I need to contact Anthony as soon as possible."

Greg narrowed his eyes and crossed his arms. "Why?"

"I have to tell him about the fracture," I said. "Gypsy needs to stay as still as possible, and she needs a splint to help hold the bone in place. Do you know how to contact him?"

"No."

He shifted his weight from foot to foot, and his chin rose higher when he looked into my eyes with intensity.

He knows where Anthony is. I kept that knowledge from my face and wrapped my arms around myself as if I were worried. I wanted to question Greg, ask everything I was sure Liam had wanted to ask yesterday, but that would blow my cover. "Can either of you think of anyone who might know where he is?"

"I'm sorry, no," Mia said, true regret in her voice. "Anthony didn't have much family, none in Ohio. I think Greg and I were the closest he had."

"'Cause everyone else treated him like crap," Greg spat.

Mia rubbed her temples. "He didn't do himself any favors, hon. His attitude made him plenty of enemies."

"He seemed a little rough around the edges," I admitted. "But I saw him with that precious dog. He didn't seem like a murderer."

"Tell that to the cops." Greg curled his lip in disgust. "They're going to sit out there forever, waiting for him to come to the only people who care if he lives or dies so they can lock him up for something he didn't do. Cops are worthless." He snarled and turned on his heel, heading for the door. "I'm out of here."

"Wait, take this!" I dug in my pack for a pen and paper and scribbled my name and cell phone number. Lifting the pen from the paper, I continued drawing, this time etching out an arcane mark above the paper's surface. I blew on the mark, pulling magic from my core and letting it follow the lines I'd drawn. It burst into brilliant rainbow of color, magic that only Peasblossom and I would see. "Take this." I held it out to Greg. "If

Anthony calls, or you think of some way to get in contact with him, please call me."

He took the card, but the nervous tension about him thickened, and he back a step. His lips parted, and for a split second, I thought he'd speak, tell me something about how I could find Anthony. Then he snapped his mouth closed and bolted for the back door.

"Greg, wait—" I started.

He didn't listen. The door slammed behind him.

Mia sighed and ran a hand through her hair before collapsing on the couch. She melted into the overstuffed headrest with an air of tired defeat. "He isn't a bad kid, I swear. This week's been really rough."

I nodded, trying to be as subtle as possible as I edged toward the door. "I heard about the murder on the Rocky River Reservation. That was the night Gypsy was there. I gather the police think Mr. Catello had something to do with it?"

"Yes." Mia's head lolled to the side as she followed my retreat. "You saw Anthony, so you can see why the cops jump to conclusions. It's his damn temper." She rubbed her hands down her face. "He didn't do it. If you could see him with Greg, you'd know."

She kept her hands on her face, but lowered them enough to look across the room at the family portrait. "After my husband's death, Greg drifted down a dark path. Always sullen at home, hardly spoke to me. Hung out with the wrong crowd. Anthony stepped up for him, took over where his father left off. He was even teaching him how to fix cars, promising him he'd give him a job if he took it seriously."

She obviously needed to talk to someone, needed to explain why Greg acted the way he did. Normally, I would feed that inclination, offer to be the one who listened. It was what a witch did best. But right now, the best thing I could do for Mia and Greg was find Anthony before the werewolves did. It was clear this family needed that man, and if I didn't get out of here now and find them, I was afraid he might not come back. Not anytime soon.

"I don't think Anthony killed that man," I told her. "You can tell a lot about a person by watching how they treat animals. Believe me, I know." I put another card on the table, writing my name and number. After a second of hesitation, I pressed another mark to the paper, similar to the one I'd used for the slip I'd given Greg. "Please let me know if you hear from him."

"I will."

I promised myself I'd check on Mia as soon as I closed the case. She was exhausted, and Greg definitely seemed on edge. Though there was no way to make raising a teenager alone an easy task, there were some coping methods I could teach her, advice I'd gathered from hundreds of mothers in the same situation. And I wanted to help.

I headed out the door, pushing my senses out in all directions to feel for the mark I'd put on the card. I needed to speak to the teenager, speak to him as Shade Renard, private investigator trying to clear Anthony's name, not as Beth, veterinarian trying to help his dog. The arcane mark I'd put on the card I gave him would let me follow him, so all I had to do was ditch the disguise and make sure I wasn't followed.

The rangers were still sitting in their car when I crossed the front porch. I felt their eyes on me as I forced myself to walk to my car without giving in to the urge to run. A quick peek in my rearview mirror assured me that the spell keeping me disguised was still in place, and I let out a breath I hadn't realized I'd been holding. I drew on my magic as I reversed out of the driveway, letting it flow out from me in a wide silver net. A tiny spark of extra-bright silver winked at me from the arcane mark. I smiled and shifted into drive, following the spell.

Ten minutes later, I was second-guessing my plan.

"This…is not a good area." Peasblossom shrank away from the

windshield, her wings pressing down against her back as she tried to make herself even smaller.

She wasn't wrong. The teenager was on foot, and didn't seem inclined to follow the street. Rather, he was crisscrossing the city like an alley cat, meandering through alleyways, across back-yards, and, at least once, climbing over a fence. If not for the mark pulling at my senses, I would have lost him a dozen times, and even with the magic, it was a close thing.

"We're not in Dresden anymore," I said under my breath. That was an understatement. This was Cleveland, a large city that made Dresden look like someone's backyard. Or possibly the far corner of someone's backyard. Buildings towered around me like forbidding sentinels of industry, casting shadows that made every doorway and corner scream "roll for initiative." It was all I could do to force myself to keep focusing on Greg and not where Greg was leading me.

The mark stopped moving. I shoved away the unease rolling through my stomach and parked the car on a side street. I waited a few minutes, making sure the mark had stopped. The last thing I needed was to end up on a mile-long foot chase through this concrete jungle.

"Now what?" Peasblossom asked.

"Now we go find Anthony."

Peasblossom held on to my hair as I got out of the car, her wings trembling as she studied the huge buildings surrounding us. "I don't like this. Not one bit. A village witch doesn't have to deal with running pell-mell through smelly, mugger-populated alleys. A village witch stays in her village and helps people. She's beloved by all, and at little personal risk to herself—or her familiar."

Adrenaline gave me the strength I needed to make my legs work, and I lurched toward the alleyway nearest the point where my mark glowed in my mind's eye. "I've chosen my path, and I won't be scared off it. As shocking as it may seem, solving crimes doesn't always mean staying in 'safe' areas."

Peasblossom hid in the collar of my coat, tucked under the protective fall of my hair. "All right, all right, but hear me out. What if you were a village witch who consults for the FBI on a strictly in-office basis? Maybe has a look-see at a crime scene now and again, detecting magical foul play and then leaving it to the Vanguard to investigate?"

I stepped over a puddle of what I hoped was stagnant rainwater. "Do you remember that half-goblin that was eating cats?"

"Yes. And I thought you judged him too harshly."

I craned my neck to give her a dark look. "That's not funny."

Peasblossom sniffed, then wrinkled her nose as if she regretted it. "It wasn't a joke. You eat cows; why is that any better than a goblin having a nibble on a cat? Cats are much more ferocious than cows, much more likely to kill a poor little pixie."

"Anyway," I said, "when I found that goblin, he'd just taken his first child. The cats weren't enough anymore, and he'd graduated to humans. If I hadn't found him, that child would be dead, reduced to a pile of excrement."

"Such a charming way to put it."

I crept along the wall of the closest building, careful not to brush against it. "I saved that child's life. I knew then that I'd found my purpose. There are bad guys out there that aren't human, and the human police are in no position to find them, let alone deal with them. I can. And I will."

"You're an amazing witch," Peasblossom said. "But you aren't a cop. You aren't even a proper PI."

"Not officially," I said. "But in terms of experience, I'm perfectly qualified. How many missing children have I found?"

"Twenty-two."

"And how many murderers have I caught?"

"Four. But those murderers were monsters—animals, not

humans. You want to be a private investigator, and that requires different training than witching."

"And I'll get that training," I promised. "If there's one thing I'm good at, it's studying." I sidled around a garbage bin, holding a hand over my nose to block out the odor as best I could.

"You'd have to be," Peasblossom agreed. "I can't swear to you how many years we spent at Mother Hazel's with you reading and studying, but I'd bet my wings it was a few decades at least."

"Is that normal?" I stepped over a lump of garbage, almost swallowing my tongue when a fat black insect scurried out from under it. I walked faster.

"Is what normal?"

"A witch's apprentice spending all her time studying? When Mother Hazel offered to be my mentor, I thought she'd be training me to use magic, but she barely taught me any spell-casting at all beyond the basics."

"There's nothing normal about Mother Hazel," Peasblossom muttered. "That old bat has gone around the bend and enjoyed the trip one too many times."

A strange sensation brushed across my senses. Fear lifted the hairs on the back of my neck, and my instincts flared, spilling adrenaline into my bloodstream. It was the universal sensation a person experienced when swimming in the ocean and feeling something brush your leg. Was that seaweed? Or a man-eating shark?

The adrenaline that surged through my body wasn't a burn in my veins—it was a solid punch against my entire body, a force that propelled me forward. I ran without making the conscious decision to do it, fled as if my life depended on it. The silver net of detection magic surrounding me heaved like a safety net saving the life of a clumsy acrobat. Or a web hefting the giant furry body of a large spider.

"Dream shard!" Peasblossom shrieked.

It wasn't so much a sound as it was a feeling, cold and hard with an edge sharp enough to draw blood. It dragged down my spine with physical pressure, driving me to run faster. I leapt over pieces of trash, broken bits of cement, and rotting wood pallets. I let go of the silver net, releasing the magic to free up every iota of rational thought I could manage.

People—I needed people. A witness, a human. Someone Arianne wouldn't want hurt; someone who would trigger the dream shard to return to its ethereal home. At least I hoped—I prayed—that was how it would work.

Somehow, in the midst of concentrating so hard on following Greg, I hadn't noticed he'd led me behind a row of factories. Dilapidated fences created a honeycomb of urban decay, littered my surroundings with obstacles and narrow entryways surrounded by broken wood or shorn metal links. My spirit sank when I realized that most people were smart enough not to wander this area. There were no crowds, no groups of people milling about, or even the occasional solitary walker to break up the empty space.

I was alone.

The dream shard's first bite sent me crashing to the ground. Invisible jaws closed over me, and my spirit bled liquid terror. I kept my eyes open, but all I saw was a cave, a dark cave with a mouth outlined by shining white teeth and fangs like glittering stalactites. Reality fell away, left me lost in the in-between as the monster tried to eat me, drinking my essence, my magic, everything that made me...me. Here and there I glimpsed the black beast that had inspired my original nightmare, the dream that had spawned this monster. Watching. Prowling.

"Shade!"

I followed Peasblossom's scream. Her little soul hung in my vision like a bright pink flame, and I charged toward that light. My feet scrabbled on loose stones, but I got my balance and threw myself into a headlong dash of desperation that sent me bolting out of the imaginary cave and back into reality.

A broken fence up ahead offered escape. I overestimated its width, hitting my shoulder hard as I dove through the gap. I cried out in pain as warm blood flowed down my arm, but continued to wrench myself through, stumbling a few steps as I regained my bearings. A warehouse towered over me, abandoned by the looks of the dusty, broken windows. If I went through the warehouse, I'd reach the main road and more people. I lurched forward.

Something struck my head from behind. Pain exploded along my skull, the sky spiraled, and something hard slammed into my back. The last thing I saw before the darkness claimed me was an angry teenage boy.

CHAPTER 13

"Holy shit, did you see that?"

"She fucking changed!"

"How did she do that?"

The shouting did not help my headache. My temples pounded like animal-skin drums pummeled too enthusiastically by a burgeoning musician. Each strike sent a sharp lance of pain straight through my skull, stabbing at my brains and shredding any train of thought I might have managed to get running. I tried to put my hands to my temples, wanting to hold my brains in, but my arms wouldn't move. A deep breath dragged the scent of old motor oil, decaying cardboard, mildew, and, over it all, the unmistakable scent of under-supervised teenage boy.

I sagged forward, and bile washed up the back of my throat. Nausea overwhelmed me, and for a small eternity, I counted my breaths, praying for the sickness to pass, or that I would develop some other means of breathing that didn't require me to smell or taste my surroundings. I had a concussion. I'd bet my broomstick on it.

"That is fucked up, man."

"That shit ain't right."

"Please, stop swearing," I managed. With Herculean effort, I wrenched my eyelids open, giving the colorful, blurry blobs the most disapproving expression I could manage. "What would your mothers say?"

Surprised quiet met my question. In the ensuing pause, my vision came into focus. The smell of teenage boy had not lied. I was surrounded by at least eight of them. Colorful blobs resolved themselves into boys ranging from thirteen to sixteen, all of them dressed in clothes that made my landlord's attire look chic.

I could forgive the dirt on their clothes and the dubious state of their hair—teenagers will be teenagers, and all that. But the nostril-burning combination of body odor and cologne was positively weaponized. No male under the age of thirty should apply his own cologne.

"What did you say to us?" a boy demanded.

I did my best to focus on him despite my teary vision. I squinted, trying to make out their expressions. Confusion, anger, and fear. The speaker was a young man, fourteen years old, tops. He wore a shirt depicting a cartoon character making a rude gesture, and his hair stood up in Cookie Monster-blue spikes.

"My dear boy," I said, my words slurred. "Cologne is not an acceptable alternative to regular bathing. If your colorful hair stands up in those spikes with no need for product, then it's time for a shower."

Pink stained the boy's cheeks, an intriguing contrast to the blue hair. I would have felt bad for singling him out, but between trying to decide which was the lesser evil—breathing through my nose or my mouth—and trying not to pass out, I had no energy for social niceties. And my head hurt. Bad.

I gave them time to figure out who would speak next while I assessed my situation. I was inside a warehouse—abandoned, if the state of deterioration was any indication. Graffiti tattooed the concrete walls, and high windows let in enough light to illuminate the far end, the scattering of boarded-up or painted-over window panes creating a patchwork effect. Barrels and crates in varying states of decay clustered against the walls here and there. I noticed with some regret that the chair I was tied to sat at the end of the warehouse opposite the entrance. I'd have to run the length of the rather large structure to escape.

"You're no vet."

I blinked, not sure if I'd missed some of the conversation. The voice was familiar...

Greg.

Pain trickled over my brain, blurring my vision as the teen in question stepped in front of the group. I concentrated on the blue hat and surrounding tufts of black hair. Yep, definitely Greg. I blinked, trying to force my eyes to work properly. His features cleared, revealing a face twisted with anger. The more my vision cleared, the more detail I could make out. For the first time, I noticed the bulge at his side under his shirt that looked too much like a weapon for my comfort.

"You're working for the cops, aren't you?" he said. "That's why you're following me. You're using me to find Anthony for the cops."

The crowd of boys erupted into furious whispers, some of them straightening to their full height, stepping forward as if they intended to continue this conversation with their fists. Several brandished weapons, chains and a few broken pieces of two-by-four. Greg seemed to be the only one armed with a real weapon, thank the gods.

"The police didn't hire me. I'm a private investigator. I'm trying to find out what happened to Oliver Dale." The mob shuffled forward, growled threats rolling out like thunder preceding a storm, but I spoke again, louder. "I know Anthony didn't kill him."

"Bullshit," Greg spat. "Then why are you looking for him? Lying to me and my mom?"

I turned to meet Greg's eyes and whimpered when my skull

threatened to fall off my shoulders. My stomach heaved, and I pressed my lips together until the threat of vomiting passed. I did my best to ignore the smell of the surrounding teenagers as I took a deep breath.

"I want to prove his innocence," I said. "But I can't do it without him." The pain throbbed harder with every passing second. I closed my eyes, but that made the nausea almost overwhelming, so I forced them open again. When I flexed my facial muscles, I recognized the tacky sensation of dried blood. Fear settled at the base of my spine. I'd hit my head hard enough to bleed. "How long was I unconscious?"

"Half an hour," Greg answered.

He stuck out his chin in defiance, but something about his voice told me he knew that wasn't a good thing. His attention flicked to my wound, then back at my face. His eyes showed more white than before. That did not bode well for my health, but it gave me hope that maybe he wasn't ready to watch me die.

I snared his gaze, held it. "I'm hurt. Untie me and let me bandage my wound."

A cacophony of protests met that suggestion.

"Fuck that."

"You think we're stupid?"

"Shoulda thought of that before you stuck your nose where it ain't wanted."

I ignored them and kept holding Greg's stare. Despite the sneers from his friends, Greg didn't seem happy with my condition. There was no sympathy in his expression, but he wasn't happy about my injury, either. "Convince me you know Anthony's innocent and *maybe* I'll untie you."

There were a few grunts of satisfaction behind him, a couple of smug smiles telling me no one believed I thought Anthony was innocent.

Unfortunately for me, I didn't have an answer. Telling Greg I wasn't ready to blame Anthony when a werewolf had been found with the victim's blood on his face wasn't an option. Telling him one of the rangers knew the truth but wasn't talking was an even worse option. I fought the urge to close my eyes, knowing it would only make me feel worse. Not for the first time, I wondered about the ocean of magic inside me. The ocean I was only beginning to learn how to harness and control. Mother Hazel had said only that the patron who'd given me my magic had left me with a burden as much as a gift. What happened to that magic if I died?

I didn't intend to find out.

Greg's jaw tightened. "You fucking lied."

His hand dropped to his side. My mind flashed to the picture in his house, the picture of Greg with his mom and Anthony, all of them armed. Dread curled at the base of my spine, and I steeled myself and reached for my magic.

"*Pax*," I whispered.

I threw the spell at Greg's waist, and golden bands of energy wrapped around the weapon, locking it into place at the teenager's side. Greg frowned, and confusion pinched the skin between his eyes as he tugged on it to no avail. He stopped pulling and his gaze slid back to me.

I met his eyes and shook my head. "Uh, uh, uh," I said softly.

His angry defiance slipped, revealing his uncertainty. "What are you?" he whispered.

"That wouldn't be a .40 in your waistband, would it, Greg?" I asked. I locked on to that doubt in his eyes, that tiny flicker of fear. My disguise was gone, so they'd all seen me change, seen Beth the veterinarian melt away to reveal Shade the private investigator. Perhaps it was time to stop being the private investigator, and start playing the scary witch. I lowered my voice, letting the pain arcing through my body lend it a rasping quality. "You will not draw that weapon, Greg."

His eyes widened. The crowd had gone dead quiet, and they all looked from Greg to me. This was good. I had Greg. I knew I had him. If the others were willing to follow, then maybe, just maybe, I could get out of here before I bled to death.

The crowd shifted, and another boy stepped forward. My hopes sank as he stood beside Greg.

"You'll keep accusing people until you find someone you can pin it on, is that it?" he snapped. "The ex-con or the young felons, right?"

The words "young felons" smacked of a teenager's exaggeration, an effort to sound tougher than he was. It was on the tip of my tongue to respond with condescension, to fix him with a witchy look I'd used to cow actual felons in the past.

I never saw him draw the gun. One minute I was locking gazes with him, and suddenly there was a very large, very real weapon pointed at my face. A hiss behind my neck sent a second shock down my spine.

Peasblossom. I'd forgotten about her. She was hiding behind my neck, and she'd obviously seen the boy point the gun at me. Tiny hands gripped the collar of my coat, her feet digging into my muscles as my tiny familiar prepared to fling herself at the gunman.

"Don't," I barked.

The boy sneered, assuming I was talking to him. "You seriously gonna act like you're in charge here?"

He cocked the gun. I wasn't an expert on firearms, but there was something so Hollywood about the gesture, like I'd fallen into an old western. Against all reason, it broke the tension in my shoulders, and I would have laughed if I wasn't about to have a heart attack.

"Chris, put it down."

Anthony Catello's voice rolled over the crowd, booming in the empty interior of the large building. The acoustics of the dilapidated structure acted like a bullhorn, and the effect was instantaneous. The boys straightened their spines, like soldiers whose superior officer had just entered the scene, and immediately fell to the sides, forming a path down the center of their group with me at the end.

Chris didn't move. He remained in front of me, gun unwavering.

I couldn't look away from the weapon, not while it was still aimed between my eyes. My peripheral vision offered me a hint of Anthony's bulging biceps, revealed by yet another black tank top underneath an open grey hoodie as he marched down the part in the crowd. His footsteps were even, determined, but not angry.

"You were going to surrender that," Anthony said, indicating Chris's gun. "What happened?"

Chris lowered the gun and looked away, but didn't give up his spot in front of me. He didn't stand as straight as the other boys, his shoulders bowing as if only barely resisting the urge to flee back into the group.

Anthony kept staring at him as if they were the only two in the room. "I thought I explained to you that you don't need a gun. All that piece of metal will get you is a short life and a guarantee you won't be remembered as anything more than a thug. Is that what you want? You want them to drag your sisters down to the morgue to identify your body? That's what that is, Chris. That's all it is. A ticket to nowhere."

Chris didn't answer. I breathed easier now that the gun was held down at his side and not aimed at me, but the danger was still there. I glanced at Anthony, but the big man didn't look at me. He had eyes only for Chris.

Anthony held out his hand. He didn't say anything, didn't try to take the gun. Just stood there with his hand out. Waiting. A lifetime later, Chris lowered the weapon into Anthony's waiting hand, his gaze locked on the warehouse floor.

Without a word, Anthony turned to Greg. "That better not be your mom's piece sticking out of your pants."

At some point during the stare-down with Chris, Greg had

gotten over his uncertainty. When he looked at me this time, there was only anger in his brown eyes, the human brain's knack for explaining the unexplainable removing all thoughts of magic and the fear that went with it. He gritted his teeth and glared at me without looking at Anthony.

"They don't care you're innocent. *She* doesn't care. They're gonna lock you up no matter what. And *she* lied. She said she was from the vet, but she's just another cop. She said she believes you're innocent, but she *lied*."

Anthony extended his hand, mirroring the silent demand he'd leveled at Chris. Greg stiffened, but didn't offer the weapon.

Anthony's jaw tightened. "Don't you dare make the same mistakes I did. You're better than that. Your dad raised you to be better than that."

Greg's eyes glittered and his throat worked as he swallowed hard. "My dad's dead."

"And you're in a hurry to join him, is that it?" Anthony put a hand on Greg's shoulder. "Your mom needs you. She already buried one man she loved. You will not make her do it again."

I knew resignation when I saw it. I released my spell and called the magic back. This time when Anthony held out his hand, Greg gave him the gun. The muscle-bound murder suspect removed the bullets from both guns before tucking them into his waistband. He put the bullets in the pocket of his sweatshirt, then went to work on the ropes tying me to the chair. The teenagers watched every movement, looking unhappy, but not malicious.

"Thanks," I mumbled.

Anthony touched my temple as he examined my head. That simple pressure made me hiss, and a fresh wave of nausea rolled over me.

"You're gonna need a doctor," he said quietly.

I fumbled at my pouch, batting at the zipper to make my fingers work. Reality tilted at an odd angle, and I stilled, waiting for the ground to right itself. "I am a doctor."

Anthony eyed me, hovering close as if waiting for me to fall over. "Sure you are."

Out of spite, I lurched out of the chair, away from Anthony. He grunted in surprise, moving too slowly to keep me from falling to my knees. Hard cement threatened to crush my kneecaps, and I hissed again. The threat of tears burned my eyes, but I blinked them back as I forced the zipper open on my pouch. My mouth felt dry and colored blobs danced in my vision. I needed a healing potion. Now.

Hysterics threatened to steal what little rational thought I had left. I stared at the floor as I rooted around for the healing potion, and my attention landed on a thick two-by-four near my chair. One end was smeared with blood. My blood. The bent head of a rusted nail stuck out from the bloody end, not enough to puncture my skull, but enough that I was sure it had been responsible for most of the blood. My stomach heaved at the thought of the infection that could be spreading through my system as I knelt here fumbling around in an enchanted pouch.

Anthony took me at my word and didn't offer help a second time. Instead, he turned to address the crowd. "I talked the talk without walking the walk. I keep telling you that you have to teach people how to treat you, but I haven't shown you how to do that."

A murmur of protest ran through the gathered crowd, but Anthony held up a hand, and they fell silent.

"The cops think I killed Oliver Dale," Anthony said, speaking as much to the boys around him as to me. "I'm a suspect because I act like the type of man who would kill someone who pissed him off. Instead of answering their questions, showing them some respect, I made it a point to be—"

"An ass," Peasblossom offered.

Anthony's eyebrows shot up, and his attention fell to where I still knelt on the floor. There was no point in pretending I hadn't spoken, since I wasn't about to reveal Peasblossom, so I ignored him and continued my search for the potion.

"Yeah," Anthony said.

My fingers closed over the small bottle, and I jerked it free. My hands shook violently now, but I managed to uncork it and gulp down the contents. Magic blossomed inside me, flowing out along my nerve endings in a blue wave. The nausea receded, the pain in my knees faded away, and when I turned my head slowly from side to side, it did not threaten to fall off.

As the pain receded, my thoughts cleared. I felt along my scalp to check for lingering injuries.

Gypsy chose that moment to dart forward, leaping at me as if I were an old friend she hadn't seen in years. I gasped as she covered me in wet dog kisses, abandoning my inspection of my wounds to save myself from drowning.

"Yes, yes, it's good to see you too." I laughed and fought not to topple backward. Blood and bone, she was a strong dog.

Gypsy's show of affection changed the mood of the room dramatically. Several of the teenagers smiled, one or two of them laughed, and even Chris seemed to relax. Gypsy's approval carried a lot of weight here.

"There will always be people who judge you before you open your mouth, people who will write you off as trash no matter how much you try to show them otherwise." Anthony pointed at each of the kids in turn. "But if you do nothing to challenge that first impression, if you don't show them the respect you want them to show you, then it won't just be the assholes of the world who write you off—it'll be the good guys too. You won't get the chance to find the rare person who will judge you on merit alone."

Gypsy was giving me the expectant look dogs reserved for people who had given them treats in the past, so I dug in my pouch for another biscuit. Her ears fell with each ball of twisty ties I pulled out, each button, each Band-Aid. By the time I'd rattled around a third glue stick, her ears lay flat against her head. With a snort of exasperation, she leaned forward and shoved most of her head into my pouch.

Two seconds later, she emerged triumphant with a dog biscuit between her teeth. She held it out for a moment, making sure I saw that she'd succeeded where I'd failed, then ended the biscuit with one happy crunch.

Snickers rippled around the room.

"To be fair, the bag is bigger on the inside," I muttered.

"I should have answered your questions from the get go," Anthony said, offering me a hand up. I accepted, and he pulled me to my feet. "I heard you say you don't think I did this. You're right. I hope you still think that when I'm done."

Unease rolled through my stomach as I remembered Liam's list of things they'd found in Anthony's apartment. "I'm listening."

"I never left the park that night. When that—" He pressed his lips together, making a visible effort not to use the first word that had come to his mind. "When the ranger sent me home, I drove around and went in another way. I wasn't gonna leave my dog behind." He met my eyes and held them. "But I didn't kill Dale."

I believed him. Unfortunately, that wasn't enough. "They found a box of guns at your apartment. And a handful of carburetors and other car parts."

"The guns were ours." It was the kid with the blue spikes. He looked younger now that he wasn't threatening me, closer to thirteen. "Anthony made us give them up if we wanted to train."

"Train for what?" As soon as I asked the question, I knew the answer. "Oh, for pity's sake, you *were* running an auto shop class, weren't you?"

Anthony nodded. "A man needs a skill if he's gonna make an honest living. There's always gonna be cars that need fixing, and no one's gonna ship them overseas for a broken carburetor."

Smart man. The more I learned about Anthony, the more certain I was that he wasn't the murderer. Unfortunately, the next most likely suspect wasn't any better. I refocused my attention on Greg. He'd been in the park that night too. And he obviously had access to a gun. Several guns, if he had access to the box at Anthony's apartment.

Anthony followed my line of sight, but to my surprise, he didn't get angry, or leap to Greg's defense. "You have to decide what kind of man you're gonna be," he said gently. "I can't make this choice for you."

Greg froze, then looked up at Anthony. A war played out over his face, anger at the world and a determination to fight it every step of the way battling against the desire to listen to Anthony, the father figure he needed so badly right now. In that moment, I saw what Mia saw, and I understood her loyalty to Anthony.

Finally, Greg squared his shoulders. "What do you want to know?"

I pointed to the weapon he'd surrendered to Anthony. "That's your mom's gun, right?"

"Yeah."

"Did you have it on the reservation when you searched for Gypsy?"

He shook his head. "No. I was going to, but I couldn't find it."

It was a weak excuse. Unless his mom could prove otherwise, there was no reason to believe Greg hadn't had access to her gun the night Oliver was murdered.

Greg read my expression. He swallowed. "I tried to get another gun when I couldn't find Mom's."

I raised my eyebrows. "Where were you going to get another gun?"

Greg looked at Chris. Chris looked at Anthony, then me. "He called me," he admitted. "But I was at my aunt's, and she took my phone when I tried to text during dinner, so I didn't get Greg's call until the next morning."

It wasn't a rock-solid alibi, but it would work for now. I let out a breath. "All right. I believe you."

Anthony faced the boys. I knew from the look on his face what he was going to say next, and they weren't going to like it. "I'm turning myself in."

A roar of protest rose, but he raised a hand for quiet. "No. This is the way it has to be. I need to clear my name the right way." He nodded to me. "I'll walk you to your car."

I was guessing he knew damn well he couldn't clear his name of everything. He knew the rangers had searched his house, knew they had the guns. He was in serious trouble for that, even if they cleared him of the murder. As much as I wanted to believe the werewolves would keep an open mind, I feared Anthony would end up a sacrificial lamb—however unintentionally.

Not if I can help it, I promised myself.

CHAPTER 14

"I'm hungry. Can we go to the café?"

I stood beside my car, waving to Anthony as he retreated into the urban jungle to finish saying his goodbyes to the kids. He offered me that odd chin-jutting thing some men did instead of waving and then disappeared behind a fence.

"Yes, we can go to the café." I glanced down at my clothes and winced. My leggings gaped in two large tears, and I did not want to know what had caused the stains turning the bright red a dark brown. I rattled off a spell, a minor flex of my magic, and the tears in my clothing knitted together and the stains melted away. A cool breeze caressed my cheeks, now clean of sweat and grime. Mother Hazel would never have approved the frivolous use of magic, but I was having a bad day, and I didn't care.

"Yes, yes, you're lovely again, nice to see you've mastered the Cinderella spells, now let's go."

"Your concern is overwhelming."

I climbed into the car, smiling as Peasblossom dove straight for the GPS and found the address she wanted among the saved locations. It was a small café we'd discovered on our first case, an Otherworld sanctuary in the heart of the city. It was one of the few places Peasblossom could order for herself and enjoy her meal without hiding in a plant, or inside my bag.

I fastened my seatbelt and checked my mirrors, but my attention kept wandering back to where Anthony had disappeared. I couldn't get his face out of my head, that somber look when he'd announced his intention to turn himself in.

"Are you thinking of the dream shard?" Peasblossom asked. She flattened herself over the GPS, looking out the windows with an uneasy expression. "I don't feel anything. Do you?"

"No, no, it's not the dream shard." Though now she'd mentioned it, I was in more of a hurry to have a go at downtown traffic. "I can't help thinking of those boys. What will they do when Anthony is in jail?"

"You don't think the wolves will believe he didn't kill Oliver?"

I pulled onto the street and followed the GPS's mechanical instructions. "Liam is not my favorite person right now, but he's not a bad man, or a bad cop. I think eventually he'll admit that Anthony didn't do it. It's too hard for a human to lie to a werewolf."

"So what's the problem?"

"He's got Anthony dead to rights on the weapons possession, so he'll arrest him if only to hold him. Eventually, he'll realize Anthony didn't commit the murder, but there's no guarantee how soon that'll happen, and until then, Anthony will be at the mercy of three very stressed-out werewolves. We need new evidence. Now." I let my head fall against the headrest. "I wish I'd gotten that wizard's information. I'd like to talk to him."

"Perhaps his number is in Blake's cell phone."

"How does that help m— What are you doing?"

Peasblossom tugged at the zipper on my pouch, opening it enough for her to climb inside.

"You'll get lost in there again," I warned her, keeping my focus on the road.

Something black nudged its way out of the pack, followed by

a grunting pink pixie. The object fell into my lap, and I stared. "Is that...?"

"Blake's cell phone." Peasblossom leaned her folded arms on the zippered edge of my bag, her feet kicking inside the enchanted pouch. "I took it when they were being mean to you."

"You..." I should have given her a lecture about the dangers of stealing from werewolf law enforcement. But I was too proud of her. "You're brilliant."

"I know." She climbed out of the pouch and sat on my lap with the phone balanced in front of her. "What was the wizard's name again?"

"Vincent. Vincent Aegis."

She tapped on the phone. "Nope."

"Is he under 'wizard'?"

More taps. "No."

I bit my lip. "What did he call him, the nickname? Wince? Try that."

"Found him."

I continued navigating toward the café as Peasblossom called the wizard, setting the phone to speaker. Vincent answered on the second ring.

"Aegis Analysts, how can I help you?"

"Hi, Vincent, this is Shade. Shade Renard. We met yesterday?"

Silence dragged out for a minute, and when he spoke again, his voice held more caution. "Yes. Yes, I remember. How can I help you, Ms. Renard?"

"Shade, please. I have...concerns about the case. Could we meet?"

"I'm sorry, Ms. Renard. Shade. I handed in my final report an hour ago. My participation in this case is over. I'm only a crime scene analyst, not a detective."

His tone said even more clearly than his words that he did not want to be involved. I was guessing he hadn't wanted to be involved from the moment he'd found out about Stephen's circumstances. "I understand. But I'm concerned the pack may not have attributed the correct weight to a few key pieces of evidence." I paused. "Anthony Catello is about to turn himself in. Do you understand why I'm...worried?"

Vincent cleared his throat. "I believe so. But I don't think I can help you. I'm only the crime scene analyst."

He said the last line the way most people said "don't shoot the messenger." I gripped the steering wheel tighter, willing him to listen. "If you would just meet with me? Ten minutes, that's all I ask."

There was a short, uncomfortable silence. "Did Sergeant Osbourne approve this request?"

"Liam understands that when Mother Hazel assigns someone a task—or in this case, a murder investigation—one has no choice but to see it through, and to do everything one can to be triumphant."

There was a strangled sound on the other end of the phone— a common reaction to the mention of Mother Hazel's name. "Where shall we meet?"

"Do you know Goodfellows?"

"I'm five minutes away."

"I'll meet you there. Thank you."

"You're welcome."

His tone when he said "you're welcome" made it sound more like "if you say so." I didn't let that bother me. Vincent was obviously a lab man, not a field man, and Liam would have been an intimidating boss even for someone who didn't prefer to stay behind a microscope.

I wasn't far from the café, and it took only a few minutes before it appeared on my right. I pulled into the parking lot and chose an empty parking space by the door. I walked inside and was immediately greeted with the earthy scent of the brick walls, the combination smell of napkins and silverware, and a mouth-watering concoction of cooking meat and vegetables that declared today's special was beef vegetable soup. As soon as the doors closed behind us, Peasblossom leapt out of my shirt to stand on my head with her hands on her hips.

The sprite standing at the short hostess podium turned her focus to the pixie, brushing a lock of pale blue hair behind her pointed ear. "Table or a booth?"

"A booth!" Peasblossom declared.

"Excellent choice." The waitress smiled at me and gestured for us to follow her.

"I want honey—a big cup, not the little portion people get with their tea," Peasblossom told her.

"And for you?" the waitress asked me.

"Tea." I took a deep breath through my nose and sighed. "And perhaps a cup of beef vegetable soup?"

"Coming right up," the sprite said.

I settled into the booth, letting out a long sigh as I eased against the cushioned seat. My eyes drifted closed, and I placed my hands flat on the table, needing that solid anchor to keep myself from floating away. Today had turned out to be a lot more exciting than I'd expected, and it was catching up to me. Stress tightened the muscles between my shoulder blades, and my thoughts had twisted into a chaotic jumble of what-ifs and but-whys. I had to relax, and that meant organizing my thoughts. It was time to take notes. I unzipped my pouch and reached in to feel for a notebook.

"Shade?"

I paused in the middle of balancing a picture frame amidst a pile of loose beads I'd pulled from my pouch. Vincent stood beside my booth, his hand wrapped around the top of a walking cane that I would have bet my last Post-it note was actually his staff under a glamour.

"Oh, hi, Vincent. Thank you for coming." I gestured to the seat opposite me. "Please, sit down."

"My pleasure. Though I don't see how I can help you." He

accepted the invitation to sit, though his gaze lingered on the growing mess of random objects on the table in front of me. "Lost something?"

"Not exactly." I shoved my hand farther into the pouch and let out a little sound of triumph as my fingers found the notebook I'd been looking for.

Vincent arched an eyebrow at me as I held it aloft. "Success."

"Indeed." I set it down as the waitress arrived with my order. "Now, I need a pen…"

"If I may?" Vincent said. He smiled at the waitress. "Have you a pen my associate might use?"

The sprite smiled and put a pen down beside my cup of soup. "Just leave it behind when you're done."

"Excellent. And tea for me? Best just bring the pot."

She nodded and left to fetch his order. I gathered all the debris and shoved it back into the pouch. "I'm glad you're here. I really do need your help."

Vincent shifted uncomfortably in his seat, fingers dancing over the edges of his brown wool coat. "Yes, well, I'm not sure what more I can offer you beyond what was in my report."

I put the pen to paper, scribbling out "Opportunity" at the top of the page. "Well, as things stand, we have three suspects based on opportunity. Stephen, Anthony, and Greg."

Vincent shifted uneasily, the fingers of both hands drumming on the table's surface. "Stephen is not in the clear, then?"

"Not yet."

"Don't forget Mia." Peasblossom's voice was thick with honey, her words almost unintelligible. "Women can be murderers too."

Vincent followed the sound of the pixie's voice like a man in a horror movie turning to see where the strange sound is coming from. He closed his eyes when he saw Peasblossom sitting with her legs wrapped around a ramekin of honey, both arms deep in the sticky stuff.

"That's Peasblossom," I told him. "She's my familiar."

"I see." He took a slow, deep breath, then forced his eyes open. "How do you do?"

"How do I do what?" Peasblossom frowned, one honey-laden hand pausing halfway to her mouth.

Vincent's eye twitched. He tore his gaze from the pixie and met my eyes. "I'm sorry, you were saying?"

I added Mia's name to the list. Peasblossom was right. I hadn't considered Mia, but maybe I should. Greg had called Anthony when Gypsy escaped, but no one had asked him if he'd called his mom too. In fact…

I crossed out Anthony and Greg.

Vincent leaned forward. "They're no longer suspects? I thought…"

"I spoke with them today. I'm convinced neither of them shot Oliver Dale."

Vincent pulled at the collar of his mint-green button-up shirt where it poked out of his coat. "May I ask what convinced you?"

Being a wizard, Vincent would have understood if I'd told him it was a gut instinct. Wizards weren't unlike witches in that respect, and we learned early not to ignore our inner voices. But I'd already had one man insinuate that my ovaries somehow guided my investigation, so I wasn't in the most trusting mood.

So instead, I related my experience in the warehouse. "They didn't have to let me go. Anthony could have stood there and waited for Chris to shoot me, or Greg could have shot me while I was unconscious. There were a lot of boys in that warehouse, lots of suspects for when the cops found my body."

"I see." The waitress brought his tea and left the pot. Vincent poured himself a cup with the desperation of a man who needed tea to breathe.

I looked down at my list, staring at the two names left. "We have no proof that Mia was there before Greg called her to come pick him up. And we have no motive for Stephen."

Vincent didn't look away from his tea.

"I think it was Mia," Peasblossom said. She shoved her hand in her mouth again, smearing almost as much honey over her face as she got in her mouth. "Women are vicious."

"She has access to a gun. No alibi." I tapped the pen on the paper. "She had a strong motive. Not only does she care about Gypsy, but Oliver was blocking her promotions. That's serious business for a single mom with a teenage boy to feed."

Vincent said nothing. I noted with some interest he was already pouring his second cup of tea.

"Then there's Stephen. He was there, and he had the right caliber weapon. He also had the victim's blood on his face. What do you think, Vincent?"

"I'm not a detective. I would not presume to—"

"Stephen's story is pathetic," I said evenly. "You know it is. And Liam refuses to let me interview him at all."

"Ms. Renard, please—"

"Oliver was shot, but Stephen omitted that fact. Liam asserts that there may have been predation before Stephen found the body, a barghest or a coyote. You're the crime scene analyst, so you tell me, does that story hold water?"

The wizard winced, clutching his cup of tea as if it were his only anchor to this world. "No. No, it does not hold water."

I dropped the pen and leaned forward. "You're certain?"

He nodded. "I'll show you." He dug in the pocket of his pants and withdrew a phone. "It's in the gallery somewhere..." After squinting at the screen, he poked at the buttons and frowned.

"Oh, for pity's sake, I'll do it."

Peasblossom slogged across the table, leaving sticky foot-prints in her wake, and grabbed the edge of the wizard's phone. Vincent's jaw dropped as she tugged it out of his grip and let it fall to the table. Honey dotted his screen in thick smears as she tapped at the phone, accessing the gallery and pulling up a video previewed by an image of a forest scene.

"There," Peasblossom announced.

JENNIFER BLACKSTREAM

I cleared my throat. I almost tried a "Cinderella" spell on it, but electronics could be tricky. Electricity and magic were both energy, and sometimes using a spell on an electronic item was akin to using a charger that gave off a higher voltage than the device could handle. Accidents happened. Instead, I dug in my pouch until I unearthed a handful of wet wipes.

I carried a lot of those.

Vincent pressed his lips together, cleaning his phone as best he could before handing it to me.

"Press play and you'll see my analysis for yourself."

I nodded and tapped the button to play the video. The sound was too low to hear what was said, but the picture said enough. Oliver Dale's body—what remained of it—lay on the grass. Bright lights illuminated the scene. A man's hand appeared in the picture—I guessed Vincent's, based on the silver ring on his thumb. He waved his hand, and my eyebrows rose. Smoke flowed out from his fingertips, rolling over the ground and the body. It sank into every surface it touched, simmering down to a fine silver sheen. After a few breathless seconds, plumes of smoke shot into the air, each one taking shape as I watched.

"That's amazing," I whispered.

"It's a spell of my own creation." Excitement threaded through Vincent's voice, and for the first time since he'd arrived, he didn't sound like a prisoner submitting to an interrogation. "The magic seeks biological evidence, hair, skin, saliva, and so forth. The shapes you see forming manifest from the creature who left the sample."

"How much information does it give you?"

Vincent shook his head. "Not much. Species and gender. But such is the unreliability of magic. Chemistry and science are much more helpful. After I make notes about the effects, I follow the magic to the individual samples and collect them for more detailed and proper analysis at my lab."

"So you have a lab report to include in the file in case this turns out to be mundane," I guessed.

"Precisely."

"How did you make the magic show up on video?"

A grin lifted the corners of his mouth. "That is impressive, isn't it?" He wagged a finger at me. "Here is a perfect example of why chemistry and science are the skills to master. As a crime scene analyst, it is important for others to witness as much of my process as possible, for corroboration. Magic unseen is unproven, little more than my word against that of a suspect. For this spell, I tied it to dry ice. The magic takes the place of hot water, activating the powder, and giving a visual of the spell that is visible on a recording."

"Fascinating." I hesitated. "Don't you worry that these videos could end up in the wrong hands? Put on the internet?"

He snorted. "Not at all. All it takes is a word to a magician and there'll be thousands of trained eyes studying every aspect. It's only a matter of time before one of them 'figures it out' and puts his own video up revealing 'how the trick was done.'" He smiled. "Magicians. Crafty buggers. They can already replicate half the spells we know, superficially, and if you give them another few centuries, mark my words, they'll have the other half."

"I heard a rumor recently that the Vanguard had hired a magician for that very reason," I said, studying the video. "I'd brushed it off as ridiculous, but if what you say is true..."

"Wouldn't surprise me at all."

I opened my mouth to say more, but something kept nagging at me as I watched Vincent's spell unfold on the screen. I studied the puffs of smoke, focusing on the ones over the body. The most prominent shape kept changing—from wolf to man. What concerned me the most were the shapes I didn't see. I met Vincent's eyes. "There was no barghest. No coyote."

"No." Vincent took a deep breath. "No, I fear my spell found no such evidence."

"And you shared this information with Liam."

"I did. But the spell isn't foolproof. One sample can obscure another. Sergeant Osbourne insisted that if another beast got to the body before Stephen, that evidence could have been covered or even consumed by Stephen himself. It is possible. The magic requires a biological sample to give an impression of the creature it came from."

"So if the barghest saliva was on the body, but Stephen ate that part of the body, he would have consumed the sample and the spell wouldn't pick it up."

"Yes. And given how much of the body Stephen...consumed, it is possible."

"But not likely."

Vincent's shoulder sagged. "No. Not likely." He rubbed a hand over his jaw, scratching at the greyish-brown five o' clock shadow. "And science has failed Stephen as well. I've found nothing to suggest any creature, mundane or other, laid jaws on that body before Officer Reid."

I leaned against the booth. "Stephen knew Oliver Dale was shot, and he didn't tell anyone. Why?"

"Mother Ren—Shade. I am not a—"

"You don't have to be a detective to use common sense," I snapped. "Why are you being difficult? Your own magic is telling you Liam is wrong. Stephen lied."

"They are good men," Vincent insisted. "I have worked with them for many years."

"Good men can still do bad things."

"Stephen had no reason to kill Oliver Dale."

"That we know of," I said. "Liam won't allow me to question him."

"He said you could; he just refused to wait for you," Peas-blossom pointed out.

"Still." I shook my head. "I don't understand why he's so standoffish with me."

"Well, it is in his nature to be reserved," Vincent pointed out. "He is not only a police officer of significant rank, he's also the alpha of his pack. That's a great deal of responsibility."

"So he's like this with everyone?" I asked.

"He is more relaxed among his pack mates, I'm certain. But I would venture a theory that he is never truly relaxed, not as you or I would be among friends. As alpha, he must maintain some distance, some…authority, at all times." He took another sip of tea. "In fact, it is my understanding that the only person an alpha can be completely at ease with is a mate."

"I'm not asking him to be completely at ease around me," I said. "I'm only asking he respect me. That he show me the same courtesy he shows his rangers."

Vincent leaned back in his seat, one hand still cradling his half-empty teacup. "If I might make an observation?"

"Please do." I ate some of my soup, sighing in pleasure at the flavor of beef and assorted vegetables in a perfectly seasoned tomato broth.

"Your mentor assigned you to this case, I'm guessing without the enthusiastic consent of the pack?"

My shoulders slumped and I swallowed my soup. "Yes."

"And you have been apologetic for that. You feel like an intruder, and you are aware your participation is…less than desired?"

"Agreed." I wagged my spoon at Vincent. "But I have insisted on participating. And I don't think Liam would argue that I've been too accommodating to his wishes."

"But you feel bad for being where you're not wanted. You are still waiting for them to approve." Vincent poured himself another cup of tea. "Werewolves, as a general rule, respond to strength. Stop apologizing. Stop feeling like a third wheel. Be yourself. I believe Sergeant Osbourne will respond to that."

I considered that. To an extent, I felt I did stand up to Liam. But perhaps Vincent was right. Perhaps I needed to stop asking permission, or even forgiveness. Maybe I needed to smack him again. That thought made me sit up as I thought of what else I'd wanted to talk to Vincent about.

"Has Liam talked to you about me?"

Vincent didn't look up from his tea. "In what way?"

That was a yes. I put my spoon down and pushed my soup away. "What did he say?"

"I'm not sure what you're getting at."

I shared a look with Peasblossom, then drummed my fingers on the table. "Let's try this another way. Since I've been around the werewolves, I've discovered that I have an...odd reaction to their energy."

"Oh?" Vincent stared harder at his tea, as if it were suddenly the most interesting thing in the world.

"Yes. I'm embarrassed to say I've actually caught myself leaning on Liam, not once, but twice."

"You're a witch—you are more sensitive to auras in general," Vincent said lightly. "If you find the auras of shifters pleasant, I see nothing wrong with that. I'm sorry if it's caused you discomfort."

I watched his face closely. "It's causing me more than discomfort. Liam accused me of trying to siphon off his energy."

The wizard didn't react. So Liam had told him.

"What did he tell you about it?" I asked.

Vincent sighed and released his tea, letting his hands go limp on the table. "He did come to me today and ask if I had a means to monitor if someone were using magic to affect him."

"Did he say why?"

"No, but it does not take a wizard to guess it had something to do with you. Liam does not work with many magic users, and he wouldn't come to me for such an item if I were the one concerning him. To the best of my knowledge, none of the suspects in this case were magic users, so that left you."

I clenched my hands into fists. "I've done nothing to Liam to justify his suspicions. I would never use magic to influence him like that, and I would certainly never try to siphon off someone's—"

I froze. Mocking laughter filled my head, past sins taunting me with my own words. I wilted in my seat, staring down at the table as the memories threatened to drag me into the past. Liam couldn't possibly know of my previous crimes.

"Shade?" Vincent asked gently.

Something sticky made the back of my hand itch. I looked up to find Peasblossom with one hand on top of mine, her pink face pinched with concern. I tried to give her a reassuring smile, but I couldn't manage it. Instead, I looked at Vincent.

"I haven't been using magic on Liam," I said, my voice so low that even I almost missed it.

"I gave Liam an enchanted stone," Vincent said. "I told him it would glow if you were guilty of the crime he suspected you of."

I snorted, thinking back to our confrontation earlier. "So he baited me on purpose to make me angry, then touched me to see if I'd try anything. That explains that." I drew invisible patterns on the tabletop with my finger, still trying to fight back the images from the past, and all the emotional baggage that came with it. "I still don't understand why I'm affected by his energy, though."

"Is it Liam, or shifters in general that you find so enticing?" Vincent asked.

I thought about that. Stephen's energy had been too violent at the time; there'd been nothing comforting about it. And Blake didn't usually stand very close to me for the short amounts of time I'd been in his presence. Sonar kept even more of a distance than Blake. I shrugged. "I don't know."

"Well," Vincent said, tapping one finger on the rim of his teacup, "I'm assuming there is nothing in your past that would predispose you to feeling drawn to shifters?"

I barked out a laugh. "No."

He nodded. "Well, in that case, it's possible that this is a holdover from a previous life. Perhaps you had a special relationship to a shifter, then—or perhaps you were a shifter. Has Mother Hazel ever encouraged you to try a past life regression?"

"No." I shook my head vehemently. "In point of fact, she's forbidden it."

"Indeed?" Vincent raised his eyebrows. "Interesting."

I shook my head and sat up in my seat. "Never mind; none of that matters now. I'm not trying to siphon off Liam's energy, and if your stone works, then he should have realized that by now, or will soon. In any case, we're here to solve a murder." I nodded, as much to myself as to Vincent. "I'm going to get a look inside Oliver's apartment. Maybe I'll find something there to connect him to Stephen." I looked at Vincent. "I could use your spells. Will you come with me?"

Vincent opened his mouth, but before he could respond, a feminine voice interrupted.

"Planning to break into someone else's home, are you? Will you be burning this gentleman's house down as well?"

That voice. I froze, keeping my hands pressed flat to the table in the universal "don't shoot me, I'm unarmed" position. "Hello, Arianne."

The sorceress stood beside my booth, in my peripheral vision, but just enough out of sight I couldn't see her hands, couldn't see if she were readying a spell. Every nerve in my body screamed in anticipation, a panicked urge to run as fast as I could shaking my legs. I turned my head, slowly so as to appear as nonthreatening as possible.

Arianne wore a stunning gown that somehow looked as if it could be worn to bed as easily as to a formal occasion. It hugged her slim curves, the sleeves plunging down like the dresses I'd seen so often when I was a girl in a different world. Somehow she made it look modern.

"What are you doing here, witchling?" Arianne demanded, her

voice cold. "I wouldn't have thought you daring enough to seek me out again after our last encounter."

"I'm not here to see you," I said. "I—"

"You are far from Dresden," Arianne said. "You are less than three blocks from my business—my business you nearly burned to the ground."

I wanted to point out I'd only set a bed on fire, and said fire had been extinguished by her sprinkler system before too much damage had been done. I'd also been fighting for my life when I did it. But Arianne didn't appear to be in an understanding mood, so I kept those thoughts to myself.

I shifted on the bench seat. "So... How've you been?"

"I have been dealing with the fallout that comes from having the FBI stomping through one's business, hauling out a dead body. As if that were not enough, you put me in the sights of that insufferable *sidhe*." Her mouth twisted in disgust. "He's come around twice now, trying to convince me to help him with that ridiculous tattoo." She crossed her arms, fingers dancing over her biceps in a motion that could all too easily turn into a spell.

Again, I had to swallow back information that would hurt me more than help. The *sidhe* she referred to was Flint Valencia—a *leannan sidhe* who used his seductive abilities a little too freely. He'd taken an unhealthy interest in me during my last case, and the tattoo Arianne spoke of was my attempt to protect myself from him. Nothing cooled one's hormones like an enchanted spider tattoo that moved like the real thing over the would-be seducer's face...

"Arianne, I am so sorry for what happened at your hotel. It was irresponsible of me, completely inexcusable. I hope you can forgive me. I would like us to be friends."

Arianne gaped at me, the open-mouthed expression some-what at odds with the elegance of her dress. "Friends? *Friends?* I am not friends with those who threaten my business, who nearly bring death and destruction on those I hold dear. I—"

She froze as if she'd said more than she wanted to. I blinked. Death and destruction to those she held dear? I hadn't hurt anyone that I knew of.

An unpleasant smile curled her lips. "Tell me, witchling. Have you had any interesting dreams lately?"

I fought not to react, curling my hand around my still-warm tea. I'd already known Arianne was the one who'd sent the dream shard after me, so that was no surprise. And I wouldn't give her the satisfaction of knowing just how badly she'd scared me.

"No more than usual," I said.

Her smile widened. "So nice to hear it. Well, I must say goodbye now." She pivoted and walked a few steps before pausing. "Be careful, Mother Renard. Rocky River Reservation is full of shadows and things that go bump in the night. I wouldn't want anything to happen to Mother Hazel's precious protégée."

It wasn't until the door shut behind Arianne that I realized Peasblossom was no longer sitting next to my hand. I looked around, then tensed. With a groan, I found the sticky pixie tucked under my arm—attached to my shirt.

"She's not very nice," Peasblossom mumbled. She walked back to her honey, then squeaked when her wings stuck to my shirt, glued in place by honey residue.

I cleared my throat and drew on my magic to clean away the tacky substance. "No, she's not." I turned to face Vincent. "I apologize for—"

The wizard was gone. Vanished like a coward during my tête-à-tête with the dream sorceress.

"Didn't waste time escaping, did he?" Peasblossom clucked her tongue, her eyes still locked on the remaining honey. "Sissy wizard."

"It makes me wonder how he ended up in this field." I signaled our waitress. "Could I get a to-go container, please?"

"We're leaving already?" Peasblossom held out her arms for

the honey, and only my two-fingered grip on her skirt kept her from launching herself face first.

"Anthony turned himself in. I don't want him to be in the tender care of the werewolves any longer than necessary. Let's go see Oliver Dale's apartment."

"And if you don't find anything?"

I sighed. "Then we must talk to Stephen. Whether his alpha likes it or not."

CHAPTER 15

I didn't have the authority to ask the building manager to let me into Oliver Dale's apartment. Fortunately, my lock-picking skills exceeded most—mostly because people summoned a village witch for help in any situation, including after they'd locked themselves out of their house. Mrs. Patel locked herself out of her house so often that I'd taken her on as a locksmith apprentice, and now she helped me with some of the calls I got.

The door creaked as I swung it open, and that small sound grated on my nerves. *I have a right to be here*, I reminded myself. *It's all part of the investigation.*

"It stinks in here," Peasblossom complained.

I wrinkled my nose. "Silver polish. Cheap silver polish."

"And you made Liam stay in here while you chatted with Anthony. No wonder the cranky cop refused to return so you could snoop around."

I conceded the point. Though in my defense, Liam hadn't said anything about silver, and he could have waited in the hallway while I looked around. Too late now.

I shook off thoughts of what the werewolf alpha would have to say about me breaking into the victim's apartment and crept farther inside. Boxes piled up on the far end of the room announced the landlord's intention to clear it out for a new tenant. Lucky for me, it seemed he hadn't started yet. The boxes were empty, only a few of them stuffed with bubble wrap and brown paper for packing the more fragile possessions.

As I reached the center of the living room, I had to stop and stare.

"Not a humble man, was he?" Peasblossom muttered.

It was the understatement of the year. Floating shelves covered the entire living room wall, each shelf laden with a picture or trophy or plaque. A couple held framed certificates. Half the trophies were from school, awards for athletics, mostly football. The plaques were from work, those odd glass constructions congratulating Oliver Dale for efficiency and—of all things—teamwork.

"No wonder Mia hates him." Peasblossom studied the trophies. "Ha! This one's from Pee-Wee Football!"

"He saved every award he ever got, and took the time to display each one of them." I walked the perimeter of the room, ghosting my hand over a solid oak credenza burdened with more tributes to the great and powerful Oliver Dale. "There's not a single picture of anyone else anywhere. No family, no friends. Nothing."

"You already knew he had no family, and by now you should guess he had no friends." Peasblossom squinted at the label on a plaque. "This one's dated last month."

A bookshelf near the far wall caught my eye, and I strode over to it. The first shelf bowed under the weight of yearbooks and school mementos, including a stuffed eagle with a football sewn to its foot. I pulled a yearbook out at random and opened it up.

As I'd expected, high school had been a grand time for Oliver. There were pictures of him everywhere, most of them featuring a handsome youth in a football uniform. Oliver scoring a touchdown, Oliver celebrating a win surrounded by screaming fans,

Oliver half hugging a cheerleader as she draped her scantily clad body around him. Arrogance filled his features, screamed out of the image in the jut of his chin and the fact that in none of the pictures was he smiling at anyone else. No, Oliver's attention remained on the camera. Posing as if he already knew he'd been keeping that photo forever and he wanted to capture as much of his glory as possible. The final picture showed him hefting a college sweatshirt into the air, but I couldn't make out the whole name.

"The Golden Boy of North Olmsted," I murmured. I glanced at the trophies again. "He rode his fame till the end, didn't he?"

On a whim, I flipped through the photos, looking for Stephen Reid. No luck. I tried the other yearbooks, accounting for a possible difference in age, but still no Stephen. I looked around for a college yearbook, but couldn't find one. That seemed strange.

"He was a jerk as a kid too," Peasblossom said from her perch on my shoulder. She pointed to the pictures. "He drew wings on a lot of them. Is that supposed to be some creepy 'I wish they were dead' thing? Like giving them their wings?"

"No, I don't think so. The school's mascot is the eagle. Those wings are printed around certain pictures to indicate those students participated in the athletics program." I arched an eyebrow at some other pictures. "Those notes, however, are handwritten."

Oliver had not been any kinder back then than he'd been at the time of his death. Several of the girls' pictures had...well, Oliver's "thoughts" on how the ladies had...performed. Romantically speaking. Some girls had Oliver's helpful comments about what they needed to make them "layable," and most of the boys' pictures had his estimation of their shortcomings and why they weren't as wonderful as Oliver himself.

"What does that word mean?" Peasblossom asked, pointing to

a word above a picture of a particularly well-developed young lady.

My cheeks warmed, and I slammed the book shut, missing Peasblossom's outstretched hand by a hair. "Never mind. The point is, Stephen didn't go to school with Oliver."

Peasblossom glowered at me, the hand I'd nearly missed crushing tucked against her body. She gave me one last dirty look, then flew off in a huff. I should have felt bad. She was older than me, and by all rights, I shouldn't treat her like a child. But she was just so innocent sometimes, so childlike. It was hard to remember how old she was. I glanced at the book and my cheeks burned. Besides, there were some words that just weren't appropriate. For anyone.

Shaking off the slimy feeling induced by Oliver's high-school vocabulary, I reached for my magic and threw it outward in a thin silver net. The magic tingled against my senses, probing the room for any sign of magic.

Nothing. Not a glimmer or a sparkle, nothing to suggest Oliver had anything even as simple as a lucky charm.

For a while, I stood there, staring at the wall of Oliver Worship. A light weight landed on my shoulder, tugging on a lock of my hair. "What's wrong?"

"Why did she assign me this case?"

"What?"

I glanced at Peasblossom and nodded toward the yearbooks, the wall. "Everything we discover about this man, this victim, paints him in a horrible light. He loved himself and hated everyone else. He was cruel to animals and unpleasant to anyone who crossed his path."

Peasblossom stroked the shell of my ear. "Isn't it important to solve murders even when the victim is a bad person?"

Peasblossom's voice lacked judgment, but the words still stung. "It's not that. Look at our suspects. Three of the four are human. And then there's the investigation. So far, everything we've accomplished could have been achieved by a human investigator. Even the victim was human. If Liam's right, and Stephen is innocent... I don't understand why she wanted me working this murder."

"Beats me," Peasblossom said. "Who can say why that daffy witch does anything?"

I dismissed the spell with a wave of disgust and left the apartment, locking up behind me. "There's got to be something I'm missing."

"I'm sorry?"

I startled and glanced to the side. Rosie, Anthony's neighbor, stood outside her apartment with her arms full of groceries.

"Were you talking to me?" she asked.

I gave her a weak smile. "Sorry. No, I was just talking to myself."

She smiled. "I do that all the time."

I returned the smile and took a few steps toward her. "Can I help with those?"

She glanced at the paper bag of groceries in one arm and the three plastic bags hanging from the other, weighing down the hand trying to put the key in the lock. "If you wouldn't mind?"

I took the bag and stood beside her as she shifted the other bags in her grip and slid the key into the lock. The door swung open, taking her keys with it, and she grunted in frustration.

"Thank you." She stumbled inside, leaving the keys behind in the door and trudging toward the dining table with a little more momentum than she'd intended. She eased the bags down, careful not to smash any fragile contents, then accepted the last bag from me before retrieving her keys and closing the apartment door.

"You're welcome." I paused, watching her inspect the bags before unloading the contents onto the table. "Could I ask you a question?"

"Certainly. Can I offer you a drink?"

"No thank you." I took my cell phone out of the side pocket of my pouch and tapped a few buttons before holding it up to Rosie. "Do you recognize this man?"

She looked at Stephen's picture for a moment, her brow furrowed, then shook her head. "I'm sorry. Should I?"

I sighed and replaced the phone. "I guess not. I was just wondering if he was a friend of Oliver's."

Rosie snorted and lifted a tub of chocolate ice cream out of a damp plastic bag. "Not likely. He didn't seem to have any friends."

"Well, he's a police officer too. Is there any chance he responded to a complaint? Maybe Oliver met him that way?"

"Not that I saw." She paused with the freezer open, the tub of ice cream forgotten in her grasp. "Wait a minute. Oliver might have had one friend. At least he said he did. A cop."

"Did he mention a name? Stephen Reid?"

Rosie shook her head and put the ice cream on the top shelf of the freezer. "He never gave a name. Just liked to brag about it. Any time someone threatened to call the cops on him the way he did on everyone else, he'd laugh and say go ahead, that his 'friend' would take care of it. He bragged that he hadn't got so much as a speeding ticket since college."

My pulse skipped a beat, and I leaned forward. "Can you remember anything else he might have said about this person, anything that might help me find them?"

"No." She closed the freezer and returned to the shopping bags. "I wish I could be more help. I don't even know if he and the cop were really friends. To be honest, it'd be easier to believe he was blackmailing someone."

"Blackmailing a cop?"

She shrugged and carried a bag of cherries to the fridge. "He wouldn't have been above something underhanded like that. A man down the hall moved out a few months ago. There was a rumor that Oliver caught him violating his lease. Something stupid like letting a friend stay with him for too long. Supposedly, Oliver threatened to report him to the landlord if he didn't give up his highly coveted front-row parking space. That's not the same thing as blackmailing a cop, but…"

I didn't disagree with her. Generally speaking, someone willing to resort to blackmailing someone else didn't discriminate. If Oliver would blackmail someone in the building, there was no reason to think he wouldn't blackmail a cop, given the right leverage. So Oliver had a connection with someone on the force, and it could have been blackmail.

Still, that could be a coincidence. Just because one of my suspects was a cop didn't mean he was the one Rosie had mentioned. For all I knew, Oliver had been lying about his supposed cop associate. Or he may have had a friend in the local police, unrelated to the rangers. I closed my eyes and rubbed my temples. I needed more information.

I needed to talk to Stephen.

I opened my eyes and smiled at Rosie. "Well, I should be going."

She gave me an apologetic smile and leaned against the fridge. "I'm sorry I couldn't be of more help."

"You've already been a big help, more than you know."

I waved goodbye and let myself out. Peasblossom waited until we were in the hallway before speaking. "How can we confirm if Oliver was blackmailing Stephen?"

I tripped over the last step, my heart leaping into my throat as I pinwheeled my arms in a desperate attempt to land on my feet. Peasblossom clung to my hair like a heavy barrette, growling at me when I regained my balance.

"Slow down before you get us killed."

"You can *fly*," I pointed out for the millionth time. I put a hand over my racing heart, relearning how to breathe. I needed to watch where I was going.

"You can drink water," she responded. "Doesn't stop you from guzzling Coke."

I ignored the jab and continued down the stairs. "We're going to see Stephen." I exited the apartment building and headed for my car.

"He won't let you in," Peasblossom said. She jumped to the passenger seat as soon as I sat down, turning on the GPS even as she disparaged my plan.

"Oh, yes, he will. I'm done letting werewolves shut me out of this investigation. He'll talk to me, or he can bloody well wait for someone else to take that collar off."

"Liam will be cross." The GPS beeped as she called up Stephen's address from the list of recent destinations. "The one thing he's been crystal clear about is that he doesn't want a witch interrogating his wolf."

"Well, he had a chance to be present when I talked to him and he passed, so he can live with the consequences."

I held on to that confidence on the drive to Stephen's, but all the same, I was relieved to find his driveway empty. I'd been fairly certain Liam would still be questioning Anthony, but I'd had no guarantee. There'd been a significant chance that the alpha would be here, telling Stephen they had a suspect. And Peasblossom was right: if Liam ever suspected I would question Stephen, he'd be here to stop me in a heartbeat.

I knocked harder than I'd meant to, the adrenaline pumping through my system acting in much the same way as too much espresso. The door swung open. The werewolf in question towered over me, still wearing the rumpled T-shirt and jeans he'd worn yesterday. He hadn't combed his hair, and it hung haphazardly over his head, giving the impression he'd just woken up. As soon as he saw me, Stephen's jaw tightened.

"Sergeant Osbourne told me not to talk to you."

It didn't take a witch to see he was upset, and in pain. It was to be expected when he wore that collar, especially given the circumstances under which he'd come to put it on. The fact that, despite his obvious distress, I couldn't feel the hum of his aura, couldn't feel his energy at all, made my stomach twist.

"You have a lot of nerve looking at me like that when you're the one that put this thing on me." His voice was a low rasp, almost a growl. He tightened his grip on the doorframe until his knuckles turned white. He looked like he wanted to say more, but he swallowed it back.

I found my voice just in time. "I know about Oliver's 'friend.'"

Stephen froze, the door halting a split second before it would have clicked shut. Stephen pulled it open, and when he looked at me this time, his face was a blank mask.

"Oliver's friend?"

I nodded. "We need to talk."

He shifted from one foot to another, his hand braced on the edge of the doorframe. "Liam doesn't want me talking to you."

The words lacked the ring of finality they'd had the first time. It felt like progress, so I stood straighter. "Your alpha is very protective. But I assure you, I'm not here to manipulate you, or magically bully you into a confession. I'm here for the truth." I met his gaze and held it. "You and I both understand it would behoove you if we spoke privately before Liam figures it out."

An eerie quiet settled over his body, and he dropped his arm from the doorframe. "All right. Come in."

He held the door open for me, but he didn't step back more than a foot. His position and the narrow doorway forced me to brush against him as I entered. His chest rose and fell as he inhaled deeply. Scenting me. Probably to see if I was lying. Or nervous.

An abrupt sizzle of energy erupted where our bodies touched, the hum of his aura seething against the barrier of the collar's binding. My nerves spasmed, and I pressed against him before I could stop myself, chasing that energy. As soon as I realized what I was doing, I overcompensated and leaned away.

It would have been too much to ask that he not notice my

reaction. I felt his scrutiny on me as I passed him to enter the room, the weight of an assessing stare. Great. All I needed was another werewolf convinced I was trying to siphon off his life-force. Or flirt with him. I smoothed my hands down my coat, straightening the collar. Well, at least that answered my question. It was shifters in general, not just Liam.

I jumped at the ominous sound of the deadbolt sliding into place.

"You shouldn't have let him get between you and the exit," Peasblossom whispered, once again using my ear as a microphone. "No one else knows you're here!"

My stomach dropped, but I forced myself to stand tall and turn to meet Stephen's gaze. "He can't hurt me. The collar would send him into unconsciousness if he tried."

I didn't bother to whisper, since he'd hear me anyway. Just as he'd heard Peasblossom.

"And besides, I'm here to help. Isn't that right, Stephen?"

The bound werewolf stood in front of the door, watching me. Now that I'd brushed against him, I couldn't get rid of that sensation of his aura against mine, the chaotic heat of his beast trapped inside him. Liam hadn't been kidding when he'd said requesting the collar had been serious. I couldn't imagine it was having the best effect on Stephen.

"I heard about your deal with your mentor," Stephen said finally. He stalked around the grey couch, moving with a predator's even grace. He sat down on the section between me and the door. "I can't think of anything a witch—or any other creature—wouldn't do for an unlimited, unqualified favor from Mother Hazel."

Fear made way for anger, and I snapped my mouth shut, swallowing a sharp retort as I reflected on the gossipy natures of werewolf packs. *Worse than kindergartners.* "If you understand my mentor at all, then you'll know what she would do if she suspected I'd sacrificed my principles to get that favor. She doesn't want just any answer. She wants the right one."

Stephen drew a finger down the arm of the couch. "Is that why you're here? You want me to give you the answer?"

"I think I already know the answer," I responded evenly. "I'm here because I want to give you a chance to provide…context."

He fell silent, but he didn't look away from me. Over and over, he drew his finger over the surface of the couch arm. Something about the movement, the drag of his fingernail over the material, made me imagine a claw on that hand. It provided images of what that claw would do if it were dragged down something softer than the couch. Meatier. Something that bled.

His brown eyes remained plain, ordinary brown, no hint of wolf gold, but that wasn't as comforting as it might have been if he hadn't been wearing the collar. "Did your mentor specify an outcome?"

I tore my attention from the couch. "Specify an outcome?"

"Does getting that favor require only that you figure out how Oliver Dale died, or did your mentor specify you need a conviction? Did she dictate a specific punishment?"

He'd said "how Oliver Dale died" not "who killed Oliver Dale." He wasn't admitting anything yet, was waiting to see how much I knew.

I circled my end of the sectional couch to sit opposite him with the coffee table between us. I hadn't been lying when I told Peasblossom he couldn't attack me with that collar on—the magic would disable him before he could raise a hand to me. But just because my brain knew that, didn't mean my instincts weren't calmer with a piece of furniture between us.

"Mother Hazel would never do that," I said. "She knows, perhaps better than anyone, that there are always circumstances to consider. One punishment does not fit all."

Stephen tilted his face up, and his nostrils flared. Scenting whether I was lying.

"Why don't you tell me what happened," I said, "and we'll go from there. Give me the story—*your* story."

"Why don't you tell me what you think happened, and I'll tell you if you're right?" he countered.

I leaned forward, bracing my forearms on my knees. "If you don't want to talk to me, that's fine. I can call Liam right now, and we can all sit down and chat about Oliver's police friend together."

A muscle in Stephen's jaw worked as he clenched his teeth. "If you call Liam, he's going to be pissed you came here and tried to talk to me without his permission."

"Then he'll be angry with both of us," I said. I met his eyes. "The difference is, when this is all over, I'm going home to tell my mentor I did what she asked me to do. You, on the other hand, will remain here. With an alpha you lied to." I tilted my head. "Do you really think he's going to have that collar removed if you don't tell him the truth about what happened?"

There. In his eyes. I could see Stephen's fear now, see the knowledge that I was right. Liam wouldn't have the collar removed as long as he believed Stephen was lying.

"Stephen," I said softly, "let me help you. Tell me what happened—everything that happened. Tell me why you did what you did. I promise you, I will help if I can." I shook my head. "You do not want to wear that collar longer than necessary."

He looked away, but only for a second. Then his gaze was back on mine, boring a hole right through me. "The deal you made with your mentor. Do you have to tell Liam the truth for it to qualify?"

"I—" I frowned. "No. I have to solve the case, but she didn't say anything about telling Liam."

"You don't have to report it, don't have to see that formal charges are filed? There's nothing about punishing the guilty party?"

There was a hint of desperation in his voice now, but I didn't understand why. It didn't matter if I told Liam or not—the fact remained that Stephen wouldn't get that collar off until his alpha believed he'd come out with the whole truth.

He pressed his hand against the arm of the couch, gripping it until the metal frame groaned. "I'll make you a deal. I'll tell you what happened, but in return, I want your word that once I tell you, you'll leave. You'll leave, and you won't say anything to Liam. And you'll tell me who told you."

He wanted to know who'd told me about Oliver's "friend" on the police force. And he wanted me to leave without sharing the information with Liam. I bit my lip. It would satisfy Mother Hazel. And it wasn't as if I owed Liam anything. He'd made it clear he wanted me gone anyway. But Anthony…

"I will agree," I said slowly, "but with the stipulation that if someone else is charged with this crime, and if they are in danger of being punished for something they didn't do, then I will share what is necessary to clear them."

Stephen pressed his lips together. "Fine."

I nodded, my pulse racing as I leaned closer. "Tell me what happened."

"You need to understand the context first," Stephen said. He leaned back against the cushions, rubbing his hands over his thighs. "See, Oliver was a big shot in high school. Football star, good looks. He had it all, and his classmates worshiped him. Charmed life doesn't even begin to cover it."

He met my eyes then. "The problem is, high school isn't real. It doesn't prepare you for real life, and when you're treated like a god, it prepares you even less. For some people, that means depression afterward, this deep hole you fall into when you realize that no one cares you were a star athlete in school. For others, it means they get a taste of power, a taste of what it's like to believe you're better than everyone else." He jabbed a finger at me, tension squeezing the muscles between his shoulders. "Those are the people who become dangerous."

"Oliver Dale was dangerous?"

Stephen stared at a random spot on the carpet. "He was never a nice person, even in high school when he had everything going for him. Everything came too easily to him, and when he realized that wasn't the case for everyone else, it gave him an inflated sense of self-importance. He treated people like shit, and most of them didn't even care. Being near him gave them a contact cool, so they let him get away with it. And when he graduated, he expected that adulation to keep coming indefinitely."

"But real life isn't like that."

Stephen snorted. "No. But he didn't even get to real life before he learned that. He went to college and they put him in his place. He may have ruled North Olmsted, but college is full of high school stars, and Oliver wasn't even in the top ten. He came home with his tail between his legs."

I held my breath, afraid to interrupt lest I stop him from continuing. We were getting to the heart of it. I could feel it.

"He came home a lot meaner than he'd left. He wasn't just arrogant now—he was angry, and he was cruel. People tried to cut him a break—I think they realized he'd had a hard awakening —but he didn't appreciate it. One by one, people stopped trying to help, stopped caring."

He fell silent, staring into space as if he were looking into the past. He clasped his hands around his knees until his knuckles turned white. I waited, but when the silence dragged on, I gave him a little prod.

"Not everyone stopped caring," I said gently.

Stephen's gaze lifted to my face, and the intensity there shoved me back in my seat. "He didn't deserve it. He had a hundred chances, and he blew them all. You know how many times his tantrums could have got him arrested?" He shook his head in disgust. "There's no reason for a good person to lose everything they've worked for just because they didn't give up on someone. Didn't see him for the monster he was and just leave him to deal with his own mess."

"I agree." I sat forward in my seat, my forearms braced on my legs. "I've seen it, what you described. People who fight to find the good in someone and suffer an unimaginable price. I'll admit, I did the same thing for Oliver at first. I thought he can't be all bad. Mother Hazel assigned me his murder; there must be good inside him, a reason she cares." I shook my head. "But now I think *you're* the reason. I think she put me on this case so I would be here to listen to you. To understand."

Stephen rubbed a hand over his jaw, scratching at his beard. "And if someone did shoot Oliver to stop him, shoot him because he was a danger to others—what sort of punishment would that person deserve?"

"That won't be up to me."

He sat on the edge of the couch, leaning closer. "But you see that he had to be stopped? It was only a matter of time before he killed someone. He was hanging a dog."

"Is that what finally pushed you over the edge?" I asked. "Seeing him trying to hang Gypsy? Is that when you decided enough was enough?"

Stephen went still. The emotion on his face drained away, and he looked at me from the same empty mask he'd worn before. "What do you mean?"

Frustration curled my hands into fists. I was losing him. "You said you tried to see good in him. You clung to that hope for a long time; you helped him get out of all those charges. What changed? What happened that night that pushed you over the edge?"

Stephen stood, rubbing his hands on the sides of his jeans. "This was a bad idea."

"No, it wasn't," I said, standing to match his stance. "You want the truth to come out, I know you do. Tell me, and I'll try to help." I took a step closer. "I saw the yearbooks. He used people, and you're right, he treated them as if they existed only for his convenience." I thought of the pictures in the yearbook, the little notes. "He seemed particularly crass with women. Was it Emma? Did Oliver try to hurt her?"

Something snapped inside Stephen. Every muscle in his body tensed, and he half ran for the door. "You need to leave. Now."

"Wait, why?" I held my ground, refusing to move when he jerked open the front door. "Stephen, talk to me. Is that it? Did he threaten Emma?"

"I need you to leave. I have to think." His grip shifted on the doorknob, and he shifted his weight from foot to foot.

"Stephen, I know you care about Emma. If Oliver threatened you, no one would blame you for protecting her. You have to understand that."

He snarled at me then, lips pulling back to reveal white teeth. He didn't shift, couldn't shift, but my brain was all too willing to remind me of what he really was. What those teeth would look like as soon as that collar came off.

"Get out," he said, his voice a low rumble.

I came around the couch, moving as slowly as I could without making him angrier, as my mind whirled to think of some way to reach him, to make him talk to me. He'd been so close. So close to telling me what really happening, confiding in me. What had happened to make him change his mind?

Pain traced lines across his face, a sign he was losing his temper, and the collar was reminding him of his new limitations. "I won't ask you again. Get out."

He couldn't hurt me. I knew it, and he knew it. I closed my hands into fists, fighting my frustration, my desire for the truth that was within my grasp. I had magic at my disposal. There were plenty of things I could do to him, ways I could make him talk.

If I wanted to be that kind of witch.

I left before I had to decide.

CHAPTER 16

"Peasblossom, at what point would you say the panic started?"

I walked to my car, the skin between my shoulder blades itching with the need to turn and see if Stephen was glaring at me through the window. If anyone but Mother Hazel had created that collar, I'd have readied a spell. What had scared him? Why was he so angry?

"When you mentioned the yearbooks," Peasblossom said immediately. "You said you saw the yearbooks, you know how he treated people, and then you asked him if Oliver tried to hurt Emma."

"If Oliver tried to hurt Emma, then Stephen would have told Liam that, and that would have been the end of it. No one would blame him for defending her, even if they weren't dating."

"If Oliver...*hurt* Emma," Peasblossom said slowly, "then maybe Emma doesn't want anyone to know."

I considered that. Emma had looked like a wreck when I'd seen her the next day. Very upset. I'd assumed it was just the reaction of a dog lover to almost seeing a dog hanged, but what if that wasn't it?

"If that's true, and Emma really doesn't want that to come out, then we need another way to tie Stephen to Oliver. The way he was talking, it sounded personal." I unlocked the car and opened the door. "I must have missed something in those yearbooks."

Peasblossom fluttered in to sit on the dashboard. "If you did, then he knows it."

I froze with the key halfway to the ignition. "He'll go after the yearbooks."

"Yes, he will." She leapt from the dashboard down to the passenger seat and grabbed the GPS. "We have to get them first."

The GPS screen lit up as Peasblossom prepared to enter Oliver's address, her tiny palms flat as she pressed the buttons. I reversed out of the driveway with my attention still on those front curtains, looking for the werewolf.

"He can't leave," I murmured. "He'll get someone else to fetch them." The mechanical voice gave me instructions, and I turned out of Stephen's allotment.

"What do you think you missed?" Peasblossom asked, leaning against the seat with the GPS balanced in her lap.

I pressed my lips together and shook my head. "Werewolves age slower than humans, but that doesn't mean they don't change at all when they age. A lot of people look nothing like their year-book picture. I could have looked right at him and missed it. And a lot of werewolves don't show up for picture day, just so they can avoid having a record of their face next to their name."

"Makes it harder to say it's a relative and not them if someone notices," Peasblossom said. "So maybe he's in one of the student-submitted pictures?"

I bit my lip. "You could be right. Whatever the reason, he tensed when I brought up the yearbooks. There's something in those books he doesn't want us to see."

"Someone might have written something about him," Peasblossom suggested. "Humans like signing books, and that one had all sorts of scribbles in it."

I gripped the steering wheel, teeth gritted in frustration.

"Damn it, that means we need Oliver Dale's books. We can't just find another copy. If the person he calls to retrieve them is closer than we are…"

"Don't drive faster!" Peasblossom said. "Safety first!"

"Yes, yes." I eased my foot off the gas. She was right; getting in an accident certainly wouldn't get us there any faster.

"I wonder why he liked Oliver?" Peasblossom put the GPS down and climbed onto the armrest. "Stephen doesn't strike me as the friendly, ever-optimistic sort."

I winced as she grabbed my shirt, tiny fingers stabbing me through the thin cotton weave. "He doesn't, does he?" I drummed my fingers against the steering wheel. "Which means it probably wasn't something as simple as being classmates. We're missing something, something important. Something connects him to Oliver; we just have to find it."

We stopped at a red light, and I mentally ran over everything I knew about Stephen and the victim. Which wasn't much. "Everyone has been telling me since I first showed up that Stephen is a good man. I thought it was a general opinion, but what if it's something more? What if Stephen did something that impressed his peers?"

"Like saved someone's life?"

"Perhaps. Say he did save Oliver's life. If he risked his life to save him, then it would make sense he'd want to believe Oliver Dale was a decent person. Even need to believe it. Remember two summers ago when Susan pulled George out of the river?"

Peasblossom snorted. "Not that he deserved it. He only fell in because he was trying to push little Joseph in and Joseph moved at the last minute."

"Exactly. Susan saved his life, but he was still a bully after that, wasn't he? Always picking on kids. But she wouldn't hear a word spoken against him, always insisted that deep down he was just scared. Part of her needed to believe he was a good person, otherwise all the trouble he caused after she pulled him out of that river would have felt like her fault."

"Did we look at the teachers' photos?" Peasblossom asked.

I almost smacked myself in the head. "No. No, we didn't. Blood and bones, what was I thinking?"

"Seems like you weren't thinking much at all, if you ask me."

I ignored the insult. I might have deserved it.

Every mile stretched into an eternity. By the time I pulled into the parking lot of Oliver's apartment building, I was jumping out of my skin. Peasblossom squeaked a protest as she tumbled off my shoulder in my haste to get out, her legs scrabbling against my upper arm as she tried to regain her perch. I didn't bother to remind her—again—that she had wings. Her complaints were nothing but white noise as I dashed up the stairs to Oliver's apartment.

It took three attempts to pick the lock this time, my hands shaking from the rush of adrenaline. When the door swung open, I half fell into the small entry hallway, my heart pounding so loud that I didn't even hear Peasblossom anymore. I fought back a sneeze as the scent of silver polish assaulted me again and stumbled inside toward the bookcase.

A quick glance told me I was too late.

"No, no, no." I ran to the bookcase, staring in dismay at the large gap where the yearbooks had been. They were gone. I removed the biographies that had fallen over into the vacated space, some small, irrational part of me praying that the yearbooks had fallen over, all four somehow hiding themselves behind a different book. No such luck.

"So someone is helping him," Peasblossom said. "But who?"

I put my fingers to my temples, trying to concentrate. *Think, think, think.* My gaze landed on the eagle holding the football, and I stared at it, letting it hold my focus while my mind spun down all the different possibilities. Someone was helping Stephen. Someone

JENNIFER BLACKSTREAM

had taken the yearbooks for him. He'd called them, told them to take the yearbooks. Phone records? No, that would take too long. Who would he call? Why didn't he want me to see the yearbooks?

The stuffed eagle stared at me.

"He couldn't have asked anyone from his pack," I said. "They would think he was covering up evidence. So who would he trust to help hi—" I shot to my feet, eyes widening. "Emma."

"Emma?"

"I would find out if anyone there had a connection to Oliver Dale. I'd look at church attendance, gyms, even high school. I would keep looking until I found a connection."

Emma's words came floating back, and I cursed and headed for the door. "She tried to tell me. She didn't want to turn him in, but her conscience got the better of her. She told me everything I needed to figure it out, and I was too dense to listen."

"She must love him to help him get away with murder."

"Romance is never irrelevant." I closed the door to Oliver's apartment, hesitating a second before leaving it unlocked. I took a few steps down the hallway, then paused when I heard voices coming from inside Anthony's apartment. On a hunch, I knocked on the door.

The sound was louder than I'd intended, thanks to my frazzled nerves. The door opened and Rosie stood there, eyes wide with surprise.

"Shade, hi." She gave me a quick once-over. "Um, are you okay?"

"Rosie?" I leaned back and checked to make sure I had the right apartment. "What are you doing in Anthony's apartment?"

"She's helping me," Mia said.

Peasblossom slid deeper into the neck of my shirt, hiding from Rosie as Greg's mom came out from the back bedroom. Mia gave me a tired smile and hefted the box she held in her arms. "I'm keeping Gypsy until Anthony…gets things straightened out. He insisted that she have all her things."

246

I followed her gaze to a pile by the door. Huge dog bed, stack of toys, boxes containing a wide selection of treats. Gypsy had more luggage than me. "Oh my."

"I told you, she is a very spoiled dog." Mia sighed. "But we all love her. I guess you do crazy things for the ones you love."

I thought of Emma and Stephen. "That's the truth. Hey, did either of you see or hear anyone go into Oliver Dale's apartment in the last half hour or so?"

Rosie frowned. "No, I'm sorry. The landlord was there last night gathering boxes to clear the place out, but I haven't seen anyone today. Why, do you think someone broke in?"

"It would be just like Oliver to cause trouble even after he's dead," Mia growled. She dropped the box of dog necessities and crossed her arms. "Let me guess, he owed someone money and now that he's dead they're trying to collect?"

"No, no, it's just— Never mind. I'm sorry I bothered you."

I bolted down the hallway, ignoring the dumbfounded looks on Rosie and Mia's faces. I kept from tumbling head over teakettle down the stairs, but collided with my car door in my rush, grunting before pushing off enough to open the door.

"Slow down," Peasblossom wailed. "Where are we going?"

"To find Emma," I said, breathless from the mad dash. "If I hurry, we might catch her before she hides the yearbooks."

"You know where she is?"

I slid into my seat and closed the door behind me. "If she holds true to her schedule, she's on patrol on the reservation."

"And you think she'd finish her shift after stealing the yearbooks?"

"I think the reservation is close enough she might pop out to help herself to the evidence and return before she's missed."

Peasblossom squeaked as she was almost squished between my neck and the seat as I leaned back to put my seatbelt on. "Hey!" She huffed and grabbed hold of my hair with a vicious yank and then hauled herself up to sit on my head. "You can call, you know. You don't have to drive there. Call ahead and have Liam ask Emma to come to his office and hold her until you get there."

I paused with my hand halfway in the side pocket of my pouch to retrieve the keys. Peasblossom was right. As much as I hated to bring Liam in on this before I had any evidence, or even a reasonable explanation, it would be even worse if Emma destroyed the yearbooks before I could get to her. If she did think she'd gotten away with it, had gone back on patrol intending for no one to know she'd ever been missing and then destroy them later, then this was the best way.

"You're right."

"Of course I'm right," Peasblossom grumbled.

I fished my phone out of the side pocket on my pouch opposite my keys and called the main office of the Rocky River Reservation.

The secretary picked up on the second ring. "Rocky River Reservation, ranger station, Amy speaking, how may I help you?"

"Hi, Amy, this is Shade."

"Oh, hi. What can I do for you?"

"I need to speak with Sergeant Osbourne."

"He's not in his office right now. Can I take a message?"

I slumped back in my seat. "If you could just ask him to call me, that'd be fine."

"I can do that. What's your number?"

Liam already had my number, but I gave it to her anyway.

"All right, I've got it. Is there anything else I can help you with?"

I thought about it. "Could you tell me if Emma is on patrol tonight?"

Papers rustled as I assumed Amy checked the schedule. "Yes, she is."

"Could I have her cell phone number?" I asked.

Amy hesitated. "I'm not allowed to give that information out. But if you'll hold for a second, I'll call her and ask her to call you."

"W—"

Too late, Amy put me on hold and clicked over to the other line. I cursed and hung up.

"This isn't good. If Emma knows you're looking for her, she'll bolt with the yearbooks," Peasblossom pointed out.

I dug out my keys. "I don't think she's going to destroy them. She loves Stephen enough to lie to him, but I think she's a good enough cop that destroying them would be going too far. She'll probably just hide them."

Peasblossom crawled into my lap and grabbed the zipper on my pouch. "Same problem."

I rubbed my temples, trying to ease the headache I could feel forming. "Liam will never agree to search her stuff if I can't offer proof she's involved. I need physical evidence that will prove Stephen committed the murder and Emma is helping him cover it up."

"What about the wizard?"

I stared at Peasblossom and smacked her hand away from the zipper. "Yes! Yes, Vincent. He has that spell, the one that manifests images of what left behind biological samples."

"He already cast it on the crime scene—what good is it going to do to cast it again?" She tried for the zipper again.

"Not on the crime scene." I put a hand over the pouch and gave her a warning look. "You're not getting any more honey. I have some of that vegetable soup left. You can have some when we get back to the apartment."

"I don't like vegetable soup," Peasblossom whined. She furrowed her brow. "Wait, what apartment?"

"Oliver's. If he can prove Emma was there..."

"Then that might be enough to convince the alpha she's involved," Peasblossom finished. "She's not on the case, so there'd be no reason for her to be there."

I got out of the car and made my way up to Oliver's apartment at a more sedate pace than I'd left it. When I let myself in this time, I stayed in the entryway. I was fairly certain that Vincent's spell would differentiate between a human woman and a witch—at least, I hoped so, since otherwise I'd already contaminated the scene.

Vincent blessedly answered on the first ring. "Aegis Analysts, how can I help you?"

"Vincent, it's Shade."

"Ah, yes, how can I help you?"

His tone was pleasant, but I'd used that voice often enough to know what it meant. He expected me to ask him to do something he didn't want to do, and he intended to refuse and then end the conversation as quickly as possible without offending me. I called it my "how can I help you, Mrs. Harvesty" voice.

"I need your help," I told the wizard.

Vincent took a deep breath. "As I told you before, I am not a detective. I—"

"You analyze crime scenes, yes, and that's what I want you to do."

"Oh. This is another crime, then, unrelated to the Oliver Dale murder?"

I hated to destroy the note of hope in his voice, but there was nothing else for it. "No, it's still the same case. Listen, I need you to come to the victim's apartment and cast that spell from the video, the one that identifies trace evidence. Um, tell me, can it differentiate between a human and a witch?"

"I suppose I could do that. And yes, the spell can identify a witch." Confusion chased some of the hesitation from his voice. "May I ask what it is you expect to find?"

"Someone took something from the apartment, today. Within the last hour, in fact. I need to know who it was."

"As I mentioned earlier, the spell is not that detailed. I can only tell you gender and species. Science, now science could tell you everything. But that in-depth analysis takes time—"

"Yes, I understand, but right now your spell is what I need. I assume you can tell male or female, black or white?"

"Race? Well, yes, I suppose I can."

I said a small prayer of thanks. This had to be enough for Liam. "Excellent, that's exactly what I need. Will you come?"

"Of course." He hesitated. "Dare I ask if Sergeant Osbourne is aware of this request?"

My phone beeped, telling me I had a call on the other line. "He will in a second," I muttered.

"I see. Well then, I will let you attend to our diligent werewolf sergeant, and I will see you at the scene."

"You have the address?"

"I do." He paused, then added, "Good luck."

"I'll need it," I said. I steeled myself, then clicked over to answer the incoming call. "Hello?"

"Why do you need to talk to Emma?"

I leaned against the wall, trying for a casual pose in the hopes I would sound casual. "Sergeant Osbourne, how lovely to hear from you. How are things going with Anthony?"

"Why?" he barked.

I looked at Peasblossom. She shrugged, then followed it with a series of gestures that resembled charades. Or possibly a seizure. I shook my head.

"Well, it's sort of a long story." I eyed Peasblossom, then remembered the soup. I unzipped my pouch and fished around inside for the takeout container I'd taken to go from the café.

"Shade, this is not a joke. One of my officers is missing, and you called here looking for her."

I frowned as I pulled out the evidence bag with Emma's bloody sweatshirt. I'd forgotten about it. "Emma's missing?"

"Her phone is off, so we can't track her GPS. She's supposed to be on patrol, but no one has seen her for the last hour." He took a slow, calming breath. "Tell me why you wanted to call her."

I set the bag down on the floor and nudged it inside, where it wouldn't be seen by any hapless neighbors that might wander by. Abandoning the search for Peasblossom's unwanted dinner, I paced up and down the hall, trying to think of something to say that wouldn't agitate the alpha werewolf further. "I need to see some evidence from Oliver Dale's apartment. I—"

The door at the end of the hall opened and Vincent Aegis walked inside. I stopped and stared. "How did you get here so fast?"

"Gateway."

"How did who get where so fast?" Liam said.

I brushed off my questions concerning whether gateway was a thing or a person and waved a hand at Oliver's apartment. "In there."

Vincent nodded and went inside.

"What evidence?" Liam asked. "Ms. Renard, if you don't tell me what's going on…"

"Okay, fine." I glanced at the apartment, bouncing on my feet as I prayed Vincent's spell would give me results before I got to the end of this conversation. "I…visited Stephen."

Silence fell over the line. Not comforting silence, or even awkward silence. Tense silence. The sort that promises unpleasantness at the end.

"You what?" Liam's voice was deadly calm.

At least he wasn't yelling. That was a good sign, right?

"After I left you, I decided to find Anthony myself. Then things got interesting." I explained my meeting with Mia, my subsequent introduction to Greg, and the unfortunate, if intriguing, events that followed, all leading up to my conversation with Anthony. "After Anthony agreed to turn himself in, I decided it was time to talk to the only suspect I had, to this point, not been permitted to speak to."

"So you violated my orders and spoke to a member of my pack without my presence or permission. An act that violates his rights under the guidelines set down by the Vanguard."

I narrowed my eyes. "Stephen agreed to talk. And besides, as you said, they're more like guidelines than laws."

Liam was silent for a minute. I wasn't sure if it was to calm himself, or to plot my untimely demise. I hoped for the former.

"What did Stephen say?" he asked.

I slid down the wall to sit cross-legged on the carpet. "I thought he would confess," I admitted. "I thought he *did* confess. He kept going on about how Oliver Dale had been a star in high school, how it had gone to his head and twisted him into the jerk everyone's been telling us about, how he was getting worse, more violent. He talked about how there are people who can't give up on someone even when they're a lost cause. He said no one should lose everything because they couldn't give up on someone when everyone else had."

"But he didn't confess."

"No, he didn't. But when I mentioned that I'd looked through Oliver's yearbooks, he panicked. He yelled at me to get out, and suddenly he refused to talk anymore. Which is strange, because when I looked through Oliver's yearbooks, I didn't see Stephen at all."

"Stephen moved to Ohio ten years ago. He attended high school in Michigan."

I frowned. "That doesn't make any sense. Liam, I'm telling you, he went white when I mentioned those yearbooks. And then I came to Oliver's apartment straight after—I mean, I drove here as fast as I could. Those yearbooks are gone."

"And you think Emma took them."

Vincent came out of the apartment, puffs of smoke trailing in his wake. I focused on his face, ignoring all the shapes rising in the trail of his spell and what that meant about all those suspicious stains on the hall carpet.

"Hold on, I'll know for sure in a moment." I looked at Vincent. "What did you find?"

"There are two blood samples on the sweatshirt—female dog and male human."

I stared at him. "What are you talking about?"

He frowned. "The bloody sweatshirt. The one in the evidence bag. Isn't that what you wanted me to inspect?"

"No. No, I meant for you to analyze the apartment itself. I—"

"Well, it was in an *evidence* bag," Vincent said, exasperated. "A bloody sweatshirt in an evidence bag sitting in the murder victim's apartment you called me to. You can see my confusion?"

"Shade, what's going on?" Liam demanded.

I returned the phone to my ear, my mental gears spinning with the new information. "The blood on Emma's sweatshirt wasn't all Gypsy's. It was human. Male."

"Oliver Dale's?"

I looked up at the wizard. "I don't know. Vincent said he can't tell."

Vincent puffed out his chest and grabbed the lapels of his wool coat. "I bloody well can."

"But you said—"

"I said the trace spell didn't work that way. I have other spells, you know. And this is blood we're talking about, full of information, and one of the most ancient—" He stopped waving a hand through the air as if to wipe away the conversation. "Really, Mother Renard." He straightened his spine. "Tell Sergeant Osbourne that the blood on the sweatshirt matches Oliver Dale's blood type. Given time, I can run a DNA analysis and tell you for certain if it's him."

I repeated the information, but my voice sounded like it was coming from far away.

The pieces were falling into place. Details linking, revealing an image that made my stomach roll. I was vaguely aware of

Vincent saying my name, of Liam shouting into the phone. I lowered my hand and let the cell phone sag in my lap.

I knew why Mother Hazel had assigned me this case.

I knew why Stephen had lied to Liam.

And I knew who killed Oliver Dale.

CHAPTER 17

Vincent picked up my phone. I could see his mouth moving, knew he was talking to Liam, but I couldn't hear what he was saying over the rush of blood in my ears.

"Emma's sweatshirt is covered in Oliver Dale's blood," I mumbled. "She was in the forest that night." I closed my eyes. "She carries the same gun as Stephen."

"Don't rush ahead of yourself, Shade," Liam said. Vincent had switched it to speaker phone, so the alpha's voice sounded tinny and foreign. "Emma wasn't wearing the sweatshirt that night. She and Stephen were dating—it's possible she left the sweatshirt in his car."

I stared at the phone. "You're quick to defend her considering she just became an alternate suspect to your wolf you're so certain is innocent."

"I've been a cop for a long time, Shade. I don't jump to conclusions—no matter who's in the hot seat."

"You're right." I stood up, a strange numbness crawling over my body. "We need more evidence."

"Shade, what are you doing? Vincent, what is she doing?"

"She's standing up," Vincent said. He watched me as if he

expected me to break into hysterics at any moment, and he kept his voice calm, careful.

I took the phone from his hand and switched off the speaker before putting it to my ear. "I'm going to get more evidence."

"No," Liam said. "Just come to the station. I'm sending people out to search for Emma, and Blake and Sonar are heading to Stephen's house. We'll find her, and we'll get answers."

"See you soon." I hung up.

Vincent put a hand on my shoulder as if to steady me. "Are you all right?"

I tried to smile, but my mouth was too brittle. "I'm fine. I have to go to the reservation. Liam wants to... He wants to speak with me."

The wizard still looked uncertain, and he hadn't let go of my shoulder. He glanced at the apartment, the bloody evidence, then back at me. "If I might trouble you for a ride? I'd like to speak with the sergeant as well."

He was only saying that for an excuse to ride with me, so I must have looked worse than I felt. It didn't matter, though. He could come along if he wanted. "Sure."

I started walking without waiting for him, listening idly as he scrambled to retrieve the bloody sweatshirt and lock the apartment before racing down the hallway to catch up to me. Peasblossom didn't say a word, but I wasn't sure if she was just giving me space, or if she was as upset as I was.

Emma did it. Emma killed him.

Vincent remained silent as we got in the car, but the need to say something, to ask me if I was all right—again—hung heavy between us. I resisted the urge to warn him into silence, the very strong desire to use magic to ensure his silence.

Barely.

I didn't want to talk about it. I didn't want to think about the victim, and I didn't want to think about the murderer. I didn't want to think of Mother Hazel and her deal, or the sadistic reason behind my assignment to this case. I just wanted to drive, in silence. Drive to the forest to get the last piece of evidence.

Emma did it. Emma killed him.

A deep breath was my only warning that Vincent intended to start a conversation I wasn't willing to have. I spoke first.

"I have a cat."

A pause followed my announcement. Vincent fidgeted in his seat, twiddling his thumbs in his lap as he struggled for something to say. "Um, a cat, you say?"

"Yes. I didn't want a cat, but a woman from my village brought him to me."

"That's…nice?"

I stared at the road ahead, trying not to see Emma's face, not to think of the moment that would come all too soon. When we would confront her with what we knew. What she'd done. When she'd have to be taken away.

I gritted my teeth. "No, it's not nice. She brought him to me because she could tell he was in pain. She could tell there was something wrong with him."

"Always sad to see a pet suffer."

His tone suggested he wasn't just talking about the cat. I shoved thoughts of Gypsy away, tightening my grip on the steering wheel to center myself in the present. I didn't want to think about what Oliver had done to the poor dog, what he'd intended to do. What Emma had saved her from at the cost of her own future.

"A year ago, one of her cats died. Agnes. Mrs. Harvesty has a lot of cats, she always has, but Agnes was special. She'd been a favorite, and Mrs. Harvesty took her loss very hard. If I were a better witch, I'd have realized how hard she took it. But I didn't understand until she brought me Majesty."

"The cat's name is Majesty?" Vincent said. "That sets a rather bad precedent."

"Yes, I explained that to her. Lost cause, I'm afraid. In any case, unbeknownst to me, Mrs. Harvesty sought out a magic user to make certain Majesty did not suffer the same fate as Agnes."

"The same fate being…?"

"Death."

Vincent stopped fussing with his hands, his brow furrowing. "Well, that's impossible. Death is a certainty for everything but an immortal. And according to some, even immortals will eventually meet their end. I see no way for her to work out an exemption for this cat."

"All existential arguments aside, Mrs. Harvesty found a sorceress who agreed to give her what she wanted."

"What?" Shock pulled his jaw down, leaving the wizard gaping at me like an open nutcracker doll. "She hired a sorceress to…to make the cat immortal?

"That's what Mrs. Harvesty thought she was doing, but truth be told, I don't know what she did. I know that somehow the sorceress bound Majesty's life force, twisted it to feed in on itself. He's a kitten, and he'll stay a kitten. Whether it will eventually kill him is another matter."

Vincent's face blanched. "That is not good. A life force is a powerful energy, and it is meant to grow and change. To prevent it from manifesting itself, bind it in such a way… I cannot think what such a catastrophic spell would cost."

"Nothing."

He turned in his seat, facing me. There was no more fidgeting, no more uncertainty. For the first time, I caught a glimpse of a powerful wizard. A serious wizard who knew when something was very, very wrong. "Nothing?"

I nodded.

That shut him up. For a minute.

"Dresden is a small village, is it not?" he asked.

"Yes. Though we are home to the world's largest basket, so…tourists."

He didn't comment on that. "And Mother Hazel is…well

known. I believe the vast majority of the magical world was aware when she took you on as an apprentice. An apprenticeship that ended three years ago, if I recall?"

I gripped the steering wheel and made a conscious effort not to press harder on the gas pedal. "Yes. Though why my life is of interest to the greater magic community, I don't know." And I didn't like it.

If I'd been looking at Vincent, I might have been able to read the facial expression that was there and gone before I could turn. As it was, it looked like another wince in my peripheral vision.

"I'm sorry. Your life is your own, and I can understand why you'd prefer for your private life to remain private. But I must ask… Have you considered the possibility that whoever cast that spell on Majesty may have surmised that you would take possession of the cat? You being the village witch, and Mrs. Harvesty being a woman who loved her pets enough to notice when something was wrong?"

My jaw ached, and I forced myself to unclench my teeth. "Yes."

"Then you understand the danger of keeping it. That kitten is very much like a shaken soda bottle. Eventually, it will burst. And I'm not sure what that will mean for you if you're near him when it happens."

I'd thought this would be a safer topic, but now my nerves were knotting themselves into tiny bundles of pain, stabbing me in meandering lines down my arms and legs. "I was hoping you might have a look at him," I said. "Help me figure out a way to unravel the spell."

"If Mother Hazel could not do it, there is little chance I could be of help."

It was a refreshing thing for a wizard to admit to his limits so quickly. But it wasn't what I'd wanted to hear. "Mother Hazel didn't even try. She said it wasn't for her to do."

Vincent opened his mouth, then snapped it closed. He was silent for a few minutes.

"It must be very hard. Having her as your mentor. The old ones, they can be…frustrating in their perceptiveness. I'd imagine she knows more about your future then she's willing to share. Doling out little cryptic tidbits just often enough to keep you from finding peace in the present?"

Some little part of me relaxed, and I leaned my head back against my seat. "If I may say, Vincent, it's very gratifying to find someone who understands."

"I can imagine. I will examine the kitten. But I don't want to get your hopes up. In the grand scheme of things, I'm a small cog."

"Understood."

We passed the entrance to the ranger station, and he frowned, turning in his seat. "Where are we going?

"To the crime scene. There's something I need to see."

I drove as close as I could to the area near the crime scene and parked on the side of the road. The road was dark, so I turned on the hazard lights. No sense causing a crash because someone couldn't tell my car from the road in this dim light. Before opening the door, I unzipped my pouch and reached inside.

"I should mention before we get out that there's a possibility we will encounter a dream shard."

Vincent froze with his hand on the door handle. "I'm sorry? Did you say dream shard?"

I nodded, pulling out a roll of gauze, a bag of jelly beans, and a charger for some forgotten device. "You recall our little meeting with Arianne Monet at the pub?" I wanted to mention the way he'd fled like a coward upon her arrival, but held my tongue. No need to be petty.

He shifted uncomfortably, probably remembering his behavior without my reminder. "Yes."

"Well, she's still rather cross with me over a minor transgression a few weeks ago." I found the object I was looking for and pulled the wrapped package from my pouch. I peeled away the soft cotton to reveal the strange bracer Gunderson had given me. The brown leather shone dully in the moonlight, golden wheels and coils radiating gentle warmth.

Vincent leaned forward, staring at the bracer. "What is that?"

"A gift. It holds solar energy." I slipped the bracer over my arm, relieved to feel a divot beneath the leather pressing against my aura. I'd charged it in the car earlier that day during the drive to the Rocky River Reservation, and I'd worried putting it in the dark, enchanted confines of my pouch might cause the solar energy to dissipate. But it was still there, warm and persistent.

The air in the car hummed with energy as Vincent coated himself with enchanted armor. I followed his lead, casting the same spell on myself. The magic tingled against my flesh, almost distracting me from the weight at the top of my spine. I groped behind my neck, pulling a wriggling Peasblossom out of my shirt. "You stay here. I don't want you to get hurt."

"No, I want to help!" she squeaked as I held her by her dress, her body spinning as her struggles caused her to twist herself round in my grasp.

"Peasblossom, please." I cupped her in my palm, waiting for her legs to stop scrabbling for purchase. She ceased struggling and crossed her arms, glaring up at me in defiance. "I couldn't bear it if anything happened to you. I'll be right back, I promise. I'm only checking one thing."

She looked away but nodded. "Fine."

I kissed her head, then set her on the armrest between the seats. After a second of hesitation, I dug a packet of honey out of my pouch and laid it beside her in silent offering. "Shall we?" I asked Vincent.

He nodded, fingers fluttering as he smoothed down his robe before exiting the car. Night had fallen, wrapping the forest in darkness and deepening the shadows. I dipped into my magic again, then waved an arm outward, flinging balls of red energy before me. They burst into light, creating a path of dancing lanterns that moved before me as I walked. Vincent grabbed his robe with both hands, sending a wash of more tingling energy over the soft threads. A glow melted over the article of clothing, becoming increasingly bright with each passing second until it illuminated our surroundings in a twenty-foot circle.

"What do you hope to find?" he asked.

I scanned the trees ahead as we entered the forest, looking for a sign of the yellow police tape that should still mark the crime scene. We were right down the road from Gunderson's shop, so it had to be close. "I was thinking about the physical evidence. The red welts on the victim's palms, the .40 bullet, and now the victim's blood on the sweatshirt Emma brought Gypsy to the hospital in. All this time, we assumed Emma left the park before Oliver was murdered, but that's not possible. Oliver was killed while he was close enough to Gypsy for his blood to end up in her fur."

"I picked up traces of Emma at the crime scene, but I disregarded her because she was patrolling, and I would have expected to find traces of her. There were none on the body."

"So she didn't touch the body. But she touched Gypsy. And Gypsy's injuries were consistent with hanging."

Vincent made a small sound of protest in his throat. "Emma would never hang a dog to give herself an excuse to leave."

"I don't think she did anything of the sort." I spotted the yellow crime scene tape and focused my attention on the large tree at the edge of the ravine. One branch was low enough...

"Can you give me a boost?" I asked.

Vincent arched an eyebrow, but obligingly knelt down and formed a stirrup with his hands. I stepped into his grip and heaved myself up to look at the limb. A stripe carved into the bark confirmed my suspicion.

"He tried to hang her."

"Who?"

"Gypsy. Oliver tried to hang her." I got down, studying the

crime scene with fresh eyes. "She must have found him while it was happening. Maybe she warned him to stop and he didn't. So she shot him."

Before Vincent could respond, something brushed against my spine. A phantasmal touch with a physical weight that kept me from disregarding it as a breeze, or a figment of my imagination. A shiver ran through me with enough force that I stumbled forward, my back aching as if it'd been coated in a three-inch layer of solid ice. A scream blossomed in my throat, and I choked to keep it down. Fear coalesced within me, an aura so strong that it should have been visible to the naked eye. Screaming would only feed that fear, strengthen it.

Vincent whirled around, his hand sweeping out toward the dream shard. A burst of fractured light exploded from his finger-tips in a rainbow of colors, leaping at the creature like a living sparkler.

The dream shard had no body, at least nothing visible. Like most incorporeal nightmares, it undulated and changed, more of a shadow you saw in your peripheral vision, only to disappear if you looked directly at it. The only parts of it that seemed solid were the bright silver eyes and the stark white teeth and claws where its mouth and paws should be. The nightmare roared, and the sound echoed not just on the physical plane, but the astral plane. It boomed inside my head, driving me back a step. I raised my hand, curling my fingers into a fist. I aimed the bracer at the dream shard, centering it on the shadowy mass under the shining white fangs.

Brilliant gold sunlight pulsed outward in a solid beam, striking the beast in its chest. It screamed again, writhing in the air.

Crimson energy shot like an elongated fireball from Vincent's palm, exploding against the dream shard in near-perfect unison with the sunlight from my bracer. Orange and yellow sparks rained over its body and it opened its jaws in another scream. "It's dazed," Vincent yelled. "Hit it again!"

I didn't realize I'd covered my ears to block out that horrible screaming. I forced my arms down and flexed my will. More golden sunlight flooded into the small tube at the top of the bracer, and I readied my second shot. The dream shard's midsection was no longer so intangible. Blood and blistered flesh hovered where my first attack had hit it. I aimed for that wound.

Something rolled out from the dream shard, as if it had thrown a piece of its own body. I backed away, my attention locked on the piece of black shadow as it continued toward me, firming into something more tangible than shadow. Dark streaks spread out from a round body, bending into two rows of segmented legs before landing on the ground. Four legs on each side. Fur covered the creature in a rolling wave, and the light from our spells glinted off eight beady eyes. It reared up, raising two thick, fur-covered fangs.

Instinct made me react before my brain had realized the terrifying reality. Sweat poured down my temples. My heart stopped, my entire body going rigid with breath-stealing fear. I couldn't move.

"Shade, it's a trick! It's not there! There's nothing there!"

The tarantula scuttled toward me, moving faster than anything that big had a right to. There was no web, no trap, but I couldn't move, couldn't scream, couldn't even breathe. My world narrowed down to nothing but that enormous furry body, those thick fangs, those glittering black eyes. It was every nightmare I'd ever had all rolled into a single monster.

And then it was on me.

"Shade!"

Peasblossom, her tiny voice so high with fear that it was more a scream than a word. Something fell into my hand, something plastic and wet. A gun. A squirt gun. My fingers seized it, instinctively tightened, pulled the trigger. A spray of water flew from the nozzle and struck the tarantula square in the face even as it reared up to plunge its fangs into my body.

Smoke hissed as the holy water burrowed into the shadowy body, and the creature scuttled back, making a sound unlike anything I'd ever heard. Vincent shouted something I couldn't quite make out over the sound of my erratic heartbeat, and purple light fired in a bolt of pure energy. Something slammed into me, Vincent's body, and we tumbled to the side and over the edge.

Rocks and sticks took turns bludgeoning and stabbing me as we rolled down to land with a painful, bone-jarring thud on the forest floor. The scent of damp leaves and rich earth filled my nostrils, helping to distract me from the image of the tarantula burned into my mind's eye.

Vincent stood and looked up at where the dream shard hissed and strained. Beneath the white glow of its fangs, I could make out an anchor made of purple light, sitting where the dream shard's body would be, holding it to that spot. Vincent screamed. Crystalline gold light exploded in a cone of sound, enveloping the dream shard, but not touching me where I lay behind the wizard. The dream shard crumpled, fangs dipping toward the ground as if it had bowed its head.

Fear still tightened the nerves in my body, making every move a fight. It was like trying to stand with a layer of iron chainmail draped over every limb.

So this was it, then. I'd answered Mother Hazel's challenge, taken the case. My bastard of a victim had been killed by a ranger saving a dog's life, and now it was my duty to put her behind bars. The justice I'd fought so hard for was to see a woman locked up because she'd refused to give up on a lost cause. Because a man hadn't shown one iota of human decency. Now I would die here too. Die at the summoned hands of a monster created by a sorceress who thought a little collateral damage to her hotel was worth more than my life.

Anger rose, red hot and welcome. I got to my feet, muscles trembling with the effort. I didn't fight the pain. I welcomed it. I focused on every bruise, every cut. I wallowed in it until the pain fed into my anger. My fury. "Let it go," I said.

"Don't be insane," Vincent snapped, his eyes wide. "We have to run!"

"Let it go!" I screamed.

I didn't know if he released the spell, or if the dream shard broke free. But it flowed down the hill, shadowy form undulating, only the fangs and claws making a sound as they clicked over the stony side of the ravine.

"You are mine," I screamed. My anger, my fear roared in my voice. "*My* nightmare. *My* dream. You are mine, not hers." I dragged in a deep breath, opening my arms as the dream shard fell on me, bracing for that wave of icy-cold fear. "And I'm taking you *back*."

Cold. Cold and ice, burrowing deep in my gut. Unlike a physical creature, the dream shard didn't tear me open so much as it plunged itself inside me, piercing not flesh, but spirit. It wasn't my skull that threatened to crack under the pressure of its fangs, but my psyche. Me.

I clenched my teeth and threw my magic around the tangle of emotions, the shreds of my mind as the creature screamed and clawed at my thoughts. There was a split second when it seemed to realize what was happening, when it understood that I wasn't fighting, wasn't trying to push it away. When it realized I was pulling it closer. Deeper inside me.

I felt the moment it realized what was happening. I felt it stop pressing forward, felt it try to retreat, to disentangle itself.

But I had it now. Arianne had used my fear, my dream to create this monster. They were mine to take if I could handle them. If I could face that much of my own fear. And so I pulled, and I held fast, and I swallowed it back. Images washed over me, terrifying images. The black cat that had started it all, the nightmare Arianne had farmed for the seed to grow the dream shard, stared at me with glowing eyes, flashing sharp fangs before leaping inside of me, splashing into my soul. I felt a feeling of completeness, of being utterly full, almost…content.

And then nothing.

CHAPTER 18

Something warm and heavy pressed against my back. A pleasant buzzing sensation vibrated against my spine, reverberating throughout my body like a soft, steady massage, seeking and destroying every pain, every knot of tension. A giant, spiky ball of ice lay trapped deep inside my core, and every breath I took pressed shards of cold into my lungs. I shrank away from that cold, that pain. Some instinct told me it was going to get worse. There was no escaping it, not even in sleep. Still, unconsciousness seemed better than waking. I tried to burrow further into the darkness, trying to hide under the shadows, away from the growing light.

"Her breathing changed. I think she's waking up."

Liam's voice. I squeezed my eyes shut tighter, fighting consciousness even as my senses stirred. I didn't want to wake up. I wanted to sleep, to press closer to that warm sensation behind me until the pleasant buzz drove deeper, broke apart the aching rock of frozen pain.

"Shade, wake up."

Liam's voice again. My brain shook off the last vestiges of sleep, rousing my body with the unwelcome realization that the warm weight pressed against me was the werewolf alpha. A tinge of awkwardness poisoned my warm, buzzy feeling, but not so much that I was willing to give it up yet. If I wasn't awake, I couldn't be embarrassed. I tried to go back to sleep.

"Ms. Renard, can you hear me?"

A second voice, also familiar. Vincent. Vincent Aegis, the wizard. A memory flashed through my mind, the wizard's face contorted with determination as magic flowed down his arm in a show of rainbow light. Amusement drew me further into wakefulness. The lab rat wizard could claim he was only an analyst, but he had power.

Lots of it.

"Shade?"

This time Liam's voice held the tone of a parent asking if you were really sick or just wanted to stay home from school—gentle and concerned with a hint of warning. I sighed and let my eyes flutter open. The light lanced my corneas, punishing me for keeping them closed for so long. I hissed and closed them again, giving myself to the count of ten before I opened them a second time.

"I'm fine," I croaked.

My voice did not sound fine. I blinked, trying to discern whether that had been my voice or if someone had spoken for me. Someone who was a hundred years old. Someone who hadn't had a non-alcoholic drink in decades. Perhaps who gargled broken glass and lemon juice for giggles.

"I sound awful."

Yep, sounded just as bad the second time. Liam didn't move, letting me stay pressed against him. "You sound good considering we thought you were dead."

Well, that didn't sound good. I blinked, trying to force my blurry vision to clear. I was in the back of an SUV. The light that had seemed so bright, so terribly intrusive, was only the vehicle's dome light. Outside, the moon shone soft and silver, almost full, but not quite.

Vincent knelt in the passenger seat, squeezed into the gap between the seats so he could offer me a bottle of water. I stared at the cap, debating whether it would be worth the effort to twist the damn thing off. Vincent seemed to read my mind. He unscrewed the cap, then handed me the open bottle. I took it, gulping down the cool fluid in a less-than-ladylike fashion.

"And this?" he offered.

I didn't take my mouth from the bottle of water as I eyed the cup in his other hand.

"A healing potion," he explained. "You suffered a rather bad beating. I did what I could, but I daresay you'll be sore." Tension drew deep creases around his eyes. "Not all of your wounds are physical."

I finished the water, ignoring the way my insides now had the uncomfortable sensation of floating in my stomach. Unsure how much room I had left, I sipped the healing potion more slowly.

"What was that thing that attacked you?" Liam asked. "I've never seen anything like it."

"A dream shard." I froze, my heart leaping into my throat. The healing potion dipped in my hand, almost spilling over the back seat of the SUV as I swiveled my head from side to side. "Peasblossom?"

"Right here!"

A tiny weight rocketed into my neck from out of nowhere, little hands wrapping around it in a ferocious hug. My shoulders slumped in relief, and I laughed, patting her back with one finger of my free hand. "Oh, thank the Goddess you're okay."

"You scared me," she whispered.

"I'm sorry." I stroked a finger between her wings. "I scared myself too."

"What's a dream shard?" Liam asked.

"A dream shard is—" I twisted around to answer him, then stopped. My cheeks warmed. "Sergeant?"

The werewolf alpha lay beside me, curled around my body to accommodate the somewhat cramped quarters of the vehicle. His brown hair was tousled, and he was shirtless. A broad expanse of tan skin called my eye down, noting the light dusting of hair over broad pectoral muscles. I had the odd, random thought that I would have expected a werewolf to be hairier.

Liam followed my gaze down to his bare chest and shrugged. "You were shaking like a paint mixer after whatever you did to that thing. When I picked you up to carry you here, you quieted." He tilted his head, his gaze taking on a considering quality as he pushed himself into a sitting position. "It was interesting, almost like you were pack. I took a chance and treated you like I would treat an injured shifter."

It wasn't until he sat up that I noticed he held something in his palm. It was the small black stone he'd had in his office, the one Vincent had given him so he could determine if I were really trying to steal his energy. I gave the stone a pointed look.

Again Liam followed my gaze. "You weren't lying," he said. There wasn't so much as a hint of apology in his voice. "Stone never so much as sparkled."

"I'm surprised you were willing to give me the skin-to-skin treatment, considering what you thought I might do." As soon as I said "skin-to-skin," I realized there was a definite draft against my spine. I patted the back of my shirt, or rather, what remained of it. My fingers met skin and shreds of cotton.

"You were almost dead, and on my territory," Liam said evenly. "I would have let you have some of my energy if it meant keeping you alive."

His voice still held that considering tone, as if he were still thinking about my reaction to his touch. "I had the same reaction to Stephen," I blurted out.

Both Vincent and Liam raised their eyebrows at that. The

blush I'd been lucky enough to avoid roared into my cheeks in a rush of heat, and I scowled. I drew my magic, ignoring the prickles of discomfort that spiraled out from that damn cold still huddled inside me, and a spell sizzled over my clothing, knitting it together. Another wave took care of the dirt and grime.

Didn't help the blush, though.

"A dream shard is a piece of a nightmare," Vincent said, picking up my explanation and blessedly taking the attention off me. "When an individual has a vivid nightmare, it takes on enough substance that an enterprising magic user with the requisite knowledge can tear off a piece and animate it. The resulting creature, a dream shard, can then be ordered about—depending on the power of whomever created it."

"That would be Arianne Monet," I said.

Vincent winced. "If that is the case, may I suggest you try to make amends before she gets it in her head to try again? The chances you could absorb a second dream shard are quite—"

"What?" I blinked, not quite processing that last part. "What do you mean, absorb a dream shard?"

"Well, that's what you did. Together we weakened it, but the creature..." His eyes went distant as he looked into the past. "It was impressive. Even weakened as it was, it went after you." The respect in his gaze chased away some of the cold inside me. "I have never had the pleasure of witnessing a person overcome a dream shard in that manner. To have faced your fear, beaten it, even when it had the added power of someone else's magic... There are few who have the courage."

I looked away, suddenly uncomfortable with the praise. "It wasn't courage. It was anger."

"Anger at me?" Liam asked. He rooted around under the blanket we were lying on and fished out his white T-shirt.

I met his gaze, trying very hard not to stare as he pulled his shirt on over his bare chest. "No. No, not at you. At Mother Hazel." I gritted my teeth and took a deep breath to force myself to calm. "I figured out why she offered me that deal. Why she set the terms she did."

"Oh?"

"Yes." I rubbed a hand over my face. "It was Emma. Emma killed Oliver Dale."

Liam tensed, then let out a slow breath. "It was the dog, wasn't it? She found Oliver hurting the dog."

"Hanging her, yes."

"Bastard."

"That's how he got the red welts on his hands. He caught Gypsy and got her leash over a low-hanging branch."

"Why?" Vincent asked, looking a little green. "Why hang her? I don't understand the urge to hurt a dog period, but hanging… That was a lot of effort to go through."

"Humans can be monsters too," I said quietly. "Stephen was right. Oliver was a very angry man. Life didn't treat him the way he thought it should, and someone was going to have to pay for that."

Vincent tapped the healing potion, a silent reminder for me to finish it. I gulped the rest down in one swallow.

"And that made you angry?" he asked.

"No. I'm angry because this was all a test." I tightened my fist around the vial. "I've wanted to be a private investigator for so long. Mother Hazel never approved, never understood. I finally did it, started my practice, made contacts. And as soon as it seemed like I was about to make it, she poisoned it. Made sure I'd get a case that would hurt no matter what happened. Either I'd fail to solve it and prove I couldn't hack it as an investigator…"

"Or you'd solve it and have to punish a good person for killing a bad one," Liam finished. He grabbed his uniform shirt and slid it on, strong hands working to fasten the buttons. "Yeah, it's one of the less pleasant aspects of the job. But it's over now."

I clenched my jaw so tight it hurt. "No, it's not."

Liam and Vincent shared a look. Then Liam looked at me.

"Shade, if you want to stay until we find Emma, I won't stop you. But I can handle it from here. You solved the case. For real. Mother Hazel can't argue that."

I let myself watch him roll up his sleeves, trying to distract myself with the pleasant sight of muscular forearms. "I don't have to find Emma. I know where she is."

Vincent sat up straighter and hit his head on the low ceiling. "You do? How?"

"Romance is always relevant," I said quietly. "She's with Stephen."

"No, she isn't," Liam said. "Blake and Sonar are there, and they've searched the place. Sonar is the best tracker we have. Emma's not there."

"Yes, she is. Stephen's the one she called after she killed a man. Stephen's the one that ordered her to stay quiet. Stephen's the one that convinced her to take the yearbooks so I wouldn't figure out the connection was between Emma and Oliver. She's there."

"And how do you think she's hiding from a werewolf?" Liam asked.

I leaned against the side of the vehicle and gestured for him to take the wheel. "Take me there, and I'll show you."

I could feel Vincent and Liam sharing looks over my head, but I didn't care. The ice left behind when I'd absorbed the dream shard provided the perfect host to incubate my growing ire toward my mentor. I would see this through, though. I would confront Emma and Stephen. I would follow the case to the end.

And then I would speak to Mother Hazel.

The drive to Stephen's was too long and too short. By the time we arrived, I was ready to fly out of the car, if only to escape the damned sympathy radiating off the two men. Poor little witch, wanted to be the knight in shining armor and ended up the executioner instead. No big, bad guy to chase down, tackle into the mud, and drag off to a well-deserved cell. Only a woman who couldn't watch a dog die. And the man who loved her enough to take the blame.

Liam knocked on the door, and Blake answered. His gaze flicked from Liam to me, his head tilted in question. Beside him, Sonar looked just as curious.

"Emma is here," Liam told him.

Blake frowned, but stepped aside so we could enter. "Sergeant, I've looked. There's no sign of her." He gestured to his canine partner. "Sonar can't find her either."

Liam scented the air as he came in. The living room was empty, so I assumed Stephen was being held deeper in the house. I looked at the couch where I'd been sitting what felt like an eternity ago. Stephen really was a good cop. Even when he'd thought I knew, he never said. He never used a pronoun, never spoke in a way that suggested he wasn't talking about himself. He hadn't spoken to anything I didn't say outright. And I'd responded with the same hypothetical tone, trying not to sound accusatory, trying to give him space. What a dance that had been. I hadn't even heard the music.

"I can smell her, but it's faint," Liam said finally. He looked at me. "No more than I'd expect, considering she's dating Stephen."

"And that's what they counted on," I said, my voice dull. I looked away from the couch, tearing my thoughts from that earlier conversation so I could draw on my magic. I poured silver over the room in a wave and watched it trickle over the floor, probing at the walls. Nothing.

I stalked into the next room, throwing out an arm to force the silver energy ahead of me. Movement to the right down the hallway told me Stephen was in the den. I ignored that room and entered a bedroom instead. The magic frothed like an ocean wave, licking up a wall beside the bed. A trace of pale white light outlined a large rectangle on the wall. A doorway.

"There," I said, pointing.

Liam followed my gesture, leaning closer as he knocked. A

hollow sound answered him, and he pressed his lips into a grim line. "Come out, Emma."

Silence.

"I can hear you breathing, Emma," Liam said, his ear close to the wall. "It's okay. Come out."

I thought I heard a sob. Then a mechanism on the other side clicked, and a section of wall swung open. Emma stood in the small panic room, her eyes swollen from crying. She was still wearing her ranger's uniform, though it was rumpled and creased. She gripped four yearbooks to her chest, her knuckles pale, as if she'd been holding them so long that she'd forgotten about them.

"Come on," Liam said quietly.

I forced myself to face Emma. I'd built the case against her, so I should have to look at her, knowing she'd go to jail now, or worse.

She swallowed hard. "I'm sorry. I wanted to tell you."

"I know." I looked away before I started crying too. "You tried to tell me."

"He made me promise not to say anything." She clutched the books harder to her chest. "It was all just a nightmare."

I knew the feeling. We all slogged through the house to the den, none of us in a terrible hurry. Stephen tensed as soon as he saw Emma, rising out of his chair as though lifted by strings.

"Don't move," Liam told him.

Stephen gritted his teeth, but obeyed the order. Emma dropped the yearbooks, and no one stopped her when she ran to Stephen and threw herself into his arms.

"I'm sorry," she said, sobbing. "I'm so sorry."

Stephen wrapped his arms around her and held her as if he'd never let her go. "It's all right," he said. "It's all right. Everything will be okay."

"How?" Blake asked, staring at Emma in bewilderment. "Where was she?"

"Behind a wall to a hidden room." I bent down and scooped up a yearbook. "I'm guessing kaava musk."

"Kaava what?"

I looked up at Emma. "Your grandmother taught you how to hide from werewolves. Yes?"

Emma nodded without taking her face out of Stephen's shirt.

Every man in the room went still at the word *werewolf*, except for Stephen.

"You…know?" Liam asked carefully, as if there were still a chance he'd misunderstood.

"She knows. She always knew." I flipped through the yearbook and found what I was looking for. "Nadège Watson?"

"Emma is my middle name," she said. "I go by Emma because no one can pronounce my real name."

I looked at the picture. No wonder I hadn't recognized her. Different first name, and she was at least fifty pounds heavier, wearing thick makeup and clothes a size too small. Above her picture was the word "pushover." I showed the page to Liam. Then I looked at Stephen. "You were talking about Emma. She's the one who tried to see the good in him, who wouldn't give up no matter what."

He nodded, rubbing small circles on Emma's back. "He took advantage."

Emma pulled her head from Stephen's chest and took a shuddering breath. Stephen tried to hold on to her, but she stepped out of his arms. "It's my fault." Tears fell down her cheeks. "I'm so sorry, Stephen."

"It's not your fault," Stephen said gruffly. "It was never your fault."

"Yes, it was." She looked at Liam. "I've known Oliver since we were kids. His mom died when he was young, and my mom used to babysit him when his dad worked." She looked from me to Liam. "Oliver's father wasn't a bad man. He just had trouble connecting emotionally. The only time he ever seemed comfortable showing affection toward his son was when Oliver would succeed at something. An A on a test, or a touchdown in football." She sighed. "Even fights at school. If Oliver won, his dad heaped on the praise. It's no wonder he got so obsessed with winning."

"He must have gotten good at football," I added.

"Yeah, he did. And you know what? He was happy in high school. He wasn't…nice, but he was happy." Emma crossed her arms over her chest. "He got a scholarship to college for football. But…"

"But being the best in a small-town high school isn't the same as making it on a college team," Liam guessed.

"He did fine," Emma said softly. "But he wasn't the best. He wasn't the star anymore, not even in the top three. And to Oliver, if he wasn't the best…" She closed her eyes. "He quit. And when he came home, he was so…angry. It was as if he felt the world owed him. Like he expected people to treat him the same way they treated him in high school. His dad got him that job at the insurance company. And he did really well."

I almost told her about how he'd undermined Mia, taken credit for other people's work whenever he could. But I didn't. It didn't matter now.

"Anyway, one night I got a call to break up a bar fight. This was before I transferred here to the rangers. It was Oliver. He'd started an all-out brawl with some college football kid, gave him a broken nose and three bruised ribs. Oliver's dad had died a few weeks before, and I…" Her voice grew even quieter. "I talked the kid out of pressing charges."

Stephen stepped closer, not touching her, but offering support. Emma fisted her hands and took a determined breath.

"I tried to help him. I thought if I could show him I was still his friend, then maybe he would let me in. Maybe he would understand he wasn't alone."

"So you helped him out. Got him out of trouble." I pushed away thoughts of how many other victims she might have talked out of pressing charges. How many people Oliver had hurt and gotten away with it.

She wrapped her arms around herself. "It was a mistake."

"Tell me what happened," Liam said.

She stared into the distance. "When Anthony told me Oliver was in the forest looking for his dog, I knew he had a right to be scared. I had to confiscate his gun and send him home, because I knew if he found Oliver…" She shook her head. "I knew what he'd probably find. And I was right. When I found Oliver, he was holding on to Gypsy's leash, watching her choke to death. I shouted at him to stop."

Her voice broke. Stephen eased closer, making sure she knew he was there, that she felt him.

"He started to lower her to the ground, but then he turned, saw it was me." Her eyes took on a haunted look, showing too much white. "He… He *laughed*. He said I wouldn't stop him. I never stopped him. I pointed my gun at him, ordered him to stop again. He… He said I'd never choose a dog's life over his. Then he pulled on the leash. All I could hear was poor Gypsy, gagging, trying to breathe." Her voice rose. "I shot him. I shot him. I had to stop him; it was *my* responsibility to stop him. If I hadn't helped him before, if I hadn't let him get away with… I knew he was escalating!"

Her voice rose in pitch, more panic thinning her voice.

"His blood sprayed over Gypsy," I said, trying to keep my voice calm. "He dropped her and she fell."

Emma nodded, swiping at her tears. "She was hurt. And Oliver was dead. I didn't know what to do. I called Stephen."

Stephen lifted his chin. "I told her to take Gypsy to the animal hospital. I made her promise not to tell anyone, to pretend she found Gypsy with her leash caught. I warned her not to say anything about Oliver."

"You ate the body to hide the gunshot wound," Blake guessed. His body language changed, became defensive. Ready for a fight.

"Yeah." Stephen shrugged. "I thought I could find another predator to finish the body off."

"To hide the evidence of your saliva on the body." Vincent nodded. "And you didn't wash the blood off your own face because you were trying to draw out predators."

"But you didn't count on the kid returning to look for the dog," Liam said. "He found the body and called it in. Then I arrived before you found a predator to take the fall."

Stephen nodded. "I swear, I thought it was time for that barghest to feed again."

A low growl crawled out of Liam's throat. "Stupid," he spat. "You almost lost your life over this. Do you understand that? The Vanguard would have arrested you."

"I couldn't let Emma go to jail because she shot that bastard," Stephen said, his voice low with the edge of a snarl.

"There were other ways! She could have pled down. Extenuating circumstances, defense of another life—"

"A dog's life," Stephen snapped. "Even with extenuating circumstances, she would have gone to jail for five years, minimum. She doesn't deserve that."

"And now she'll go for longer because she covered it up!"

Stephen slid an arm around Emma and pulled her against him. Emma stared into space as if watching a replay of that night, watching it all happen again.

"No," Stephen said. "You can't turn her in to the humans. There's no explaining what happened."

"You and I both know they'll chalk the predation up to a coyote or some such nonsense," Liam said flatly. "Reports will be adjusted. Nothing about the original crime is too hard to explain."

"She's one of ours," Stephen said, his voice gruff. "Shifter or not, she's pack."

Liam shoved a hand through his hair. He looked at Emma,

and there was real sorrow in his eyes. "I know it feels that way. But she's human. She's out of my jurisdiction."

Stephen tightened his hold. "No. This isn't right. She wanted to confess. I wouldn't let her."

"I know." Liam shook his head. "You know how this has to end."

Emma nodded. "I'm ready."

I felt like I would throw up. This wasn't how it was supposed to go. She didn't deserve this. Neither of them did.

Emma took a step forward, then stopped. "Stephen is free to go now, right?" She looked at me. "The collar?"

"Stephen will answer for lying." Liam let out a deep breath and nodded at me. "But you can remove the collar. I don't need help to discipline him for this."

The cold inside me radiated out, as if my body had turned brittle and would splinter into a thousand pieces. This was not what I wanted. Not what I'd expected. I shuffled over to Stephen and touched the collar, unlocking it with a press of magic. *"Salvo."*

The collar clicked and fell into my waiting hand. Stephen's aura roared over me, all that fury writhing like a pit of snakes, hot enough that I stumbled back a step. I unzipped my pouch and shoved the collar inside, seeing images of throwing the wretched piece of metal and leather into Mother Hazel's face the next time I saw her.

As I backed away, Stephen breathed something into Emma's ear. She tensed, but said nothing.

"Come on, Emma," Liam said. "Stephen will be fine, I promise."

Emma hissed as if in pain, pressing harder against Stephen as his arms tightened around her. Blake and Liam jerked, their nostrils flaring. My heart skipped a beat. We all darted forward as one, but we were too late.

We all knew we were too late.

CHAPTER 19

Liam snarled.

Emma's shoulder was bleeding. Sweat beaded on her temples and her breathing grew ragged. I grabbed her, pulling her away from Stephen. He let me take her, defiance shining the jut of his chin. A jaw that extended farther and was full of more teeth than a human should have. An image from a nightmare.

Liam snatched Stephen's shoulder, the muscles in his forearm flexing as he shook him like a rag doll. "What have you done?" he demanded.

Stephen stared at his alpha, eyes shining with the gold of his beast. His fingertips had sprouted claws, but he kept his hands at his sides. "She's pack now. She's not going anywhere."

I shut them out and put all my focus on Emma. My heart pounded in my ears, my thoughts a chaotic mess that defied logic. "Emma, look at me. Do you understand what he did?"

Emma trembled, but there was no fear in her voice when she said, "Yes." Her skin looked waxen, and blood stained the collar of her uniform.

I clenched my teeth, my brain offering flashes of what the future held in store for her. Learning to balance two natures was no simple task, not something to enter into lightly. As bad a decision as it was, I didn't think it was one that had been made in the spur of the moment. "You talked about this with him. Before tonight."

"Yes." She touched the wound and hissed lightly.

I nodded. "Is this what you want?"

She met my gaze, and her eyes were too bright. The fever was already taking her, her body temperature rising as her beast came alive inside her. "I want to stay with Stephen."

"You're a witch," Liam snapped. "Can't you stop this?"

I looked at him over Emma's bowed body, letting the truth show in my eyes. "You know I can't."

The alpha turned his glare to Vincent, but the wizard raised his hands. "If she won't fight it, I can't fight it for her."

Liam swore a blue streak and shook Stephen again, harder this time. Blake stood beside Stephen as if ready to restrain him, but Stephen stared at Liam with a triumphant look he would have been smarter to hide. "She's pack," he said again. "She's not going anywhere."

It wasn't until that moment that I realized how young Stephen really was. Not in age, but in maturity. I pulled Emma closer, dragging her back with me as, all at once, a change came over Liam.

Not anger. More like…resignation. A quiet resignation born out of frustration and anger that had nowhere to go. He stared at Stephen as if reading something written on the back of his skull, or maybe across his soul. Finally, he nodded. He let go of Stephen and walked away. Slowly, he began unbuttoning his shirt.

"I was wrong about you," he said. "I was very, very wrong. It's my fault we arrived at this point." He shrugged out of the uniform shirt and draped it over the back of the couch. "I'm going to rectify the situation now."

Stephen didn't look away, and barely moved. Emma tried to take a step toward him, but Sonar moved in front of her, blocking her way. The German shepherd glamour she wore changed her size and coloring, but the expression on her wolfish face was clear. Grim determination. Peasblossom hugged my neck, and I knew she felt something coming. I patted her back between her wings.

"All this time, I thought what you needed was encouragement and guidance." Liam grabbed the hem of his white undershirt and pulled it over his head. "You were naturally good at so many things, and when you didn't press for more, didn't work to get to that next level, I thought you just needed someone to show you how much more you could be with a little more effort. A little more dedication."

Liam had the body of a forty-five-year-old man. A forty-five-year-old man who used his desk chair for extra storage, who spent most of his life outdoors walking as a man or running as a wolf. Now that I wasn't half-dead, I couldn't help but notice the toned lines of his muscles, the solid outline of his pecs, and the smooth swells of his biceps. Not gym muscles. Work muscles. He had an alpha's body.

The hot auras of the agitated shifters pressed against my skin, and the sight of the half-naked alpha drove that heat a little deeper into my body. This time it wasn't just the warm, fuzzy comfort that drew me. It was arousal. And I didn't bother to fight it. It was a welcome distraction from the tension. The knowledge that something bad was coming. Something very bad.

"Blake, stand outside," Liam said. "Make sure no one interferes."

Blake nodded. Without looking at Stephen or Emma, he retreated. A beta wolf, the alpha's *stallari*, leading by example. Obeying the word of the *kongur*.

Blake's attitude seemed to drive home Stephen's realization of what was happening. He set his jaw and grabbed his shirt, tearing it from his body as easily as if it were made of tissue paper.

Emma's breathing quickened. I looked down, but her reaction wasn't driven by arousal. It was panic.

"What are you doing?" she asked, her voice too high. "Sergeant?"

Liam never took his eyes off Stephen. "I misjudged you. Your problem isn't that you don't *want* more. It's not that you're content to stay an officer, stay a mid-ranking member of the pack." His eyes flashed with a hint of gold. "It's that you think more will fall into your lap. You think you're already good enough to be alpha, to be *kongur*. You think as soon as you decide to try for it, you'll win. You'll just decide to start your own pack and people will fall into line behind you. Because everything else has come easily to you, so why not?" He laughed, and again, there was no humor in it. "It seems you and Oliver share that flaw."

My jaw dropped, but I snapped it closed. It was a fair point.

Stephen's eyes burned brightly, a savage gold that promised violence. But to his credit, he didn't rise to the bait. "Emma is staying with me," he said, his voice low, almost a growl.

Liam's mouth tilted up at the corner, a sad amusement that shoved all thoughts of his muscular body from my mind. I'd guessed what he was doing, where this was going. But that quirk of his mouth, that amusement that was more sadness than humor, stole my breath. I'd seen that look two months ago. On the face of a father whose son had been arrested—again—on drug-related charges. He'd finally decided enough was enough. He wouldn't bail his son out again, wouldn't save him from the consequences of his choices. I'd sat with him three nights in a row after his son went to jail. Listening to stories about his son as a young boy. Offering silent support for his decision. A shoulder to cry on. It wasn't until I saw that look on Liam's face that I truly understood what it meant to be alpha.

"All this time, I've been encouraging you," Liam said softly. "When what I should have been doing was showing you just how far you have to go."

"No time like the present," Stephen said. "That is, if you're done with the speech?"

Stephen had already shucked out of his pants, and now he stood naked and burning with adrenaline-infused energy. I could feel his aura from across the room, feel how ready he was to fight. He looked at Emma and smiled. Reassuring. Confident. He thought he was going to win.

I looked at that sadness in Liam's face, and I knew Stephen was wrong.

By the time Liam took his pants off, I was no longer in a state to appreciate his body, to let my arousal protect me from the chaos on the horizon. I wanted to leave. Now.

"We need to get her out of here," I told Sonar, gesturing to Emma.

"No," Liam said.

I snapped my attention back to him. His voice was quiet, but firm, and he'd wiped the emotion from his face. His blue eyes were gone, burned away by the sizzling gold I saw now.

"What?" I asked.

"She needs to stay," Liam said. "She needs to understand what Stephen has done. The reality of the consequences of her decision."

"Bastard," Stephen said, hands curling into fists at his sides. "You're being cruel."

Liam didn't justify his decision, didn't explain himself. He was alpha. *Kongur*. He didn't have to.

Sonar shifted her weight, settling on four heavy brown paws as if preparing to stop Emma from bolting. I didn't think she meant to stop her from running out of the house, so much as she would stop Emma from going to Stephen. Trying to help him.

"If it's all right," I said softly, "I'll stay as well. To...explain." I kept my eyes firmly on the floor. Submissive, asking his permission. The room burned with shifter energy, and this was not the time to challenge Liam's authority, even in a small way.

Liam never took his eyes from Stephen. "You may stay."

He didn't warn me not to interfere. It was probably the most respect he'd shown me since I met him.

"What's happening?" Emma demanded. She tried to stand up straight, but winced and folded again. Sweat poured down her forehead. I put a hand on her back, rubbing up and down her spine. She would change soon, full moon or not. With this much energy in the room, she'd have changed already if this wasn't her first time. Her body didn't know how to do it yet, and it would take a while for her flesh to figure it out. But it would figure it out soon.

Stephen changed first. He closed his hands into fists and dove into his shift. Fur washed back over his body, covering carved muscles with smooth brown fur. Muscles and bones popped and reformed beneath his skin. The sound made my stomach turn, but he didn't appear to be in pain. He landed hard on all fours, his chest rising and falling rapidly as he regained his breath, golden eyes locked on his alpha.

"Stephen disobeyed his alpha," I said, trying to sound calm, informative, not emotional. "Packs have a strict hierarchy. Liam is more relaxed than some alphas, but his authority is still absolute. Stephen lied to him, then he turned you without permission." I swallowed hard. "Then he openly defied an order."

Stephen's shift had been impressive, well executed and smooth. The sign of a lycanthrope who'd found harmony between his human half and his wolf. Liam was right. Someday Stephen would have made a strong alpha.

Liam's shift made it look like choppy scene from a low-budget horror movie.

The alpha of the Rocky River pack didn't shift into wolf form —he became a wolf. One minute he was standing on two feet, and the next, his weight fell toward the ground, re-forming on four legs with such natural grace that my eyes never saw the process. Silver fur spread over his body, flaring out around his neck and shoulders. Just like that, he stood facing Stephen, regal, full of cold confidence that came not from his own estimation of his abilities, but from experience.

Lots and lots of experience.

"So now they're going to fight?" Emma stared at me, then back at Stephen and Liam. I saw the urge to stop them, the urge to tell them this wasn't how humans settled things.

I put a hand on her shoulder. "Don't interfere," I said quietly. "It has to be this way." I clenched my teeth to avoid trying to explain it further. Dammit, Stephen should have told her all this. She should have understood more about what it meant to be pack before she gave permission for what he'd done.

Stephen lowered his head and took a step forward, eyes searching Liam for some sign of weakness, the best opportunity for attack. Liam pulled his lips back to expose his teeth and let out a low growl. A warning.

It didn't have the desired effect. Stephen crept to the side, his weight balanced on all four paws, ready to spring in whatever direction provided the best angle for attack. Liam stood still, watching, letting Stephen make the first move.

Stephen shot across the floor like a brown bullet, firing straight into Liam's left flank. I jumped, caught off guard even though I'd been waiting for it. Blood and bones, Stephen was fast. He slammed into Liam's side, trying to knock him to the ground to gain the dominant position.

Liam moved with the momentum, swinging his body around and curling his head to the side to grab Stephen's neck as he passed. Using Stephen's body weight against him, Liam dragged him into his own spin, then used that leverage to throw Stephen to the ground. As Stephen's back hit the floor, Liam put a paw on his chest and leaned in, mouth open to reveal glistening fangs. Ferocity twisted his features into something vicious, something deadly. Liam's black lips rose higher, exposing the full length of his canines. The expression pulled his nose back, shortening his muzzle and making his jaws appear even more powerful.

Stephen's ears fell to the sides, sticking out like horns. His muzzle broadened as he mirrored Liam's fierce expression, not giving in, not submitting. He snapped at the alpha, darting his head forward in an attempt to bite Liam's nose and gain control of his jaws.

Liam pressed harder with the paw on Stephen's chest—and tore down.

Emma screamed, and I looked away, grabbing her shoulder to force her to turn as well. I was too slow to keep the image from burning itself into my brain, an image of blood spreading over the pale brown fur of Stephen's belly. A pained yelp stabbed at my ears. Emma struggled against me, trying to turn and see what was happening. I tightened my hold, but then remembered what Liam had said.

"She needs to stay. She needs to understand what Stephen has done. The reality of the consequences of her decision."

I gritted my teeth and let go. Emma tried to run forward, a cop's instinct driving her to put herself in the path of danger to save someone else. Sonar gave a sharp bark and rose, using her paws to push Emma back. Emma stumbled, staring at Sonar as if she'd never seen the dog before. Something heavy hit the wall, and the sound of broken drywall scratched at my ears. The fight continued.

Trembling seized Emma's shoulders, and she turned back to Sonar with renewed determination. *"Sitzen!"* she said, pointing at the floor.

I blinked at the German command, shocked for a moment before I remembered Emma didn't know what Sonar was.

Growls and snarling erupted to my side, but I didn't look. Emma needed to learn this lesson. I didn't. I knew what was happening.

Desperation pulled Emma's features into a mask of near-panic. She tried to push past Sonar again, driven by another sound of pain from Stephen, a growl, and then a snap of toothy jaws. This time, Sonar snapped at her, giving her a gentle but firm bite on her hand as Emma tried to edge around her.

Emma jerked her hand back with a high-pitched sound of pain, her jaw hanging open.

"Sitzen!" she said again, pointing at the floor.

"She's not going to sit," I told her gently. "She's pack. And her alpha told her you're not to leave, and you're not to interfere."

"She's..." Emma stared at Sonar. "You're a werewolf?"

Sonar didn't say anything, didn't make a sound. Her silence made the heavy panting that much louder. I paused, trying to listen over the sound of my own heartbeat. No growling. No flesh hitting flesh. Just panting.

Emma clapped a hand over her mouth, smothering a cry of dismay. My stomach clenched, and I turned to see the fight's result.

Liam stood over Stephen, once again in human form. Blood dripped into his eye from a deep cut across his forehead. He ignored it as he looked down at Stephen, still in wolf form. The brown wolf was injured—badly. The rip down his stomach looked deeper than before, and I saw the shine of his intestines bulging out of the deepest point. One of Stephen's eyes was ruined, a mess of blood and that thin liquid that filled the ocular organ. It would heal when he shifted, but it would take a while to regain full sight. His breathing sounded irregular, and it took all my self-control not to offer my healing services then and there.

"Why are you just standing there?" Emma screamed. Her shoulders tensed, and this time when she tried to go to Stephen, it was with a clear intention to use physical force against Sonar if necessary. Her brown eyes lightened, and I caught a flash of gold.

"Stay. There." Liam's voice remained even, but there was an authority in his tone that cracked over Emma as if he'd shouted.

She stumbled back and bowed her head. Her eyes widened as if her reaction surprised her.

She opened her mouth, but before she could get a word out, she bent in half with a choking sound somewhere between a groan and a whimper.

"I'm going to get cleaned up and then we'll take her to Laura's," Liam told Sonar. "Watch her."

"She's going to change soon," Peasblossom whispered in my ear.

I nodded, but didn't interfere. Emma was learning the hard way how different her life would be now. She'd have to obey her alpha as a shifter even more than she'd obeyed her sergeant as a human. And she'd have to rely on her pack for comfort, guidance, and protection.

I had no place here now.

I hadn't noticed that Vincent had left the room, but it must have been before the fight. Probably right after Liam's speech, when the wizard would have guessed what was coming. I found him standing on the stoop, smoking a pipe that looked comically large. Blake stood on the other side of the porch. Silent.

"I've called a taxi," Vincent said. He took another puff on the pipe. "I'm happy to share."

"Thank you," I said.

He offered me the pipe, but I waved it off.

"I know what happened here!" Emma shouted.

I hadn't even heard Liam speak. Vincent and I both tensed, then very deliberately tried to relax.

"You tried to kill him," Emma continued, hysteria projecting her voice through the screen door. "I'm the one who shot Oliver, I'm the one who deserved to be punished, but you almost killed him because he *disobeyed* you!"

Vincent winced. "She doesn't say that with the right tone," he said, sounding pained.

"No," I said.

"She doesn't understand what it means yet," Peasblossom said, her voice sounding tiny even for her. "She doesn't understand it's different now."

I tried not to listen, but now that I knew they were talking, I couldn't help hearing the low tone of Liam's voice as he talked to Emma, probably explaining what was going to happen now. Telling her she had no choice.

"I'm not going anywhere!" Emma snapped. "He's hurt. He could die."

More low murmurs from Liam. I took a few quick steps toward the street, looking down the block. "Come on, taxi," I mumbled.

"You know he won't hurt her," Vincent said calmly.

"Emma is a strong woman, and right now she's feeling guilty, angry, frustrated, and helpless," I replied. "She's also very close to her first shift, thanks to her heightened emotions and the very unfortunate circumstances under which she was turned." I rose on tiptoes, knowing full well that it wouldn't help me see the cab coming. "If you think she's going to go quietly, then you need to meet more women."

A scream of outrage chased me closer to the street, and I sagged with relief as the taxi's headlights came down the road. Vincent followed, tapping out the contents of his pipe before joining me at the bottom of the driveway.

I closed the door behind me, cuddling Peasblossom as she hugged my neck.

"We are not running away," Vincent said after a long, quiet minute. "Even if we stayed, our presence, and certainly any aid we might offer, would only make things worse."

He was right. I knew he was right.

But I was going to dream about Stephen's bloody, half-eviscerated body tonight. I was going to hear Emma's cries in my sleep. I leaned my head back against the seat and scoffed.

What sleep?

CHAPTER 20

"So, did you solve the crime?"

I wasn't surprised to find Mother Hazel in my house, sitting in the dark waiting for me like a serial killer from a horror movie. Now that it was over and I could see the big picture, I was certain she'd known how it would end from the beginning. And of course she'd have known it was over. It was only logical that she'd show up here, present herself for the conclusion of our deal.

It didn't make it any easier to handle.

I closed my hands around my keys, letting the pain of the metal digging into my palm center me, keep me from giving the old crone a piece of my mind. With seething calm, I closed the door behind me.

"Yes. Yes, I solved the crime."

I walked through the dining room and into the kitchen without looking at the living room couch where my mentor sat, neat as you please. I couldn't look at her. Not when Emma's teary face and gold-flecked eyes still filled my mind. Not when the sound of flesh meeting flesh and grunts of pain still reverberated in my ears. I snatched a cold can of Coke from the fridge, gripping it as if I could punish it for all the turmoil churning inside me. The crack and hiss of freshly opened soda soothed my nerves, and I tilted it back in one long, defiant swig.

"Did the werewolf do it?"

She'd moved into the kitchen. A predator stalking prey. I glared at her over the rim of my can, taking another long, slow sip before answering.

"No. It was a ranger, a human woman. A good woman. She shot him to save a dog's life."

Aluminum groaned, and I forced myself to relax my grip before I doused myself in soda. *Don't give her what she wants. No emotion.*

"So you got justice for Oliver Dale."

I gulped down more soda, ignoring the burn in my nostrils as carbonation flooded my system. "Yes, I got justice for Oliver Dale. Justice for a bastard. A man who hated everyone." I shrugged, a rough, jerky motion. "Hated kids, hated people. Hated dogs." I pointed at her with the hand holding the can of Coke. "I got justice for a man who only loved himself—no, no, not loved. Worshiped."

"And I can only assume you are filled with satisfaction? Content with that bone-deep pleasure that comes from fulfilling one's true purpose?"

Her eyes bored into mine, watching me with that damned stare that looked right past your skin to your soul. I lifted my chin and took another drink, holding her eyes the whole time. *Read my soul, damn your eyes.*

"The werewolf ate the body to save the woman from jail," I told her. "He loves her. And she loves him. In fact, they love each another so much that when their plan failed, she let him turn her."

Mother Hazel arched an eyebrow. "She allowed this?"

"Yes, yes she did. It turns out her grandmother knew of the Otherworld, so it wasn't as foreign to her as most. Dating a werewolf didn't seem strange. She wasn't familiar enough with the Otherworld to understand the extent of what she'd agreed to."

I paced, giving in to the energy building inside me. The anger.

"They did it so they could stay together. Pack mates, all that." I paused my pacing to point at her. "I know what you're thinking. Stupid, right? Bloody insane. Because that's not how it worked out. No happy ending for the murderers. She's being sent to live with one of the females and he's to remain home—collared—until he rebuilds the trust with his alpha. You know how long that will take. Oh, Liam would like you to contact him about adjusting the spell in the collar. You know, for the long term."

"I'll tend to it tomorrow." Mother Hazel's expression still hadn't changed. She didn't care about the details of the case. "You seem upset."

I laughed, a short, humorless sound. "Do I? Well, dearie me, why could that be?"

She didn't rise to that bait. "Tell me, at what point did you know the sort of man Oliver was?"

I started to take another drink, then realized the can was empty. I stalked to the trash, slamming the pedal down so hard that the lid flew open to smash the wall behind it. Plastic made a popping sound that promised a repair would be necessary if I wanted that pedal to function again. *Sod it.*

"Oh, it was clear from the beginning. Everyone hated him, and he hated everyone." I tore open the fridge and grabbed another soda. "And if you're thinking he had some sad story about how he came to be that way, forget it. He was a spoiled high school athlete who got angry when the ass-kissing stopped after graduation."

Mother Hazel snorted, dismissing the idea she ever would have asked for a sad story to explain the man Oliver had been. "Was there a time when you could have blamed a less than shining example of humanity instead?"

I started to say no, but reconsidered. "One suspect seemed

like a bad man, but he turned out all right."

"But you kept investigating. You did not believe the worst of this bad person?"

Irritation scalded my veins as if my blood had turned to molten lead. She was trying to teach me something. I *hated* it when she tried to teach me something. It always involved twisting my emotions into the most painful knots imaginable and leaving me to sort through the mess.

"No, I didn't believe the worst of him. Yes, he turned out to be a decent human being—unlike the victim. Now, if you don't mind, I'd like to drink my soda and try to forget the werewolf who's probably lying bloody and unconscious on his bed. I'd like to forget the alpha who's likely sitting next to him with his head in his hands thinking of the mess he's made of his life, all that wasted potential. I'd like to avoid thinking about the human ranger whose entire life changed in wild and scary ways because she stood up to a bully. I want to forget this entire mess and go to bed."

Mother Hazel smiled. "You might be a good investigator after all." She moved to the door, opened it, and paused before exiting. "If you still want to be one."

I hurled the can of Coke at the door as soon as it closed behind her, my entire body shaking with rage. Soda sprayed everywhere, coating the door, the walls, and the floor. I stared at the trickling, sticky liquid, my vision tinged red.

"I knew it," I whispered. "I knew she did this on purpose. Chose a despicable victim. I'll bet she knew who did it all along and wanted to see if I'd go through with it, or let them get away."

"It's okay, Shade," Peasblossom said.

I twitched, having forgotten about the pixie, she'd been so silent. Tears blurred my vision. "No, it's not all right. None of this is all right." I went to the kitchen to fetch a wet rag to clean up the mess I'd made. "This isn't how I'm supposed to feel after solving a case. I won, dammit." I sank to my knees on the floor, landing hard enough to send pain shooting into my bones. "I'm supposed to be happy."

Peasblossom fluttered over to the counter, putting all her weight into tearing a paper towel from the roll. She wet it in the sink and returned to help me clean up my mess, dabbing at the droplets that had reached the ceiling. She pretended she didn't hear me crying.

My phone rang. The sudden noise in the silence stabbed through my thoughts like a hot spear, and I almost flung it across the room just to take the edge off the surge of adrenaline. I threw the soda-soaked rag to the floor and swiped the screen to answer, not bothering to check the caller ID.

"Hello?" I snapped.

"Hello, Mother Renard. I hope I didn't wake you?"

Kylie. I sat back on my heels, wet rag forgotten in my lap. "Kylie. No, you didn't wake me. I was…tidying up. How can I help you?"

"I heard what happened. With Emma."

I closed my eyes. "I'm sorry."

"Why? You did your job, even though it was difficult. Even though you like Emma."

I narrowed my eyes. Instinct was screaming at me, telling me there was something coming. "I appreciate your understanding. Is that what you called for? To talk about Emma?"

"No. No, I called for another reason. It's just…" She paused, as if choosing her words. "Mother Hazel has taught you the importance of performing your duties, no matter the pleasantness or unpleasantness of the task, yes? That's what you did today."

"Yes," I said. "Why?"

"I work hard to find the truth. I do what I can to balance my karmic scales. I believe I am a good person. However, I love no one, and am loved by no one."

I fought the urge to stare at the phone, as if this were some dream. "What are you saying?"

"Someday, I will be a ghoul. I do not want that change to take away all the good I've worked for, all the effort I've put in to redeeming my soul. Whatever's left of it."

My lips parted and it took me two tries to speak. "Are you asking me to—"

"I'm asking you to do your duty when the time comes," she whispered. "However unpleasant it might be. Can you do that for me, Mother Renard?"

I slumped over, narrowly avoiding dropping the phone. She was asking me to kill her before she turned. I did not need this. Not tonight, not now.

"Mother Renard?"

"Yes." My voice held no emotion. Yay me. "Yes, I'll help you. When the time comes."

"Thank you."

She hung up. No goodbye, no transition. Just confirmed that I would kill her and hung up.

"Shade?" Peasblossom said. "Are you okay?"

My phone rang again. My nerves, raw as they were, tightened so that I swiped to answer the phone, pressed it to my ear, and snarled into the phone. "What?"

"Ms. Renard?"

Andy. I froze, my fingers tightening into a cage around the phone. "And—Agent Bradford?"

His voice was as I remembered it, clear and professional. He had a voice that would have betrayed him as a cop even if I hadn't known he was FBI.

"Yes. I'm calling because I need your help, your input, on a case. A few cases. I need your insight. How soon can you get here?"

I pulled my phone away from my ear, checking the number. Yes, it was Agent Bradford. I looked at Peasblossom where she sat on the top edge of the door. Her pink eyes were wide, and she shrugged.

She'd heard it too. Not a dream.

"Now?" I asked. I checked the time. Eleven o'clock. What could he need help with at this hour?

"Oh, good. I'll text you the address."

"I didn't mean—" I stopped and shook my head. Andy had called me. Weeks of no response, and now he was calling me for help. The FBI calling me for help. It was everything I wanted. Only, suddenly, I wasn't sure I wanted it at all.

"Ms. Renard? Are you still there?"

"Text me the address."

It hadn't been the answer I'd intended to give. And as I hung up and sat there staring at the green new text alert on my phone, it occurred to me that I'd agreed to a two-hour drive, a commitment that would last past midnight. "I am an idiot."

"Yes you are," Peasblossom said. She fluttered down from the doorframe to perch on my knee. "I want you to bring my travel bed."

I sighed. "Why not? One of us should get some sleep."

"And it might as well be me."

I grabbed another Coke from the fridge, reconsidered, and grabbed two. Majesty was nowhere to be found, so I ignored Peasblossom's snickers long enough to heat a dish of cat food, and left it in the center of the floor for him. A stop in the bedroom to grab the bed from Peasblossom's dollhouse, and I was ready to go.

It was strange not having Peasblossom to talk to on the drive. It made the interior of the car darker, somehow, the quiet... quieter. I tried the radio, then turned it off. I wasn't in the mood for it. Any of it.

"My, this all looks familiar." I sighed and leaned my head against the headrest, looking at the same construction cones I'd passed less than two hours ago. If he'd called a little sooner, perhaps I would still have been in the area.

I groped for the first can of Coke, popping it open without my usual satisfaction. I had a decision to make. Mother Hazel owed me a favor. Anything I wanted. All I had to do was confirm I wanted it. Confirm I'd accepted my prize, despite my earlier anger. She probably thought I was giving up. Maybe I was.

"Do you still want to be an investigator?" I asked myself. "Do you want more cases like this one? Watch more good people ruin their lives in one moment?" A surge of anger rushed through me and I slammed my hand on the steering wheel. "He was *hanging a dog.*"

"Oi, you're loud." Peasblossom sat up in her silky pink sleeping bag, shoving the tiny sleep mask I'd made for her farther up her head so she could squint at me. "What's wrong?"

"Nothing. I'm sorry. Go back to sleep."

Peasblossom huffed out a sigh and smoothed her blanket over her lap. "They'll be fine. All of them."

"You don't know that. Thinking you're all right with becoming a werewolf isn't the same as being one." I pressed my lips together. "Emma was upset she shot him. He treated her like dirt and she still feels bad."

"You think that's a bad sign?"

"All the werewolves we've met that were really happy. What do they have in common?"

"Good flea medication?"

"No." I rolled my eyes. "They were at peace with both sides of themselves. They gave their instincts and their drive to succeed the same respect they gave their social side, the side that obeys society's laws."

"And you don't think Emma has that balance."

"No. I don't. I think if Emma were at peace with the part of herself her beast will personify, she would have stood up to Oliver much sooner. And she wouldn't feel poorly for having killed him, because she did it saving another life." My vision blurred and I blinked back tears. "And they tore her away from Stephen, the man she trusted to guide her through this."

"Sergeant Osbourne is a good man. If he sees this separation is too detrimental, he'll put them back together."

"You're right."

Peasblossom crossed her arms behind her head, lying back down on her sleeping bag. "You know, Mother Hazel always says everything is a witch's business."

"Yes, I know," I said, then took another fortifying sip of Coke.

"Well, I suppose that means it's your business to check in on Stephen and Emma from time to time. Make sure Sergeant Osbourne's methods meet your standards."

I snorted, barely refraining from getting a nose full of soda. "You want me to interfere in pack business?"

"Again," Peasblossom pointed out.

I considered that as I studied the road. Meddling in the affairs of werewolves was dangerous. Very dangerous. Unwise.

And...very witchy.

"It is my responsibility, isn't it?" I said.

"If you feel responsible for all the bad things that happened, it seems it's only right you take responsibility for seeing things through."

I considered that the rest of the way to Andy's house. There was a certain ring of logic to it. I felt guilty for my part in the whole situation, guilt that my brain recognized as ridiculous despite my heart's insistence on clinging to it. Would it be so outrageous to take responsibility for it?

I was certain Liam would think so.

Did I want to risk making the alpha angry? I already had a dream sorceress sending nightmares after me. Did I need to add an alpha werewolf to that list?

By the time I pulled into Andy's driveway, I wasn't any closer to reaching a decision. Worse, I'd finished both sodas, and was in rather desperate need of a restroom.

I knocked on the door with more enthusiasm than I intended,

and when Andy opened the door, I spoke before he could get a word out.

"Bathroom?"

He blinked, then pointed at a small staircase. "Down those stairs on the left."

I nodded and proceeded as quickly as I could without falling down the stairs. A few minutes later, relieved and refreshed, I found Andy sitting at a bar across from the bathroom. We were on the lower level of a split-level home, and the room I walked into now was spacious, with only two pillars in the center to break up the large space. The bar stuck out from the east wall, with two small windows at the top of the wall on either side. The opposite side sported a large sliding glass door, and if it hadn't been nighttime, natural light would have flooded the room.

It was a testament to how scattered my thoughts were that I didn't notice the files until Andy got up from the bar and paced to the far wall. Once I noticed them, I couldn't help but stare. There had to be at least twenty piles lining the wall from one end of the room to another, and at least ten thick files in each pile. I stared as Andy knelt down and lifted one file, paged through it, then put it back down. He walked to the end of the line of files and chose another one. Again, he paged through it and put it back.

"What is all this?" I asked.

Andy didn't look up. "Unsolved cases. Some solved, but possibly solved wrong." He closed the file and looked up at me. "I was hoping you'd go through them with me and tell me if there's any chance something Otherworld is holding it up."

"You want me to..." I gaped at the files. "That's a lot of files."

He nodded and pointed to the far end. "I've organized them by date, with the oldest cases down there leading up to the most recent cases here. Open cases are on the bottom of the piles, closed cases on top."

"Why the solved cases on top?"

He met my eyes. "Those convictions might have put the wrong person behind bars."

I walked over to the piles and lifted the first folder. I opened the folder and found a picture of a brown-haired man with striking blue eyes that bored right through me. Doubt bit me, hard. All these files held the lives of real people. What if there were more Emmas here? Was I ready to commit to a path filled with more evenings like this one?

"Andy, I'll be honest. I'm not sure I'll keep going with private investigations."

He frowned and looked up from his file, seeming to notice my mood for the first time. His attention slid from my hair, in wild disarray from all the tugging I'd done, to my clothes still wrinkled and soda-stained from my earlier tantrum. "Bad day?"

"Yeah." I put the file down and smoothed my hair back from my face. "I solved a murder today. The victim was a complete bastard. Evil, even. And the woman who shot him... She's a good person. I don't blame her—I mean, I understand why she did it."

"And you arrested her anyway?"

I looked away. "Yes. Well, sort of. It's complicated, as werewolves are, but... Let's say she's being punished."

Andy set his file down on the pile nearest him, then frowned, picked it up again, and put it on the pile next to it. Then he took a step closer.

"And now you feel like crap? You wanted to let her get away with it."

I nodded without looking at him. "Yes."

"Could you have let her get away with it?"

I bit my lip, considering that for a second. "I think so."

"But you didn't."

"No." The word came out harsher than I'd intended, but I was in no mood to field the same question fifty times.

"Good." Andy nodded.

"What?" My temper sparked, fueled by all the caffeine and the resulting jitters. "What's that supposed to mean?"

"It means—"

"I've been calling you for weeks, and you couldn't pick up the phone, to return a single phone call. You call me tonight just before the witching hour, asking me to drive two hours to help you without so much as one question about how I'm doing, or how busy I am, or even a fleeting thought to how tired I might be, and now you're going to stand there and take satisfaction in my misery?"

Andy blinked, then looked at the sliding glass door as if just noticing the late hour. "What time is it?"

"After midnight," I said. I jabbed a finger at Peasblossom, who'd carried her sleeping bag to the top of a stack of folders. "She should be in bed."

"I am in bed," she grumbled. "And if you'd stop shouting, I could be asleep."

Andy avoided looking at Peasblossom. He ran a hand through his hair, drawing my attention to the fact it was wet, as if he'd showered before I arrived. Now that I'd noticed, I realized he smelled good, that strong scent of body wash before it faded.

Concentrate, I told myself.

"I'm sorry. I didn't realize it was so late. I've been working on this"—he gestured at the files—"and I guess I got tunnel vision. And I'm sorry I didn't return your calls. I was thinking things through, and I didn't want to talk until I knew what I'd say."

"And you decided what you would say is 'help me'?"

He considered me for a long minute. "The last time we spoke, you were bound and determined to be a private investigator. You wanted to catch bad guys—alone, if I recall."

I took a breath to answer, but he held up a hand.

"I won't beat you up over magically drugging me and ditching me again. I understand why you did it. I'm letting it go. I want to talk about the future. A future where we help each other. I'll bring you cases; you help me deal with the Otherworld."

"I told you, I'm not even sure I'll keep doing this."

"Then at least let me explain what I meant when I said it's good you feel like crap." He took another step closer, holding my gaze. "If you like every victim, hate every murderer, and are happy and at peace after every case, then you're only doing your job for half the population. The fact is, bad things don't just happen to good people. Sometimes they happen to bad people. And sometimes good people do bad things. Justice only works if everyone gets it. Sometimes you'll hate the victim and love the murderer. You'll be angry and depressed after you solve those cases, and that sucks, but it also means you're getting justice for everyone. It's a lesson that takes some cops decades to come to grips with. So in a way, you're ahead of the curve. Which tells me you're following the path you were meant to take."

His words sank in, and the knots twisting my stomach, eased, released. I could breathe easier now, though I still felt like crying. I guessed that was a good thing.

I looked around at the case files. "These are all cases you think might have ties to the Otherworld?"

"Yes."

I nodded. "Mind if I make a quick phone call?"

"Go ahead."

I called Mother Hazel. The old crone answered on the fifth ring.

"Yes?"

"Hi, Mother Hazel?" I smiled. "You owe me a favor."

****

Finished? Want to talk about what you just read? Join the Magic, Murder, and Mayhem Book Club, a Facebook group where we discuss the Blood Trails series. You know you have an opinion. Share it…

ABOUT THE AUTHOR

USA Today bestselling author Jennifer Blackstream is...odd. Putting aside the fact that she writes her own author bio in third person, she also sleeps with a stuffed My Little Pony that her grandmother bought her as a joke for her 23rd birthday, and she enjoys listening to Fraggle Rock soundtracks whether or not her children are in the car.

Jennifer makes it a point to spend at least one night a week with her sibling binge-watching whatever show they're currently plowing through, and she ferociously guards quality time with her son and daughter. She cooks when she has the sanity for it and tries very hard not to let her arachnophobia keep her out of her basement on laundry day.

Jennifer's influences include Terry Pratchett (for wit), Laurell K. Hamilton (for sexual tension), Jim Butcher (for roguish flair), and Kim Harrison (for mythos). She is currently writing the series of her heart and her dreams, the series that has been percolating in her brain for the last decade...Blood Trails. An Urban Fantasy Mystery series that will combine the classic whodunit spirit with a contemporary fantasy setting. Expect mystery, magic, and mayhem, with characters that will make you laugh, cry, and stare at the screen with your jaw hanging down to the floor. Well, that's how they affect Jennifer anyway...

DID YOU FIND A TYPO?

I hate typos. Really, they upset me on a deeply emotional level. If you find a typo in one of my books, please contact me through my website at www.jenniferblackstream.com. I have a monthly drawing in which I pick a name from those who have submitted typos, and I award said winner with a $25 gift certificate.

Death to typos!

JB

98061053R00193

Made in the USA
Columbia, SC
17 June 2018